"Adam, wait!"

She ran toward the ba... door, struggling with... dark, and her eyes ad...

She saw him finally. He was sitting on a bale of straw, cuddling the orphan lamb in his arms. She was surprised by the lump that rose in her throat at the sight.

She joined him, and her arm crept around his shoulders. "Such a tough guy," she murmured, resting her head against his.

Adam felt the silky tickle of Paige's hair. The spiciness of the scent she wore struggled with the odors of lamb and straw and won, and he turned to kiss her. Afterward he wondered if every kiss they shared would feel new.

In a minute the lamb was a woolly heap on the straw beside them, and Adam had Paige in his arms.

"I thought we'd decided this was a bad idea," she said, gasping.

"I'm developing a new philosophy," he responded. "Every idea should be followed up on. Otherwise how will we know where it might have led?"

Dear Reader,

When two people fall in love, the world is suddenly new and exciting, and it's that same excitement we bring to you in Silhouette Intimate Moments. These are stories with scope, with grandeur. The characters lead the lives we all dream of, and everything they do reflects the wonder of being in love.

Longer and more sensuous than most romances, Silhouette Intimate Moments novels take you away from everyday life and let you share the magic of love. Adventure, glamour, drama, even suspense— these are the passwords that let you into a world where love has a power beyond the ordinary, where the best authors in the field today create stories of love and commitment that will stay with you always.

In coming months look for novels by your favorite authors: Maura Seger, Parris Afton Bonds, Linda Howard and Nora Roberts, to name just a few. And whenever you buy books, look for all the Silhouette Intimate Moments, love stories *for* today's women *by* today's women.

Leslie J. Wainger
Senior Editor
Silhouette Books

Emilie Richards

Smoke Screen

Silhouette Intimate Moments

Published by Silhouette Books New York

America's Publisher of Contemporary Romance

SILHOUETTE BOOKS
300 East 42nd St., New York, N.Y. 10017

ISBN: 0-373-07261-9

First Silhouette Books printing November 1988

Printed in the U.S.A.

EMILIE RICHARDS

believes that opposites attract, and her marriage is vivid proof. "When we met," the author says, "the *only* thing my husband and I could agree on was that we were very much in love. Fortunately, we haven't changed our minds about that in all the years we've been together."

The couple lives in New Orleans with their four children, who span from toddler to teenager. Emilie has put her master's degree in family development to good use—raising her own brood, working for Head Start, counseling in a mental health clinic and serving in VISTA.

Though her first book was written in snatches with an infant on her lap, Emilie now writes five hours a day and "rejoices in the opportunity to create, to grow and to have such a good time."

Maori Glossary

haka - Chants of defiance accompanied by movements of the hands and feet

hangi - An earth oven in which food is cooked

hapu - A large family grouping within a tribe

hongi - The pressing of noses in the traditional Maori salute

iwi - Tribe

kaihana - Cousin

kai-tiaki - Guardian

koauau - An elaborately carved flute with three finger holes

marae - Ceremonial ground around a meeting-house

matua whangai - Adoptive parent/godparent

mauri - Spiritual essence; symbol of fertility, vitality

mokopuna - Grandchild, may be grandchild of siblings or cousins

ngakau Maori - The Maori heart; pride in being Maori; understanding of Maori ways

noa - Free from restriction; ordinary, not sacred

pa - Fortress

pataka - Storehouse

poi - A light ball on a string swung to a song; a graceful dance

poutokomanawa - Heart post supporting the ridge-pole of a meeting house

puhi - High-born girl whose chasitity was guarded until an advantageous marriage could be arranged

tama - Son; boy

tamahine - Daughter; eldest niece

tangata whenua - Person who is connected with a place through a line of ancestors

tangihanga - Funeral wake

tapu - Sacred

tohunga - Priest

whakapapa - Genealogy

whare hui - Meeting house

He Whakamuri-Aroha

Aha te hau e maene ki to kiri?
E kore pea koe e ingo mai ki to hoa,
I piri ai korua i to korua moenga,
I awhi ai korua,
I tangi ai korua
Tena taku aroha
Ma te hau e kawe ki a koe,
Huri mai to aroha,
Tangi mai ki to moenga,
I moe ai korua.
Kia pupuke-a-wai to aroha.

What wind is this blowing softly to your skin?
Will you not incline towards your companion,
To whom you clung when sleeping together,
Whom you clasped in your arms,
Who shared your griefs.
When the wind bears to you this my love,
Incline hither thy love,
Sighing for the couch where both slept,
Let your love burst forth,
As the water-spring from its source.

This is a ritual chant or *karakia* sung by a Maori *tohunga* or priest to help a man win back the love of a woman he has lost to the fairies.

Chapter 1

She shouldn't have come. Not to New Zealand, not to Waimauri, and most especially not to this place.

Paige Duvall leaned against the sleek, straight trunk of a tree—a tree like none she'd ever leaned on before—and asked herself once more just what she was doing hiking in a country where her only companion was fear—fear and sucking, spitting mud pools that threatened to strip the very flesh off her bones.

She took a deep, calming breath and was rewarded by the acrid, nostril-taunting smell of sulphur. So much for the sweet rewards of fresh air, so much for the benefits of exploring Godzone. Godzone? No, somehow she had ventured into Hell, and the damnedest part of it was that she had been warned.

She remembered the words of the old man at the Waimauri dairy yesterday. "So you're from the States. And you've come to see about the thermals." He had been understandably curious. "I should think the house there's a bit of a shambles."

Paige had appreciated his talent for understatement. "A bit," she'd acknowledged, tongue in cheek. "But I'm managing." And she was, if you could count eating meals out of cans and huddling under four quilts because she couldn't figure out how to turn on the heat.

Her answer hadn't dimmed the old man's curiosity. "Done any bushwalking?"

"Not much. I've been too busy trying to keep warm and dry."

The old man had laughed. "Ah yeah. It'll warm up in a month or two. You Yanks, your seasons are turned around." He had filled a bag with odds and ends, then set a bottle of cream-rich milk on top of the rest of her groceries. "You've been warned about wandering around in the thermals by yourself?"

She hadn't been, but the dairyman's next words made up for the lack. "If all the people who died in the Waimauri thermals stood up at the same time and cheered, it'd look like a rugby match in Eden Park." He had pushed the bag across the narrow wooden counter. "Don't go in alone, miss."

But today she had done exactly that.

It wasn't that she hadn't believed the man. She knew little about the strange country she was now exploring, but she did know enough not to underestimate boiling geysers and steaming mud pools. She just hadn't intended to come this far. She had planned to skirt the edges, scan the scenery, then decide if she wanted to hire a guide to explore farther. Instead she had become caught up in her discoveries, promising herself that she would turn around at the next bend, the next ridge. Now she wasn't sure how to get back.

Through a haze of drifting vapors, Paige could see the haloed sun overhead. She shaded her eyes and checked her watch. The watch was a recent gift from an unlikely source, the wife of the man she had planned to marry. Now the delicate gold band sparkled against her creamy olive skin, reminding her of promises kept and broken. On a more mundane level it also reminded her that if she didn't find her way out soon, she might be one of the dairyman's cheering skeletons.

Just when had she strayed off the path—if she could call the misbegotten tangle of scorched grass garnished by the sharp, low branches of manuka shrub a path? For all she knew, she was still on it, and alive or dead the path was leading her inevitably to the netherworld.

Lost in the Waimauri thermals, and these thermals weren't extravagant wool underwear from a yuppie mail-order catalog. They were an area of such bizarre geological formations that if someone discovered her in the midst of this foul-smelling mist and undulating, steaming earth, he would probably be brandishing a pitchfork. And at this point, she might be glad to see Lucifer himself.

"Welcome to the scenic wonders of New Zealand," Paige said out loud, a grimace stretching her generous bottom lip.

"Welcome? You must be the rare visitor who appreciates our local attractions."

Startled, Paige looked up to see the outline of a man obscured by the steam rising from the shore of a rust-tinted pond to her right. For just a moment she wondered if she *had* called up the devil himself.

She took a step forward, but as she watched, he walked toward her, materializing out of the mist, a disembodied wraith solidifying slowly into flesh and bones and man.

"Would you like me to leave you alone?" he asked with the politely clipped New Zealand accent that she was just beginning to decipher with ease.

Caught exactly at the convergence of relief, curiosity and fascination, Paige scrutinized him before she answered.

He was dark—dark hair, dark eyes, skin a rich hue that proclaimed his Maori blood. His eyebrows were a thick slash of black across a wide forehead broken by a shiny thatch of midnight hair that just skimmed his collar. His features were hawklike, lines and angles and sweeping planes, and his taut, lean body was composed of lines and angles, too. Lines and angles clothed in khaki chinos and a black pullover sweater distributed over a frame that towered inches over her own.

"No, I don't want to be left alone," she said, shuddering at the thought. "What I want is a good, stiff drink."

Without a smile he pulled a silver flask from the side of his belt and held it out to her. Paige swept her eyes up to his, cocking her head as if to ask permission. "Do I have to sell my soul for this?"

He smiled a little, just a faint twist of his lips, but she took the flask, unscrewing the top with a graceful twirl. Two swigs later she realized it was tea. Hot and strong and laced with nothing more potent than sugar.

"A good start," she said wryly, wiping her mouth with the back of her hand before she handed the flask back.

"You're shivering."

"I started shivering when I got off the plane in Auckland."

He stretched out his hand and lifted the hem of her sweater, rubbing his fingers across the knit. "Cotton," he said, and the word sounded like the vilest profanity. "Cotton and silk. Small wonder you're freezing."

"Worse than freezing, I'm lost."

"Suppose you tell me what you're doing here in the first place. Didn't you see the signs?"

She *had* seen the signs. Danger. No Trespassing. Proceed At Your Own Risk. She had ignored them. She had ignored subtler versions of signs like them all her life. This wasn't the first time she had found herself in Hell because of it.

"This place belongs to me," she said.

"Pardon?"

"It's mine, or rather, my mother's." She gestured to the weird landscape surrounding them. "As far as you can see, and farther still. I knew Duvall Development owned a chunk of the world, but until this week, I didn't know we owned Hades, too."

He frowned. "You're American."

"Guilty as charged."

"This is New Zealand."

And she knew exactly what he meant. So why, if she was an American, had she wrapped her greedy little fingers around a chunk of Godzone? She imagined her deliverer was experiencing what she did every time she realized just exactly how much of the good old U.S. was owned by Arab sheiks.

"My mother is a Kiwi," she said. "The land came to her recently at the death of a relative."

"Jane Abbott."

"That's right. And I'm here to evaluate it."

"Gold in the mud pools? Uranium in the geysers?"

"Land, Mr...." Her voice trailed off when she realized she didn't know his name. "I'm Paige Duvall," she said, holding out her hand.

His hesitation was so slight that a less observant person might not have noticed it. "Adam Tomoana." He took her hand, wrapping it in his own.

In the second before he withdrew she felt the rough texture of calluses and the strength that could crush her delicate bones to dust.

"Were you bushwalking, Mr. Tomoana?" she asked, using the dairyman's phrase. It conjured images of a grown man leaping from shrub to shrub.

"Trespassing."

She was surprised at the bitterness in the word. "True, but it was lucky for me you were. Now you can point me out of here."

"I'll take you back."

She heard no pleasure in his voice, just a bitter resignation. It spoiled her pleasure at his rescue. "Thank you, but I got this far by myself, so if you'll show me which direction to go, I'll get myself out of here."

One expressive eyebrow rose. "Oh? And you're certain your luck will hold again?"

She was beginning to dislike him. "Luck had little to do with it, Mr. Tomoana. I was very careful."

"Not careful enough to keep from getting lost."

She shrugged.

He turned and started through the mists. "Perhaps it wasn't luck. Perhaps your footsteps were guided," he said cynically.

"Guided?" she called after him, interested despite herself.

He stopped at precisely the point where he would have disappeared from her view and motioned her toward him. "Our dead ancestors," he said darkly.

She frowned. "What's that supposed to mean?"

He said something in a language so fluid it seemed to slip through the pores of her skin and infuse warmth into her chilled body. He paused, and then with a short, frustrated exhalation of air, he repeated his words in English. "Yours and mine, Miss Duvall," he said shortly. "We're cousins."

Not exactly cousins. Adam allowed himself a small smile. At least, not cousins in the Pakeha way. Still, his words had produced the desired effect. Miss Paige Duvall had said nothing more. She trudged along behind him, keeping up the pace he set without so much as stumbling on the rock-strewn path.

Adam didn't even need to glance behind him to know exactly how close she was, how determined to match his stride, and how irritated. He didn't have to glance at her to know that none of those things would show on her face.

Nothing showed on Paige Duvall's face. Not fear that she was lost in a place unlike any she had seen before, not surprise that a man had materialized out of the mists to rescue her, not anger that the man dared to herald their blood bond. The face was inscrutable, but the woman was not.

He could read every emotion in the veins of her long, slender neck, in the movement of her shoulders, in the nearly invisible shudders of her gloriously perfect body. He could read the way she tossed the short, gleaming mass of black hair off her face and the way one delicately arched eyebrow lifted as she worked to conceal her thoughts.

He could read her. For what it was worth.

Adam crested a hill and stopped, waiting for Paige to catch up to him. "If you're tired, we can rest. But we're almost there."

"I don't think this is the way I came."

He turned and admired her mixture of haughty displeasure and exhaustion. If she hadn't been warm since arriving on the North Island, she was warm now. A thin sheen of perspiration decorated the smooth skin of her forehead. "Perhaps we should go back and let you lead us home, then," he said politely.

He watched her body tense. "I'm not going back. I've seen enough geothermal activity to last me for the day."

"Have you seen enough of New Zealand, too?"

Paige heard the challenge. "Why do you dislike me?"

He was surprised that she had cut so quickly to the point, and he felt a moment of reluctant admiration. She was going to save them both time. "It's not you I dislike, cousin," he said, watching to see her reaction. "It's what you stand for, what your coming here means."

Paige lowered herself to the ground and rested her head against a tree trunk. "I have no cousins in New Zealand," she said, closing her eyes. "My mother was an only child, raised here in Waimauri. Both her parents are dead. My father was raised in New Orleans. My only living relative in New Zealand was a distant relation of my mother's, a woman named Jane Abbott, and she died last year leaving this—" she raised her hand as if words had failed her "—this place to my mother. So you have me confused with someone else."

"Do I?" Adam watched Paige as she rested. She had grown into an extraordinarily beautiful woman, but then, she had been an extraordinarily beautiful child, a child wrenched from all of them by the untimely appearance of her father. Even now he remembered the sound of her grandmother's weeping.

Maori and Pakeha. Polynesian and Caucasian. Brown-skinned and light. How strange that a mixture of blood could produce the rare, perfect creature sitting so placidly in front of him, her lies no more than words she had been taught to believe.

"Do you dislike me because I'm an American and I own part of your country?" Paige opened her eyes to find that he'd been staring at her. "Well, rest easy. I don't want it. I've come to sell it back."

"Have you?"

Strangely, it irritated Paige that she couldn't read his tone. *She* was the unfathomable one. She wasn't sure she liked having her own inscrutability reflected back at her. "How far are we from the house where I'm staying?" She stood, brushing off the seat of her pants.

"Over that ridge." Adam pointed to the next hill. "And through the grove." He said no more, just waited for a bellbird to cease its melodious chiming before he turned and started back the way they had come.

He had been swallowed by the thick, scrubby forest before Paige realized he was leaving her. "Adam?" She heard his first name roll off her tongue and wondered why it had come so easily. There was no answer. "Thank you," she called into the silence.

The bellbird's sweet chimes were her only answer.

The Maoris had called it Aotearoa—the land of the long white cloud. The first Europeans on its shores had called it New Zealand—originally Nieuw Zeeland, after a province in Holland. Modern day Kiwis affectionately called it Godzone—for reasons they kept to themselves. Huddled under a blanket in front of a smoking fireplace, Paige shivered and wondered what insanity had brought her to this place where sheep vastly outnumbered people, and people seemed content with nothing more than the simplest pleasures.

Some of her reasons for being here were obvious. Someone from Duvall Development had to evaluate this, the most peculiar of their vast real estate holdings. Despite her father's resistance, she had felt that person should be her, because in some strange way, this place was part of her heritage.

And then there had been her need to get away from everything familiar and find herself again.

"Are you there, Paige Duvall?" she asked, leaning over to pour herself a shot of brandy. "If you are, please show yourself so I can pack up and go back home."

In the resulting silence, the brandy spread like indolent fire through her bloodstream. Paige tried to concentrate on her body's response, because it was better than concentrating on her loneliness. And she *was* lonely. Soul-shuddering, dead-center-of-the-bones lonely. Lonelier than she had ever been in a life where loneliness had been the status quo.

Only now, for some reason, it felt different. If loneliness had hurt before, she had been able to tell herself it didn't matter. Now it mattered, and no incantation to the contrary could help.

"So what did you expect?" she asked herself, sipping the last drops from the glass. "You just lost your best friend."

Strangely enough, that part hurt more than losing the man she had planned to marry—even though they were one and the same person. Granger Sheridan, friend, lover, confidant. Granger of the warm gray eyes and the easy grin. Granger with whom she had believed she had a chance to build a life.

Granger was gone now, reunited with the woman he had loved for ten long years, and Paige was left alone, her heart unbroken but somehow . . . emptied. She had loved Granger, but she had loved his friendship most of all. And Granger had loved her, but it had been Julianna he had burned for, Julianna for whom he had almost given his life.

Somehow Paige didn't inspire that kind of devotion in men. She hadn't inspired it in Granger, and she hadn't inspired it in her ex-husband. She was a woman men thought they wanted to possess, but once they discovered how impossible that was, they lost interest. Only Granger hadn't wanted to own her, and perhaps that had been because he had loved another.

That thought made her add another inch of brandy to her empty glass. No, she wasn't a woman who aroused great passion. Nor was she a woman who stimulated male bravado. Not usually, anyway. Of course, there had been the strong, silent man who had rescued her today.

"Adam Tomoana." Spoken aloud, the name had all the smoky warmth and full-bodied texture of the expensive brandy she was drinking. It was civilized, with just a hint of earthier, untamed pleasures beneath its cultured surface.

Paige doubted Adam's actions in the thermals qualified as risking his life. He had been perfectly at home amid the steam and smoke, and leading her to safety had seemed almost more of an excuse to get rid of her than to protect her. She had been an intruder, even though the land belonged to her family, and Adam, who had no legal claim to the land, had seemed to belong to it.

He had called her "cousin." She wondered what he had meant. She was no more his cousin than the New Zealand prime minister was her uncle. She had no relatives in New Zealand, and she certainly wasn't Maori, although Adam probably wasn't fully Maori, either. She remembered reading that many New Zealanders claimed Maori blood, Maori mixed with Pakeha, as they called white-skinned New Zealanders. The Kiwis claimed to be proud of their mixed heritage. If they truly were, it was a model the rest of the world might want to take note of.

Cousins, though? No, she was as alone here as she could possibly be. That was part of the reason she had come. No family, no one to ask questions, no one to give her advice, no one to tell her they were sorry that her life had taken another downward spiral.

Paige looked at her empty glass and wondered when the brandy in it had disappeared. Lately she had begun to enjoy the taste of liquor too much. Was this how her mother had started? Had Ann Duvall looked down at her glass at the beginning of her slow slide into alcoholism and wondered when the liquor in it had vanished? Paige shook her head, repressing a shudder, and screwed the top back on the bottle. She had grown up watching the agonizing deterioration of the mother she adored; it had been the ultimate lesson on the merits of sobriety. There were no solutions to life's disappointments at the bottom of a bottle of brandy.

In all probability, there were no solutions to life's disappointments period.

She was immediately ashamed that she was giving in to the sadness that had been trying to claim her since she had said goodbye to Granger in Honolulu two weeks before. She gave herself a mental shake. She stood, stretching her cramped body.

"And on that note of self-pity, Paige Duvall stands, gathers her four quilts around her as protection against the New Zealand night and calmly finds her way to bed."

It was early; she didn't really feel like sleeping, but since the Waimauri nightlife consisted of one hotel pub that closed its doors at ten and a public hot bath that showed movies while families lounged in steaming outdoor pools, her choices were limited.

Limited, but apparently not as limited as she had first thought. The timid knocking on her door proved that. Paige dropped her quilts and straightened the cotton-silk-blend sweater that Adam Tomoana had reviled. She brushed her hair back from her face as she strolled through the three-room cottage to the door.

A little boy stood on the front steps, surrounded by the mists of the chill night. Paige guessed he was no older than four, a sturdy little cherub with curling wisps of black hair framing a dark, serious face.

Since her conversation with children had been limited to "Hello," "Goodbye," and "What's your favorite television show?" she cleared her throat and tried the first.

The little boy's answer was to hold out a package wrapped in brown paper.

Paige was puzzled. "Is that for me?"

He nodded.

"I didn't order anything."

He moved backward without answering.

"But then, you're not the standard delivery boy type, are you?" She took the package from his hands. As he stepped backward again she tore the paper, lifting out an ivory sweater replete with intricate, twisting cables and honeycomb designs. The wool was soft as a cloud and as heavy as the New Zealand dew.

Paige squatted down so that she and the little boy were at eye level. He promptly stepped backward once more, as if he were afraid she might grab and shake him.

Although his expression hadn't changed, Paige sensed his fear. "Did I scare you?" she asked softly. "I'm sorry." She tried to think of something else to say to reassure him, but she had no idea how to comfort a little boy. "Will you tell me who sent this?"

"Granny."

She nodded. "Does your granny have a name?"

"Granny."

Paige smiled. "And a lovely name it is. Can you tell me why she sent the sweater to me?"

He pretended to shiver, wrapping his arms around his chest.

Paige understood the pantomime. "She was afraid I was cold?"

The cherub nodded.

Paige cocked her head, searching the boy's angelic features. "And how did she know?"

There was no answer, no pantomime. The little boy just turned and stepped off the porch. In a moment he had vanished into the night mists. Paige started to go after him, but she knew it was useless. The little boy knew where he was going. She didn't. After a minute she climbed the steps of the porch and went inside.

In the tiny bedroom she shivered, wishing, not for the first time, that her mother's cousin had left an electric blanket as part of her bequest. Her hands clenched on the little boy's mysterious gift; then she shrugged. Whoever had sent it wanted her to wear it. Paige slipped off her expensive designer sweater and let the ivory wool slide down over her silk blouse. Almost immediately she was more comfortable, so comfortable in fact that she actually felt sleepy. Suddenly the bed looked more inviting than it had in days.

As she lay down, fully clothed and warmer than she'd been since stepping off the plane in Auckland, Paige realized that for the second time in one day she'd been rescued by a beguiling male stranger.

Chapter 2

Adam listened to the soft click of his grandmother's knitting needles as they transformed wool from the sheep he'd raised into a garment a princess would be proud to wear.

"I'm waiting, Adam."

"What is it you want to know, Granny?"

"Tell me again how she looked."

"She has blond curly hair and big blue eyes," he began.

He waited for the fluid, softly spoken words of condemnation to cease. He smiled fondly at the old woman and began again. "Dark hair, black, I suppose. She wears it short. It tickles her cheeks, but not her forehead."

"You noticed a lot," the old woman said slyly.

"She has dark eyes, too. They're Maori eyes, big, tilted a little."

"Like her mother's," his grandmother interrupted. "Ann had eyes that made my heart sing."

Adam's heart hadn't sung a thing, but he went on, knowing Mihi Tomoana wouldn't let him rest until he'd finished. "She had pale skin, but not Pakeha pale, creamier. She's tall and slender."

"Pretty?"

Even Adam had to admit that pretty wasn't on the same list as the words describing Paige Duvall. She was stunning, breathtaking, elegantly dazzling. "Pretty? I suppose."

"And, of course, you didn't really notice," the old woman countered, looping a small ball of gray wool over the ivory wool already on her needles.

Adam bent and kissed her forehead. "She'll wonder where the jumper came from. I should imagine she'll be here tomorrow to thank you for it. It won't take her long to hunt you down."

"E kore e ngaro, he takere waka nui."

Adam straightened and smiled. "But unlike the proverb, you're not a canoe, only a woman who doesn't want to stay hidden, anyway."

A smile merged into the countless wrinkles around the old woman's mouth. "And you are only my grandson who wants to stay hidden forever," she said in English. "Perhaps Paige Duvall will change your mind, *ne*?"

Adam felt a tug at his pant legs. He glanced down, knowing who he would find. He held out his arms, and his son climbed unhesitatingly into them. The little boy smelled like soap and toothpaste, warm milk and sunshine. He rested his shining black curls against his father's shoulder and slipped his thumb in his mouth.

"We have company," Adam told Mihi.

"You think you must tell me Jeremy is out of bed again?"

"What should we do?" Even as he asked the question, Adam moved toward the hall that would take him to the little boy's bedroom.

"Just love him," Mihi Tomoana answered. "I promise you, someday it will be enough."

"An electric blanket for a double bed and a pair of those wool socks in the corner." Paige pointed to a shelf behind the shopkeeper's head. The woman held up a pair of light blue knee socks, and Paige nodded. "And do you have raincoats?"

Paige followed the shopkeeper's directions to the far side of the store and riffled through the oiled canvas slickers. She had awakened that morning determined to stay in Waimauri until plans for selling the thermals were settled. Until that moment, she had contemplated transacting all further business from the comfort of her New Orleans condominium, but something about the early morning birdsong and the sunshine flowing like the purest clover honey through her window had made her decision.

She had come to New Zealand for more than real estate transactions. If she went home now, the temptation to throw herself back into the fast lane would be overwhelming. She didn't need a return to the frantic pace she had kept before Granger had come into her life. If she didn't know what she needed instead, at least here she had the time and the space to think about it.

"Anything else?"

Paige handed a navy slicker to the young woman and shook her head. At least now she was going to be comfortable while she contemplated her navel. "Oh, there is one thing," she said as the shopkeeper added up her purchases on a cash register that belonged in a museum. "I wonder if you might know the origin of this sweater." She held the ivory wool away from her blouse. "It was given to me by a little boy last night, but I don't now who he was or why he gave it to me."

The shopkeeper leaned over the wooden counter. "It's a lovely jumper, isn't it? Hand knit. Turn around, won't you, and I'll just have a look."

Paige turned, filing away the term "jumper" as she did.

"Ah yeah. Just as I thought. It's one of Mihi Tomoana's, from Four Hill Farm. When you take it off, look at the back, Mihi always knits four hills—actually they look like pyramids—on the backside of all her jumpers. You're lucky to have one. Sometimes she sells them in the shop across the way. They cost a pretty penny."

"Do you know who the little boy might have been?"

"Probably Adam's son, Jeremy. Curly black hair? Shy?"

Paige nodded.

"Fetching little fellow, but he's seen some bad times. I'm surprised he got close enough to you to give you the jumper."

Paige realized she was more intrigued than ever. She would have liked to ask more questions, but she knew better than to gossip in a town as small as Waimauri. There was only one more thing she had to know. "I'd like to thank Mrs. Tomoana. Could you tell me how to get to Four Hill Farm?"

With the directions in her head and her parcel under her arm, Paige left the shop and started toward her car. Halfway there her path was blocked by a six foot, blond obstacle.

"Miss Duvall?"

Paige lifted her eyes to meet the obstacle's. His were blue and admiring under expensive, lightly tinted glasses. "Yes?"

"My name is Hamish Armstrong. I was just on my way to your house when someone pointed you out."

Paige was surprised that she was so well known, but then, Waimauri was a small town in a small country. And she was a stranger. "What can I do for you, Mr. Armstrong?" She moved to the edge of the sidewalk to let a group of schoolchildren pass.

"This might take some time. Would you have some tea with me while we talk?"

She cocked her head, assessing the man before her. Besides Aryan good looks, Hamish Armstrong had a smile that was so perfect she suspected an orthodontist's intervention. He was probably in his late thirties, although his tanned, tennis-pro body seemed to belong to a younger man. Only the fine lines around his eyes and the hint of a receding hairline betrayed his true age.

"Would you mind telling me what this is about?"

"Certainly not. I work for Pacific Outreach Corporation. We're interested in property your family owns."

"The thermals?"

"Right."

"Tea sounds like a good idea, Mr. Armstrong."

Minutes later, settled in the Waimauri tearoom, Paige waited for Hamish to bring a tray to their table. After a childhood spent in Europe she was readjusting to a nation that faithfully took leisurely breaks for morning and afternoon tea. Teatime was nothing like the coffee breaks the Duvall Development staff had always taken. Here no one gulped down a steaming cup of coffee at their desk while munching a candy bar. There were probably places in New Zealand—Auckland and Wellington, perhaps—where the fast pace of the Western world had intruded and people cheerfully ruined their health in the name of progress. In Waimauri, however, tea was a welcome pause in the day's routine for nourishment and relaxation.

"I'm afraid this probably isn't what you're used to," Hamish apologized, setting a pot of tea in front of Paige. "The scones are hot, though, and the jam here is homemade."

Paige realized she was starving. "It looks wonderful. I'm probably going to embarrass myself." She reached for a scone and broke it open, inhaling the fresh-from-the-oven aroma.

Hamish removed his glasses and folded them into his shirt pocket. "Are you enjoying New Zealand?"

Paige had to stop and think. "I don't know," she said finally.

Hamish laughed and took a scone for himself. "All business, huh?"

"Actually, I'm afraid I've been hibernating."

"Have you been to see the thermals?"

"I've seen enough to know I need a guide."

"They can be tricky." Hamish offered Paige the raspberry jam and watched as she spread it on her scone. "Try some cream on it, too."

Paige smiled and spread thickened cream over the jam. "Like this?"

He nodded. "Now you can say you've had a real Kiwi-style Devonshire tea."

"What's your interest in the thermals, Mr. Armstrong?"

"Still all business. I understand why Duvall Development sent you," Hamish said with a flash of his perfect teeth. "Call me Hamish, won't you?"

Paige nodded. She waited for him to get to the point.

"Have you been to Rotorua, Miss Duvall?"

"I came through Rotorua on my drive from Auckland." Paige sipped her tea and thought about that trip. She had gotten off the DC-10 from Honolulu to discover an airport like many she had been in and a lovely, medium-size city that could have been plopped down intact in the United States and not seemed out of place.

She had spent that night in Auckland in a well-run modern hotel and rented a car the next morning to take her to Waimauri. It was only on the long drive south that she had begun to take in the essence of New Zealand.

New Zealand was green, sheep-covered hills—irregular sweeps of emerald velvet trimmed with zigzagging rows of trees. New Zealand was an absence of fast-food restaurants and shopping malls, and a proliferation of rural towns, each with its own distinctive character. New Zealand was upside down and backward, from the side of the road she drove on to the numbers on the telephone dial. And yet as she'd driven on the wide, modern highway toward Waimauri, she had wondered if "backward" was the best word to use. This was, after all, the nation that had proclaimed itself a nuclear-free zone.

Her second night had been spent in Rotorua, where she'd found a different New Zealand. The city, which in its infancy had been nicknamed "Rotten Egg Town," smelled of sulfur and catered to tourists. There were expensive hotels and natural spas that tapped into the vast geothermal resources for heating. Paige imagined there was another Rotorua, one she hadn't had time to see, but aside from wallowing shamelessly in the bubbling hot bath adjacent to her hotel room, she had left the city without experiencing any of its attractions.

Then she had found her way to Waimauri.

"What did you think of Rotorua?"

Paige pulled herself back to the present. "I didn't have much of a chance to see it. It seemed like an interesting place."

"It's the major tourist attraction in New Zealand. Did you go to Whakarewarewa? Ohinemutu? Government Gardens?" He watched as Paige shook her head. "There are only two other countries in the world with anything similar. Iceland and your Yellowstone Park."

Paige thought she might understand what he was leading up to. "And you believe there's room for more tourism?"

Hamish leaned back in his chair, his eyes approving. "Rotorua's expanded as far as it can. They've tapped into their geothermal field until there's nothing more to get from it."

"Just how do you want to develop the Waimauri thermals, Mr. Armstrong?"

"Hamish."

"Hamish," she acknowledged. "I am right? That is what you want to do?"

He wove his fingers together and rested his chin on them. "Rotorua's a tourist town. People come in for a night or two, tour here and there, maybe take in one of the Maori shows at their hotel, fish a little in the lake, then they head back where they came from." He paused. "Anyone can see Rotorua," he said at last. "Anyone."

Paige lifted an eyebrow. "And you object to that?"

He made an absolutely-not gesture with his hands. "It's fine with me, but there's always room for a little something different, too, isn't there?"

Paige started on her second scone. She waited silently for him to tell her about "something different."

"I represent a group of Australian investors who would like to build a world-class resort here in Waimauri."

Paige was surprised she hadn't placed Hamish's accent, but then, there were many Australian accents, just like there were many American ones. Hamish's was almost British in its careful precision. "So you're not from New Zealand."

"Sydney. We already have resorts outside of Perth and Sydney, and one in Fiji. Perhaps you've heard of Palm Island?"

"I've heard of it." Paige tried to remember just what she had heard, but the kind of development Hamish was talking about was so foreign to the sturdy, middle-class condominiums and suburban housing her father's company dealt in that she hadn't paid much attention. All she remembered was that it was one of the crowning jewels in Fijian tourism.

"What we have in mind for Waimauri is something smaller, of course. After all, we can't take over the whole North Island, can we?"

"I imagine the Kiwis would object if you tried," Paige said dryly.

"We want to combine old-world elegance with modern technology. Some of the pools in the Waimauri thermals are said to have healing properties. We'd be catering to the very rich—the very old, very rich. We'd have a full staff of physicians, physiotherapists, nutritionists. We'd offer the finest, freshest New Zealand foods, the latest therapies, and all the scenic wonders within a hundred miles." He paused. "We'd boost the local economy one hundred percent. Everyone would benefit."

Paige smiled. "Just how would Duvall Development benefit?"

Hamish named a figure that made her eyes widen.

"Is that American, New Zealand, or Australian dollars?" she asked.

"American."

"If the thermals have all that potential," Paige said, struggling not to show her excitement, "what makes you think we would want to sell them? Why wouldn't Duvall Development want to develop them and reap the profit?"

"May I speak frankly?"

Paige nodded.

"Because, Miss Duvall, your company doesn't have the expertise, and you don't have any kind of reputation here in the Pacific. Oh, you could do it, but not on the same scale we can. And when you were done, you'd come out with less than we're offering for the land."

"And why are you offering so much?"

"To keep you from doing what you just suggested. We plan to make a fortune. We're happy to share."

Paige knew from experience that no one in the cutthroat world of real estate development was happy to share. If Hamish and his group of investors could have stolen the land right out from under Duvall Development's nose, she knew they would have. On the other hand, Hamish was showing keen business sense by not underestimating Duvall. He had done his homework.

"And you're prepared to make this offer right on the spot?" she asked.

"The necessary papers can be drawn up in a day's time."

Paige considered Hamish's words at the same time she surreptitiously examined him. He was trying hard to appear nonchalant, as hard as she had tried when he had mentioned the money his investors were willing to pay. But she was too experienced and too astute not to see subtle signs of tension. Hamish Armstrong wanted the Waimauri thermals as badly as she wanted peace of mind. And she wasn't going to give them to him. Not yet.

"You understand that I'll have to talk to my father about this," she murmured, looking at her new watch in the time-honored signal for concluding a meeting. "Will you be in Waimauri a few more days, or is there someplace else I should reach you?"

He took his glasses out of his pocket and slipped them on. Paige noticed the designer emblem on the thin gold frames. Somehow it fit with the mental picture she was forming of him.

"I'm staying at a hotel in Rotorua." Hamish pulled out a business card and wrote a number on the back. "If you leave a message, I'll be back in touch immediately."

Paige let the corners of her mouth turn up in a lazy smile. "I'll be in touch."

"Perhaps I could interest you in dinner while you're thinking over my offer?" He held up his hands to stall off her refusal. "No business. Just," he hesitated, "pleasure? It's only too rarely that I have such a beautiful business adversary."

There was something about Hamish Armstrong that wasn't quite what it seemed. Paige sensed a shrewdness that was somehow at odds with his polished manners. He interested her because she didn't understand him, and that was rare. She had an intuitive sense about people that almost never failed her.

"Dinner sounds nice," she said.

"Tomorrow night?"

She nodded. "Shall I meet you in Rotorua?"

They made plans as he walked her to her car. She was on the road heading toward Four Hill Farm before she began to have regrets.

"You'll fall on your head, then what will I tell Granny?" Adam ruffled his son's hair, supporting him with a hand on his shoulder as he did. Jeremy Tomoana was perched on the top rail of the wooden fence surrounding the small front yard of the brick farmhouse, and Jeremy never stayed perched for long. Adam was hovering just close enough to make a grab for the little boy if he decided sitting wasn't as much fun as walking along the edge.

"Granny won't know."

"She will if I take you inside screaming."

Jeremy didn't answer, but Adam hadn't expected him to. The real surprise had been the complete sentence he'd spoken first. Jeremy was given to either silence or one-word answers. Adam felt victorious if the little boy forgot his fears long enough to speak at all. In the year and a half Jeremy had been with him, Adam had learned not to be uncomfortable with his son's lack of responses. Jeremy's silences, like the nightmares that haunted him each night, would fade with time. Adam had to believe that.

"I've got to finish nailing these boards to the post, *e tama*. Would you like to help?" Adam watched Jeremy consider his offer. Jeremy considered everything; it almost broke his father's heart. At four, his spontaneity had already vanished, leaving an old man inhabiting a child's body.

Finally, gravely, he nodded. Adam held out his arms, and Jeremy circled his neck with his hands to be lifted down. Only Adam didn't lift him down. He hugged the child against him and buried his face in his hair. *"Taku aroha ki a koe,"* he whispered against the soft curls. "I love you."

The hug was interrupted by the wheeze of a car climbing the steep hill leading to their house. Adam turned, Jeremy still in his arms, and watched the car approach. "Well, she found us."

Jeremy's arm tightened around his neck.

"No, she didn't hurt you last night, and she's not going to hurt you today," Adam reassured him. "Last night you weren't scared. You took the jumper up to the porch by yourself. Remember?"

Jeremy squirmed, trying to get down, and Adam let him go. As he watched, the little boy ran up the path to the house and disappeared inside. At almost the same moment Adam heard the slam of Paige's car door. He wanted to go after his son, but he knew it was too late. With a sigh of resignation he started toward her.

Paige brushed a strand of hair back from her eyes, tucking it behind an ear, where it promptly escaped again. She gave up the struggle as useless and waited for Adam to reach her. He was wearing a gray wool jacket trimmed and lined in sheepskin. Unbuttoned, it showed a burgundy flannel shirt tucked into well-worn blue jeans. He looked less like Lucifer and more like the New Zealand farmer that he was, although the change in no way diminished him. He was a powerful man, a man who throbbed with good health and vitality, and Paige felt something odd trace along her nerve endings as he came closer.

"I see you found us."

Paige wished he would smile, just so that she could measure the effect. She suspected that if he did, only a seismograph could chart the resulting vibrations. "Did you know I'd come?"

One corner of his mouth turned up. "I suspected you were too well bred not to."

"The sweat—jumper was beautiful. I wanted to thank Mrs. Tomoana for it."

"You've been busy today."

She nodded. "Detective work. But then, if you'd just given it to me yourself, told me who it was from, and told me why, I wouldn't have had to ask questions all over town until I found my answers."

One shaggy eyebrow rose in inquiry. "All over town?"

Paige smiled. "An exaggeration."

"I intended to give it to you, but my son insisted on doing it by himself." He didn't add how out of character Jeremy's insistence had been. Adam had never seen the little boy willingly approach a stranger, particularly a female stranger. He suspected Jeremy's reason, and it made something clench deep inside him.

"Were you there?"

Adam nodded.

"He's a beautiful little boy. I'm sure you and your wife are very proud of him."

Adam rarely had to respond to such comments, because Waimauri was a small community and everyone in it knew Jeremy's history. He tried to keep his voice even. "I have no wife. Jeremy and I live here with my grandmother. Come inside and I'll introduce you to her so you can say your thank-you."

Paige read his sudden tension and knew immediately that it wasn't the tragic loss of his wife that had made the cold fire flash in his midnight eyes. "I'd like to thank Jeremy, too. Will he be there?"

"I doubt it," Adam said curtly.

She knew she was trespassing in territory as treacherous as the thermals, but she felt compelled to go on. "I wanted to assure him I wouldn't hurt him. He seemed afraid of me last night."

"There's nothing you could say to him, Miss Duvall, that would convince him you mean him no harm. He's suffered too much at the hands of his mother to believe anything a woman says." Adam turned and started toward the path.

Paige watched the stiff set of his body as he neared the house. "And you, Adam," she said too softly for him to hear, "you've suffered too much, too, haven't you?" Surprised that it should matter to her, she started after him.

Chapter 3

The inside of Adam's house was dark and cool, with the entwined scents of bayberry and roasting lamb perfuming the air. Paige waited on the threshold for her eyes to adjust to the dim light before she stepped into the hallway. The floor at her feet was a highly polished dark wood, and a staircase of the same wood rose in front of her. The cream-colored walls were freshly painted, and framed photographs of laughing men and women decorated them in random, colorful groupings.

She walked behind Adam, admiring the house as they went. Each room was scrupulously neat and tastefully decorated with subtle prints and beautifully refinished antique furniture. "You have a lovely home, Adam," she complimented him. "Just the kind of house to raise a little boy in."

He turned, as if trying to discover if she were patronizing him. "Hardly what you're used to."

"How do you know what I'm used to?" she countered. "You know nothing about me."

Adam took in the way she kept her big, dark eyes carefully blank, but he knew he had hurt her. He realized he was still caught up in her remarks about Jeremy's mother. When would Sheila's destructiveness end? "Well, I know you're an American city girl," he struggled to sound pleasant.

"I'm sure the American part is obvious, but how do you know I'm a city girl?"

He could have told her that he knew everything about her, including her genealogy, but there was no point. Apparently she had no memory of the time she had once spent in New Zealand, and no knowledge of their ties.

"No country girl wears designer clothes to visit a sheep farm."

She looked down at the dark tweed pants, one of the simplest pieces of clothing she owned. "This is what we wear on American sheep farms," she said with a self-mocking grimace.

"It suits the jumper."

She was surprised. His words could almost have passed for a compliment.

"Granny's in the kitchen. We're just about to have tea."

Paige took a quick glance at her watch and realized it was noon. Her timing couldn't have been much worse. "I'll just tell her thank-you and go. I didn't realize—"

"You'll stay," Adam said in a tone that brooked no resistance. "She'll have it no other way."

Paige wanted to tell him that she'd just eaten and couldn't possibly handle another bite, but even as she opened her mouth to say the words, she realized that despite the scones she had shared with Hamish, she was hungry again. And the smells coming from the kitchen were mouth-watering.

Adam pushed a swinging wooden door, and Paige followed him through it. She listened as he spoke a language she didn't understand to the old woman standing by a large stainless-steel stove.

Mihi Tomoana was time itself. Paige could no more have guessed her age than she could have guessed what Adam was saying to her. Her face was square, with strong, prominent bones that, despite the ravages of age, were the most assertive aspect of her countenance. Her skin was brown and wrinkled, and her hair snow white, caught back from her face in a tidy bun. Her features were blunt, obviously Polynesian in origin, but nothing like her grandson's. She was tiny, but sturdy, and as Adam spoke, her face was wreathed in smiles.

It was only as Mihi started toward her that Paige realized she was blind.

"Do you know how to *hongi*?" Adam asked Paige.

She blinked. "I don't think so."

Adam said something to his grandmother, and the old woman laughed. "I'll teach you," Mihi said in English. "Come." She held out her hands, and Paige took them. "Bend over."

Paige did, and the old woman leaned toward her. Their noses touched, then their foreheads. Mihi stepped backward, dropping Paige's hands.

"So tall," Mihi said, shaking her head, "but then, your mother was tall."

"You knew my mother?"

"Does she never speak of anyone from Waimauri?"

"Mother lives in the present." *From one bottle of scotch to the next,* Paige added silently, knowing that sharing that bit of information with Mihi Tomoana would be unkind. "She's said very little about her life in New Zealand."

"After tea I'll see if you look like her," Mihi said. "But for now, perhaps you'd like to freshen up."

"I really didn't mean to come at mealtime," Paige began.

"You are welcome here any time of the day or night. Ann's daughter is always welcome in my home. Come, I'll show you where you can wash your hands."

"I'll see if I can ferret out Jeremy," Adam told them.

"Tell him I said he must come," Mihi told her grandson.

When Paige emerged from the bathroom, Mihi was carrying a casserole into the small dining room off the kitchen. "Have a seat, dear, and wait for Adam and Jeremy."

"Is there anything I can do?" Paige rarely did anything more domestic than pop the cork on French champagne, but now, in addition to sheer good manners, there was something about the warm, fragrantly pleasant kitchen that made her want to lend a hand.

"Not a thing. I have everything arranged just so, and if anyone else comes in and changes the least little thing, I get confused."

Paige had almost forgotten that Adam's grandmother was blind. Mihi was so efficient, so sure of herself, that it was almost as if the filmy dark eyes could see every detail of the kitchen. Only the way her eyes failed to focus gave her away.

"Jeremy, say hello to Miss Duvall."

"Paige, please," Paige said, turning at the sound of Adam's voice. "Hello, Jeremy." She smiled at the little boy. "I'm glad to see you again."

Jeremy hid his face against his father's flannel shirt.

"Jeremy," Mihi said in a stern voice. "Greet our guest."

"H'lo." The voice was muffled, but the word was unmistakable.

Paige cleared her throat. She knew she should do something more, say something more, but she felt much like she had in the thermals. If she took the wrong step, she might be in worse trouble yet.

"Let's eat," Mihi said, saving her from fashioning a response. "Jeremy, you may show Paige where to sit. She'll be right between you and your father, across from me."

Adam set Jeremy down, and the little boy skirted the edges of the kitchen, staying as far from Paige as possible. In the dining room he pointed to a chair, and Paige, who had followed him at a discreet distance, nodded. "Thank you."

Adam came around behind her and pulled out her chair. She let him seat her; then he took his place beside her. Jeremy was on her left, perched on the far edge of his chair like a sparrow about to take flight.

With a knife as wickedly sharp as a machete, Adam began to carve the roast lamb, while Mihi passed a platter of steamed carrots, parsnips and whole new potatoes. Then came a divided dish with a variety of salads. When Paige finally had the courage to look down at her plate, she saw a week's worth of calories.

"I haven't seen so much food in one place since I left the States." She picked up her fork when she realized everyone else was already eating. "This looks and smells wonderful."

"How have you been cooking?" Mihi asked, a frown distorting her forehead. "Have you discovered the secrets of Jane's old stove?"

"No. I got just far enough to figure out that it *was* a stove." Paige tackled the lamb to find that it was as mildly flavored as the finest veal.

"If you're not using the stove, what are you using?" Adam asked.

"A can opener," she said wryly, "and the tearoom in town when I really get hungry."

Mihi clucked disparagingly. "You could almost boil water on the steam radiators in that house. Use them to heat food for yourself."

"That's something else I haven't figured how to work," Paige admitted.

"You don't have any heat?"

"It's supposed to be spring. And I hadn't planned to stay very long."

Adam raised an eyebrow. "City girl," he said sweetly.

Paige felt a peculiar rush of warmth at his words. He was teasing her, and the moment, free from cynicism and distrust, was very nice. "I freely admit it," she said, aiming her smile at him.

Adam felt the smile like a punch in his stomach. Already he knew enough about Paige to know that smiles that unaffected were rare. She was relaxed, and she was enjoying herself. Considering her background, he wouldn't have thought it was possible.

"Adam will show you how to operate the heat and the stove," Mihi said firmly.

"Will you show me how to cook, too?" she asked him.

Mihi was incredulous. "You don't cook? Ann's daughter doesn't cook?"

"Ann doesn't cook," Paige said, defending herself. "I've never seen Mother do anything more complicated than spread pâté on a cracker."

"Ah, once she was the finest cook in Waimauri. Her mother taught her, and her mother could take the toughest cut of mutton and make it tender enough to put on the queen's table."

Paige tried to imagine such a thing. "Apparently she's been hiding her talents."

"You really don't cook?" Adam asked.

"I really don't. Do you?" Paige lifted her gaze from her plate to meet his. "Or don't Kiwi men stoop that low?"

The smile he shot her would have been a nine on the Richter scale. Paige was almost bowled over. "I cook," he said. "Maybe one day I'll cook for you."

The meal continued, with Jeremy sitting as far from Paige as possible and Mihi asking questions about Paige's reactions to New Zealand. It was only after they had all finished that Paige realized she still hadn't thanked Mihi for the sweater.

Mihi giggled when she did, a lilting, girlish sound that momentarily transformed her into the Maori maiden she must once have been. "I'm glad you like it, and I hope it keeps you warm."

"I'm wearing it now. In fact, I've hardly taken it off."

Mihi waved aside her praise. "Will you call me Granny like Adam and Jeremy do?"

Paige realized Adam was watching her intently, and, in her own way, Mihi was watching her, too. "I'd like that."

Mihi dropped her napkin on the table and stood. "Good. Now I want to see you."

Paige stood, too, unsure how this miracle was going to be accomplished. Hesitantly she followed Mihi into a large, comfortable room furnished with upholstered furniture supplemented by more of the antiques she had noticed earlier. Mihi settled herself on the sofa, then patted the seat beside her.

Paige sat, and Mihi put her hands on her shoulders. Then she stroked her fingertips up Paige's neck to her face. Very slowly she began to explore her features. "There are only so many things I can tell from your voice," she murmured. "I want to be sure I know you." She laughed. "Ah, that worries you, does it? You don't like to have people know you. In that way, too, you're very like your mother. And like Adam."

Paige tried not to stiffen, but she knew Mihi was picking up her tension. She wasn't comfortable being touched this way. Even at the rare moments of real intimacy in her life, she had resisted this kind of petting.

"You have your mother's eyes and your father's nose. The mouth is your grandmother's." Mihi laughed again. "The chin is your own, child, unless it comes from your father's family."

Paige realized Mihi was full of surprises. "You knew my father?"

Mihi shook her head. "I saw him once, before I lost my sight. Life hasn't been simple for you, has it?"

"It's not supposed to be, is it?"

"Once it was simpler. People knew where they belonged—and to whom." Mihi lifted her hands to Paige's hair. "Lovely," she said admiringly. "Black."

Paige wondered how she had known. "Yes."

"And your eyes are dark, too."

Paige nodded. She looked up and saw Adam, arms folded across his chest, leaning on the doorjamb watching them. Jeremy was peeking out from behind him.

"Ko Hine-titama koe, matawai ana te whatu i te tirohanga."

Paige was sure her confusion showed on her face because Mihi laughed, and Adam explained. "She said you are like the Dawn Maid. The eye glistens when gazing upon you. Granny enjoys keeping the old Maori proverbs alive."

"She's as lovely as you said." Mihi turned in Adam's direction. "Now take her home and show her how to heat her house." Her hands fluttered to her side.

"Thank you for everything." Paige felt disconnected from something important, but she didn't know what. On a whim she leaned over and kissed the old woman's cheek. "I'm very glad to know you."

"Granny."

"Granny." Paige stood.

"Come back soon."

"I'm going to leave Jeremy here." Adam pushed himself away from the doorjamb. "He could do with a nap."

"No," the little boy wailed.

"Yes," his father answered calmly. "I'll be back, *e tama*. I always come back."

Jeremy wrapped his arms around his father's leg.

"You know, Adam, I've been doing fine without heat. And I bought an electric blanket today, so I'll be comfortable at night." Paige eyed Jeremy's defiant little face and wished that it were some other woman who was going to take his father away.

"He'll be fine." Adam bent over and pried Jeremy's fingers loose. "Jeremy, go to your room. Granny will tuck you in for your nap, and I'll be back by the time you wake up."

Two crystalline teardrops spilled down the little boy's cheeks, but Adam ignored them. "I always come back," he repeated.

Without another word, Jeremy fled the room.

"Are you sure you should leave?"

Paige's question was softly spoken, but Adam heard the distress behind it. He grimaced, knowing that at some point he was going to have to explain Jeremy's behavior. Irrationally he was angry at her for making it necessary. "If you're ready, we can go," he said, and he knew he sounded as irritated as he felt.

Her chin lifted an inch. "I'm ready."

"You drive as though you're used to this side of the road."

Paige spared Adam a quick glance before she focused on the road in front of her again. "I was educated in Switzerland. I learned to drive from an English count, the brother of a schoolmate, on one of my holidays. When I got back to the States, I had to be taught all over again. To this day I feel more at home with the steering wheel over here."

Adam shifted, his legs cramped. "You've seen a lot of the world, then."

"Europe and some of Asia. This is my first trip to the Southern Hemisphere."

Adam could have disputed that, but he didn't.

"Have you traveled much?" Paige asked in return.

"I've seen most of Europe, and I've spent holidays in Australia and Colorado."

"Colorado?"

"On a sheep ranch. Comparing techniques."

Paige wondered how many American sheep ranchers were so well traveled. She was learning that people from this part of the world dealt with their relative isolation by taking long and varied holidays. They had a richness of experience and an appreciation for variety because of it.

"Well, I think we're here." She pulled the little rental car to one side of the gravel drive and turned off the engine.

Adam stared out the windshield at the small clapboard bungalow. "Are you finding the house comfortable, other than the temperature?"

"Comfortable enough after I gave it a good cleaning."

"You've cleaned it, you've bought an electric blanket. Are you planning to stay a while?"

"I wasn't at first." Paige opened her door and stepped out into the sunshine. She finished explaining as they walked toward the house. "I didn't realize just how large the thermals were, or how potentially profitable. I thought I'd just look them over, relax a few days, then head back home."

"Potentially profitable?"

Paige thought about Hamish's offer for the first time since she had driven up to Adam's house. "Land is valuable, Adam." She realized she had used his given name, but somehow it seemed appropriate now. "My father always says its the only thing they're not making more of, though when I watch the way developers dredge our coasts, I wonder about that, too."

"And you think the thermals might be valuable?"

"Might be." Paige pushed the door open. There was no lock, no key to the little bungalow. She couldn't shake the feeling that she would walk in one day and find everything gone, but when she'd questioned someone in town about security, they had laughed and walked away muttering.

"And what if they're not? What if you can only get a pittance for all your trouble? Will your trip here have been a waste of time?"

"You know, when you ask a question, I always feel like you're really asking another." She hugged herself, suddenly chilly now that she was out of the sun. "Do you do that to disconcert me? I don't disconcert easily."

"I ask questions to get answers. Isn't that the usual reason?"

"Why don't you like me, Adam? Is it because I'm an American? I can't help that, any more than I can help the fact that a relative of my mother's died and left her this property."

"There are things you *can* help."

Now she was truly puzzled. It bothered her to be treated so abruptly. She had no reason to want his respect or affection, but she did anyway. She wondered what loneliness was doing to her good sense. "What things can I help?" she asked, poker-faced.

"You can be sure the land's not exploited."

Paige relaxed a little. She had been through enough discussions of this ilk to know what was coming. "Duvall Development has a policy of cooperating as fully as possible on any environmental concerns. We have an ecologist on our staff who does nothing except study the environmental impact of all our developments."

"But you're not going to develop the thermals yourselves, are you?"

"We take into consideration the reputation of any company we sell property to. And there must be laws in New Zealand like there are in most countries protecting the land."

"Are there laws protecting legends, Miss Duvall?"

She stared at him, thrown off guard. "Legends?"

Adam took a deep breath. "I think you'd better show me your radiators, and I'll get started fixing them."

She struggled to make sense of their conversation. "You ask questions under questions and expound in riddles. You're a frustrating man, Adam, and I really wish you'd stop calling me Miss Duvall."

He was sure he didn't feel like smiling, but the familiar tightening of his mouth was unmistakable.

"You're smiling at me," she warned. "You're going to ruin your image."

Despite everything, he knew she was a very easy woman to smile at. That thought was enough to wipe the smile right off his face. "Your radiators?"

Paige realized they were still standing in the hallway. She smothered a frustrated sigh. "There's one in the bedroom and one in the living room. But they're both turned on. I don't think that's where the trouble is."

The trouble, it turned out, was in the complicated set of valves and dials on the back porch. Adam made a few adjustments, and the radiators began to hiss. "The heat comes from the thermals," he explained. "Years ago somebody sunk a bore nearby and piped the steam. You're heating your house for free."

Paige thought about her conversation with Hamish. "I've been told that most of the energy in Rotorua is supplied that way."

"Were you also told that in the last thirty years they've gone from 130 geysers down to six, and that dozens of natural springs and mud pools have disappeared? Some physicists believe that all the geysers are destined to stop in the next four years."

Paige gave a low whistle. "What a shame that would be."

"Wouldn't it?" Adam said cynically.

"All that because they've harnessed the steam?"

"That's the theory."

"I can see why you might be worried about the thermals here," Paige conceded.

"No you can't."

She felt a surge of anger, something she rarely allowed herself. She had discovered a long time ago that anger gave other people power, and that was something she couldn't afford.

She hesitated just long enough to get herself under careful control. "I appreciate your help," she said coldly. "I'd like to pay you for your time."

"Would you?" Adam straightened and turned to her. "And would you like to pay me for guiding you back from the thermals, and for the jumper, and perhaps even for the meal we shared?"

"If it would wipe that supercilious, holier-than-thou expression off your face, I certainly would."

Adam's eyes narrowed, and Paige felt a flicker of alarm. Abruptly she remembered what a powerfully built man he was. Adam didn't move, however. Instead his mouth twitched, and then, unbelievably, he smiled again. "Holier than thou?"

"I'm sorry," she murmured, no apology in her voice.

"For what?"

He was still smiling, and despite herself, Paige smiled, too. "For not adding that you're the most difficult, contrary man I've ever had the pleasure to know."

"Pleasure?" He moved a little closer. "Has it been a pleasure . . . Paige?"

"Not yet, but I have the most ridiculous feeling that if you let us, we might be friends."

"Granny would certainly approve of that."

"Well, what do you think? Shall we try to share more than sarcastic retorts, or are we both so jaded that it's not going to be worth the effort?"

Unwillingly he felt himself being drawn to her. He wanted to put her in the category of rich American, out-to-own-the-world, but he couldn't. Beneath her aloof, elegant exterior there was a fragile woman who needed friendship and warmth and the security of the roots that had been denied her. Defeated, he rested his hands on her shoulders and drew her near. Then his nose and forehead touched hers. He could feel her stiffen, then relax, as if she had forced her muscles to respond. She smelled like spring flowers, and in the instant before he drew away, he knew the smooth, melting warmth of her skin.

"Friends help each other because they need help," he said, his hands dropping to his sides.

Paige tried to still her response to the *hongi*. She was lonely; Adam was a very attractive man. Her feelings were natural. "I appreciate your fixing the heat. Please let me know if I can return the favor."

"You may have that chance."

She tried to fathom his fathomless eyes. "When? How?"

"It's too soon to say yet. But I may be coming to you with a proposition." He smiled lazily at the slight change in her expression. "A business proposition," he added. "If you'd do me the courtesy of listening, I'd consider it a favor returned."

"I always listen to business."

"Good." Adam stepped back. "Jeremy's waiting. I need to get home."

"He won't be asleep."

"What do you mean?"

She was surprised that her thoughts had been said out loud. "Only that I remember being Jeremy's age, waiting for my parents to come home. Even if it was early morning before they got in, I'd stay awake until I heard them come down the hall. Then I'd finally shut my eyes." She wondered why she had shared that small piece of her childhood. She shrugged. "As worried as Jeremy was, he'll be awake when you get there."

"Even when I'm there he rarely sleeps."

Paige didn't know what to say, but Adam didn't seem to want to respond anyway. He started toward the door. "If you have any more trouble with the heat, I'll be glad to look at it again."

He was gone before she even thought to offer him a ride home.

Chapter 4

No one could say that the Kiwis cut corners on phone booths. Paige stood in a wood-and-glass model, circa early twentieth century, and wondered if she ought to give a cocktail party while she was waiting for her call home to go through. The booth was large enough; in fact, she could almost envision a grand piano in the corner.

She needed that kind of a lift. She wasn't looking forward to this discussion with her father. Carter Duvall was not a man who liked to be crossed, and Carter had said he didn't want her coming to New Zealand. "Let somebody else handle this one, Paige," he had told her somewhere between his desk and office door when she had brought it up. "I need you on more important business." Then he had neglected to tell her what that more important business might be.

She hadn't intended to pursue the Waimauri property, not until her vacation with Granger in Honolulu had fallen through, anyway. Then she had needed to take her mind off her personal disappointment, and somehow, New Zealand had seemed like the answer. Her secretary had been instructed to inform Carter when and if he seemed to be in a good mood. Paige hoped Lucy had found an opportunity by now.

"I'll hold," she promised the operator as she drummed her fingers in a hard-rock rhythm against the glass. She listened as the phone whirred and clicked; then she heard her mother's voice.

"Hello, Mother," she said, trying to remind herself that she didn't have to shout. There was a faint hesitation as her voice was transmitted, then an enthusiastic response from the other end.

"Darling. Where are you? Are you still in Honolulu? I tried to reach you last night and this morning, but they told me that number had been disconnected."

Paige drummed her fingers louder in frustration. Either Lucy hadn't found Carter in a good mood in the days since Paige had come to New Zealand, or Carter hadn't told his wife where their daughter was. "I left Honolulu the Wednesday before last. I'm in Waimauri, New Zealand."

There was a longer silence than necessary. "Why?" Ann asked at last.

"I'm checking on the property you inherited, Mother. I'm staying at the house."

"Does your father know?"

Paige recognized her mother's Carter-must-be-placated voice. "I don't know if he does or not," Paige said, irritated, "but I'm calling to tell him now. Is he there?"

"Paige, come home. You shouldn't be there."

Paige could almost hear her mother reaching for the cut-glass decanter that stood on the table beside the parlor telephone. She imagined the tingle of ice cubes and the splash of expensively mellow scotch. "Mother, is Father there?"

Another extended silence was followed by a sigh. "Don't stir up trouble, darling. New Zealand is too far away. Come home."

Paige wondered what New Zealand was too far away from. Too far from the United States, or too far from her mother's life? Perhaps what had seemed like a whim on her father's part was more. "I need to speak to Father," she repeated.

"Just a moment."

Paige heard the hurt in her mother's tone, and she was sorry to have put it there. But she was too old to blindly follow bad advice just because it had been given by a parent. She wasn't going to leave New Zealand without a plan for the thermals firmly in place.

And she wasn't going to leave Waimauri without some answers to questions that were beginning to seem important.

Cousin.

She wished she could call her mother back to the phone and ask if Adam's suggestion that they were related had any basis in fact. Did she have family here, family that her mother had never acknowledged? Adam's blood was Maori and Pakeha. Did they have a common English ancestor? Had there been a family spat her mother didn't want her to know about?

Her thoughts were interrupted by her father's voice.

"What the hell are you doing in New Zealand?"

"Playing cricket with kiwi birds," she said pleasantly. "And hello to you, Father mine."

"Right now I'm your boss, not your father. Get on the next plane home, Paige, or your job is a memory."

"I'm fine, thanks, and how are you? Improved your golf score any? Bought and sold any continents?" There was a short silence, and Paige tapped her fingers, waiting.

"I wouldn't stand for this from anyone else."

"The advantages of daughterhood."

There was a rumble across oceans, but Paige knew it was her father trying to suppress a laugh. Carter Duvall was any man's definition of a bastard, but he had two weaknesses: his daughter and his wife. "Come home, daughter," he said more pleasantly. "Come home and I'll buy you a continent."

"Thanks, but I'll settle for selling part of an island. Listen to this." She told him about her conversation with Hamish Armstrong, ending with the price Hamish had quoted.

"You've done well," Carter admitted grudgingly. "Now come home and let me send someone more experienced with this kind of deal to finish up negotiations."

"Just what are you and Mother trying to hide?"

There was a short silence, followed by profanity that made even Paige, who was used to Carter's language, take notice.

"You know, you just insulted your own mother," she said when he'd finished. "And possibly your grandmother, but you went so fast, I couldn't say for sure."

"We aren't hiding anything," he shouted. "New Zealand's history. And there's no point in you being there. The future counts, not the past."

"An excellent slogan. I'll have it chiseled on your headstone. In the meantime, I'm not going to tolerate you sending someone 'more experienced' to finish anything. This deal's mine, Carter. I'll come back when I've made a successful sale." She paused. "And when I find out what you're so worried about."

She could have heard his slam of the telephone receiver without the phone company's help.

* * *

Late that afternoon, dressed in an ice-pink, wool jersey dress with frivolously expensive eelskin shoes and belt, Paige began the hour drive to Rotorua to meet Hamish for dinner. Lush, verdant hills rolled back from both sides of the road, broken only by an occasional tree and more than occasional sheep, some with newborn lambs who frolicked in the deepening shadows.

After her phone call she had spent the day browsing through the library for books that detailed the history of New Zealand, particularly the volcanic region of which Waimauri was a part. Her reading had begun as an exercise in trying to understand the area, but it had quickly evolved into fascination.

She had followed the story of the Maoris coming to the islands sometime around the fourteenth century and their struggle to survive in a climate unlike their native *Hawaiki*, now thought to be one of the group known as the Society Islands, of which Tahiti was a part. She had learned about the eight canoes that had landed, and how descendants of the people from each canoe had formed tribes. She had read the fascinating, often violent history of a people who had almost been extinguished after their encounters with the Europeans who followed them centuries later to "civilize" the islands.

Reading about the European settlers had been interesting, too. North of Auckland, the Bay of Islands had harbored a colony of the worst reprobates in the South Pacific, pirates and whalers and convicts escaped from Australia's penal colonies. There had been an unconscionable rape of the North Island forests, and a flourishing market in Maori tattooed and preserved heads. The Europeans had brought a Christianity they didn't always practice, along with muskets and liquor and diseases that the Maoris had no immunity against.

It wasn't until 1839 that Britain began to sort things out, sending 19,000 stable settlers to begin a colony. But it was another twenty-five years before the fierce wars between the Maoris and Pakehas ended, leaving a Maori population decimated by war and poverty and the attendant problems of alcoholism and malnutrition.

Luckily the story hadn't finished there. Both Maoris and Pakehas had thrived and flourished since the turn of the century. Paige had been left with a growing sense of excitement at discovering more about this country whose heritage was rich in folklore and tradition, and whose contemporary commitment to fair play and equality was a model for nations everywhere.

Carter might believe she had no reason to stay in New Zealand, but more than ever, she knew he was wrong.

And more than ever she believed Carter was hiding something. Whatever it was, she intended to find out the truth before she went home.

In the meantime she was looking forward to sizing up Hamish a little better. If she had sometimes felt that she was a vice president of Duvall Development solely because the company belonged to her father, she couldn't feel that way after she left New Zealand. Negotiating the future of the thermals fell under the heading of proving herself.

She put Carter out of her mind, and immediately another man filled it. Unfortunately it wasn't the first time she had thought of Adam that day. He was a confusing man, and he provoked confusing feelings in her. She was no twittering virgin whose heart beat faster at velvet dark eyes and masculine arrogance; she was a divorcée who had known her share of men, even if she had never fallen into the casual sexual habits of the women in her crowd. So why did her mind keep straying back to Adam? He had nothing to offer her, just as she had nothing to offer him, even if he were interested.

And yet he was undeniably the most arresting man she had met in a long time. Her attraction to him was classic. He was a man of mystery, a man whose secrets were more compelling than other men's candor, a man whose depths begged to be explored. Even Granger had not affected her this way. Granger had been a known quantity, a man she had understood and loved for his compassion and warmth. Adam showed neither of those qualities, yet she had the feeling that those closest to him saw both.

She could rationalize her interest in Adam as loneliness, as something to enliven the simple life she was living, but neither analysis was complimentary to Adam or to her. The truth was more complex, so complex that she didn't understand it all. Paige forced Adam out of her mind. For the rest of the trip she counted sheep and kept her eye on a dwindling fuel tank.

Rotorua's downtown was laid out with British precision. She found her way to the hotel where she was meeting Hamish and turned her car over to the valet. As she waited in the lobby, she admired a carved wooden panel done by a Maori craftsman.

"Like it?"

Paige turned around and smiled at an elegantly attired Hamish. "I don't know that I understand it, but yes, it's wonderful."

"They've got carvings like this all over New Zealand if you know where to look."

"Where do you look?"

"Meeting houses. Churches. The Maoris do some smaller carvings for the tourist trade, but usually today's carvers can't keep up with the demands of their own people."

"You've done your homework."

"I have, actually. We need to understand this part of New Zealand to be certain we make full use of the thermals." He smiled. "If you sell them to us."

"We'll have to see about that, won't we?"

Hamish took her arm. "No business tonight. I've neglected to tell you how lovely you look. I'll be the envy of every man in the dining room."

Paige let Hamish guide her through the hotel lobby to the lounge. She wasn't oblivious to the heads that turned. With his blond good looks, Hamish made a striking companion.

"I took the liberty of purchasing tickets for the *hangi* feast and concert tonight. I thought that if you hadn't seen one you might enjoy it." Hamish seated her at a small table and signaled the waitress.

"I haven't seen one. What is it, exactly?"

"The *hangi* is a special underground oven that the Maoris use. They steam all sorts of food in it, then serve them buffet style. After the feast there's a troupe of Maori singers who entertain."

"Have you been before?"

"Several times." Hamish smiled almost sheepishly. "When you see the women, you'll understand why a bachelor might be tempted to go back more than once."

Paige wasn't sure if Hamish was just trying to slyly tell her he was single, or if he was really that impressed, but either way, the *hangi* sounded interesting. Sipping drinks, they chatted about their lives, although when they finally made their way into the banquet hall, Paige realized she knew little more about Hamish than she had originally. He had been an executive with Pacific Outreach Corporation for five years, and his special expertise was the design and development of future projects. He was a native Australian, although his parents were from Germany and Scotland, and he had grown up in a tiny town in Queensland where his parents had run a butcher shop. Beyond that, Hamish Armstrong was a skillfully camouflaged unknown.

They arrived in the banquet hall just in time to follow the tall-hatted chef poolside to open the steam pit where their dinner had been prepared. Back in the banquet hall, they were seated at one of a number of long tables with other guests, and then, after a humorous introduction to the fare by their Maori host and a blessing in the Maori language, they went to the buffet to heap their plates from a variety of dishes including marinated raw fish, mussels, and Maori chicken, a local seabird.

The meal progressed with chatting among guests. Four different countries were represented at their table alone, and the friendly atmosphere set by their host prevailed. Over boysenberries and fresh cream, Paige lifted her eyes from her plate to see Adam standing beside her.

"Adam," she said, caught off guard. "I didn't know you were here."

"I wasn't. One of the performers asked me to come and see the show tonight." Adam's gaze traveled to Hamish. He didn't smile. "Hello, Armstrong," he said without enthusiasm. "You're no slouch, I'll give you credit for that."

Hamish nodded curtly.

"I gather you two know each other," Paige said, mystified that the vibrations between the two men were this strong. Hostility almost shimmered in the air.

"We do," Adam acknowledged. "Do you mind if I join you here at the end of the table?"

Paige was interested in Hamish's answer, but he only shrugged. "Of course you may," she said. "You'll have a good seat for the performance."

Adam pulled out his chair with lazy grace and draped his long body over it. "Have you been to one of our concert parties before, Paige?"

"No. I'm looking forward to it. The meal was delicious."

"Someday you'll have to come to a real Maori feast."

"The Maori people excel at cooking and singing," Hamish said, as if he were instructing Paige, "but they're behind in other areas. Wouldn't you say so, Tomoana?"

Paige refused to be insulted on Adam's behalf. She knew him well enough to know he could take care of himself. Settling back in her seat, she waited for the sparks to fly.

"In areas like avarice and fraud?" Adam asked politely. "I'm afraid you may be right. The Maoris have trouble cheating their neighbors or claiming everything they see as their own. It's set us back tremendously."

"I wouldn't want you to think I was criticizing," Hamish said, holding his hands palm-out as if to push away the thought. "There's a certain sweetness in simplicity."

"What do you think about that, Paige?" Adam asked, raising one shaggy brow.

"The only Maoris I know personally are anything but simple or sweet," she said, locking her gaze to his.

She saw the approval in his eyes before he spoke. "Insightful." He stopped, then grinned. "For an American," he added.

"We can't all be Maoris. We have to work with what we've got."

"You might be surprised," Adam said, his high-voltage grin disappearing.

Paige was used to Adam's swift changes of mood and his enigmatic answers, but this time she couldn't let it pass.

"What do you mean?"

Adam reached across the table and covered her hand, which was still holding the spoon she'd been using for her dessert. He guided the spoon back into the bowl of cream.

"'Things are seldom what they seem. Skim milk masquerades as cream,'" he recited in his resonant voice. He let the cream drip off her spoon for several seconds before he moved his hand. "There's another line from that song, too. Something about jackdaws strutting in peacock feathers." His gaze flicked to Hamish. "Are you a Gilbert and Sullivan fan, Armstrong?"

Paige didn't understand anything any better, but she knew she had to close the open rift between the two men, even though she was irritated with Hamish for goading Adam. "I was Yum-Yum in *The Mikado* in my senior year of high school," she said, switching the subject to herself. "It was a small girl's school. Both my roommates had to sing men's parts."

"Then you sing?" Adam asked.

"Only a little. The director thought I looked exotic enough to play Yum-Yum. I think he was sorry when I opened my mouth." She pushed her bowl away. "I can't eat another bite. That was delicious, Hamish. I'm glad you thought of this."

Hamish's pale eyes signaled his disapproval of her interruption, but he gave her a chilly nod. Before more hostility could erupt, their host appeared to introduce the show. Paige clapped along with everyone else as the troupe of Maori singers came out to perform.

The women were dressed in thin-strapped bodices of intricately woven red, black and white design, with matching headbands adorned with white feathers. Their red skirts were covered with an outer skirt made of individual reedlike fibers in a white and black stripe that rippled and clicked as they moved. The men wore similar reed skirts over dark shorts, but they were bare-chested. All were bare-footed.

Paige was unexpectedly stirred as the troupe began to sing. Performed in the Maori language, their songs were melodic and beautifully harmonized, with the men keeping a driving chant-like beat while the women carried the melody. They danced as they sang, and the movements and sound were hypnotic. She had expected a tourist show, but this was something more. It was the song of a people who had adapted their ways under the pressure of another civilization, yet it was a song filled with the beauty and joy of their own unique contribution to the country that was now New Zealand.

"What do you think?" Adam asked, leaning forward so that his question was a whisper only she could hear.

"Wonderful." Paige didn't take her eyes from the stage. For a moment she was overwhelmed by dèjá vu. "I feel like I've heard them before. I must have heard a recording somewhere."

"Perhaps."

"Who did you come to see?"

"The woman on the far right."

Paige examined her. She was the youngest and the prettiest of the five women, with waving black hair that rippled over the top of her dancing skirt and a smile that no man would be immune to. "She's lovely."

"You'll enjoy the *poi* dances."

She did. The *poi* was a lightweight ball on a string that was swung in graceful arcs as the women sang. The men were featured in the *haka*, rhythmically shouted chants of defiance that were accompanied by sharp, aggressive jabs of the hands and feet.

For an hour Paige listened, spellbound. When the lights were turned on again and everyone stood to sing "Now is the Hour," the traditional Maori farewell, she was sorry the concert was over.

"Would you like to meet Hira and the others?" Adam asked, switching his gaze to Hamish to include him, too.

"I'm afraid I have to use the telephone," Hamish said, looking at his watch. "Shall I help you get your car, Paige?"

Paige would have liked to meet the performers, but she also knew where her social duty lay. "Thank you," she told Adam, "but I should probably be getting back now. It's a long drive at night."

Hamish said a cool goodbye to Adam and walked Paige to the front desk to call for her car.

She considered letting the hostility at dinner drop, but since she and Hamish were going to be doing some intense business negotiations, she decided to probe a little. She'd found from experience that little things could ruin the most substantial deals.

"I couldn't help noticing that you and Adam don't like each other," she said as they waited for the valet to bring her car around. "I was surprised you knew him, since you aren't from Waimauri."

"You might as well know," Hamish said with a smile that didn't quite reach his eyes, "that he and I have had words about the thermals."

Paige was glad she had played her hunch and opened the subject. "Do you mind telling me why?"

"He came to me when he heard I was asking questions about the area. He has some cockamamy story about them being scared ground or some such rot. What it comes down to, I'm sure, is that he and his people are afraid of progress. They don't know the difference between a first-class resort and a tourist trap, and no matter how hard I tried to explain, he didn't understand."

Paige was intrigued, although she didn't tell Hamish. Adam wasn't a man who would have trouble understanding anything. If he was antagonistic to Hamish's plans, then he had reasons. Some of his more cryptic remarks began to make sense, as did the feud between the two men.

"Well, I hope it didn't spoil your evening," she said, holding out her hand. "I certainly enjoyed the meal and concert, and I appreciate your arranging it."

"I'm glad you could come." He squeezed her hand before he released it. "I'll be in touch soon."

"Not too soon," she warned. "I'm going to need a guided tour of the thermals before I can begin any negotiations. I've got to see them for myself."

"When are you planning to do that?"

"Just as soon as I can find someone who's willing to take me in."

"I'm sure I can find someone for you."

But Paige already had a person in mind. She watched Hamish closely for his reaction. "To be honest, I intend to ask Adam. If he can't find the time, I'll see if he knows someone else."

Hamish nodded but, as she'd expected, his expression mirrored his disapproval. "Then you have my number here at the hotel?"

"I do." She turned at the sound of tires squealing and watched as the attendant parked her rental car in front of the hotel. "I'll call you in a day or two. Thanks again for dinner."

"My pleasure."

She doubted that, but she smiled anyway as she slid under the steering wheel.

Paige was out on the road before she remembered that she had forgotten to ask where the closest service station might be. Her gas gauge was too close to empty for comfort, and although she had seen several stations off the highway between Rotorua and Waimauri, she wasn't sure they would be open. She swung back into the drive in front of the hotel, hoping to find the valet.

Instead she found Adam embracing the lovely young Maori girl who had been one of the evening's entertainers. Paige was back on the road in seconds, determined to locate a station by herself.

"Come on, Hira. Pat's hardly worth all these tears." Adam's arms tightened around Hira's back, and he pulled her into the shadows. He wondered what he had ever done to deserve being saddled with a weeping woman.

"But I love him!"

Adam tried to remember what it was like to be as young as Hira and as captivated by another person. A million years ago, when he'd believed he loved Jeremy's mother, had his feelings been this intense? "You love someone who makes you cry this way?"

Hira moved away and wiped her eyes. "I wish I didn't!"

"Hira, there's hardly a single man for two hundred kilometers who doesn't worship at your dancing bare feet," Adam said, trying to make her smile. "Go home, make a list of all the times Pat's made you cry, and then forget him."

Hira sniffed, and, sighing, Adam handed her his handkerchief. "Really, Hira, he's best forgotten."

"You can talk!" Hira blew her nose and stuffed the handkerchief in the pocket of the jeans that had replaced her dancing costume. "You keep him on at your farm, you post his bail at the cop shop when he's gone off on a binge, you lie to his mother—"

"I don't lie, sometimes I just forget to tell her things."

"You protect him!"

"He's Granny's *mokopuna*," he reminded her gently. "My cousin."

"Does Granny know he's a ratbag?"

"Ratbag?" Adam smiled, encouraging her to do the same through her tears. "I'm afraid Granny loves him, too. In fact, Pat's always been surrounded by people who love him. It's one of his problems."

"I'd like to wring his neck."

Adam imagined that if Hira found Pat, her hands would go around his neck in a far different embrace. "When he shows up again, tell him I said he doesn't deserve you." Adam kissed her forehead. "Now go home, and forget about Pat tonight."

Adam watched Hira swivel her narrow hips in a naturally provocative movement as she disappeared around the back of the building where her car was parked. He had long since realized that Pat hadn't been born with good sense, but his cousin's latest rejection of Hira was proof once more.

Hira had fallen in love with Pat the moment she had first seen him. Hira had been fifteen, Pat sixteen, and even then Pat had been relentlessly charming. They had taken one look at each other, and an alliance that was still the talk of the family had been formed.

Through the years, the alliance had changed until it was apparent to Adam that the two young people had been lovers for some time, but Pat still refused to marry Hira, even though he claimed he loved her. One minute he treated her like the most precious of gifts, the next he ignored her or broke his promises to her as he had tonight. Pat was supposed to have come with Adam to see Hira perform. He hadn't shown up, just as he hadn't shown up for his job at Four Hill Farm for the past two days. If history was any indication, he wouldn't show up for the rest of the week, either.

Adam shoved his hands in his pockets and started down the sidewalk toward his car. Pat and Hira would have to work out their own problems. In the meantime there was nothing he could do except deliver his usual lecture when a charmingly repentant Pat showed up next week to reclaim his job. Pat was family, Adam's own bones. Tradition decreed that he help him and help him and help him some more. It was one of those Maori traditions that Hamish Armstrong probably wouldn't understand. And tonight was one of those times when Adam wasn't sure the Hamishes of the world weren't right.

Pulling onto the road, he thought about the other family member he was required to help, the family member who didn't know she was one. Paige had been breathtakingly beautiful tonight. He hadn't seen her in a dress before, but he'd found it hard to concentrate on anything except the way the pale pink fabric had clung to the softly rounded contours of her body. The dress was probably worth more than his prize ram, and the pearls in her earlobes and circling her throat were probably worth more than all his spring lambs. She had looked just like what she was, a stunning, wealthy American who was as out of place in Waimauri as he would be in her New Orleans.

And still he found himself thinking of her at the oddest times. *"Makere te weka i te mahanga e hoki ano?"* he muttered. Granny wasn't the only one who thought in proverbs. They were simple phrases signifying loftier philosophy, and Adam knew them all. "Would the *weka* return to the snare it escaped?" he chided himself out loud. Not if the *weka* had any sense. Of course, if the snare was hidden under pale pink and pearls, how could anything as stupid as a parrot resist?

He was lucky he wasn't a parrot. He had fallen for pale pink and pearls once before, and it had gotten him heartache and a son so terrified that even now Adam found himself speeding to get home in case Jeremy awakened.

Preparing to pass, Adam was almost on top of the car in front of him before he realized it belonged to Paige. For a moment he wondered if he'd summoned her out of his thoughts. Then he realized she was driving so slowly that something had to be wrong. Honking, he blinked his lights several times and motioned her over to the side of the road.

Paige stepped out of the car when she realized it was Adam who had come to her rescue. It galled her to need his help for yet the third time. She waited for his condemnation.

Adam opened his door and got out. "If I hadn't ridden with you, I'd think you were afraid to drive."

"I'm low on gas. I only saw one station in Rotorua that was still open, and they had just sold out. I think I'll make it if I take it slowly."

Adam knew Paige wouldn't ask for help, just as she hadn't asked him to lead her home through the thermals or to fix the heat in her house. She was proud and arrogant and entirely too calm for a woman alone in a foreign country with an empty petrol tank. And just like every other time he'd helped her, she rose another notch in his estimation. She was pale pink and pearls, but she was also finely tempered steel.

Adam leaned against the car, crossing his arms in front of him. "Didn't your mother ever tell you what happens to women who run out of petrol on dark country roads?"

"The darkest country road my mother ever expected me to be on was St. Charles Avenue," she said dryly. She realized he didn't understand. "One of the main thoroughfares in New Orleans. I was raised to be a debutante, not an executive, and certainly not an executive surrounded by sheep." She waved to the pasture behind her.

"Sheep?" He said the word as if he didn't know it. "Not sheep. Romneys. Some of New Zealand's best. They're producers of meat and wool."

Paige shrugged. "Then I was perfectly safe. I wouldn't have starved or frozen if I'd had to spend the night here."

Adam laughed, and the sound surprised them both. "What does it take to scare you?"

She knew. The answer was the sound of her heart beating double-time, just as it had the moment she had realized it was Adam getting out of the car. The answer was that peculiar thrill of anticipation she had experienced knowing she was going to see him again. "I don't scare easily," she said, knowing it was a lie. "If I'd run out of gas, I would have gone to sleep in the car until someone came along to help."

He gave a mock bow. "I suppose I saved you a step. I'll follow you in. If you stall, we can siphon some petrol out of my tank to get you home."

"I saw the way you were barreling down the road. Aren't you in a hurry to get somewhere? Home to Jeremy?"

"I'll get there quicker if we start now." He pushed himself away from the car. "Next time ask somebody where to find a station."

"I started to...." Her voice trailed off.

Adam waited.

Paige decided to continue. It was just as well Adam had a woman in his life anyway. "I went back to the hotel to ask, but I thought I might be interrupting something if I got out of the car."

The corners of his mouth turned up as he realized she had seen him with Hira. "Oh, you would have been, and I would have been grateful. You could have helped me comfort my lovelorn niece."

Paige didn't let her eyes flicker. "I'll remember that next time."

Adam appreciated how well she controlled herself, but he wondered if she realized her creamy skin was tinting a delicate rose. His eyes trailed down to her mouth. She had just moistened her lips, and they were a dewy, darker shade of the same color. He wished there was something about her to criticize.

Back in her car, Paige drove at the agonizingly slow pace she had set earlier, aware, as she did, that she was keeping Adam from Jeremy. Her hands gripped the wheel, but she kept her foot light on the accelerator, determined not to have to ask Adam for more help.

She wondered if he knew anything about the strange mixture of feelings she had experienced when he had said that the lovely young singer was his niece. She had felt both relief and disappointment, and she wasn't sure which had been the stronger.

The lamp she had left on for her return glowed in the window when she finally drove up to her house. Adam pulled up beside her and got out of his car at the same time she got out of hers. He read her gas gauge through the window.

"I'll be over tomorrow morning with petrol," he told her, going back to his own car. "You won't make it into town to get any."

Resigned, she nodded. "You don't want to do it now to save yourself time?"

He slammed his door, then motioned her to his window. Paige strolled over, puzzled. Adam pointed to his own gauge. It stood one hair past empty. "And I knew where an open station was," he said.

She was delighted. "Then you had no excuse."

"Only that I had my mind on something else." His eyes lingered just a second too long on hers before he started the engine and backed down her driveway.

Chapter 5

After an endless night, luminescent layers of silver and gold shot through the New Zealand darkness, testimony that day would come, and soon. Paige sat on the front porch, bundled in a blanket against the cold, and urged the sun to hurry.

She had awakened hours before in the grip of a terrifying nightmare, and now it seemed only the sun could burn away the malaise that was left. Sleep was impossible; she wouldn't take the chance that another dream might occur. Eyes wide open, she stared at the horizon and counted sun rays.

The sound of a vehicle on the road in front of her house broke the early morning stillness. Somewhere nearby the flutelike trills of a magpie answered the grinding of gears as the vehicle, a battered truck, turned into Paige's driveway. She pulled her blanket closer, but she didn't go inside. Nothing could entice her back to the scene of her nightmare.

The truck stopped, the engine died, and the resulting vacuum was filled by the pathetic baaing of four sheep in the back. The truck door slammed, and they baaed louder.

"Were you waiting for me?" Adam asked, hands in his pockets, surprise on his face.

Paige shivered. The question asked too much. "I'm afraid I had Jeremy's problem," she said, too exhausted and too hung over from fear for their usual verbal fencing. "Nightmares."

Adam didn't want to be drawn to Paige. He had come to fill her petrol tank, not probe the terrors of her night. He held himself rigid, fighting his urge to comfort her. "It looks as if you're trying Jeremy's cure, too."

"If you don't sleep, you don't dream."

"If you don't sleep, you don't get any work done." Adam went around to the back of the truck, shoved one of the bleating sheep aside and lifted out a large can.

"And you've never had a nightmare?"

There had been nights after Sheila disappeared, taking his unborn child with her, when Adam hadn't slept at all. Only that memory kept him from snapping back at Paige. He glanced in her direction and saw her eyelids drift closed, as if she were too tired to pretend she was anything she wasn't.

He was beside her before he even realized he was moving in her direction. He lowered himself to the porch step, careful not to touch her. He kept his resignation out of his voice. "Sometimes it helps to tell somebody about it."

Surprised, Paige opened her eyes and turned to him. "Does Jeremy tell you his?"

"He doesn't have to. I know what he dreams."

"I told my mother about this dream once. I never told her again."

"Then you've had it before."

Her head barely moved in affirmation. "Why are you here so early?"

"It's not early."

"Who are your friends?" She nodded toward the truck.

"I'm moving them to the pasture closest to my house. I don't like the look of one of them, and it's the first time the other three have been bred, so I want to keep an eye on them. They may be lambing early."

"Do you know all your sheep so well?"

"These are some I'm cross-breeding. They're an experiment."

She lowered her voice to a whisper. "Do they know?"

His laughter filled some of her emptiness. "I've got tea," he said, standing. "If you'll get cups we can sit here and watch the dawn together."

Touched by his obvious attempt to cheer her, Paige rose and went into the house, coming back with two pottery mugs. Adam poured steaming tea from a vacuum bottle for both of them, and they sat together once more.

Adam watched Paige tuck the blanket back around herself. "You don't have a robe?"

"They take too much room in a suitcase. Don't tell Granny. She'd probably knit me one if she knew. I don't usually sit outside before the sun comes up, anyway."

He tried not to think about what was under the blanket. "I know you don't use the wood stove, but don't you at least have a jug to heat water in?"

"One of those plug-in kettles? I do. I just didn't want to be inside that long."

Adam leaned back against the top step. "Tell me about the dream."

Cradling her cup in her hands, Paige tried to think of a polite way to refuse. Then she realized she really didn't want to. "Other people's fears don't bore you?"

Adam was beginning to think nothing about Paige could bore him. He was beginning to wish that were different. "Tell me."

She sighed. "It's always the same. I'm in a room full of people, looking up at them like a small child would. Someone touches my hair, someone else smiles at me, and I feel happy. There's music, someone is singing, and I'm trying to sing with her. Then everything is quiet." She stopped to take a sip of the sweetened tea. Then another. The next part was harder to tell. "Then I'm outside, on a green somewhere. A hand reaches for me, and I reach up to hold it, but when I do, the hand begins to shrivel until it's nothing but bones. All the flesh is gone, but still it holds on. Then the hand begins to drag me away. I hear people talking, but no one tries to help. Someone screams and screams, and finally I wake up and realize I'm the one screaming." She paused. "Or trying to scream," she continued finally, "but no sound is really coming out."

And the family had wondered if she remembered them. Adam tried to make himself speak, but the words grew in his throat until they were too immense.

Paige turned. Even to her own ears she sounded upset. "I'd like to understand. I have the dream often enough to wonder what's causing it."

He swallowed the words he couldn't speak and asked a question instead. "Have you ever asked anyone to help you?"

"You mean a professional, like a psychiatrist? No. Maybe I should. That's the traditional response, isn't it? Something goes wrong and you hire somebody to fix it for you. If you have enough money you can fix anything. Even nightmares."

"You dislike having money?"

"Of course not. Look how happy it's made me." She set her mug down with a thump. Her hand was shaking. "Adam, this isn't me sitting here saying these things. Go away."

He knew he should. Instead he slid his arm around her, pulling her closer. "I've had nightmares, too." He felt her resistance and refused to honor it. "Come here."

Paige sensed the blanket slip off her shoulders. She made a grab for it, but it fell between them. Adam ignored it, tugging her to lean against him. "Let me warm you," he insisted gently. "Give in, Paige. Just for a moment."

Her cheek rested against the rough wool of his jacket. He was little more than a stranger, yet she felt she'd known him all her life. And right now she needed comfort too badly to worry about proprieties. Adam's arms held her tighter, and the fingertips of one hand traveled the length of her back. She felt the rumble of laughter.

"I've been trying not to imagine what you had on under that blanket. Do you always sleep in a windcheater?" He pulled the sweatshirt away from her skin.

"'New Zealand, Home of 70,000,000 Nuclear Free Sheep,'" she quoted the logo emblazoned on her chest. "It beats my silk nightgowns all to hell."

Adam wanted to disagree, but at the moment it didn't seem prudent. He was already fighting his reaction to having her so close. His hand moved to her hair, and the short, silky strands clung to his fingers as he brushed it back from her face.

"It wasn't just the nightmare was it, *kaihana*?" he asked softly. "You've been hurt. That's why you came here."

"It's nothing I can't handle." She rubbed her cheek against his jacket. "What did you call me?"

"Cousin."

"You've called me cousin before."

"Yes."

"Why?"

Paige was struggling with too much to struggle with more. And his grandmother had decreed that she not be told the truth. Adam told her what he could. "Jane Abbott was a very distant relation. We claim and value kinship here in a way that you probably don't. I can tell you the name of hundreds of people in my family, and Jane was one of them."

"Then you think of me as a cousin even though the relationship is probably untraceable?"

His fingers stopped smoothing her hair and lingered for just a moment on her cheek. "I've never had a cousin I've thought of quite this way," he said dryly.

Somewhere she found the strength and good sense to try to put some distance between them. She lifted her head. "It is early, even though you don't think so, and I know I'm keeping you from your work."

He didn't let her go. Their faces were only inches apart. "Was it a man who hurt you?"

She countered instead of answering. "Was it Jeremy's mother who hurt you?"

"Sheila was a woman who damaged everything she touched."

Paige felt strangely pleased that he had answered. She could do no less. "Granger was a man who healed, but I wasn't the woman who needed his touch."

"You need someone's." Adam framed her face. "You have for a long time, haven't you?"

"I don't think I was meant to have what Americans call a 'meaningful relationship.'" She examined her own voice and found no traces of self-pity. She was encouraged and managed a smile. "I think I'm more the type to have a long series of doomed affairs."

If there hadn't been just the faintest note of wistfulness in her words, he might have laughed. As it was, his hands threaded through her hair. "I think you're afraid."

"Any sensible person is afraid, Adam. It's a big, bad world out there. Don't they teach you that here?" She tried to pull away, but she didn't try hard.

Adam knew he should let Paige go. He tried to tell himself that kissing her was a bad idea, but he didn't try hard enough. "Here they teach us to take care of our own."

She watched him move closer. "Does this qualify as taking care of me?" she asked softly.

"You decide." His lips took hers gently, blocking all protests. She tasted like sweetened tea and sunrise. She tasted like warm, sweet woman. His unsteady fingers traveled slowly through her hair until he could feel the velvety softness of the back of her neck against his fingertips. Lightly, he caressed the faint hollow before he withdrew his mouth from hers.

"I don't think you're taking care of either of us." She was shaken by the gentle power of his touch. Lucifer had kissed her like the sweetest angel.

Adam worked to form an ordinary invitation when he felt anything but ordinary. "Come have breakfast at my house."

She had expected something very different. A proposition, more kisses, perhaps an angry withdrawal. "Breakfast?"

He raised an eyebrow. "You call it something else?"

"Adam, what's happening here?"

"I'm going to fill your tank with petrol, then I'm going to take you to my house, and Granny's going to serve us breakfast. Jeremy will probably cower, and Granny will probably flutter like an old hen. That's 'what's happening.'" He said the last two words with an excellent imitation of her Louisiana drawl.

"I'd better not."

Adam stood and held out a hand. "You don't want to be alone here, Paige. Believe me, I know."

She had been kissed by more than a few men, but no kiss had affected her this way. She took his hand and let him help her stand. His gaze traveled slowly down to her legs.

"And you sleep in jeans, too? Expensive jeans?"

"I sit on the front porch in jeans."

"Will you ride with me or take your own car?"

"I'd better change."

"Don't. Come the way you are."

"My hair's a mess." She ran her fingers over it.

Adam knew they had to leave before he kissed her again. "I like it that way. You need an imperfection or two."

On a whim, she stretched on tiptoe and ruffled his. "You could stand an imperfection or two yourself, cousin."

"*Kaihana.* Cousin."

"*Kaihana.*"

As he drove, Adam wondered if Paige had any idea how much self-control it had taken not to pull her into his arms and kiss her with the full force of the desire she had ignited. His body ached from restraint.

And still he hadn't shown enough. He never should have touched her at all. If she had needed comfort, he should have taken her home to Granny. His regrets were overwhelming.

There would be no excuse good enough to make him touch Paige again. Now he knew the pleasure that touching could bring. Now he knew the frustration.

Paige sensed that Adam's silence wasn't comfortable or ordinary. If she was still trying to untangle the unexpected intimacy of his kiss, Adam seemed to have untangled and dismissed it. She resorted to small talk. "Is the land we're passing part of your farm?"

"Yes."

She turned to stare out the window when a movement in the side mirror caught her eye. "Adam, there's a dog chasing us."

Adam glanced out his rearview mirror and shook his head in disgust. He braked and got out, waiting for the short-haired, black mutt to catch up. The dog halted several feet away, sank down to his belly and slithered the rest of the distance like a snake.

"Come meet my latest defeat," Adam told Paige. "This is Cornwall. Cornwall, meet Paige."

Paige slammed her door to join Adam and the trembling dog. "What on earth is he afraid of?"

"This." Adam put his foot under the dog's jaw and lifted it gently. His words, spoken in Maori, were less gentle.

"That's it?"

"He knows what I'm saying."

"He's your pet?"

"Never a pet. He's a sheepdog."

"I thought he was some kind of mutt, part Doberman maybe."

"Border collie, black Labrador mix. A Huntaway. New Zealand's greatest labor-saving device. Except this one." He bounced his foot gently so that the dog's head bobbed. "This one is a throwaway."

Adam gave a piercing whistle and pointed, and the dog turned and, shaggy tail between its legs, ran back the way it had come.

"I hope you never plan to reject me like that." Paige watched the dog until it was nothing more than a blur. "What did he do wrong?"

"He left his post."

"Court-martialed." Paige went back around the truck and got in. In a moment they were back on the road.

Adam checked his mirror again. "Cornwall's from the best stock. His mother's a champion, and his father was my best dog until he died. Apparently both of them had some aberrant genes that produced Cornwall."

"He seems lovable."

"He's not supposed to be lovable. He's supposed to be efficient. You haven't seen him down your way, have you?"

"No. Will he be visiting?"

"He'd better not."

In a minute they were at the bottom of the hill leading up to Adam's house, in three, up the hill amid much grinding of gears. Paige laid her hand on Adam's arm as he started to open his door. She liked the way he felt, strong, hard, all wiry, rangy muscle and bone. What she didn't like was the way he tensed at her touch. "Is there anything I should do to make Jeremy more comfortable? I haven't had much experience with kids. I really don't know what to do."

"There's nothing you *can* do," he said gruffly.

Paige withdrew her hand. She wondered where Adam's gentleness had gone. There had been moments on her porch when he had been a different person. On the trip over, he had become the remote New Zealand sheep farmer, and she had become the woman he was forced to rescue once more. She felt disappointment and something more elemental, as if an unspoken promise had been broken. She realized she had been foolish to let down her guard with him. She wouldn't be so foolish again.

Adam opened the house door for her, and Paige stepped in, confronting a small figure in bright red flannel pajamas. Jeremy sat in the middle of the hallway, spinning a beautiful wooden top. Paige didn't move any closer, afraid she would frighten him. Instead she watched the top, its intricately carved designs whirling in symmetrical patterns. "What a beautiful toy," she told Adam, knowing Jeremy would overhear. "I've never seen one like it."

"Thank you."

She turned her gaze to him. "You made it?"

He shrugged. "He plays with it when he wakes and finds I'm not here. I've been told he can watch it spin for hours."

Mihi came into the hallway and greeted them. "Adam's carved a top for each child in the family. After we eat, perhaps he'll show you the flutes he makes, too."

Jeremy seemed to become aware of Paige's presence and fled with his precious toy. But not before she could see how beautifully crafted it was.

One memorable breakfast later, Paige followed Adam into his office, where he displayed some of his handiwork on the wall over his desk. The flutes were as intricately carved as the top. Of varying sizes with three finger holes, each was covered with designs that heightened the beauty of the dark wood. He took down one of the largest and handed it to her. "This is a *koauau*."

Paige fondled the shining wood, letting her fingers linger in the elaborate spiraling grooves. "Do you play it?"

Adam held out his hand, and she gave the flute to him. He put it to his mouth, and in a moment his office was filled with music. The sound was primitive, each note sliding into the next with no pattern that Paige could discern. And yet when he was done, she realized the song had the chillingly perfect beauty of a spider web whose pattern can only be recognized when it's completed.

She tried to shake off the spell of the music, but it had tugged at emotions she couldn't identify. "That was wonderful," she said finally, her voice husky. "Is that a Maori song?"

"I like to think so. We're an adaptable people. A musical people, too. When the Europeans came, we liked the sounds they made, so we adopted them as our own. There's nothing much left of our old music. That was my idea of what our songs must have sounded like."

"You keep the old traditions alive, yet you're very much a twentieth-century man."

Adam didn't want her to understand him. He wanted distance. "Perhaps I believe that some of the old traditions have more value than some of the new." He hung the flute on the wall behind him.

She heard the dismissal. He thought she was an insensitive little rich girl who believed the world had sprung to life the moment she had been born. Worse, he believed she only saw value in familiar things. "Why are you trying to convince yourself I'm so shallow?" she asked softly. "I'm not."

"I don't know what you mean."

Paige tried not to let her hurt show. Since they had gotten in his truck, he had tried to cut himself off from her. She was tired of trying to find out why. "I think I'd like to walk home. The exercise will do me good. I know you walked here from my house once. Is there a shortcut?"

"Through the thermals."

She tried to joke. "That might be even shorter than I need. I'd like to live to see New Orleans again."

Adam was stone-faced. "I'll take you back. I've got to go into town anyway."

She wished she didn't have to face another ride with him, but she knew she had little choice. It was Adam or scalding geysers. She found Mihi and said goodbye before she followed Adam to the car.

As unapproachable as he had suddenly become, Paige knew that the trip back to her house was probably her only chance to ask him to guide her through the thermals. Obviously he knew them as well or better than anyone. At the least she had to ask him for the name of someone else if he wasn't interested. Adam was her only resource.

"I didn't even realize your property bordered the thermals," she began when they were halfway to her house and the silence had extended until it was uncomfortable. "I was fooled by the hills."

"You have a bit to learn about your thermals yet."

Mentally she thanked him for the introduction, if not for the snideness of his comment. "I'm hoping you'll agree to teach me some more."

Adam realized just how dangerous getting that close to her would be. He could still taste her on his lips, could still feel the warmth of her body seeping into his. He knew his aloofness was hurting her, but he knew how much more both of them would be hurt if he didn't establish distance.

Paige listened to Adam's silence and thought about how much it said. "I need a guide," she said finally. "I can't make any decisions about selling the thermals to Hamish's corporation without seeing them myself. Maybe you could suggest someone else who could do it."

"No."

"Thanks for considering it," she drawled, turning to watch the passing scenery.

Silently, Adam cursed their situation. "I can't suggest anyone else because there isn't anyone reliable who knows them the way I do."

"Reliable? Someone's going to strand me beside a boiling mud pool?"

"I have a cousin, Pat Tomoana, who knows the thermals. But Pat tends to forget about commitments he makes."

"He sounds better than no one."

Adam knew he was trapped as surely as if he had been caught in the middle of the thermals after dark. Paige had to be shown the area, and she had to have the right guide. He wouldn't have lifted a finger to help her sell them to Hamish Armstrong, but there wasn't anything he wouldn't do to help her assess them for a different reason.

"I'll guide you."

"Thanks, but I think I'll find someone else," she said politely.

Adam's car made easy work of the gentle slope to Paige's front door. He turned off the engine, then put his hand on her arm to keep her from getting out. "I said I'd take you through, and I will."

Paige shook off Adam's hand. "You've already done too much. I can't ask for any other favors, and you've already told me how you feel about being paid."

"You'll be doing me a favor if you let me."

She turned to him, hand still on the door handle. She was sick of his games. "What am I supposed to think about you, *kaihana*? One minute I'm *persona non grata*, the next you're telling me that a favor I need is really a favor *you* need. Can't you make up your mind?"

She was flushed, and more than a little angry, even though the polite smile on her lips belied it. Adam knew she had a right to her anger, and an equal right to an explanation. Silently he cursed again. "What do you see when you look at me?"

"I didn't get much sleep last night, so I may not be too good at guessing games."

"Just tell me what you see."

"Is this some sort of ink-blot test? Snakes in the squiggles, rocket ships in the smudges?" Paige let her eyes travel from Adam's face down to his feet. "I see a man, Adam. What do you want me to say? That I see a sheep farmer? That I see the father of a little boy and the grandson of a wonderful old woman? That I see a person whose blood combines two ancient and honorable cultures? That I see an exasperating, angry cousin-fifty-times-removed who can't be pleasant for more than a half hour at a time?"

"Do you see a man who wants you?"

She was taken aback. "No. No sign of that man anywhere," she said finally.

"Good." Adam opened his door and came around to help her out.

Paige regarded him warily.

Adam leaned against his car. "Let me tell you about Sheila."

"You don't have to."

"I think I do."

She stood in front of him, arms folded, waiting.

"My brothers married young and happily. They picked flowers for their wives, their wives cooked for them. I thought all marriages were like theirs, and I wanted to marry, too, except I never seemed to fall in love. When I met Sheila, I thought I'd finally found my wife. Only it wasn't that way. Sheila lived with me, but she refused marriage. She claimed she wasn't ready. She needed time. As it turned out, what she needed was a man with no Maori blood.''

Paige frowned. "I thought New Zealand was free of that sort of racism."

"Racism exists wherever there's more than one race. The government can't legislate what's in a person's heart. When Sheila found she was pregnant, she left me. I did everything I could to trace her, but she just disappeared. Three years later I got a call from the authorities in another city. Sheila had abandoned our child to them, giving them my name. It seems that the older Jeremy grew, the more Maori he looked. Sheila was ashamed of him. When the authorities began to uncover his history, they found a long record of neglect. Apparently, Sheila's favorite way to care for our son was to lock him in her apartment while she went out by herself. Sometimes she remembered to leave him something to eat, sometimes she didn't. The Jeremy you've seen is a healthy little boy compared to the Jeremy I saw that first day."

Paige didn't even want to think about what Jeremy must have suffered. She knew Adam wasn't asking for pity, but she wasn't sure what he *was* asking for. Understanding? Patience? Distance?

"I'm sorry," she said carefully.

He silently applauded the understatement, considering that for once her face clearly showed her horror.

"Now tell me what it has to do with me," she asked.

"Tell me about Granger."

"Granger is only part of my story."

"I have time."

She told him, hoping never to speak of it again. "I was married once. Only Sim didn't pick flowers for me, and I didn't cook for him. We saw each other at parties, mostly. Sometimes we'd leave together, sometimes Sim would leave with another woman. After a while, I learned to hope it would be the latter, because when we were together he didn't have the compassion to keep silent about his affairs or the fact that he'd married me because he had already gone through his own fortune. Finally my father bought me an uncontested divorce with a photo of Sim and a girl who was underage. He told Sim he could have the photo or the police could. For once Sim showed some sense."

"Why did you marry him?"

Paige shrugged. "My parents approved of him. I wanted something substantial in my life. And, of course, Sim gave me substantial problems, so I guess I got what I'd asked for. Then there was Granger.'' Her expression softened. "He was everything fine and good, only he still loved the woman he'd been separated from for ten years. I haven't heard from him since I got here, but I've heard from his wife. They're back together, and I think they'll stay that way."

"And if they don't?"

"Granger and I will never be anything but friends."

He reached out for her, but not to give comfort. "Tell me what you felt when I kissed you this morning."

Startled, she tried to resist, but he tugged her closer. "Let go of me, Adam."

"Tell me you felt nothing."

"I didn't feel as angry as I do now, that's for certain."

"I'll tell you what I felt. You slipped inside me. I don't want you there."

Her breath caught. She lifted her head proudly, emotions concealed. "I don't want you, but if by telling me your life story you're accusing me of being anything like Sheila..."

He pushed her away. "You refuse to see what's in front of your eyes."

"What are you talking about?"

He took a deep breath and clamped his lips shut.

She exploded. "I'm tired of your riddles. Shut the damn door inside you, Adam. I don't want to spend any time there, and I don't want to spend any time with you. I'll find somebody else to guide me through the thermals." She turned and started toward the house.

His answer was the slam of his car door.

Chapter 6

The *marae* stood between two hills on a fifteen-acre reserve at Waimauri's edge. Adam parked his car beside a dozen others and walked back along the fence to the gateway. The *marae* proper was a long, brilliantly green expanse of grass leading to the *whare hui* or meeting house, a one-story, rectangular building of one room with a deep gabled porch across the front and a single door and window in the front wall.

The meeting house in Waimauri was a more elaborate building than some in other towns. Built in the late nineteenth century, it had a steeply pitched roof and was richly decorated with traditional carving, reed paneling and rafter patterns. More important than its decorations, however, was what it symbolized. The meeting house was, in essence, the body of one of Adam's ancestors. Its ridgepole was his ancestor's backbone; at the junction of two bargeboard arms there was a carved representation of his face. The front window was his eye, and when Adam stepped through the door, he stepped into his ancestor's chest, enclosed by rafter ribs and held up by a *poutokomanawa*, or heart post.

Once the *marae*, both land and meeting house, had been the village living room, where Maoris gathered during their free time to socialize and conduct the business of the *marae*. Now, as well as for ceremonial occasions, it was used for many of the same purposes as other halls, for club and committee meetings, recreation and politics, and discussions of local issues.

Today the *marae* was being used for the latter. Adam greeted other *tangata whenua*, or *marae* members who, like him, had the right of *marae* usage because of lineage. He counted fifty men and women, including two tribal elders who had come a distance for this meeting.

Seated in the large hall, Adam listened to the official greetings given by several men. Although the purpose of the meeting was to discuss Hamish Armstrong's plans for the thermals, other subjects were dealt with first. Worldwide, the Maori people were recognized and saluted for their great oratory. Today, as always, grievances and disagreements would be brought into the open in a forthright manner. The rule was that nothing that was said in a *marae* was considered to be offensive. Disagreements were meant to be argued through to an amicable consensus.

Adam waited until he was called on, then stood to make his presentation. He spoke in Maori, as the other speakers had. Succinctly he explained what most of them already knew: Hamish Armstrong, representing Pacific Outreach Corporation, was negotiating with one Paige Duvall from Duvall Development in the United States for the purchase of the geothermal property that had once belonged to Jane Abbott. Pacific Outreach's stated intention was to build an exclusive health resort using the thermals as both an energy source and an attraction for their guests.

"And now, perhaps I should speak for a moment about Duvall Development and how they have come to own the property," Adam continued. "As all of you know, the thermals were originally Maori land, owned and cared for under the auspices of this *marae*. Then, more than a generation ago, the land was alienated, taken by the government, and sold to meet a tax debt. The land was purchased by the Abbott family and held by their descendants. The most recent descendant to hold title is Ann Abbott Duvall, whose American husband owns Duvall Development. As custodians of the land, the Abbott family has never sold portions or in any way developed the thermals. The land has been ours while not being legally recognized as such.

"Now that relationship has been threatened." Adam paused to let his words settle a moment. "We have relaxed under the goodwill of the Abbott family, but now we must step forth and once more take control of something that belongs to us in every way but legally. Just as the thermals were sold away from us, we must buy them back. If we don't, we'll see destruction and def-amation of something we view as sacred.''

Adam looked around and saw the nodding of heads. He also saw frowns. He knew those frowning probably had the best business sense. If they banded together to buy the thermals, it would take every penny each of them could beg and borrow.

"There is an added complication," he continued when the silence had gone on long enough. "The woman who has come to negotiate is the daughter of Ann Abbott, and she has been raised an American. New Zealand is the country of her moth-er's birth, nothing more.'' Adam had been debating his next sentence, since he had known he would have to utter it. He was still uncertain whether he was handling this correctly. It was too late, however, to back away now.

"Apparently, Paige Duvall doesn't realize her mother is Maori, and that by virtue of her own birth, she is Maori, too.'' He ignored the low buzz of voices. "Many of you know that her mother left Waimauri to return only once when her daughter was a small child. Many of you also know of her father's op-position to that trip.'' Adam knew that the elders, particularly, were reviewing that day almost a quarter of a century before when the child, Paige, had been brutally ripped away from the family she was just beginning to know. He remembered it all too clearly himself. He remembered the feel of his small, girl cous-in's hand, the tiny perfection of her nose, the dancing darkness of her eyes. He remembered her screams as her father dragged her away. All too clearly he remembered his own humiliation.

"Before you ask why I haven't told her," he went on, "let me assure you that keeping it a secret wasn't my idea. My grand-mother, Mihi Tomoana, asked that it be that way. Now I'm asking each of you to honor her desire in this matter. Miss Du-vall claims to view us as an ancient and honorable culture, just as she views the Pakehas. But she feels no connection. My grandmother believes Miss Duvall will remember the past one day, and that if she doesn't, it's because she doesn't want to. Although I'm not sure I agree, I do know that nothing will be served by acquainting her with something that's been hidden for twenty-four years. If we do, it will seem that we are asking her to give us special consideration because of our blood ties. It will confuse the issue and possibly go against the best interests of all of us. Miss Duvall is a businesswoman. Negotiations must be carried out on that level.'' Adam sat down.

As he had expected, discussion was strident and lengthy. He had proposed two controversial topics. Fortunately this wasn't the first time that buying the thermals had been discussed. In fact, it was almost the only thing that had been discussed since Jane Abbott's death. A final decision would be reached today, and Adam was sure he knew what it would be.

He wished he was as sure about his second proposal, both whether it was the right thing to ask of the others and whether it was the right thing for Paige.

He didn't know if she had absorbed her father's prejudices or her mother's nearly fatal ambivalence, or whether she was simply unable to recognize the obvious. Whatever was behind the secret of Paige's ancestry, she was within inches of the truth, and yet she didn't seem able to take that final step and see what was right in front of her.

Adam listened to the discussion and prepared to support whatever the prevailing opinion might be. For too long he had carried the problem of the thermals and Paige Duvall by himself. Now the problems belonged to them all.

Paige sat down to a late lunch of New Zealand cheese and a dark bread that tasted as if it had just come from the baker's oven. The small grocery store in Waimauri carried only the basics, but everything was fresh and wholesome. She didn't miss the greater variety available at home, but she did have to fight a craving for Cajun food.

The day had meandered by at snail speed. She had phoned Hamish at his hotel to take him up on his offer to find her a guide, but he had been out. On a whim she had decided not to leave a message, and since she knew Adam was in town, she had driven back to Four Hill Farm to talk to Mihi about a guide. Mihi had been gone, too.

Jeremy had been there, though, in the company of a middle-aged Maori woman who had immediately befriended Paige and told her stories about Waimauri people she seemed to expect her to know. The woman had been effusively warm with Jeremy, as well, and the little boy had looked like a rabbit caught in a snare. Each time he sidled away, the woman grabbed him for an overpowering hug. Paige had left quickly, knowing the last thing he needed was one more person to fuss over him.

Until she found someone to take her through the thermals, Paige knew she was stuck in Waimauri. Yesterday that hadn't seemed so bad; today it seemed intolerable. Now she knew she didn't need the complication of Adam Tomoana in her life. If she was going to suffer through another doomed affair, she would do it on her own turf with a man she understood. A man who couldn't hurt her.

Paige was just putting away the bread and cheese in the old-fashioned refrigerator when a howl like a coyote's split the air. She fumbled with the refrigerator latch, shoving it tightly against the door before she ran to the front porch.

Adam's throwaway Huntaway sat on the steps, his bushy tail beating a staccato rhythm.

"Cornwall."

The tail beat faster.

Paige knew as much about dogs as she did about children, and for a moment she just stared. "Go away," she said at last. "Go home, go back to work, go play with your sheep."

Cornwall moved up to the porch, then rolled on his back and stuck all four legs in the air.

"Fabulous." Paige slapped her hands on her hips and made her voice stern. "Go home, Cornwall." She wished she could whistle. Cornwall had seemed to understand Adam's whistles. She wished she spoke Maori for the same reason.

Cornwall rolled back to his feet and sat up, extending one paw.

"Who taught you all these tricks? Not Adam, that's for sure." Paige fought down the impulse to take the expressive paw in her hand. "Do you jump through hoops, too?"

As if he had tired of the small talk, Cornwall trotted into the house through the still-open door.

"Hey, come back here, you. You weren't invited. All I need is for Adam to find out I'm entertaining you." Paige followed the dog inside. "Shoo. Go away."

Cornwall circled the room as if taking inventory, then, settling on the sofa as the most comfortable spot, jumped on it and lounged against the cushions.

"Did you want tea, too?" Hesitantly, Paige approached the dog. "Or do you want a chunk of human flesh?"

Cornwall closed his eyes.

Paige stopped in front of the sofa, reluctant to try to move a sleeping dog. She knew her proverbs, too.

"Make yourself at home," she said, shrugging. "I can always sit on a chair."

Cornwall sighed.

Adam would be furious if he found out Cornwall was snoozing comfortably on her sofa. Paige smiled at the thought.

The smile was short-lived. A car with the peculiar chug-snort engine she had learned to identify as Adam's was coming up her driveway.

"Save yourself," she told the sleeping dog. "I've never seen you before in my life."

As she expected, Cornwall slept on.

She wondered how Adam would feel about being entertained on her front porch. Drawing her shoulders back to face the challenge, she went to answer the door.

Adam hadn't come alone. The man standing on the porch beside him was as old as Mihi and as darkly wizened as a Greek olive. Power radiated from him, and when Paige's eyes met his, she felt strangely chastened, like a small child who's just been caught telling a lie.

She might have found a way to leave Adam standing on the porch, but there was no way she could fail to extend hospitality to the old man. "Come in, please." She opened the door wider. "I'd better warn you, though, you may not like what you see."

Adam raised an eyebrow. As always, he liked what he saw far too well. Paige was wearing trousers and a short-sleeved sweater of deepest turquoise; more interesting, her cheeks were flushed a becoming rose. He pulled his eyes from her and surveyed the room to see where the problem lay. They settled on Cornwall.

"May I introduce Henare Poutapu?" Adam asked, his gaze returning to Paige. "Henare, this is Paige Duvall."

Paige refused to look at Adam. She extended her hand and felt the old man's wrap around it momentarily. "I'm pleased to meet you. Won't you please sit down?" She gestured to the chair. "Adam, why don't you sit with your dog?" She stressed the last two words. "I'm sure he won't bite you."

"He won't. He's leaving."

Cornwall's eyes opened as if he knew he had been given his cue. He took one look at Henare Poutapu and the fur rose on his back in a belated threat. He growled.

Adam called his name, then whistled a short series of blasts. With wounded dignity, Cornwall stretched, keeping his eyes on Henare, then proudly planted his feet on the ground. One more blast had him running full speed out the door.

"Just brush the dog hair off the sofa," Paige said, trying not to smile. "May I get either of you tea?"

Still standing, both men shook their heads. Paige lowered herself to a chair so that they could sit.

"We've come to discuss the thermals," Adam began.

Paige wanted to remind him that she had canceled her request to have him guide her, but she knew that would be petty, particularly since they weren't alone. "What would you like to discuss?"

"We would like to buy them from you."

She sat back. Adam was always full of surprises, and this was no less astounding than some of his others. "Really."

Adam gave credit where it was due. Paige was doing a remarkable job of pretending everything was exactly as it should be. He would have thought to look at her that every day of her life had been spent exactly this way. "Before we make our offer, I want to explain why."

"I'd like that."

He wanted to kiss the complacency off her face. He wondered how many kisses it would take, how long before she ignited and showed the fire that he knew smoldered deep inside her. It was too bad that he would never know.

"The thermals are part of our tribal heritage," he began, pulling himself back to the subject at hand with difficulty. "One of our stories says that after the Arawa canoe landed, the great priest Ngatoroirangi set off to explore. He reached the summit of Mount Tongariro, but there he suffered so greatly from the cold that he implored the goddesses in his homeland, Hawaiki, to send some of their warmth. They threw fireballs across the water, and the fireballs skipped across the land, touching down at all the places where geothermal areas now exist. Our ancestors believed the thermals were the natural habitat for our spirit gods."

"Much more colorful than the geological explanation," Paige said.

Adam nodded, unsmiling. "Through the centuries, each geological peculiarity assumed importance in our traditions and our folklore. The thermals here are no exception."

"Then you're saying they had significance today?"

"They're filled with legend, with history. Their destruction would be a kind of death for us."

Paige began to have an uneasy feeling in the pit of her stomach. She turned to look at Mr. Poutapu and had the same experience she'd had when meeting him. Under his unflinching gaze she felt like a recalcitrant child.

"If this is true, why were the thermals owned freehold by the Abbott family?" she asked, turning almost gratefully back to Adam.

He gave her part of the speech he had used in the meeting house. Then he continued. "I believe originally the Abbott family intended someday to deed the property back to the Maori Land Board. There were advantages to owning it, however, and they neglected to do so. Jane Abbott had talked about doing it as a bequest, but she died suddenly and apparently without leaving a will."

"This is valuable land."

"More valuable to us than to anyone."

"If it's historic, perhaps the New Zealand government might consider purchasing it as a park."

"We don't want a park. We don't want a resort. We want to keep the land as it's always been. Active. Alive. Ours."

"And you want to buy it as such?"

Adam nodded. "There's one more story to tell."

Paige tried not to be caught up in the velvet spell of his thickly lashed midnight eyes. She didn't want to be drawn to Adam; she wanted to forget he existed. Impatiently she waited for him to finish and leave.

"There's a tribal legend that hidden somewhere in the thermals is a *mauri*." He spelled the word so she would see it was like the name of the town. "*Mauri* means many things in our language: life principle, source of the emotions, talisman. It signifies both a type of totara timber and the moon on the twenty-ninth day. Because of the wide variety of definitions, there have always been a wide variety of explanations for the town's name."

"In my country names easily become obscure, too."

She was polite to the nth degree. Adam supposed it was for the best, but he yearned for a spark of interest to enliven her eyes, even though he'd worked to extinguish that spark this morning. "There is always one correct explanation," he went on. "And in this case *mauri* refers to a talisman, an idol that's hidden somewhere deep in the thermals. I've spent the years of my adult life looking for it, and men before me have done the same. It's still there."

"How do you know it exists?"

"The legend tells us."

"Every culture has its legends. Cities of gold, fountains of youth. Aren't they more important for what they say about the people who've believed them than for their accuracy?"

"If you're a philosopher or a sociologist, perhaps. If you're an archaeologist or a historian, not necessarily. In that case, the unearthing of the legend, the verifying, is more important."

"But if all those hours have been spent, and nothing has come of them..."

"You haven't seen the thermals, not really. You've barely been past the edge."

She couldn't resist. "Not for lack of trying."

Adam didn't miss a beat. "When you see them in their entirety, you'll see why we haven't been successful as yet. But we will be." He turned to Henare Poutapu and began a rapid, fluent Maori exchange with him.

Paige listened and waited. She wondered how much of her conversation with Adam the old man had understood.

Adam turned back to her. "Henare would like me to tell you the legend. Then we'll tell you our offer. But first, do you understand anything about the way the Maori community organizes itself?"

"Only a little."

"We're very aware of our ancestors. In pre-European times, we were even more aware. For instance, each of us knows the canoe that carried our ancestors here, and the name of the tribe or *iwi* we're part of. Beyond that, we break it down even farther, into *hapu* or subtribes. The Maori people who live around Waimauri are almost all members of the same *hapu*, which means we have a common ancestor of many generations ago from whom we can trace our descent."

Paige had the distinct feeling that Henare Poutapu's eyes were boring a hole in the side of her head. She kept her own eyes firmly fixed on Adam.

"Hundreds of years ago, an ancestress of our *hapu*, Hori-i-rangi, died, and after her death she assumed the status of a goddess. Paiaka, a chief of our tribe built a *pa*—a fortress—on the top of the Tihi O Tonga ridge outside Rotorua. The image of Horo-i-rangi was cut into the cliff face and venerated as a *mauri*. The image wasn't worshiped. A *mauri* is a symbol, in this case a symbol of the fertility of the surrounding forests. It was believed that making offerings to her would assure that birds would be plentiful. The gifts were laid in a *pataka* or storehouse carved in the rock beside her image, and it was a very sacred place. The *mauri* and the *pataka* were protected by guardians throughout the generations."

Despite her intention to stay detached, Paige found her imagination caught up in the story. "Is this the *mauri* Waimauri's named for?"

"Yes and no." Adam tried not to notice the way her dark eyes sparkled. "The last guardian, Rangiriri, decided to cut the *mauri* out of the cliffside in order to preserve it. The *mauri* had been discovered, and there were fears it might be destroyed. First, the *mauri* was placed on a tiny islet in a stream, but later it was handed over to the Auckland Museum for safekeeping.''

"And it's not there anymore?"

"It's there. Its twin isn't. You see, there's long been a legend that there were two carvings of Horo-i-rangi. One outside the *pataka* on the Tihi O Tonga ridge, one carved into a cliffside here in the thermals. Because only the *tohungas* or priests ever approached the *mauri*, few people knew the truth. Now it's said that at the time Rangiriri cut out that cliffside *mauri* and took it to the stream, the other was still hiding here in the thermals, where it had been for many generations."

"'Hiding here in the thermals' is rather vague, isn't it?"

Adam nodded, glancing at Henare to exchange a few sentences before he turned back to Paige. "We have a little more to go on, but not much. The *tohunga* who was its last guardian was a clever man. He left enough description to make us believe the *mauri* exists, and little enough to make it nearly impossible to find."

"Apparently he didn't want it found."

"I like to think he wanted it found by the right people."

Against her better judgment, Paige smiled. "And you're the right people?"

"I've yet to find it. But I will."

She paused to put all the information together. "If the *mauri* were found, would you still want the property? Or would you want to remove the *mauri* and place it in a museum?"

"The property," Henare said the word with a verbal grimace, "is ours. It will never cease to be ours because it is our history, our heritage, ourselves. The *mauri* is ours, too, and it won't be removed."

Paige's questions about the old man's knowledge of English were answered. "Both of you must know," she said, turning to include him, "that I'm only a representative of Duvall Development. I don't make the final decision about this. I'll have to take all offers back to my father for his consideration."

"And your mother?" Henare asked.

Paige was surprised that Ann Abbott had entered the conversation. "Mother has nothing to do with business. I'm sure she'll turn this over to my father to handle."

"She has no interest in an inheritance?"

"She has no interest in New Zealand," Paige said frankly. "I don't know why, but to my knowledge she hasn't been back since she married my father thirty years ago."

Adam tensed, and his eyes sought Henare's. Henare did nothing more than signal him to make their offer. "The official committee of our *hapu* has empowered me to make you a bid for the land."

Paige listened carefully, hoping that Adam's offer would be as generous as Hamish's had been. She wanted to sell the land to his *hapu*. Even if the offer was a little less, she thought she could rationalize the sale to her father. But the amount Adam quoted was far less than Hamish's had been. She listened to the details of how the money would be raised, how management would be divided, how the deed would read. When Adam finished, she shook her head regretfully.

"Adam, you know I've had another offer. It was substantially higher than that."

He had known it probably would be, but he had hoped. "Then we'll find a way to meet or exceed your other offer."

"Can you really do that?" She sat forward a little, forgetting for a moment that she was trying to stay as far away from him as possible. "We're talking about a lot of money. And if I wait too long, I might lose my other bid. Pacific Outreach Corporation might find another property."

"We'll apply to the Arawa Tribal Trust Board for the difference."

"How long will that take? And will you be assured of getting the money?"

For the first time since arriving with Henare, Adam showed his frustration. "Everything takes time, Paige. Are you in such a hurry that you can't even let us try?"

Paige was irritated, but she tried not to show it. She had made a decision not to let Adam get under her skin. "I'm a business-woman working for a large company that values time almost as much as it values land. How do I explain that I'm waiting for an offer that might never come when I have an excellent offer already?"

"Then you won't wait?"

"I didn't say that." Without realizing what she was doing, she ran her fingers through her hair in frustration, tumbling it around her face. For a moment she forgot Henare was there. "Would you stop putting words in my mouth and expecting the worst? And please stop pretending you know what's going on in my head. No one knows me that well."

"I apologize," Adam said with a slight smile. "But tell me in what way I was wrong. You'll wait for us to make our application to the board?"

"I'll wait, but not indefinitely." Paige sat back in her chair. "You have three weeks."

"We'll need at least six."

"I'll give you four. Then I'll take all the information back to my father and let him decide." She hesitated, but she knew she had no choice other than to ask *him* for something now. "In exchange for the time, I'd like you to arrange a guide into the thermals. If you can't, I'll ask Hamish to find me someone."

"I've told you I'll guide you."

"You've told me other things, too, including how little you want to spend time with me."

She said the words casually, but from Adam's perspective, they dripped with feeling. Henare saved him from answering. "There is no one else in Waimauri who can show them to you the way Adam can. If you really want to see them, you have no choice." He stood. "Thank you for listening to us, Miss Duvall. Adam, I'll wait for you outside."

Paige stood, too, but Henare was gone before she could say anything else to him. Adam came to stand beside her. "Then you'll let me take you in?"

"Can I trust you not to leave me beside a mud pool?"

"Only if you stop sniping at me."

"I don't snipe," she said haughtily.

"Kei runga te korero, kei raro te rahurahu."

"Meaning?"

"Loosely? Under honeyed words lies mischief."

"Don't expect either honey or mischief. I need a guide. You need a well-informed source to plead your cause. *Quid pro quo.* I give, you get. And vice versa. Nothing more. If you can be polite, I can be polite."

Standing this close to her, Adam wondered if a thin shield of politeness would be protection for either of them. They were going to be forced to spend time together. They could pretend an aloofness neither of them felt, but he wondered just how far it would get them.

Now wasn't the time to worry. Now they had to call a truce. There would be plenty of long, lonely nights in the weeks to come for regrets.

"Then you'll let me take you in?" he repeated.

"I will, and thank you."

Adam nodded. He was in the doorway before he spoke again. "We'll start early. Wear sturdy hiking shoes and bring your bathers. That's a swimsuit to you." He stepped out on the porch, then turned. "Oh, and Paige..."

"Yes?"

There was the barest sparkle in his eyes. "If you're desperate for a pet, you might want to inquire in town. Cornwall hardly suits you."

Chapter 7

Cornwall, you just don't suit me."

Paige stood on her front porch combing her sleep-tumbled hair back from her face with widely spaced fingers. Cornwall stood on the front porch gazing yearningly toward her door.

"No dog suits me. No *animal* suits me, especially not at five a.m." She yawned, then covered it with a fist. "Shoo."

Cornwall didn't move.

"If I go inside and leave you here, you're going to howl, aren't you?" She wasn't sure she could bear to listen to Cornwall's pathetic pleas again. He had jolted her out of bed minutes ago. There was no telling what she might do to him if he woke her once more.

Yesterday, Adam had solved the Cornwall problem by two short whistle blasts. Paige shrugged. Pointing a finger in the direction from which Cornwall had come, she gave two weak whistles. In a second Cornwall was standing on his hind legs, front legs on her nightgown, trying to reach her face with his tongue. The impact was enough to send Paige sprawling. Cornwall took advantage of her loss of dignity by springing on to her now available lap and covering her face with what passed for kisses.

Paige shielded her face with her arms.

"I'm beginning to think you live on this porch."

Paige didn't need to uncover her eyes to know who was there. "Go away, Adam, and take this monster you bred with you!"

"Cornwall!" Adam gave two sharp whistle blasts, and Cornwall retreated to the porch's edge.

Paige wiped her face with her sweatshirt-clad arms and addressed her remarks to the sheepish sheepdog. "Today I'm going to buy you a collar and a chain." She looked up at Adam. "And I'm going to show *you* how to use them."

The smile on his face could have lit the morning sky if the newly risen sun hadn't been lighting it already. Too late, she realized what he was smiling at.

"Fine, Adam." She stood, brushing off the skirt of her nightgown. "So you don't see a woman in a silk nightgown and a sweatshirt every day of your life. I'm glad I could make your morning."

"The latest in haute couture?"

"The latest solution to traveling light. What are you doing here?"

"I told you I'd be by early."

"You're going to have to learn the distinction between civilized early and *un*civilized early." She pulled the oversized sweatshirt lower to cover her hips. "What time do you get up, anyway?"

"The minute I have to and not a minute before." His eyes traveled down to the diaphanous white silk covering her legs. He wasn't sure whether to thank or curse the designer who had slit the gown up to her thigh. "What is it between you and Cornwall, anyway?"

Her eyes narrowed. "I encourage him. You know. I leave a trail of steak bones between your house and mine. I lure him here with promises of pretty little French poodles and solid gold fire hydrants."

"I'm going to have to get rid of him if he doesn't shape up quickly."

"I'm sure some nice old lady in Waimauri would love to have him as a pet." Paige watched Adam's smile disappear. "Somehow I get the feeling that's not exactly what you have in mind."

"He's not a city dog. He's a country dog, and he's used to roaming. If he starts roaming and scattering another sheepman's mob, he's going to find himself at the lethal end of a shotgun. And then I'll be the one who gets the blame. Better my shotgun."

"Somebody taught him his stupid tricks. Give Cornwall to them."

"My cousin Pat is irresponsible enough to teach him the tricks and too irresponsible to live with the consequences." Adam shoved his hands in the back pockets of his black trousers. "I'll make certain Cornwall's locked in the shed at night so he doesn't bother you again."

Paige fought her wave of pity for the dog, but it was no use. "I'm sure he won't be back." And if he did reappear, Adam was going to be the last person to know. Paige didn't want Cornwall's death on her conscience. "Come have some coffee while I change."

Adam signaled Cornwall and pointed, and Cornwall headed toward home. Then Adam followed Paige inside.

He concentrated on the house, trying to ignore the way the thin silk outlined her hips as she walked. He had been here only yesterday, but now he paid attention to the changes she had made since arriving. He was startled to realize how many there were.

The spinster primness of the little bungalow had been transformed by the clever rearranging of furniture and the placement of accents she had probably found in old cabinets. In the corner a vase filled with wildflowers decorated a newly polished table; on the mantel a glass bowl held an assortment of ripe fruit. An afghan of brightly colored squares hid the worn back of a sofa, and crocheted doilies embellished the backs and arms of all the chairs. Even the windowpanes shone like flawless diamonds.

"You've spent some time fixing this place up." Adam stood in the doorway and watched Paige plug in the percolator.

"I'll be here a while. I wanted to be comfortable."

"Then you plan to stay the four weeks?"

She had spent the greater part of the last afternoon trying to decide exactly that. In the end one thing had persuaded her: there was nothing to go home to, or for. "I plan to stay."

"Won't you be missed?"

Paige supposed the answer was at the root of her discontent. Her absence would be noted, but would she be missed? She shrugged. "Not really. I completed everything else I was working on before I came here. If I go home, I'll be immersed in busywork someone else could just as easily do." She didn't add that she was also certain that once she left New Zealand, her father would probably find a way to keep her from completing this transaction.

"You're going to be bored."

"Apparently you know me better than I know myself." She folded her arms and turned to him, leaning on the counter. "Maybe you can inform me when I start feeling bored. Without your insight, I might not notice."

He kept his eyes on her face, studiously trying to ignore the leg so elegantly revealed through the slit of her gown. "How are you going to spend your time, then?"

"I'm going to help you look for the *mauri*."

He hadn't expected that. "You think so?"

"Yes." She turned back to the counter at the sound of the coffee perking. "Let me get you a cup, then I'll change. Shall I make anything to take with us?"

"I've packed some food."

She reached up into the cabinet, hiking her gown higher. "I'll be right back. Make yourself at home."

Adam averted his eyes. He felt anything except at home. The temperature of his blood rivaled the hottest springs in the thermals. After she left the room he wanted to call out and tell her to forget about the swim he had mentioned yesterday. The gown had been hard enough to take; he didn't want to see her in a bikini.

Instead he leaned on the counter, sipping weak coffee and wondering why the only thing he had felt when she'd said she was staying was relief.

The hills they crossed were the same ones Adam had led Paige over the day they had met. Now, as then, Paige's long legs barely kept up with the pace he set. She was in good physical condition. At home she spent the mandatory hours at an Uptown health club, swimming and working out, but even that hadn't prepared her for this near-jog over New Zealand's fertile countryside.

She concentrated on birdcalls instead of her breathing. She was learning to identify New Zealand's birds. If it was a useless skill for an American, she didn't care. She had hardly been aware of the existence of birds before she had come to Waimauri, but now their trills and songs woke her in the morning and lullabied her to sleep at night. On impulse, she had even bought a bird book.

"Have you ever seen a kiwi in the wild?" she asked, three paces behind Adam.

He had been waiting for complaints, not for questions about ornithology. "No. They still live in the forests, but they're shy."

"For good reason. I guess hiding is their only defense." Paige took advantage of Adam's slowed pace and caught up with him. "They've been badly cheated. What fun is it to be a flightless bird?"

"About as much fun as to be a helpless child."

Paige knew Adam was thinking about Jeremy, and she could see the parallels. She had wanted to ask him more about the little boy, but she hadn't known how to broach the subject. Now, as gently as she could, she did. "Why do you suppose Jeremy brought the jumper to my door that day? He's frightened of me now, but when he first came to the door—"

"He was hoping you were Sheila."

She was silently shocked.

Adam went on, ignoring her expression. "Jeremy knew I was taking a present to a woman. Apparently, in his little head, there was only one woman I'd be giving presents to. He's been looking for Sheila everywhere since the day she left him. No matter how she mistreated him, she's his mother."

There was nothing she could say to make the horror go away. Like the New Zealand kiwi that had never known a predator until the arrival of man, helpless little Jeremy had been completely at the mercy of careless whims of his mother. And still he loved her.

"He'll find a woman he can trust." As she said it, she hoped it was true.

"My family tries."

Paige thought about the exuberantly warm woman who had been taking care of Jeremy. Somehow she doubted that kind of demanding affection was what the little boy needed. But then, who was she to say?

"Do you recognize this?" Adam asked, changing the subject.

The vegetation had changed subtly as they'd walked. Now it was sparser, and scrub had replaced the pasture land and tall trees. "We're getting close to the edge of the thermals," Paige answered.

"You weren't very far when I found you."

"I felt like I was. If you hadn't found me, I might still be standing in the same spot."

"Before we go any farther, I want a promise."

Suspiciously she waited.

"Don't get cocky because you're getting a guided tour. You'd be a bloody fool to think you could come back on your own after one trip in with me."

"Not one trip, Adam. Many trips. I want to come when you look for the *mauri*. I told you."

"No."

"We're discussing property owned by my family," she reminded him. "I have a perfect right to be here anytime I choose."

"Not with me as guide."

"You, on the the other hand, have no right to be here unless I give my permission." She said the words politely, but they were backed by her most rigid posture.

"And how do you intend to keep me out?"

"I don't. I intend to come with you."

He let out a frustrated sigh. "Why?"

Her answer was hard to form. Part of it was because she wanted to know all she could about the property to be sure she negotiated a good deal, but there was more, too. "I guess it's mostly because I'm intrigued," she said at last, her chin lifted defiantly. "I don't intrigue easily."

He wanted to tell her what he thought about bored little rich girls who needed new toys, but even as he opened his mouth to say the words, he knew they weren't true. Paige wasn't a bored little rich girl. She was a woman struggling to find meaning in her life. He couldn't fault her for that, because he knew better than she did why so much of her life had been meaningless.

"What intrigues you?" he asked, more harshly than he'd intended.

"Adam, I'm not trying to become part of something that's not mine," she said, misinterpreting the emotion she saw on his face. "And I know the thermals aren't really mine, that it's an accident my family owns them. It's just that the *mauri* is important for you and the people of your *hapu*. I guess I'm looking for something important, too. Maybe if I help you find the *mauri*, I'll find something for myself, too."

Adam felt Paige slip inside him again, a feeling he'd never known with anyone except a big-eyed, black-haired cousin who once upon a time had trustingly placed her hand in his. Only then he'd been too young to see the dangers.

He turned away, angry, afraid, resigned. "I can't keep you from coming," he said gruffly.

Paige wondered why she felt disappointed. She shouldn't have expected Adam to understand. Apparently she hadn't yet shoved yesterday morning far enough away. The man she had glimpsed on her front porch was best forgotten. "Then you'll let me know when you're looking?"

"When it's convenient."

She recognized a compromise when she heard one. "Fine. I just hope it's convenient more than once or twice."

Adam set the pace again, but their way was often barred by the branches of shrubs and by rocks too large to step over. Paige was grateful they were walking slower, but she was learning again how poorly prepared she was for this kind of physical test. She was just about to swallow her pride and ask him if they could rest when he stopped again.

"When I found you, you were over the ridge, down in the Valley of Regrets," he said, pointing to their left.

"If I liked country-western music, I'd hum along." She laughed at his expression. "I rarely make jokes, Adam. You ought to be safe for the rest of the day. Tell me about the Valley of Regrets."

"Better yet, that's where we'll start."

She put her hand on his arm before he could move away. "Can you give me a minute? I'd like to catch my breath."

"You've done well." Adam watched her eyes light with pleasure in the brief unguarded moment right after he spoke. He was surprised that such a small compliment would please her. He knew just from looking at her how often men must have sung her praises.

Paige leaned against a tree and filled her lungs. Once in the thermals, she wasn't sure if she would want to breathe again. "I've read what I could about this area, so I understand a little of how it was formed. The thermals are caused by volcanic eruptions, aren't they?"

Nodding, Adam explained further. "The eruptions form basins called calderas, which are produced when the roofs of underground chambers of magma collapse."

"Magma?" She struggled to remember her college geology.

"Molten rock. Calderas follow the climax of a cycle of major volcanic activity. We know of four in the central North Island. By world standards, our volcanoes are very young, so many of the landforms haven't been modified by erosion."

"And that would make them important, wouldn't it?"

"Geologists love New Zealand."

"How much have these particular thermals been studied?"

"We see teams in here from time to time. Students doing dissertations, professors doing textbooks. This area is fairly small compared to others, though, and there aren't any phenomena here that the other, better known, areas don't have, too. I'd never get rich leading expeditions."

"Why you? Because your property backs up to the other side?"

"My family has lived here for generations. I've been taught every inch of the land. Once my ancestors knew the location of the *mauri*."

She asked the logical question. "Why didn't someone pass on the secret?"

"Generations ago the *tohunga* who knew the location had only one son. The son married an Englishwoman, and apparently his father felt there was no longer anyone he could trust the secret to. It died with him. Are you ready?"

"I guess so."

Adam strode away. He didn't want to discuss tribal history with Paige. It was too tempting to tell her that the *tohunga* had been her great-great-grandfather.

Paige carefully followed Adam up the ridge and down into the tiny valley. Loose stones made balancing tricky, and she was forced to duck under the branches of the manuka shrub. The air had been tinged with the smell of sulphur since they had passed out of the denser forest, but now it grew stronger still. One minute the area was sparsely forested but normal in appearance, the next they were in hell.

The Valley of Regrets had been well named. Paige was glad to be able to examine it without fear of ending up there permanently. Directly in front of her the ground bubbled like a witch's cauldron; to her right the scorched grass gave way to a spurting stream of water, not a geyser, but certainly not a spring like any she'd ever seen, either. The path seemed to wind to her left, but when she took a step in that direction, Adam held her back.

"I wouldn't." He reached down and lifted a long branch that was lying on the ground beside him. "Watch." He drew it back over his shoulder like a spear, then let it fly. It landed on the "path" she'd planned to take and lodged with the hissing noise of an overheated radiator.

"Lovely spot. Just right for a picnic." Paige tried to suppress a shiver but didn't succeed.

"You were right over there." He pointed to a tree on the other side of the bubbling ground. "Actually, you were fairly safe. The only logical way for you to go would have been back over that hill, around through those trees and out of the thermals."

"Why don't I feel vastly relieved?"

"Because you're an intelligent woman."

She knew she hadn't shown much intelligence the day she had tried to explore by herself. "I was warned people have died in here."

"It's a warning to keep in mind. All the thermal areas have their dangers. Scalding mud, poison gas."

"Gas?"

Adam took an audible breath. "Smell the sulphur in the air? That's hydrogen sulphide, five times as toxic as carbon monoxide and almost as lethal as cyanide."

Paige wanted to hold her nose. "Why are we still alive, then?"

"It's safe in this proportion. Concentrated, it can kill in minutes. Sulphide's denser than oxygen, so it hugs the ground, accumulating in hollows close to its source. Excavations, poorly designed swimming pools, houses without adequate underfloor ventilation."

"Air that's dangerous to breathe, ground that steams under your feet. It's a surprise to me that anyone settled here."

"I imagine it's a surprise that you've got a fight on your hands for this piece of ground, too."

"It is." Paige tried to figure out what to do next. "If we can't go straight, and we can't go right or left, where do we go?"

"We're going right. Do you mind getting wet?"

"I mind getting scalded."

"It's more like a hot shower. Come on. Just stay right behind me and do what I do."

The spurting spring emptied into a small, bubbling pond. There was a narrow pathway between the two, and, as Adam had predicted, they did get wet from the resulting spray, but the water was comfortably warm. "Why does the pond bubble, then, if the water feeding into it isn't hot?" Paige asked when Adam had led her to a rocky clearing.

"The pond's really fed by a hot spring beneath it."

"And is that what made the mud bubble back there?"

"Mud pools form when steam and gas are released under a mixture of rainwater and mud created by reaction of the rock with acidic fumes. When the weather's been dry, the mud forms steep-sided cones, and when it's wet, as it has been lately, the mud looks like lakes of lava." Adam reached out and wiped a drop of water off the tip of Paige's nose. "In the bigger, really spectacular boiling mud pools, you can see both, and the activity is even more dramatic than this one."

"Is the whole area this bizarre?"

"Some more, some less. It's probably the parts that seem normal that are the most dangerous, because they seduce you into believing you're safe. And you're never safe here."

Paige wondered if Adam was trying to scare her into abandoning her quest for the *mauri*. "Not even if you know the area as well as you do?"

"Not if you take it for granted. Things can change rapidly in a thermal area. Do you know about the eruption of Mount Tarawera in 1886?"

Paige shook her head.

"I brought some scones for breakfast. There's a pretty little pool not too far from here. Let's go sit there and I'll tell you about it."

Paige had known that Adam regarded the thermals as something special to his heritage, but she'd had no idea he would find them so personally fascinating. He had grown up here, but still the bizarre landscape seemed as interesting to him as it was to her. So interesting, in fact, that he was forgetting, at least momentarily, to hide his enthusiasm. She wondered if this unguarded Adam was the Adam other people saw, or if this was just one of the rare times in his life when he felt free to be himself.

She followed him along the rock-strewn path, stopping once to comment on yellowish smoke rising between two large boulders.

"Fumaroles," he explained. "Hell's chimneys. You'll see more than a few today."

The pool was a bright, clear green, and at Adam's encouragement, Paige trailed her fingers through the water. It was icy cold. Pongas, medium-sized, palmlike trees with lush fern branches, lined the far side, and it was easy to forget that they were relaxing in an area of incredible geological anomalies.

Adam took napkin-wrapped scones out of his small backpack and handed one to Paige. Hot tea from a vacuum bottle followed, along with juicy oranges. She settled comfortably on the wide strip of grass leading down to the pool and waited for him to join her. He draped himself in front of her with perfectly coordinated masculine grace. Against her will, she thought of their kiss on her front porch and wondered what it would be like to have Adam kiss her in earnest. He had made it clear she would never know, and for a moment she let herself feel disappointment.

She tried to shake the feeling with small talk. "This isn't the pool you were talking about swimming in, was it?"

"Not unless you want to turn blue. You'd freeze."

"You could revive me over a fumarole."

He laughed, watching with fascination as her small white teeth severed a section of orange. "What do you think of all this so far?"

"I'm impressed." She waited, but when he didn't say anything she decided to take a risk. "I don't like knowing I have any control over what's going to happen to this place. No one should own the thermals. They should own themselves."

"No one ever really owns the land. We say, *'Whatu-ngarongaro he tangata, toitu he kainga.'* People pass away, but places still remain. Long after you and I are gone, the thermals will still be here, unless they're destroyed by careless usage."

In more ways than one, they were on dangerous ground. Paige changed the subject. "Tell me about Mount Tarawera."

Adam tried to shake off the feeling that he should pull Paige into his arms and dispense with small talk. He had known it was going to be hard to spend this time around her; he hadn't known that he would find everything she did provocative. An expressive sweep of her hand sent his blood pressure higher; her tongue darting out to lick drops of juice from her bottom lip was almost too much to bear. Apparently his long-enforced celibacy was taking a greater toll than he had ever imagined.

Paige watched fire kindle in Adam's eyes, and her own response was immediate. She tried to tell herself that what she felt was the classic rebound syndrome. She couldn't possibly be over Granger this soon; her attraction to Adam was just a need to feel alive again. Even as the thoughts went through her head, her heart began to pound.

Adam watched a slow flush warm her skin. Her lashes swept down as she reached for another orange slice, and he knew she had looked away because she, too, was fighting for control.

"Do you know what a volcano is?" he asked in a low voice.

"Vaguely," she said, her gaze focused on the orange.

"I understand them intimately," he said with a derisive laugh. "The heat, and the unbearable pressure, and, finally, the explosion."

Paige lifted her head and reluctantly met his eyes. She could read the heat and the unbearable pressure in the inky depths. With no conscious choice, she felt herself sway toward him.

Adam damned himself for letting his composure slip away. He felt more than saw Paige move, and it took all his self-control to remain still. He forced himself to sound nonchalant. "Have you ever heard of the pink and white terraces?"

She had only moved an inch or two, but Paige felt as if she had reached out to Adam and been rejected in return. She tensed, wondering if she would ever learn. Grasping the orange slice, she turned away from him to gaze at the water. "No. Should I have?"

"They weren't too far from here. Once they were considered the eighth wonder of the world." Adam's eyes lingered on the proud curve of Paige's neck, the tension in her shoulders, and he silently asked her forgiveness. He went on because it was all he could do. "The terraces were formed from sinter, a precipitate of silica. In this case, the sinter was deposited in steps. Thousands of tourists visited every year before Mount Tarawera erupted and buried the terraces. As a consolation prize, an eight hundred foot deep hot lake was formed. The village of Te Wairoa was buried, too, and a hundred and fifty-three people lost their lives."

Paige turned back to him, her face innocent of expression. "A tragedy."

"They've uncovered parts of the village, and you can take a tour of it. It's a lesson on talking anything for granted."

"Could something like that happen here?"

"It's unlikely anything quite that spectacular could. But nothing ever stays the same. The thermals are alive. I've watched them change since I was a boy. And just when Jeremy begins to know them, they'll change again."

Paige unwrapped her scone and began to eat, washing down bites with hot tea. Somewhere overhead a bird sang, and in the distance she could hear the sound of rushing water. She concentrated on everything except Adam.

Adam watched Paige ignore him, and, like everything else about her, it fascinated him. He knew he had become obsessed with her, an obsession that would lead to nothing except pain for both of them. And yet each time he drew back from her, it seemed to bring them closer. Everything seemed to bring them closer.

"Do you hear that?" he asked as she finished the last of her scone.

Paige listened closely, identifying a new sound. It seemed to come from below them, a faint keening followed by an emphatic gurgle. "What is it?"

"Papa, the earth mother."

She listened again. "She's crying."

Adam was surprised at her perception. "She cries for Rangi, the sky father. Once they were together, clasped in each other's arms. Then they were separated by their son, Tane, who pushed the sky far above the earth. When Papa cries for Rangi, the earth groans in anguish. When Rangi cries for Papa, his tears come to us as rain.''

Paige met Adam's eyes for the first time since she had felt his rejection. ''All creation myths are beautiful, aren't they?''

''Not all are tragic love stories.''

''I guess love's always the best story.'' Paige watched Adam fight his awareness of her again. When she could stand it no longer, she stood and went to the pond's edge to scoop water to wash her face. She straightened and felt Adam behind her. She wanted to turn, but she knew better. Through the heavy wool of her sweater, she felt his hands rest lightly on her shoulders.

''I used to believe in love,'' he said quietly.

''So did I.''

They stood that way for a long moment; then Paige felt the cool morning air where his hands had been. She turned; Adam was just stuffing the last of their picnic in his backpack. He looked up at her, and his eyes were shuttered. ''There's more to see.''

She nodded and followed him back to the path.

Chapter 8

Paige was tired again by the time they reached the hot pool where Adam wanted to swim. He had acquainted her with more fumaroles, gushing springs and strangely formed mineral deposits than she had known existed. She had waited patiently for a geyser that never went off and thrown small sticks into another boiling mud pool, only to watch them sink forever out of sight.

Adam had spoken little, other than to give detailed speeches about each geological phenomenon. If Paige had spoken about anything, it would have been about the tension between them and what they should do about it. And since those weren't thoughts she *could* speak, she had remained silent.

Now she sank down to the ground and rested her chin on her knees. The hot pool poured steam into the morning air, where it condensed into visible droplets. The ground around the pool was scattered with wildflowers and ferns, and the pool itself was crystal clear and brilliantly blue. "Can we really swim here?" she asked doubtfully. "In New Orleans we boil crawfish in water that doesn't look any hotter than this."

Adam favored her with an arrogant smile. "Shall I go first?"

"Would it be to your advantage to get rid of me?"

He grunted, and she knew it was an answer she could interpret either way. "I guess I'll have to trust you," she said, sitting straighter. Crossing her arms, she pulled the sweater over her head.

Adam's mouth went dry as Paige began to unbutton her blouse. Rationally he knew she was probably wearing a bathing suit under her clothes, but some irrational part of him was still praying.

Paige stood and stripped off her pleated wool pants. It was strange to be standing in the cold air naked except for the sleek, French-cut bathing suit. She reached up to twist her hair into a knot, then laughed at herself. "Now that's a habit for you. I cut my hair almost a year ago, but I still forget sometimes."

Adam turned his gaze from the sight of her. For a moment he'd filled his eyes with the sumptuous curves of her breasts and hips, the tiny circle of her waist, the long, exquisite length of her legs. Now he forced himself to sound nonchalant when he felt anything but. "I can imagine you with long hair." And he could. Long, black pigtails framing dancing dark eyes.

Paige watched Adam undress. She was sure he swam in the pool often, and just as sure that when he did, he didn't bother with a suit. She wished she could be a bird in the cabbage tree beside her at one of those moments. Adam naked would be a study in masculine beauty.

He turned, and she made herself breathe. Adam in a swimsuit was a study in masculine beauty. The untanned portions of his body were the same creamy olive as hers. His shoulders were broader than she had realized, tapering down to a narrow waist and flat stomach. His cut-off jeans hung low over slender hips and taut, muscular thighs. His chest was finely matted with hair as silky as a butterfly's cocoon. She wished she could explore him with her hands.

She pulled herself back to reality. The only exploration she would do that day was of the thermals. "Well, who goes first?" she asked, suddenly cold.

Adam saw her shiver and wondered how much of it was the temperature and how much the tension. He held out his hand without weighing the consequences. He wanted her to be warm. He wanted to be warm. "I'll help you in. It's a shock at first."

Hesitantly she slipped her hand inside his.

Adam led her down to the water's edge and walked in as if the temperature was of no concern. Paige followed, but her lips clamped shut in painful surprise as the water covered her feet.

Adam felt her hand jerk, and he stopped, waiting for her to adjust. "You'll get used to it."

Paige inched in until the water came up to her knees. She resisted looking down to see if her body was still covered with skin.

"After the first jolt, the temperature seems more bearable." Adam lowered himself into the water so everything but his head was covered. He tugged lightly on her hand. "Coming?"

"This can't be healthy."

"On the contrary, your friend Armstrong is banking that this spring and others like it are healthy to the tune of millions of dollars of tourist business. He'll come in and pipe it into a concrete shell, chlorinate it and count his money."

"Who would pay to be boiled alive?"

Adam tugged again. With a sigh Paige shut her eyes and lowered herself into the water. Adam felt her hand tense in his. "Give it a minute, and if you don't like it, we'll go."

She waited, counting slowly to sixty, but by thirty, the water was beginning to feel more comfortable. By forty, she opened her eyes. "Am I getting used to it, or have all my nerves short-circuited?"

Adam wished his nerves *would* short-circuit. It would make it easier to be close to her. "A hot pool like this one figures in another Maori love story."

Paige could feel the heat penetrating her bones. "Is it as sad as the last one? Tears from the sky and agonized cries from the earth?"

"Do you like happy endings, *kaihana*?"

"I like them, I just don't believe them."

"I'll tell you this story, and you can decide whether to believe it or not. There's a spot at the edge just made for stories." Adam led her to a shallow, sandy shelf that sloped down to deeper water. He sat while she considered how to make herself comfortable. Before she could decide or he could think clearly, Adam spread his legs and pulled her to sit between them. He circled her with his arm, forcing her to lie back against him. His wrist brushed her breasts, and she could feel her nipples harden from the contact. For a moment she couldn't breathe.

"Comfortable?" he asked.

"Not at all."

Harsh laughter rumbled against her back. He began his story before he could begin something else. "In the middle of Lake Rotorua, there's an island, Mokoia Island, that figures in Arawa history. Did you see it when you were there?"

She knew better than to draw attention to her reaction. She forced herself to breathe. "I didn't see the lake except from a distance."

"I'll take you there someday, and we'll swim in a hot pool like this one. It's the one where Hinemoa and Tutanekai swam." His arms tightened until she was his prisoner.

"Tell me about them," she said, trying to relax.

"Tutanekai was the stepson of Whakaue, and he had three elder brothers who resented him because Tutanekai was illegitimate—"

"Haven't you left something out?"

He backtracked. She had turned her head, and her cheek was warm satin against his chest. "Tutanekai's mother fell in love with another man while her husband was away from home. But being an understanding, gracious sort, he accepted the child of that union when he returned."

She managed to stop herself from snuggling closer. "Are all Maori men that understanding?"

"I wouldn't attempt to find out." His mouth skimmed her hair in a kiss she couldn't feel. "Tutanekai grew up on Mokoia Island, a handsome, strong young man, skilled in every way. At the same time, at Owhata across the lake, there was a beautiful young maiden named Hinemoa, the daughter of a very influential chief. Because of her high rank, Hinemoa was made a *puhi*, which means she was declared *tapu*. She couldn't sleep with any man nor choose her own husband as most women were allowed to do. She had to let her *hapu* choose a husband for her. When she reached maturity, many young men came to ask for Hinemoa's hand, including all the elder brothers of Tutanekai. But her father refused them all."

"So she was destined to live a virgin?"

"Not so. Our people have always gathered for meetings. In those days, we did the same. Hinemoa saw Tutanekai at one of those meetings and fell in love. Tutanekai fell just as hard. Because of Tutanekai's lowly birth, they couldn't even speak to each other, but each time they met they conveyed their feelings with their eyes."

Paige stirred in his arms.

He held her tighter. "Tutanekai was so unhappy about this state of affairs that every night he would sit with his good friend Tiki on the beach of Mokoia Island and play sad music on his flute. All the way across the water Hinemoa would hear him, and sadness would fill her, too."

"A flute like yours?"

"I copied mine from one in the Auckland Museum that's said to have been Tutanekai's."

Paige remembered the sad melody Adam had played for her, and she knew how Hinemoa must have felt. "Go on."

"After many nights of this, Hinemoa knew she could never marry anyone except Tutanekai. Her people began to suspect as much, and, worried that she might try to go to Tutanekai, they began to pull their canoes well up onto the beach at dusk to keep Hinemoa at home. Finally, it was more than Hinemoa could bear. She decided that if she couldn't use a canoe to reach Tutanekai, she would swim. The next night she told her people she was going to the *whare tapere*, which was the place where games were played and dances performed, but instead she went to the cooking house, where she stole six calabashes."

"Calabashes?"

"Hollow gourds used for storage, or transporting drinking water. Hinemoa fashioned them into primitive water wings, took off her clothes, slipped into the water and began to swim the mile to Mokoia Island." Adam brushed Paige's hair with his lips again. "Shall I tell you the rest of the story?"

"Umm . . . Please."

His hands slowly traveled down to her hips and rested there. "After a very long, tiring swim, she made it, guided all the while by Tutanekai's music. When she climbed up on the beach, however, she was alone and very cold, so she headed right for the warm bathing pool called Waikimihia, which was just below Tutanekai's house, to rest. After she had warmed up, she realized she was in a bit of a predicament because her clothes were on the beach at Owhata, and she was beginning to feel shy."

"A fine time to think of that."

His fingers fanned out to caress the firm flesh of her thighs. "Shall I go on?"

Paige felt her pulse begin to speed. Her oxygen supply had stopped at the touch of his roving hands. "Please," she said in a breathy voice.

"About that time, Tutanekai began to get thirsty, and he sent his slave down to the lake for water. When Hinemoa heard someone passing, she called out and asked in a gruff voice who the water was for. The slave replied it was for Tutanekai, and Hinemoa, secluded from his sight, reached out, grabbed the calabash and broke it. The slave went back inside and reported what had happened, and Tutanekai sent him back to the lake with another calabash. The same thing happened again. This time when the slave returned to tell Tutanekai, Tutanekai was furious, so, grabbing his best feathered cloak and a weapon made of greenstone, he marched down to the pool to fight the stranger who dared to break his calabashes.''

Paige covered Adam's hands with hers. halting their progress. ''It's a good thing she brought her own along to replace them.''

''I don't think Tutanekai was too worried about his calabashes, *kaihana*. When he arrived at the pool he issued a challenge, but there was no answer. Hinemoa had moved to a spot where a small overhanging rock gave her cover. Tutanekai felt along the edge of the pool until he reached the place. Catching her by the hair, he pulled her clear and shouted, 'Who are you? Who dares to annoy me?' She answered, 'It is I, Hinemoa, who has come to you.' Tutanekai lifted her from the water, and I'm sure he thought he had never seen anything so beautiful. Then he covered her with his cloak and led her to his house, where he took her to his bed, and thus they were married.''

Paige had a sudden longing for the good old days. ''It was that simple?''

''The next day her family, suspecting what had happened, came to the island, but because Hinemoa had shown so much courage, they couldn't be angry with her. There was feasting and rejoicing, and a lasting peace was made between the two families.''

''A much happier ending than Shakespeare would have given it.''

''Tutanekai and Hinemoa lived on Mokoia Island for some years, but later they moved to the summit of Tihi o Tonga. It's said that Tutanekai was the chief who had steps carved in the face of the cliff there, leading to the cave where Horo-i-rangi was kept.''

Paige turned so she could see his face. ''Did Tutanekai have anything to do with the Horo-i-rangi you're looking for?''

''I don't know. The story is too obscure.''

''It would make sense, wouldn't it, that a man as much in love as Tutanekai would see fertility and the life force in a carved stone goddess?''

''It would.'' Adam reluctantly lifted his hands from her legs and brushed her hair back from her face, framing it with his palms. ''Did you like the story?''

She had found the story strangely touching, especially hearing it with Adam's arms around her. ''I'm glad you told me.''

''And the happy ending?''

"Reserved for legends."

Adam wanted to kiss away her cynicism. Instead his hands moved to her shoulders, and he lifted her so that he could move away. If he held her for one more moment, he might never let her go.

He struck out for the middle of the pool. Paige watched him until he turned and waited; then she followed. The pool wasn't large, but by the time she joined him, she was tired. The heat of the water after the long hike made her feel boneless and good for nothing.

"Feel the difference in the temperature." Adam stood straight, his head barely above water. He stretched out a hand to help hold her up.

"It's cooler here. Why?"

"We're farther from the spring itself."

Paige lay back in the water and closed her eyes, half-floating. A warm feeling of well-being overlay the awareness he had kindled. "You must come here often."

"Not as often as I'd like. I don't have the time."

Paige thought about Adam's words. She hadn't given much thought to the time he was taking out of his schedule to guide her. He was a man with a large farm and a small son, and both needed his full attention. She wondered if she was so used to getting what she wanted that she just assumed others should be at her beck and call. An apology seemed in order. She moved a little closer.

"You know, I've taken up more of your time since I came here than I have a right to. I'm sure you must have a hundred other things you should be doing right now."

"Two hundred. But none more important than this."

"Someone else could have taken me through."

"I wanted you to see the thermals with me."

She knew he meant because he could give her the most comprehensive tour, but she liked the way the words had sounded, anyway. "I wanted to see them with you, too," she admitted.

"You hid that fact well."

"You made me angry."

"It might have been safer if you'd stayed that way."

She straightened, no longer relaxed. Without a word she swam to a shallower spot.

Adam joined her. "And now I've made you angry again."

"Do we need anger to keep our distance from each other? We're not children. You've made it clear you want our relationship to be purely business. I'm happy to oblige."

Adam straightened, too. "*Are* you happy?" he asked, one lifted brow signaling his distrust. "I shouldn't have thought so, but then, maybe I misread what happens to you when I touch you."

For a moment Paige's usual candor deserted her. She wanted to tell him that he had misread her, but Adam wasn't a man to be lied to. She made herself meet his gaze squarely. "I respond to you. But you're not the first man I've responded to, and you won't be the last. I've seen too much to think the world revolves around the chemistry between a man and a woman."

Adam knew he should applaud, but he had never felt less in the mood. Instead he felt anger at the men who were responsible for making her belittle the potent attraction between them. Somewhere she had learned to expect nothing from any man except a fleeting physical release. He wanted to prove to her that more was possible, even if he knew it was wrong to try.

"Not a very romantic sentiment for a woman who likes happily-ever-afters," he said at last, schooling himself to sound calm.

"Romance?" She forced a laugh. "My husband bled it out of me, one drop at a time."

"And what replaced it?" He moved a step closer.

"Good sense." Paige stood perfectly still, but her heart beat faster.

"Sheila bled me dry. Apparently, I wasn't as lucky as you were."

"What do you mean?"

"No one transfused me with good sense." He took another step.

"Then we're lucky I've acquired enough for both of us."

He shook his head as he moved closer still. "I'm beginning to think there isn't enough good sense in the world to keep us apart."

"Adam, no."

"No what? No, there isn't enough good sense? No, you don't want this?"

"Maybe I should remind you of yesterday's lecture. *You* don't want *me* remember?" She stood her ground, but it took all her strength to do so. She wanted to retreat from the new feral gleam in his eye and the pounding of her own heart.

"I'm beginning to think what I want isn't the issue." He reached for her, splashing water around her shoulders as he did. "I'm beginning to think we have no choice." His arms entwined around her back, but instead of the kiss she had expected, he just pulled her through the water until she was leaning against him. He held her as if he wasn't sure whether to shake her or kiss her.

If Adam had kissed her, Paige would have resisted. But his restraint was enough to catch her off guard. His body was as tense as hers, and she knew he was fighting himself. Still he held her as if she were fragile glass. Fragile glass about to shatter. "I never know what you'll do next," she said, her words strangely like a groan.

"You're a woman of the world. Can't you guess?"

"Not with you. You might stand here holding me like a brother forever."

He pulled her closer and ground his hips against hers. "Do I feel like a brother, *kaihana*?"

"You don't feel like a cousin, either." Paige lifted her face to his. "You feel like a man who wants a woman."

"And do all the men you respond to feel this way?"

"It's possible I exaggerated the number."

His lips curved slowly in a dark, secret smile. "And will you be thinking of any of them when I kiss you?"

"I imagine that when you kiss me, I won't be thinking at all."

"Both of us had better be thinking, or it won't stop at a kiss." Adam bent his head and took her mouth with his, not gently, as he had kissed her on the porch, but with the passion that had built slowly in him since that moment. The battle he had fought only heightened what he was feeling now. He filled his senses with the essence of her, the full, sweet flavor of her mouth, the sleek warmth of her body, the subtle spicy fragrance that was as much a part of her as the blood coursing through her veins. His hands learned her ripe curves, and the rest of his body learned the pain of denial.

Paige leaned into Adam, her lips parting under the insistent pressure of his. She wanted to suppress her response, just as she suppressed the expression of all her feelings, but Adam made that impossible. In seconds he broke through defenses it had taken her a lifetime to perfect. As the kiss deepened, she let herself move against him, learning his strength and his warmth by degrees until her arms were clasped around his waist and her body was bonded to his.

Only then did he end the kiss. He pulled her head to his shoulder and tightened his arms around her. "The world may not revolve around us, *kaihana*, but our own worlds are spinning out of control."

She heard his battle for control. She tried to pretend the kiss had been less than it had. "We both know how little this meant. We're diversions for each other, nothing more."

Adam heard her words. At the same time he felt her arms tighten spasmodically around him. They mocked her denial and proclaimed her need. "Not diversions," he reassured her. "And not substitutes."

"What, then?" She forced herself to unwrap her arms and push him away.

"Something that has no name." He waited until she was almost out of reach, then easily pulled her back to him. This time his fingers tightened on her shoulders to hold her still. Her mouth eluded his for only a moment; then she was locked in his embrace again. In another moment, she was embracing him.

Desire ran through her in hot, shuddering waves, and she felt the full strength of Adam's answering desire as she pressed against him. She knew in that moment how much she wanted him and how wrong it would be to have what she wanted. He could hurt her, and, just as surely, she could hurt him. They were not diversions, not substitutes.

"Something that has no name?" She moaned the words as he lifted her and trailed kissed down her neck to the soft flesh about her bathing suit. "Adam, the name is tormentors." Her knees gave way as he nudged aside the strap of her suit. "Haven't both of us had enough torment not to want more?"

And because he knew that, in the end, that was exactly what they would bring each other, he stilled, his fingers biting into her waist for control. He was suddenly cold, as if the water had been transformed into an icy spring. His cheek fell against her chest, and he listened to the speeding rhythm of her heart. Her skin was wet satin, and for just a moment he let himself mourn what would never be.

Paige anchored her fingers in his hair as his fingers loosened and he let her slide fully back into the water. Her hand was unsteady, and although he had managed to wipe all traces of expression off his face, somehow she was unable to do the same. Her eyes shone with vulnerability, and Adam knew that for the rest of his life, he would remember the way they searched his face.

Little by little she regained control, covering what she felt. Finally she stepped away. "I've used up enough of your day. We'd better be getting back."

He knew that would be best, but as she turned to head to shore, he grabbed her hand and held her still. "I would never willingly bring you torment, *kaihana*."

"What would you bring me, then?" she asked softly. When he didn't—or couldn't—answer, she pulled her hand from his and left the water.

Paige and Adam tried to avoid touching each other for the rest of the morning. What conversation they made was strained and polite, as if they had never progressed beyond being strangers.

Although the areas of the thermals Adam had initially shown her had been filled with interesting phenomena, there had been natural pathways leading to them. Adam had explained that these were the areas local people visited, and, with a knowledgeable guide, they were safe enough.

There were other areas, however, vast uncharted territory where few ventured, only those who, like Adam, knew and respected the land's idiosyncracies. Here there were no paths. The land was as treacherous as a quicksand-filled swamp, its dangers hidden by the thin shells of rocks, the seeming innocence of glistening silent pools. Adam understood that the rocks would give way to roiling cauldrons and the silent pools could spurt boiling water from hidden fissures. He warned Paige as they explored.

Adam guided her through one such area, coaching her on where to place her feet, where not to touch. Paige had believed his warnings, but as they walked along a steaming cliff stratified with all the colors of the earth, she developed a profound respect for his knowledge.

"I was in Hawaii when Hurricane Eve struck," she said, hesitantly accepting his hand as they crossed a narrow ledge leading to an innocent grassy plain. "I thought I'd discovered all I needed to know about Mother Nature's fury."

"There's always something to learn." Adam dropped Paige's hand, then leapt a narrow crevice. Turning, he held out his arms to her. "Don't look down. I'll catch you."

Without thinking, she leapt. She felt his arms tighten around her momentarily. Then he moved away. If he'd felt anything at all, he didn't show it. "Do you know where we are?" he asked.

She shook her head.

"We're on the other side. After a short walk we'll be on my pasture land."

Disappointment that their morning together had ended filled her. Hiding it, she spun slowly, as if trying to get her bearings. "I'm thoroughly turned around."

Adam continued in the lecture mode he had been using since their swim. "We circled several times. Loosely, the thermals are bottle-shaped. If the bottle lay on the ground, your house would be at the lower middle. My land is on the upper top. One of the easiest ways for either of us to enter is at the bottleneck, on either side of the Valley of Regrets."

"How much did I see?"

"About three big sips."

"I've seen a blowup of the area. The thermals didn't seem that big."

"If you could cover them by auto or even in a logical progression on foot, they wouldn't seem so large. But we had to backtrack constantly. We were actually near your house when we swam."

She hadn't realized. "How long will it take me to see the rest?"

"Another day or two to see even the highlights."

"Where do you search for the *mauri*?"

"We didn't see that area today."

"When will we?"

He was no longer the lecturer. One eyebrow lifted, as if the cynical Adam had reasserted himself. "How wise will it be to spend that time together?"

She tossed her head. "We'll manage. Neither of us lacks self-control. We proved that today."

"Is that what we proved?"

"I want to help you look for the *mauri*. I hope you're not going to go back on your word."

"Never."

"Good, then I'll wait to hear from you."

He smiled his most taunting smile. "Are you saying goodbye for the day?"

She became aware that she was far from home, and the way back was through the thermals. "I'm at your mercy, aren't I?"

"What a pleasure that would be." His smile warmed for a moment, then disappeared. "Granny's expecting us for tea. Then I'll drive you home."

"Aren't you tired of feeding me?"

Adam turned and started through the field. He was tired of nothing about her, but telling her wouldn't change a thing.

"Don't fish for compliments. Just come home with me and have tea."

And because she had no choice, she followed.

In minutes Four Hill Farm spread out before them. By the time they reached the pasture nearest the house, Paige was exhausted. Since they were just in time to see two of Adam's workers transfer a mob of sheep from that pasture to another, she rested, leaning on the wooden fence to watch the remarkable maneuverings of two dogs who looked like Cornwall. Adam observed with her.

"It's a pretty sight, isn't it?" Paige asked as she watched the dogs and men work the sheep, entranced. "Those dogs have more sense than half the people I know."

Adam was surprised by her obvious enjoyment of a spectacle he never tired of himself. "Those dogs have more sense than one of the men working them." He whistled sharply after the dogs had succeeded in moving the sheep in the right direction. One of the men turned, and Adam beckoned.

"Be glad you don't speak Maori," he said as the young man walked toward them.

Paige turned to him, puzzled, but she understood immediately when Adam began a harangue that would have been unmistakable in any language.

She compared the two men as the volume of their conversation increased. The younger man was dark-haired, like Adam, but he was stockier and smiled easily. His eyes were the same midnight hue, but even when he smiled, they were lit with rebellion.

The argument ceased abruptly, although Paige would have bet that neither man was satisfied. There was a short silence before Adam spoke in English. "Paige Duvall, I'd like to introduce my cousin, Pat Tomoana."

She held out her hand politely, but Pat smiled and shook his head, wiping his hands on his trousers. "You don't want to shake," he protested boyishly. "I smell like an old leg of mutton."

"Does Granny know you're back?" Adam asked.

"I stopped by and saw her this morning before I came up here."

"And Hira?"

"She's forgiven me. You should do the same, cousin."

"And if someday I don't?"

Pat shrugged. "We're family."

"Don't count on the old ways to protect you forever."

Pat seemed to be struggling to look remorseful. "I won't do it again."

"And don't count on me believing that." Adam pushed himself away from the fence. "Ready, Paige?"

She smiled her goodbye to Pat, then followed Adam down the hill toward his house. "I think I'd do just about anything not to be on the other end of one of your lectures," she commented. From the corner of her eye she could see the muscle in Adam's clenched jaw still jumping in anger.

"He was lucky it was only a lecture."

"Hira was the singer at the *hangi*, wasn't she?"

"My niece."

Paige put together what she knew and what she'd heard. This was obviously a family drama, and not just the first act. Families fascinated her. She had never had enough of her own to understand what made them fight or stay together. She had grown up watching other people's from afar and wondering.

"You stick by our own, don't you?" Paige wasn't prepared for the strange look Adam gave her. The question had been rhetorical.

Adam's answer—if he had planned to make one—was interrupted by a high-pitched shout from the yard behind the house. Paige watched as Jeremy barreled across the ground at top speed to throw himself into his father's arms. She had a sudden, perverse inclination to hug the child herself. Dressed in dark overalls and a plaid shirt, Jeremy was the same sturdy male cherub she had met on her front porch. With his face aglow with love for his father, he stirred maternal feelings she hadn't even known she'd had.

Wrapped in his devotion for his son, Adam stirred feelings in her, too. She liked seeing him this way: relaxed, careless about showing love, proud of the little boy in his arms. She felt a bond, as if something was right about their being together. It was different from the strong physical attraction she felt, but just as overwhelming. And possibly more dangerous.

"Say hello to Miss Duvall, Jeremy," Adam prompted after Jeremy had settled down.

Jeremy obeyed with a one-syllable hello.

Paige murmured her response without quite looking at him, watching out of the corner of her eye, as she waited for him to move as far away from her as his father's arms would allow. Instead she saw that Jeremy was watching her inquisitively. Faced with the chance to begin establishing a relationship with the little boy, she was at a loss for what to do.

Just as she was sure she ought to say something, anything, to break the silence, a bell rang from the direction of the house. "We're here just in time," Adam said. He set Jeremy on the ground. "Run ahead and tell Granny we're coming."

Jeremy said something in Maori, and Adam smiled. "Yes, she's going to eat with us. But I promise she won't eat you."

Paige peeked at the little boy just in time to see a fleeting smile cross his face. His eyes held hers for just a second before he scurried down the rest of the hill. "Did he smile at me?" she asked when Jeremy was out of earshot.

Adam glanced at her curiously. "Would you have noticed?"

"I like children. I just don't know what to do with them."

"Much the way you feel about dogs?"

"Much the way I feel about you," she added dryly. "I like you, Adam, but damned if I know what to do with you."

"Or about me."

She nodded. "Or about you." She stopped at the feel of his hand on her arm. Each separate finger seemed to mark her skin.

"We'll swim together again."

"No, I—"

"We'll swim together again," he repeated. "We'll protest what's happening between us and swear we're stronger than it is. And then, finally, we'll realize we aren't stronger at all. And when that day comes, *kaihana*, you'll know what to do with me, and I with you."

Chapter 9

Paige pressed her nose to Mihi's as Adam looked on. The old woman seemed tired, and Paige regretted accepting Adam's summons to lunch.

"I'll just be a moment getting everything on the table," Mihi told them as she headed toward the kitchen.

Paige turned to Adam. "I wish she'd let me help."

"I wondered if you were still speaking to me."

She cocked her head. Not a word had been exchanged since Adam's surprising declaration. "How was I supposed to answer you?"

"A simple yes would have been nice."

"Nice, but not necessarily true." As soon as the words were out of her mouth, Paige regretted them. They were as firm as a dish of chocolate mousse. "Not true at all," she amended.

Adam laid the back of his hand against her cheek. "I suppose we'll see."

She didn't want to move away. But she did. All she had to do was succumb to one more touch, one more caress, one more kiss. Then his prediction would come true. She would know what to do with him, and he with her.

But neither of them would know what to do afterward.

Jeremy came into the room, and instead of leaving as soon as he realized Paige was there, he sidled along the wall, keeping his eyes on her until he came to a chair. Settling himself, he took his wooden top out of his pocket and, pulling the braided cord, began to spin it on the flat chair arm.

Paige moved a little closer to watch, and they stood that way until Mihi called them to eat.

They had almost finished their meal when a knock on the door brought Adam to his feet. Pat strode in and murmured something in Maori. Adam ran his hand through his hair in frustration as he turned to Paige. "*Kaihana*, can you wait to be driven home? I've an emergency to deal with."

Not for the first time, she wished she spoke Maori. "Of course."

"Thank you." He passed Mihi, giving her a quick kiss on the cheek before he disappeared.

"I hope everything's all right," Paige said.

"One of his ewes is dying. She's part of a special line he's been breeding."

Paige remembered the sheep Adam had brought in from a far pasture. "One of the ones about to give birth?"

"The lamb was born a few minutes before Pat came to get Adam, but the mother isn't going to make it."

"What will happen to the baby?"

Mihi looked sad. "I'm afraid the baby will die, too. I've raised a few by hand, but it's not a job I have the strength for these days. Unless another ewe accepts the lamb, I'm afraid Adam will have to dispose of it."

Paige wondered what made her accept lamb on the dinner table, while the idea of a motherless lamb dying made her shudder. "Surely someone would want it. Maybe Adam could give it to someone else to raise and keep."

"Do you know how many lambs are born each year in New Zealand, dear? I'm afraid it wouldn't be much of a gift."

Paige heard a rustling noise as Jeremy got up from the table. He flashed a grin at her before he left, carrying his own plate into the kitchen. She was startled by more than his burst of spontaneity. Not only had Jeremy smiled at her, the smile had been exactly like one of his father's. And her heart was reacting almost the same way. Lifting her eyes to Mihi's, she wanted to tell her what had happened, but Mihi was already nodding.

"The child is beginning to accept you."

"How did you know?"

Mihi answered with a question. "When did Adam begin to call you '*kaihana*'?"

"He called me cousin the first time we met. *Kaihana* came a little later. Adam says he's related to the Abbott family very distantly."

Mihi laughed again. "*Very* distantly. How do you like being his cousin?"

"He's an infuriating man."

Mihi stood and motioned Paige to follow her into the kitchen. "I'm prejudiced, of course, but I think there are women all over the island who would like to have Adam say '*kaihana*' to them in just the same way."

"You *are* prejudiced."

"You would be a good match for him. Adam is used to getting what he wants. You wouldn't give it to him easily."

Paige could think of one time when Adam hadn't gotten what he had wanted, and the thought sobered her. "He's been hurt, and so have I. That doesn't make us good for each other, it makes us suspicious. Suspicion breeds nothing but more of the same."

"You aren't suspicious of him, nor he of you. You're only suspicious of what you feel, for you haven't felt it since you were children."

"What do you mean?"

Mihi stopped in the kitchen, rolling up the sleeves of her blouse to begin washing the dishes. "Think back to when you were a child, dear. Did you ever have the feeling that someone knew you so well they were a part of you?"

"A best friend? Not really." Paige took the plate Mihi had carefully set in the dish rack and found a dish towel, ignoring Mihi's protests.

Mihi gave up. "You don't remember a best friend?"

"I'm told I was a shy child. I don't really remember anything before I started school. Then I was far from home and lonely. By the time I adjusted, I found that life was easiest if you were friends with everyone, but not a special friend to anyone."

"Your mother shouldn't have sent you away."

Paige wondered how much she could say without giving away her mother's secret. Mihi didn't need the burden. "My mother was ill," she said finally. "She couldn't really take care of me. I was better off in school."

"I know about your mother's illness."

Paige was silent, wondering if Mihi really did.

"Is it something you're ashamed of?" Mihi asked finally.

"No. I just wonder how you know."

"The world is a much smaller place than you think, dear. And once I knew your mother well."

"She's had the best help money can buy. Sometimes she's well, sometimes she only lives for the next drink."

"And that baffles you."

As always, Paige marveled at how much Mihi understood although her sight was gone. Mihi could hear things in her voice that Paige didn't even realize were there. "I suppose it used to baffle me," she admitted. "I think I began to understand it when my own life seemed to be going nowhere except wrong. Then I could understand the support Mother found in a bottle."

"You drank too much?"

"No, but I might have, if I hadn't had my mother's example to warn me." Paige dried another dish, surprised she had shared something so personal. Even in her most intimate relationships she never spoke about her mother's problem or her realizations about herself.

"That's one of the most important things about family," Mihi said. "They teach us what we can be, and they teach us what we shouldn't be, and they teach us all the in-betweens. When we cut ourselves off, we lose that."

"You're in no danger there. From what I can tell, you and Adam are related to almost everyone in New Zealand."

Mihi cackled good-naturedly. "And you find that strange?"

"Strangely different."

"We Maoris call our interest in family *whanaungatanga* and yes, I suppose it seems peculiar to someone who wasn't raised among us. We aren't related to more people. It's only that we know the people we're related to and treat them so." She paused. "Would it scare you to have so many people close to you?"

"I think it might. Does it scare Jeremy?"

"It does. That's one of the reasons he's warming up to you. You keep your distance and let him make the advances. You understand children."

Paige laughed. "Jeremy scares me to death! If I keep my distance, it's because I have no idea what to do or say."

"You know more than you think. You're just what he needs."

Paige reached for the last of the dishes. "I'll be gone before long. Does he need another woman who'll leave him?"

"Perhaps you won't go. I think you like Waimauri more than you know."

Paige couldn't imagine staying in the tiny town. Sometimes even New Orleans seemed too small, too parochial, for her.

"I'm afraid I'm someone who's always off to the next adventure." The next party, the next exciting "in" spot, the next place where she could temporarily lose herself. Even the vice presidency of Duvall Development was a figurehead position, guaranteed to keep her on the move and in the social whirl. And if lately that had seemed more like running than anything else . . .

"The best adventures are right here." Mihi put her fist over her heart.

Paige reached for another dish. "By far the most dangerous, too."

"Nothing worth having comes without risk. Jeremy is finding that out now. That's why, even though he's scared to death, he's reaching out to you."

"How could his mother have treated him that way?" Paige asked with a sudden burst of anger. "I can't understand someone lucky enough to have that beautiful child treating him so badly. If he'd been mine—" She stopped, confused at what she'd been about to say.

"If he'd been yours, you would have given him all the love you've always wanted to give somebody. I know, dear. But it's not too late to begin what his own mother couldn't."

"I'm not equipped—"

"And Jeremy's father needs you just as much. Perhaps even more. You have to forget the person you've worked so hard to become all these years and be the person you really are."

Paige was stunned into silence. She wanted to tell Mihi that her advice was an old woman's fantasy, and yet she had nothing except profound respect for this particular old woman. Rarely in Paige's twenty-nine years had anyone thought enough of her to give her advice.

"Don't be angry at me, dear," Mihi went on at last. "At my age, there just isn't time to beat around the bush."

The kitchen door opened, and Adam entered, a bedraggled clump of white wool in his arms. He muttered something in Maori as he slammed the door behind him.

Mihi answered, inclining her head toward Paige. In English she said, "I told her where you'd gone."

Adam nodded to Paige. "The ewe was dead by the time I got there. I brought the lamb back, just on the chance Hira might want to raise it for me. Pat's ringing her now."

Paige dried her hands and walked to the center of the room, peering at the lamb from a safe distance. "It's so small."

"Not small enough. The mother just couldn't birth it. If I have any more defeats like this one, I won't do any more breeding. The lambs may just be too big for their mothers."

The lamb gave a pitiful baa, as if it wanted to disagree.

"You've hurt her feelings." Paige moved closer. "Do you think Hira will take her for you?"

"She might, if she's going to be home. But Pat thinks her troupe is going on tour in a few days."

"Shouldn't you feed her now or something? She looks hungry."

Adam's sigh was audible forbearance. "She is not a she. She is a he, and frankly, *kaihana*, hunger is the last thing he has to worry about right now."

Paige winced, well aware what he meant. "Maybe Hira—"

Pat sauntered into the room, kissing Mihi's cheek before he turned. "Hira's leaving tomorrow."

Paige watched sadness flicker across Adam's face. "Well, we tried. You want him, Pat?"

Pat laughed. "I hate sheep."

"I've noticed." Adam turned toward the door.

Paige swallowed. "Adam?"

She heard his next sigh even though his back was turned. "What is it?"

"Umm . . . What are you going to do with him?"

"Do you really want me to tell you, *kaihana*?"

"Suppose somebody raised him for you? Would he just end up on the table as Easter dinner?"

"He'd probably end up in a pen with all the little girl sheep his heart desired," Adam said sarcastically. "But discussing his future is nonsense." He opened the door and started outside.

Paige watched him go, his shoulders hunched as if, even now, he was still protecting the lamb from the cool wind. "Adam!" She started after him. "Adam, how much work is it to raise a lamb?"

Adam headed toward the barn. "Hardly any, if you're a sheep." He stopped. "Go on back to the house, please, and let me get this over with."

"What if you're not a sheep? What if you're a city girl who never even had a kitten?"

"About as much work as a baby. In other words, more than you'd want to do." He started toward the barn.

Paige watched him go. Adam was right; she had no desire to miss sleep. She had no desire to subject herself to messy feedings, messy cleanups, messy anything. She didn't like animals.

She didn't understand animals, just as she didn't understand children. She wanted no part of this.

Adam disappeared into the barn.

For a moment she stood perfectly still. Then she began to run. "Adam! Wait!"

There was no response. She pulled the big door toward her, struggling with its weight. Inside, the barn was dark and smelled of fresh straw and manure. Her eyes adjusted too slowly. "Adam, wait."

She saw him finally. He was sitting on a bale of straw, cuddling the lamb in his arms. She was surprised by the lump in her throat at the sight.

She joined him on the bale, and her arm crept around his shoulders. "Such a tough guy," she murmured, resting her head against his neck.

Adam felt the silky tickle of Paige's hair. The spiciness of the scent she wore struggled with the odors of lamb and straw and won. He turned his face to hers and kissed her. Afterward he wondered if every kiss they shared would feel new.

In his arms, the lamb baaed, then hiccuped. Paige laughed. "Once I was the queen of a Mardi Gras krewe," she said, not knowing if he would understand what that meant. "I've been featured on dozens of society pages, and once I was rumored to be sleeping with the governor of a state larger than this island. Now I'm going to be a lamb's mother."

"Were you sleeping with the governor?"

She pretended affront. "He was a Democrat."

"Do you understand anything about our political parties?"

"I don't think so."

"Good." He kissed her again. In a minute the lamb was a wooly heap on the straw beside them, and Adam had Paige in his arms.

"I thought we'd decided this was a bad idea." Paige pushed Adam away when her breath was coming in huge gulps.

"I'm developing a new philosophy. Every idea, even a bad one, should be followed up on. Otherwise, how will we know where it might have led?"

"That sounds suspiciously democratic."

From beside them, the lamb baaed again, pausing only for a breath before he repeated his cry.

Adam pulled her against his chest, kissing her hair. "You really don't have to do this, *kaihana*. There's a good chance he won't survive anyhow without his mother's milk."

"I want to try. Really, Adam, didn't you know this would happen when you brought that poor pitiful little baby into the kitchen?"

"No. You continually surprise me."

"You're not the only one I surprise."

He hugged her hard, and both of them knew the hug was three-quarters frustration. "If you can get him through the first days, then perhaps Hira will take him when she gets back."

Paige let herself be lulled by his warmth and strength. When he finally dropped his arms and bent to pick up the lamb, she felt the loss. "Will you show me what to do?"

Jeremy was outside the barn, waiting in the sunshine when they emerged. His bright-eyed gaze darted back and forth between them, as if he had to satisfy himself that all was well.

"If you're going to be a mama, you have to learn to hold your baby." Unceremoniously, Adam dumped the lamb in Paige's arms.

She clutched it tightly. "What do I do?"

"Just let all those maternal juices flow." Adam stooped to lift Jeremy up to his shoulders.

Paige held the lamb away from her body. "He smells."

"Perhaps you should give him a shampoo tonight."

She knew he was teasing, but she filed the suggestion away as a possibility. Careful not to trip, she followed Adam and Jeremy into the house.

Mihi had already fixed a milk bottle with the largest rubber nipple Paige had ever seen. She explained how to prepare fresh milk so it would be the right formula for the lamb and told her how to warm it up. Paige could see that the old woman was trying hard not to smile.

"Do I rock him and sing him to sleep, too?" Paige asked from her seat on the floor once the lamb was greedily pulling at the nipple beside her.

"I wouldn't risk it until he's housetrained." Adam laughed at her expression.

Paige stuck out her tongue.

He laughed again. "Do you know what that means here? Our warriors stuck out their tongues to properly frighten their opponents." He made a face that made her gasp. "What do you think? If you'd been a warrior, would it have worked?"

For a moment Adam had been a primeval fighting man, an enemy no man who valued his life would want to face. Paige had no doubt what her reaction would have been. "I would have dropped my spear and run the other way."

"And if I had caught you, I would have taken you prisoner." He smiled. "And then I would have killed you and eaten you."

She choked on her next words, coughing until he came over and gave her a friendly pat on the back. "Surely that tradition was no worse than burning helpless women at the stake or nailing carpenters to crosses. History always has these little things we don't want to think about, doesn't it?" He patted her back again. Without turning, he flung his next words over his shoulder. "Jeremy, why don't you come feed the lamb?"

Paige looked around for the little boy, fully expecting him to refuse. She found him standing in the doorway, looking at them with an expression that was entirely too adult. She could almost see him decide to run away, but instead he approached slowly. She watched him coming closer until she could hardly bear to think about the fear behind those short, hesitant steps. Finally he sat beside his father. Adam drew back, and Jeremy and Paige were left alone on the floor.

She had thought caring for the lamb would seem alien. But trying to relate to Jeremy without scaring him was beyond her ken entirely. Because she could think of nothing soothing to say, she just handed him the bottle, careful not to touch him.

The lamb bleated once, obviously angry that his meal had disappeared. Surprisingly, Jeremy giggled. He moved a little closer to Paige and held out the bottle. Paige guided the lamb toward him, hoping the bottle and lamb would collide.

Jeremy giggled again and moved closer to her. Without looking at the little boy, Paige talked to the lamb. "You're a hungry little fellow, aren't you? You've got to eat to grow up and be a big strong..." Her voice trailed off as she racked her brain for the appropriate title.

"Ram," Adam supplied.

"Ram," she repeated.

"Rambo," Jeremy said, as if his word were final.

Paige groaned, resisting the desire to ruffle Jeremy's hair. "Adam, don't tell me this child has seen that movie."

He stood behind her, his knees touching the back of her head. "This is New Zealand, not Mars. He hasn't seen it, but when he plays with his cousins, that's what they play."

Paige looked at Jeremy quickly, focusing on the lamb again as soon as she had seen that he was smiling. "Well, Jeremy, shall we call him Rambo, then?"

There was a long silence, and Paige realized how much she had wanted an answer. She was about to cover the long pause with more chatter when she felt a small hand rest with a butter-fly's delicacy on her arm. She turned and met the little boy's eyes.

"Rambo." Jeremy nodded, then moved closer to the lamb. "C'mere, Rambo." He held out the bottle, and the lamb grabbed it.

Paige blinked to relieve the scratchy feeling in her eyes and wondered if she was allergic to wool.

"The world would be a better place if all those bloody little bastards were eaten at birth!" Leaning on the steering wheel to free his hands, Pat made a gesture as global as his statement.

Paige held a squirming Rambo on her lap, cushioning him against each bounce of Pat's truck. Another of Adam's ewes had gone into labor, and Adam had asked Pat to drive Paige home. She had agreed, extracting a promise from Adam that if this ewe didn't survive, he would never mention the fate of its lamb to her.

The sun was already low in the sky, and the day had been long and exhausting. If Adam's predictions about Rambo came true, the night would be long and exhausting, too. Now, as Paige listened to Pat drone on about the merits of a sheepless world, her eyelids drifted shut.

They flew open again at the sound of grinding gears and squealing brakes. Somewhere she had heard that the Maori language had no profanity. Apparently no one had remembered to tell Pat. She waited until his fluent string of vowel sounds ended. "Let me guess," she said sleepily. "Something's wrong."

He grunted, thrusting open his door as he did. He had pried open the hood and tinkered with engine parts for a few minutes before, Rambo in her arms, she got out to join him. Extracting the essence of his complaints, she learned that the truck was going to take some time to fix and that Pat disliked trucks almost as much as he disliked sheep.

Yawning, Paige looked toward the horizon, shielding her eyes from the glare of the setting sun. "We're not far from my house, are we?"

"We'll get there faster if you walk than if you wait. Throw the lamb in the back and I'll drop him by when I get this fixed."

Paige looked doubtfully from Rambo to Pat and back again. "I think I'll just take him with me, thanks. He's not heavy."

With Rambo in her arms and the sack with his bottle and milk over her shoulder, she started down the road. The sun was a notch lower, her arms were strained and weak from carrying the squirming lamb, and the tender spot on her heel from the long morning hike had become a blister by the time she trudged down her own driveway. She was in no mood for what she saw.

She had company, both animal and human.

Cornwall trotted out of the woods to meet her, his enthusiasm a contrast to her lack of it. Paige suffered his loving licks purely because she had no choice. As she suffered she tried to imagine what the man standing on her porch thought of the tableau. "Down, Cornwall," she scolded under her breath. "Think of your dignity. Think of mine."

Rambo bleated and began to suck greedily on her arm. "Great. A lamb hickey." Paige held her head high and managed the rest of the driveway without limping. She climbed the front steps before she spoke again. "Hello, Hamish. Have you been waiting long?"

His smile was jovial, but his eyes under his designer glasses were less so. "Not long. I thought I'd just take a chance and see if you were at home."

"You've caught me unaware, I'm afraid. Come on in and give me a minute to get this little fellow settled." She opened the door and spoke sternly to the dog, who was still at her heels. "Cornwall, stay."

Instead he stayed at her heels, growling at Hamish as he passed. Finally he made a leap a cat would have envied and settled himself comfortably on the sofa.

"I wonder what would happen if I told him to get down." Paige walked through to the kitchen and looked around for the best place to make a warm nest for Rambo. She chose a spot not too far from the radiators and dragged a well-used blanket out of the hall closet to make a bed. Rambo's response was a pathetic baa. "You don't want to eat again, do you?" Paige straightened and slapped her hands on her hips in exasperation. Pictures of her father's face flashed through her mind. She wondered what Carter Duvall would say if he knew a deal worth a small fortune had to wait while she fed a big-eyed lamb. "Hamish," she called when it was apparent Rambo wasn't going to quiet down. "We'd better have our conversation in here."

Her words were met by a low murmur. It was a moment before she realized Hamish was talking to Cornwall, not her. Cornwall's answer was a sharp, shrill bark. She had warmed the bottle in water in the electric jug before she realized Hamish hadn't yet joined her. "Hamish?" she called. "Are you coming?"

She heard the low murmur and another bark. Abandoning the pathetic scrap of bleating wool, she went to see what was keeping Hamish. She dried the bottle on the hem of her shirt as she walked into the living room. "Why don't you come in the kitchen with me while I feed—" She stopped, startled. Cornwall was standing on all fours on the sofa, his hackles raised a full ninety degrees. Hamish was backing away.

"I don't think your dog likes me," Hamish said coldly, his eyes still on Cornwall.

"He's not mine." Paige walked toward the sofa, and Cornwall began to wag his tail. His hackles descended to eighty-five, then eighty. "What are you doing, you bad dog?" she scolded.

"Apparently he believes he's protecting you."

Cornwall growled as Hamish spoke.

"I'm protecting him. If I wasn't, I'd turn him in." She shook a finger at the dog. "Sit, Cornwall! Don't make me mad. Your friends are limited."

Cornwall wagged his tail, but he didn't sit. Paige reached out and twined her fingers in his collar, fully expecting to get nipped. Instead Cornwall allowed her to pull him off the sofa and drag him to the door. She made sure the latch was secure once he was on the other side.

"I'm so sorry," she apologized. "That's one of Adam Tomoana's sheep dogs, and for some reason I can't fathom, he's taken a liking to me."

"That wouldn't be hard to fathom," Hamish said, brushing the coat of his suit as if his long-distance encounter with the dog had somehow left it covered with fur. "What does Tomoana think about his dog guarding you?"

Paige waved away his question. "At least he's not outside chasing somebody else's sheep. Speaking of which, would you mind having our talk in the kitchen?" Without waiting for an answer, she headed back toward the progressively louder bleats echoing through the house.

Only when Rambo was sucking steadily did she look up to see if Hamish had followed her. He had, and now he lounged in the doorway, watching. "I realize," she said, "that this is not the standard place and way to do business. I apologize."

"Somehow I didn't fancy you as an animal lover."

She grimaced. "You fancied right."

"Is the lamb one of Tomoana's, too?"

"Yes."

"He has a bit of nerve asking you to care for it."

Paige pushed down her irritation. "I offered."

"I understand the Maori chief has made an offer himself."

She wondered just exactly how he knew that his was no longer the only bid for the thermals. Instead of asking, she tackled the more interesting question. "Maori chief?"

He barely lifted his shoulders, as if his words had meant nothing. "I hear Tomoana's part of some sort of aristocracy, grandson of a chief or some such."

"I don't find that difficult to believe."

"Of course, it means nothing now. This is the twentieth century."

"The twentieth century still has its share of royalty," she pointed out as mildly as she could. "Good breeding always shows, don't you think?" She would have liked to say something more pointed, but she reminded herself that even if she was sitting cross-legged on the kitchen floor feeding a baby lamb, she was still conducting a business meeting.

"Good breeding takes a back seat to good business sense in this situation."

She nodded. "I'd agree, although I'm sure you're not saying they're mutually exclusive."

His smile was thin-lipped. "Of course not, but with good breeding and good business sense, I'd like to ask you what you intend to do about the thermals."

She met his gaze, making sure her own concern about the way she was handling this didn't show. "Well, as I told you, I can't do a thing until I've thoroughly explored the land. Additionally, I have received an offer from the Maori community, which complicates matters pleasantly for Duvall Development. With all that in mind, I'm going to have to take some time to gather the information we'll need to make a decision. I expect to be able to present my father with my recommendation in about four weeks."

The same thin-lipped smile distorted his face. "Indeed?"

She lowered her eyes to the lamb, adjusting the bottle. "Indeed."

"And if I withdraw Pacific Outreach's offer?"

"Then I'll have one less offer to consider."

"Four weeks seems a bit excessive."

"Four weeks is what I require." Paige pulled the bottle from Rambo's mouth and held it up to the light. "This is an important decision. I won't be rushed."

"I'd like to know if we're actually in the running, or if you've already decided to sell to the Maoris."

Her eyes turned to his. "I'm a businesswoman, not a philanthropist. And I can assure you that my father is even more hardnosed than I am. He'll make the final decision."

"Have you considered that you might be doing the community a favor if you sold to us?" He went on before she could answer. "Not only would we bring in jobs and bolster the local economy enormously, we'd be doing the people of this area a service by making the thermals a safer place. As they are now..."

"What do you mean?"

"Only that, from what I've been told, people have died in there."

Paige had said the same thing to Adam, and his answer had been reassuring.

"And I've been told that the only people who've died shouldn't have been there in the first place. There are warning signs all along the border," she countered.

"Small comfort if you're injured or dying." Hamish shrugged. "I have to warn you, a longer delay than what you've mentioned will make your father's decision a simple one."

Paige heard the threat and inclined her head to acknowledge it. "I understand. You have deadlines, too."

For the third time he repeated the thin-lipped smile. "With that out of the way, would you like to have dinner with me tonight? I thought we might drive into Rotorua."

Paige was glad to have an excuse to say no. She didn't dislike Hamish, but there was nothing about him that made her want to spend more time with him. "I can't leave the lamb. He has to be fed frequently. I'm sorry."

"Another time, perhaps."

"Will you be staying in New Zealand, then?"

"I'll be traveling back and forth. I'll need to find backup sites."

"Of course." Paige stood. Rambo had settled into a forlorn little ball, and his eyelids had drooped shut. "Thank you for the invitation."

"I'll stay in touch."

She had no doubt of that.

They walked through the house to the front porch, where Cornwall waited, head low on outstretched paws. His eyes followed Hamish as he stepped down to the ground, but the only hostility he showed was a low growl. Paige waited until Hamish's car had pulled away before she stooped to rub the dog's ears. "Really, Cornwall. Did Adam send you here to try and squelch the deal with Hamish? Are you a spy?"

The porch vibrated from the thumps of a wagging tail.

Chapter 10

Sometime not much after dawn Paige covered her head with her pillow and tried to ignore the barks splitting the early morning stillness. Early morning. Stillness. Rambo was asleep. She'd finally been given a chance to sleep, and Cornwall was barking.

Furious, she sprang out of bed, searching sleepily for something to protect her from the morning dew. The night had been endless, plagued not by nightmares but by the pitiful baaing of a newborn lamb who seemed incapable of getting enough to eat. She had slept at most half an hour at a time, and then only lightly, expecting to be awakened any moment. Rambo hadn't once disappointed her.

Then, right before dawn, the lamb had sighed contentedly—she hadn't even known a lamb could sigh—and fallen into a deep sleep. Paige had immediately followed his example. And now Cornwall was barking.

The idiot mutt couldn't be hungry. He had dined the night before on lunch meat and cheese artistically arranged on white pottery just like the white pottery she had eaten the same meat and cheese from. He had been given a bowl of milk before bedtime, although even she knew that was a cat tradition. Apparently he was barking just to hear his own dulcet tones.

Paige muttered words she would never say louder than a mutter and snatched her nuclear-free sheep sweatshirt from the floor beside her bed, stretching it over her head and nightgown as she marched to the door. She had a suspicion that Cornwall—as dense as he was—would understand her state of mind just by looking at her.

"Stupid dogs don't live long," she bellowed, throwing the door open to find the stupid dog in question.

Beside a bristling Cornwall, the familiar figure of a man stood on her front porch. Paige blinked, as startled to find a man as she was to find this particular one. "Granger?"

"In the flesh." Granger Sheridan held out his arms, and she went unhesitatingly into them. Cornwall growled menacingly, then trotted inside when he was ignored.

"What on earth are you doing here?" she asked at last, pulling away.

"What on earth are you still doing in New Zealand?" he asked, stepping back to look at her. "Paige, do you know what you look like?"

She had a sudden vision of darkly circled eyes, hopelessly tangled hair and a dirty sweatshirt with an asinine slogan. "Absolute perfection," she said blithely. "Where's Julianna?"

"She's in the car. She's furious that I would wake you up at this time of the morning."

"A woman I could love. Go get her and bring her in. I'm going to change before she gets here."

"You may even have time for a shower," he said with a grin.

She punched him lightly on the arm before she turned and headed for the bathroom.

One shower later she was back in the living room, and this time her hug was for Julianna. Paige drew back, examining the woman who against all odds had become her friend. "You look wonderful. Granger's treating you well?"

Julianna smiled her answer. "It's you we're worried about."

Paige wondered how many women would worry about someone their husband had once planned to marry. "Why on earth are you worried about me?"

Granger stepped forward. "Carter called me."

Paige took a moment to figure out why her father would have contacted him. "He thinks we're still together?"

Granger nodded gravely. "I had to tell him."

"I wasn't keeping it a secret. I've only spoken to him once, and our phone call wasn't cordial. I just didn't get a chance to let him know what was going on in my personal life."

"He called to berate me for letting you come here."

"Father's greatest talent." Paige motioned them to seats, pushing an unrepentant Cornwall to one side so she could sit on the sofa. "I'm sorry if this was awkward for you, but don't tell me you came all this way to check up on me?"

Julianna's laugh was husky. "We're on our honeymoon."

Paige looked from Julianna to Granger, and any questions she had about how they were getting along were answered. Julianna, a petite brunette with a waist-length braid and huge blue eyes, glowed. Granger, a man whose considerable charisma resided behind a calm smile and attentive gray eyes, radiated contentment.

"Honeymoon?" Paige sat forward on her seat. "In New Zealand?"

"We're on our way to Australia. Julianna has some business to take care of there, so the trip is serving double duty. We're going to visit Dillon while we're at it, and Jody and her mother."

Paige thought of their mutual friends, stranded travelers who, like them, had been caught in the fury of Hurricane Eve. In these few days of enforced companionship they had formed a friendship as strong as any she had known. "Will you give them my love?"

"You know we will."

"And you just happened to be passing through Waimauri?" Paige asked suspiciously.

"Our flight was routed through Auckland, and we rented a car."

"Because my father called."

"Because we wanted to see you," Granger assured her.

Cornwall slunk across the sofa and plopped his head on Paige's lap. She scratched his ears. "Well, I'm thrilled to see you both. Together," she added after a significant pause.

"You got my letter? And the watch?" Julianna asked.

Paige held up her wrist, where the gold band sparkled. "It's beautiful. I wrote you, but I'll bet reading your mail hasn't been a priority."

"I'm glad you like it."

"Do you know what I like best? Happy endings." Paige examined her heart for the slight twinge that should have been there. She found nothing but genuine happiness.

A wavery baa echoed from the kitchen.

Julianna cocked her head and frowned, obviously puzzled. "That sounded like a sheep. Do they graze in your backyard?"

"In my kitchen." Paige pushed Cornwall's head off her lap and stood. "This is New Zealand. They're everywhere."

"Paige, there's a dog on your sofa and a sheep in your kitchen." Granger stood, too. "Do I bring out the straitjacket now, or just before we leave?"

"Oh, let me feed Rambo first, please." She disappeared into the kitchen.

Granger stopped as the door swung shut behind her. "Rambo?"

Julianna laughed. "Maybe her father was right to be worried."

In the kitchen, Paige knelt beside the radiator. "Don't you look pretty," she crooned. Sometime during the night—she had lost track of exactly when—she had taken Adam up on his sarcastic suggestion and bathed the lamb. Now his wool was snow white and fluffy, and a pale blue ribbon adorned his tiny neck. "Are you hungry again?"

Rambo lurched into her lap.

"You think I'm your mama, don't you, baby?" Paige hugged the warm little body, glad for a chance to sort out her feelings away from Julianna and Granger.

If she'd had a chance to anticipate this meeting, she would have built walls around her heart so thick that nothing could have penetrated them. Instead she had been taken by surprise, and the biggest surprise of all was that she felt nothing but pleasure at seeing them. She had meant everything she had said. She was glad Julianna and Granger were together.

She didn't love Granger anymore. She probably never had.

"Paige?" Granger let the door swing shut behind him.

Paige buried her cheek in Rambo's soft wool. "I'm glad you came," she said softly.

She felt him kneel behind her, his hand warm on her shoulder. "I'm glad, too."

"I wondered how I'd feel when I saw you again."

"And?"

They had been too intimate to lie to each other now. "I think I feel relieved."

He laughed softly. "Who's the man, Paige?"

For a moment she didn't know what he meant. "Man?"

"Someone's hit you like a lightning bolt. How long has it been since you thought you loved me? Three weeks? Four?"

Suddenly, Adam was as much a presence in the room as the two of them. "There is no man," she said, knowing it wasn't true.

"You were always so self-contained, so sure of yourself. You're unraveling right before my eyes. You never unraveled for me."

"You see love everywhere, Granger, because you're in love yourself."

"And I want to believe it so I won't feel guilty?"

"You have nothing to feel guilty about."

"Who's the man?"

"There is no man," she repeated.

"Then tell me, am I also imagining the lamb in your lap and the dog on your sofa?"

She laughed, hugging Rambo harder. "Yes. And if you ever tell any of our mutual friends about this, I'll haunt you."

"Is he a Kiwi?"

"The lamb?"

"The man."

"There is no man," they said together.

Paige set Rambo on the floor and stood. "Let me make you breakfast."

"You don't cook, remember? Besides, we wanted to take you out. We saw a tearoom in town as we drove through."

"If you like meat pies and scones, that's your place." Paige looked down at the lamb. "I'm afraid I'll have to decline, though. I don't think Rambo here would be welcome."

The door swung toward them. "May I come in?" Julianna asked. "Is this Rambo?" She stooped to pet him. "He's darling, Paige. But a lamb?"

"When in Rome." Paige rinsed out the jug to heat water for tea. "At least let me give you some tea before you go."

"Are we going?" Julianna asked Granger.

"I'm going into town to pick up food to bring back here. You stay and keep Paige company."

Julianna frowned. "*You* stay. I don't trust you behind the wheel of a car by yourself. He keeps driving on the wrong side of the road," she explained to Paige. "I've had more practice than he has because of the time I've spent in Australia."

Julianna was a successful fashion designer based in Honolulu and specializing in islandwear. Paige had some of Julianna's designs in her own closet, and she knew that Julianna was trying to open markets for her clothing on Australia's eastern coast.

"I'm hungry," Granger warned. "All this fresh air's made me ravenous. Be sure you come back with enough to fill me up."

Paige watched their affectionate byplay with interest. The last time she had seen Julianna and Granger, they had still been in the midst of a struggle to reestablish the relationship that had begun ten years before and died with the premature birth and death of their child. Julianna's letter had told her little more than that they were giving their marriage another try. Now the undercurrents between them told Paige everything the letter hadn't. Against all odds they had worked through the tragedy of their past to come out on the other side, stronger as individuals and as lovers.

Julianna was gone before Paige could make herself speak what she was feeling. "It's working, isn't it?"

Granger nodded. "Beyond my wildest dreams."

Paige felt suddenly lonely for Adam, which was absurd. "You had so much to overcome."

"We've both been terrified. It's made us try harder."

"Julianna seems at peace. She's radiant."

"We're thinking about having a baby."

Paige poured boiling water in the teapot. For perhaps the first time in her life she understood the desire for a child. She played devil's advocate. "So soon? Don't you need time together first?"

"Ellie would be almost ten now if she'd lived."

"And Julianna's ready?"

"She's frightened."

Paige turned. "Don't push her too hard, Granger. She has a right to be frightened."

"She's going to be frightened until she holds a healthy baby in her arms."

Paige saw his struggle, and she wanted to offer comfort. "You'll work it out." She slipped her arms around him for a hug. "I know you will."

They stood together until a noise intruded on the quiet moment. Paige lifted her head to see Adam standing in the doorway. She remembered her surprise at seeing him with Hira in his arms, and more surprise when she'd discovered Hira was his niece. Fleetingly she wondered if he would believe that Granger was her nephew.

Moving away from Granger, she inclined her head toward Adam. "Granger, I'd like you to meet a friend of mine."

Surprised, Granger looked up at Adam.

"Adam Tomoana, Granger Sheridan. 'Gray' to everyone but me," she added.

The two men shook hands, murmuring appropriate greetings.

Paige smiled at Adam, trying to dispel any tension. He was dressed in black, the way she liked him best, and his eyes were inscrutable. She looked from man to man, and she knew that later, inevitably, she would compare them and the way they made her feel. "Granger and his wife are on their way to Australia. They stopped by to be sure I was doing all right."

Adam looked around as if he expected to see another person. "Did I miss someone?" There was just a hint of disbelief in his voice.

"Julianna ran out to get us breakfast," Granger explained.

Paige realized she was enjoying the situation. "Can you stay and eat with us?" she asked Adam. "She should be back in a few minutes, and I've just made tea."

"I just came to look in on Rambo. Jeremy was wondering how he'd done." Adam squatted next to the lamb, fingering the blue satin bow.

"Jeremy?" she chided softly, squatting beside him. "Come on, tell the truth, *kaihana*, you wanted to see if I'd slept through all his pathetic little baas and starved him to death."

"Am I imagining it? Did you really give him a bath—" he leaned down and sniffed "—in expensive shampoo?"

"I dried him with my hair dryer when he came out of the tub. He's just fine."

For a moment Adam's eyes sparkled. "He'll never live it down in the pasture."

"If he lives to make it to the pasture."

"Kept you up all night, did he?"

"All night."

Adam stood and helped her to her feet. "Two of the other ewes have given birth with no difficulty, but they both had twins, so they won't be able to feed Rambo, here. There's only one to go."

"Wonderful!"

"Are you cheering from empathy for the sheep, or because you'll probably only have one lamb to raise?"

She smiled warmly. Forgetting Granger was even there, she reached up and touched Adam's cheek with her fingertips. "You would have asked me to raise another? I thought we'd made a bargain."

"I might even have supplied the shampoo." His gaze trailed down to her lips and stayed there. Then he moved away. "I'm going to search for the *mauri* on Friday. I thought you might like to come, but since you have guests . . .''

Paige had almost forgotten. She glanced at Granger and saw the speculative look in his eyes. "We're only staying for this morning," he explained. "Our plane leaves tonight."

"What will happen to Rambo if I go?" Paige asked.

"Granny and Jeremy will watch him." Adam looked from Paige to Granger. "But don't feel obligated to come along."

"You know I want to."

"Do I?"

She felt a lilting jubilation as old as time. He covered it well, but Adam was unmistakably jealous. She didn't even want to analyze how petty, how stereotypical, her feelings were. She just wanted to glory in them for a moment before she discarded them like a dutiful twentieth-century woman. She allowed herself just a hint of a smile.

"Yes, you do," she said. "You know I want to come, and you know all the reasons why."

"I'm leaving as soon as it's light. If you still want to come, meet me at my house with the lamb." Adam nodded to Granger. "Have a safe trip to Oz."

Adam was gone before Granger spoke. "If I'm not already in Oz," he said, still looking at the doorway, "and I'm not dreaming, then I think I may have just met the man."

"There is no man," Paige said, but when Granger's eyes met hers, she dissolved into laughter.

On Friday, Paige refrained from humming "Mary Had a Little Lamb" under her breath as she walked slowly up the path to Adam's front door. Rambo wobbled on unsteady legs behind her.

She had groomed the lamb almost as carefully as she had dressed herself. His blue bow had been exchanged for red; his wool was as white as the crisp curtains hanging in Adam's living room window. Paige had chosen scarlet corduroy slacks and a silver-gray sweater decorated with scarlet and yellow sunbursts for herself, and despite her best judgment, she wore new leather high-tops in the same color as the slacks. Her feet were going to suffer, but her image wasn't.

She hadn't worried so much about what to wear in years, although intuition told her that Adam never noticed what she had on unless it was made from wool. She was glad Granger wasn't here to comment. He and Julianna had gone after a visit that had been too brief. Paige hadn't realized how much she'd needed to see them; she hadn't realized how much she needed to put her past in full perspective.

She sent a brief, disorganized thank-you to a God who hadn't heard from her in years. As much as she cared for Granger and he for her, their marriage would never have worked. The essential ingredient had been missing. And she, who had ceased to believe love was important or even real, now understood that love was the force that had somehow bound Julianna and Granger to each other for ten years and would keep them together for the rest of their lives. It was as real, as basic, as unquestioned, as that.

And perhaps they didn't have a monopoly on it.

Behind her, Rambo tripped over the root of a birch tree and sprawled head first to the ground. Paige lifted him and snuggled his little warm body in her arms. "When you weigh two hundred pounds and have horns a mile long, remember this," she whispered, resting her cheek against his fuzz-covered ribs.

Adam opened the door and found her that way. It was just possible to resist Paige when she was armored with cynicism and brittle sophistication. It was impossible when the little girl he had once been so drawn to showed through.

"What is it, *kaihana*? Do you miss him already?"

For a moment Paige didn't understand. Then she registered his tone. "Are you talking about Granger?"

"Is there someone else?"

She lifted her head from Rambo's side and stared at him. "You *were* jealous, weren't you?"

"What reason do I have to be jealous?"

"An excellent question. You have no reason whatsoever."

He lifted an eyebrow. "After all, I hardly know you. Isn't that so?"

Paige shook her head in frustration. "You have nothing and no one to be jealous of. I was comforting Granger, just like you comforted your niece that day. You jumped to conclusions."

"It doesn't matter."

"It matters to me."

Adam was surprised that she was still pursuing it. "Hira is my niece. I imagine Granger was your lover. If I were a jealous man with an interest in you, my jealousy might have been fueled by finding you in his arms."

"Whatever Granger was once, now he's nothing more than my friend. His wife is my friend, too." She searched his eyes and saw that he didn't believe her. She felt a flare of anger. "And you are fast losing that designation."

"Have we ever been friends, Paige?" He reached out and took Rambo from her arms. He wanted to hurt her as he had been hurt, and he didn't even question his feelings. "Could a woman of your background ever be friends with a shepherd of Polynesian ancestry whose chief goal in life is to make a home for his bastard son?"

For a moment she couldn't believe she had heard him correctly. Then she was trembling so hard she couldn't control it. She pushed him hard, slapping her hands against his shoulders. "Damn you! How dare you accuse me of that kind of prejudice! Do you think I care about your pedigree or your son's? Or your occupation? Or your ambitions? I care about you! Or I was beginning to." She whirled and started down the path, anywhere to get away from him.

Adam caught up with her easily, gripping her shoulders. Rambo bleated unhappily behind them. "Maybe you don't love Granger anymore, but you love all the things he is." His words didn't begin to tell her of the desolation he'd felt at seeing her in another man's arms. Somehow she had crept into his dreams, and the awakening had been brutal. She could never be his. New Zealand was a diversion, a change of pace. And he was a diversion, too. He knew what it was like to be a woman's diversion, and so did his son.

Paige could see nothing but Adam's anger. "What things do I love about Granger? His honesty? His decency? His warmth? You're absolutely right, shepherd." She twisted the word so it was the cruelest slur.

"You know what I meant."

"Oh? Are you talking about his money? His social position? His American Express card?" She struggled in his arms. "Would you please let go of me?"

"You can make fun of all those things because you take them for granted."

She wrenched free and faced him. "I can make fun of them because they mean nothing!"

"What does mean something to you, then? You've had it all, haven't you? Has anything or anyone ever mattered to you? Or is your life just one casual affair after another?"

She felt as if she had been kicked in the stomach. "You can't see what's right in front of your eyes."

The eyes she challenged burned with emotion, but he said nothing.

"Don't you want to know what I mean?" she taunted.

"No."

"Too bad, because I'm going to tell you anyway. You're right, we aren't friends. Friendship has nothing to do with what's between us. I know something else, too. We're both going to be devastated if we do anything about it, and that doesn't seem to make any difference."

Adam went absolutely rigid.

"And you, Adam. What do you call what's going on between us? Is all that seething anger about our business relationship? About the coincidence that's made us neighbors? You've said we're not friends, so it can't be that."

"That's enough, *kaihana*."

She had never lost control of herself this way, but she didn't care. Twenty-nine years of feelings were pouring out, with or without her consent. "Maybe it's sex," she taunted further. "Maybe that's all that's between us. Shall we find out? It's still early. Nobody else is up. Let's go out to the barn and roll in the hay and see if we can get this out of our systems. After all, that's the only thing I'm after!"

He grabbed her shoulders and shook her. "Stop it right now!"

But she was beyond stopping. She felt the dampness of tears on her cheeks. "Damn you for making me cry! Damn you for making me think you cared! She pulled away and ran down the path. She was in her car and halfway down his driveway before Adam could make himself move.

Behind him Rambo baaed in protest.

Mihi came to stand silently in the doorway until she felt Adam's presence in front of her. *"He nui pohue toro ra raro."*

He grimaced in response. If, as the proverb said, his thoughts were as many and secret as the roots of a tree, he knew they were also gnarled into knots he couldn't untie. "You were listening?"

"I heard only the end." Mihi reached out and, with unerring instinct, touched his arm. "Go to her."

"No."

"Will pride warm your bed and your heart?"

"Both have been cold too long to matter."

"Perhaps you're right. Perhaps there's nothing left of the man you once were. Perhaps you let Sheila change all that." Mihi turned slowly. Then she stooped and felt the floor in front of her until she found Rambo. "Take her the lamb," she commanded. "You've taken everything else from her this morning. I won't have you taking this, too."

Obedience and respect were ingrained in him. He couldn't refuse. Bending, he reached down to lift Rambo from her arms. "Then I'm going to find the *mauri*."

"Would you know it if you saw it?" Mihi scoffed. "Can you recognize a thing of such value? Or will you let that slip through your fingers, too?"

Chapter 11

If nothing else was clear, one thing certainly was. Paige knew she couldn't stay in Waimauri any longer. She could not, would not, face Adam again. She had made fools of both of them. The best solution was to disappear.

The woman who had shouted and sobbed was a woman she didn't know. Paige was still shaken by the emotions that had spewed out of her like whitewater through a shattered dam. Her hands trembled as she folded clothes and placed them in her luggage. They trembled more when she came to the sweater Mihi had given her.

She sat on the bed, holding it to her cheek. It was Rambo-soft, and warm with the love that had gone into each stitch. She had never known anyone else who seemed to have all the secrets of the universe at her fingertips. Paige wondered if Mihi's wisdom had somehow been knitted into the sweater, each knitted stitch a question, each purl an answer. Perhaps now she held a world of knowledge in her hands and didn't even know it.

A sharp bark destroyed the poignancy of the moment. Paige heard the chug-snort of an automobile engine, and she let the sweater drop to her lap. Another bark was followed by the sound of footsteps on her porch. The knock at her door was loud and demanding. She knew who it would be.

Adam stood on the porch, Rambo in his arms.

"May I come in?"

Paige felt the muscles in her neck knot with the strain of holding her head high. "I'm sorry, but I'm busy."

"I brought you the lamb."

"I can see that." She made no move to take him. "I won't be able to take care of him anymore."

"Oh?"

She didn't answer. She didn't move, even though her hands flexed with the urge to snatch Rambo from his grasp.

"Then I'll tell Granny."

"Please tell her I'll be in touch."

"That has a final ring to it."

"Someone will be here at our deadline to hear your offer."

He set the struggling lamb on the porch. "Someone, but not you."

"That's right."

"You don't have to run away."

"I prefer to think I'm going back where I belong."

Her hair swung forward as she stepped back to close the door. Adam watched the glossy mass settle at one high cheekbone as he slid his foot against the doorframe. "Would an apology stop you?"

"It would embarrass me."

"Will you help me look for the *mauri*?"

"I don't believe there is a *mauri*."

"Or that I would recognize it if there were?" he asked, echoing Mihi's words.

She was still too hurt to let the warmth in his eyes sway her. "I don't know what you mean."

"Come with me." He shifted his weight forward until they were almost touching.

She shook her head slowly. "You must be kidding."

"I *was* jealous." Hesitantly he lifted his hand, and then, at the faintest glimmer of emotion in her eyes, he touched her hair. "I don't want to be jealous. I don't want to fall in love. I don't want to feel what I feel." He paused, and then told the whole truth. "I don't want to be hurt again."

She refused to let her melting heart alter her words. "Oh, surely a shepherd of mixed ancestry has no feelings."

"Shall we find out?" He smiled a little as her expression softened more. He could see her battle not to give in. He knew she was going to lose, and, strangely, it humbled him.

"I think not." Paige tipped her head to avoid Adam's pursuit, but instead the movement brought her mouth directly in line with his. At the first touch of his lips, she stiffened.

Adam felt her resistance. "Forgive me," he whispered, his lips feather-light against hers. He drew his head gently back and forth, moistening her lips with his tongue. "I don't know how to be jealous. I've never been jealous before."

"Perhaps you should be taught, then."

"I think not." He kissed her until her lips were as soft as the expression in her eyes. Then he pulled her into his arms, no longer gentle but hungry and aching, and terribly afraid. His hands slid under her sweater and up the silken skin of her back, making short work of her bra clasp. Everything his hands touched, his body ached for. Everything his body ached for, his heart embraced.

They parted at last, each breathing hard, each totally vulnerable. "I don't care how many men there have been in your life," Adam said, drawing a line from her forehead to her chin. "But when you're mine, you'll stay mine and no one else's."

She knew she was already his, but she wasn't quite ready to forgive him, or tell him so. "Perhaps that day won't come."

"Perhaps." His finger touched her lips, caressing them lightly. "Or perhaps it will come very soon."

In the end it was Cornwall who lamb-sat. Adam assured Paige that Rambo wouldn't starve if they were gone several hours. He waited patiently while she fussed over him, feeding him until he was a wooly sphere with drowsy eyes and a limp, red bow. Then he said a few choice words as Cornwall trotted merrily into the kitchen through the open door and plopped down beside the lamb for a nap.

"He *is* a sheepdog," Paige said, trying not to smile.

And Rambo, whose world was made of larger, stranger creatures than the dog, contentedly settled next to Cornwall, baaed and fell asleep.

Once out of the rolling green hills surrounding Paige's house, they hiked along a different route to the thermals. The path was shorter and steeper, leaving Paige gasping for breath by the time they paused beside a steaming stream that meandered over jagged rocks covered with mineral deposits and rainbow-hued algae.

"We're about halfway." Adam removed the backpack he carried, and stretched. Paige watched the fabric of his shirt strain against his chest. They had hardly spoken as they'd walked, and Adam had made no move to touch her. He'd acted as if nothing had ever happened between them.

She perched on the edge of a boulder near the stream, trying to figure out which Paige she was supposed to be now. The practical businesswoman Paige, who treated Adam as her tour guide? The aloof Paige, who kept her distance from everyone? Or the real Paige, who was much too vulnerable to a certain Maori man? She juggled sulphur-encrusted pebbles from hand to hand. "You've never told me how you know where to look. Are you searching systematically, or do you have clues?"

Adam settled beside her, draping his long, lean frame against another rock. "Only a description in the legend."

"Will you tell me?"

"Exactly?" He didn't wait for her answer; instead he began a fluid recitation in Maori.

"And now, the translation, please," she asked patiently when he'd finished. "I didn't quite catch it all."

He laughed, his eyes lazy and heavy-lidded. He had told her everything he felt for her and exactly what he wanted to do about it. If she did speak Maori, her cheeks would be the color of her shoes.

"The legend says that Hori-i-rangi resides where Te Po, night, and Te Rangi, day, meet. It's a place of opposites, earth and sky, fire and water, *tapu* and *noa*."

"*Tapu* and *noa*?"

"Loosely defined, *tapu* means sacred, or under religious restriction. *Noa* means free from that restriction, or ordinary. Things, places, people, actions that are *tapu* must be avoided or handled carefully according to rules. If the rules aren't obeyed, sickness or even death can occur."

"Taboo's a common enough word in English," she said, tossing a pebble to him. "The two words must come from the same source. Is there more description, or is that the end?"

"Hori-i-rangi rules over the place where Aotearoa's water has its source. As it issues from the earth, she, being female, changes it from *tapu* to *noa*, so that it's fit for human use."

"A spring, then? The mouth of a stream?"

"It would seem so." Adam shut his eyes, as if he were gathering his strength for the next part of the hike. "Once, when I was a boy, I counted the springs that I knew, everything from the spongy dampness of low-lying ground to the source of the geyser I tried to show you last time we were here. I counted forty-three possibilities. Forty-three possibilities and I still haven't found the *mauri*."

"Perhaps there are forty-four." Paige swung her legs around so that she could see him better.

"And perhaps the last *tohunga* was a man with a sense of humor. Perhaps there's nothing here except the ghosts of a different time."

She dropped her pebbles and laid her hand on his shoulder in comfort. "Maybe a man and a woman have to find it together. If it's a place of opposites..."

Without opening his eyes, he let his hands creep around her waist. "When I was a boy, I would never have accepted that. Now..."

"Were you such a chauvinist then?"

"I had no use for girls." He opened his eyes, and they crinkled in amusement. "Except for one. A cousin I met only briefly when I was still a young boy."

"And did you call her *kaihana* with that gleam in your eye?"

"I might have, although I was only nine and she was five."

"A real cousin? Not the shirttail variety like me?"

"We're all family."

"Funny, somehow you don't feel like family."

"No?" he asked with a slight smile, drawing her nearer.

"Anything but."

He held her only inches from him, his gaze sweeping her face. "She had the darkest eyes. They danced with joy at everything she saw. Her hair was black and straight. She wore it in pigtails, and when she moved, they bounced behind her. She hadn't been to a family gathering before, and she wouldn't talk to anyone but me. She slipped her little hand in mine, and I lost my heart. The other boys teased me, and I didn't even care."

She smiled, seeing the young Adam protecting the little girl. "She must have been so grateful to have you there to help her. Is she still your friend?"

"Sometimes I think so. Sometimes I don't."

Paige was disappointed. "I would have thought that kind of bond would last forever."

"Who knows? The world has a way of interfering, doesn't it?" He reached up and slipped his hands into her hair, pulling her mouth to his.

She sighed softly, giving herself up to his touch and his kiss. Both of them knew where these kisses would lead. It was a matter of time, of letting the sweetness between them grow until it was as strong as the passion they had both felt right from the beginning. Like the others they had shared, this kiss wasn't a preliminary; it was an anticipation. A promise. And when it had ended, she knew which Paige she had to be with him.

The one he could hurt.

She wondered if Adam saw any of the parallels between their own story and Hinemoa and Tutanekai's. They, too, were separated by the circumstances of their births, with continents and life-styles between them instead of *tapu* and a mile of icy lake water. She wondered whether, if she found the strength to come to Adam across those barriers, he would find the strength to accept her.

Adam saw the questions in her eyes. "What are you thinking?"

"Of Hinemoa and Tutanekai."

The day he had told her the story, he had seen the similarities. In her own way Paige was of royal birth, set aside by her father to marry well and help build the Duvall empire. The question now was whether, after one failed marriage, she would see that she, too, must follow her heart. And the question for him was whether he could accept her and trust her if she did.

"Have you noticed that nothing is ever simple between us?" Paige stroked Adam's cheek with the backs of her fingers. "You tell me a story, and I wish I could be as courageous as Hinemoa. You wonder whether, if I were, you would reach out, cover me with your feathered cloak and take me to your bed to become your wife."

He moved his cheek against her touch until her fingers rested on his lips. "Nothing is simple, because we aren't simple people," he murmured against them. "The days when things could have been simple were stolen away."

"What do you mean?"

Adam felt a familiar sting of frustration. The limitations of what he could say weighed heavily on him. "If we had come together when we were younger," he said finally, "when neither of us had been hurt, perhaps things would have been different."

She tried to imagine such a thing. "Like your cousin, perhaps," she said. "We would have met as children, climbed trees together, chased sheep."

"Gone to family gatherings."

"I would have liked that."

"Perhaps we should make up for what you missed then."

"I've grown beyond the tree-climbing stage."

"I was talking about the pleasure of belonging."

Her fingers stilled, and she searched his eyes. "I have no family here. I can't belong to something I don't have."

"Our *hapu* is having a *hui*, a family gathering to celebrate Hira's twenty-first birthday. It begins on Friday. Will you come with me?"

"But Hira hasn't invited me."

"A *hui* is open to everyone. This will be rather small, probably. Perhaps as small as three hundred people."

"My debut was smaller than that."

"Then you'll come?" Adam didn't let his concern show. There was always the possibility that someone attending might blurt out the truth to Paige. But the *hui* was part of her heritage, part of the life she had been kept from. Granny insisted it was Paige's right to be there. Adam only hoped that if the *hui* triggered memories she had buried deep inside her in the form of a nightmare, she wouldn't be alienated forever.

Paige wondered how it would be to accompany Adam to a gathering of his family. In every way she would be a stranger. "I won't know what to do," she warned him. "And I won't understand a word of it if it's in Maori."

"I'll translate when it's necessary. Will you come?"

Paige didn't know what she was agreeing to exactly, but somehow she knew Adam was inviting her to share a part of his life that had been kept from her so far. She stretched up to kiss him, lingering for a long, sweet moment. "I'll be there."

The rest of the hike wasn't as difficult as the beginning. Adam helped Paige over the hardest parts, then seemed to forget to drop her hand when they were once more on a grassy plain. The morning sun plated the landscape with twenty-four carats, and they slowed their pace, the day too special to rush through.

As they walked, they talked. Adam told Paige about his childhood, and she was surprised to learn that in Pakeha terms, Mihi wasn't his grandmother at all, but a great-aunt who had no children of her own and had taken him to live with her as her grandson when his parents had moved to a sheep station in the high country of the South Island. He had brothers and sisters scattered around the Rotorua area and some who lived near his parents. Although the family lived in different places, they were never far apart.

"Then you had two sets of parents," Paige said, trying to understand.

"Granny and her husband were my *matua whangai*. They chose me to be their grandchild, and as I grew up, I owed them my first allegiance, although I could be with my parents whenever I chose. It's not uncommon among us. Maoris take *whangai* for many reasons. In my case I was chosen because my uncle wanted to instruct me. He believed I had the *ngakau Maori*, the Maori heart, and he wanted me to learn the traditional knowledge and skills. He's the one who taught me to carve, and he's the one who passed down the story of the *mauri*. At home I was one of many children, but with Granny and Uncle, I was alone. And now Four Hill Farm is mine because of that relationship.''

He told her other things, stories of childhood escapades, loving descriptions of family members, vignettes about Jeremy's first days with him. He told her about his program for developing a new breed of sheep and what he hoped to accomplish. By the time they reached a cliff running beside the same steaming stream where they had rested before, Paige was beginning to form a clearer picture of the complex man who was Adam Tomoana.

He was a man of such fierce loyalties that to be loved by him was to know he would always be there. He was a man who would toil unceasingly, asking little in return, and what he received would invariably surprise him. His farm was one of the most successful in the Waimauri area, but he took no time for pride, although he was the proudest man she had ever known.

He was a man who would tolerate much from the people he loved, as long as he received the same loyalty he gave. And any woman who let him love her would need to understand that.

When they finally reached their destination, Paige was almost sorry.

"This is the area where I've been concentrating my search." Adam gestured in a wide arc.

She tried to remember the legend. "Day and night, earth and sky, fire and water, *tapu* and *noa*."

"You listened well."

Paige was turning in a slow circle. "The cliff shades the stream, and from the algae growing on the surface of the rocks there, I would bet that it never sees the sun. Perpetual night, even during the day."

Adam watched her, surprised that she had become involved so quickly. "Earth and sky?"

Paige frowned. "The cliff seems to reach to the sky, connecting it with the earth. Do you suppose that's what he meant?"

He shrugged. "If we find the *mauri* we'll know."

"Fire and water. The steaming spring? Seems logical."

"*Tapu* and *noa*," he finished for her.

"I don't understand the concepts well enough to guess. What do you think?"

"I don't understand how they apply here. Unless the legend is referring to Horo-i-rangi's influence on the water."

Paige walked beside the stream. "Do you know where this begins?"

"You won't like the answer."

He was right, and she liked even less what it compelled her to do. "Not straight up the cliff," she protested after Adam had explained that the stream began as a boiling spring gushing from a mysterious hole in a cave off a wide ledge hidden from their sight. "There has to be another way."

"Believe me, there's not."

"There's no path to the top?"

"There is." He teased a piece of her hair that had escaped the neat confines of an onyx comb. "We go back the way we came, cross the stream on stepping stones, then swing on a rope over a smoking chasm and pick our way carefully over the slippery terrace that culminates at the bottom of this cliff about five hundred meters that way." He pointed. "And finally we pull ourselves up hand over hand, using roots and crevices in the rocks, until we get to the path." He paused. "A path that crumbles under your feet as you walk on it," he added, as if he'd just remembered that detail. "That would take us to the top of the cliff, but then we'd have to find a way down to the ledge anyway."

"Suddenly this looks easy."

"You don't have to climb it, *kaihana*. You can wait here."

"You've been up before?"

He settled his arm along her shoulders. "Dozens of times. It's perfectly safe."

"And you've never found anything?"

"Nothing. But there is a labyrinth of boulders in the cave. Two of us could keep track of our path better than one."

"Tell me more about this cave."

She listened as he described it. The cave was wide and deep, extending back from the cliff face farther than Adam had ever attempted to go. It was hidden from view, its mouth obscured by a wind-tortured tree that leaned out over the ledge like a man perpetually contemplating suicide.

"I haven't explored it thoroughly enough," Adam finished. "I've never been convinced that Horo-i-rangi would be hidden so far into the cave. But it's possible I've been wrong."

"Are there bats in the cave?" Paige asked the question as if it didn't matter.

"Did you know bats were the only mammals in New Zealand when the Maoris came to settle the islands?"

"I don't find that encouraging."

"Neither did my Maori ancestors. They imported dogs and rats and learned to go without pork and chicken."

"If you're trying to make me forget that I'm about to climb a sheer rock face for the pleasure of having bats roost in my hair, it's not going to work."

"Then you're coming?"

She turned toward him, and his arm tightened around her. "Do you think I'd let you go alone?"

"I've been going alone for years."

"Not today."

Adam did the gentlemanly thing and let Paige begin the climb first. She told him how much she appreciated it each time she struggled to find a handgrip, each time she fumbled for a foothold. Realistically, however, she was glad to have Adam behind her. The cliff wasn't as sheer nor as high as it had seemed from the ground. The path sloped, so if she leaned into it, she could almost crawl rather than climb. With the adrenaline that pumped through her bloodstream giving her both energy and a healthy sense of caution, she fought her way to the ledge. Adam laughed at her complaints, calling encouragement from right below until she had reached a short shelf of rock obviously created by Mother Nature as a resting spot.

He pulled himself up beside her and wedged his bottom against hers.

"You're not even breathing hard." Paige fanned herself with her hand.

"No cliffs in New Orleans?"

"When I was at school in Geneva, I always managed to be in the infirmary the week they climbed Mont Blanc."

"We don't have much farther to go. Then you can rest in the cave. With the bats."

"I should take one home to round out my menagerie."

Adam pointed out the best path to the ledge, and Paige twisted, clinging to anything she could find until she was standing on the ledge waiting for him. When he was beside her, he took her hand, guiding her carefully, backs to the cliff face, until the ledge widened. "Rest a minute, then follow me," Adam told her. "The ledge widens noticeably on the other side of these rocks." He pointed to a protrusion that hid everything on the other side. "You can't see any of this from where we were on the ground, but the water coming down the cliff from the cave makes an impressive waterfall. Watch the way I maneuver past the rocks, then do the same. I'll be over here to give you a hand."

"If you've been inside the cave as far as the mouth of the spring and haven't seen any evidence of the carving, wouldn't that mean this was the wrong place?"

"It's not unknown for a *mauri* to be placed a distance away from whatever it represented. The Whanganui people placed a stone *mauri* of an eel-weir at a waterfall instead of at the weir itself to frustrate magic spells meant to deprive the *mauri* of its power. The spells couldn't be heard above the rushing water."

Anthropology lessons in midair. Paige tried not to look down, waving Adam on. "A practical people."

He seemed in no hurry. He was perfectly at home on the ledge, his balance as superior as a cat's. "So the *mauri* could be deeper inside the cave," he finished.

She waved him on again. "Adam, don't let me keep you." He laughed; then, as she watched, he leisurely crab-walked along the ledge until he reached the rocks that blocked the sight of the spring. Leaning casually against them to make a point, he smiled at her. "These are solid. Don't worry about any of them coming loose." Then, one hand securely wedged between boulders, Adam slid along the lowest rock until his right foot was in place. His right hand grabbed another rock, and his left foot followed his right. In a second he was out of sight.

"That looks easy enough." Paige took a deep breath to ready herself for the same climb. Before she could move, a deep, terrifying rumble pushed all the air from her lungs in a rush. The ledge shook. "Adam?" she shouted. The rumble was unmistakably from the area just beyond the rocks. She took a cautious step toward them, then another. "Adam!"

The rumbling ceased, and the air was suddenly deathly still. Paige edged along the ledge, her heart pounding frantically. "I'm coming!" she shouted.

"Stay where you are."

The voice was weak, but the words were definitely a command. Paige stopped in her tracks and leaned back against the cliff. "What happened? Are you all right?"

There was no answer, just the whine of something scraping against rock and another low rumble. Paige edged closer to the protruding rocks, afraid to obey Adam, afraid not to. Trembling knees slowed her progress, and she wished that just once she had climbed Mont Blanc and learned how to deal with moments like this.

She had edged close enough to grab a rock when fingertips appeared on the other side. As she watched, her heart in her throat, the fingertips became a hand, the hand an arm. Then she saw Adam's face. She stifled a cry. He was bruised and bleeding.

Before she had thought about it, she had climbed up on the rocks to help him over. On the other side, where the ledge had apparently been, was a gaping hole and nothing else except the smooth, sheer face of a cliff. If there had once been a tree guarding the mouth of a cave, it was there no longer. Her head began to spin.

"You're making this harder." Adam's fingers touched hers as if in salute. Then he pulled himself up on the rocks as she scurried backward to get out of his way. He rested momentarily, then shifted his weight until he was on the ledge beside her, leaning against the cliff. Together they inched along until the ledge widened and they could safely collapse.

Adam leaned back and closed his eyes, and Paige knelt beside him, frantically examining his face. The bruises were worse than the cuts, but one jagged gash zigzagging across his cheekbone looked as if it might be deep enough to need stitches. Now it needed cleaning.

Her mouth felt like cotton, and words were difficult to push through it. "Did you bring any first-aid supplies?"

He leaned forward, eyes still shut, and slid his pack off his shoulders. Paige took it and rummaged through, bypassing the ginger cake he'd brought for morning tea in favor of a plastic bag. Inside she found moistened towelettes, antibiotic ointment and bandages. Her hands shook as she opened the towelettes, unfolding one to begin washing his face. She swallowed hard. "I'll try not to hurt you."

"It'll remind me I'm alive."

"Do you feel well enough to tell me what happened?"

Adam admired Paige's restraint. How many other people would have waited this long before asking? He wished he could tell her more, but he knew little enough himself. One moment his feet had been on the ledge, the next they had been in midair. "The ledge fell away under my feet."

"But you said it was safe!" Paige could have slapped herself. "I'm sorry, I guess you've already thought of that."

"It *was* safe." Adam winced as she passed the towelette over a rapidly swelling lump on his forehead. "I've been over it dozens of times and never so much as a pebble has fallen."

"You told me yourself that things change rapidly here." Gently she soothed the towelette along his hairline, then opened another to begin cleaning the jagged cut. She covered it with antibiotic ointment and a plastic bandage, trying to shut out the picture of Adam falling as she did.

"Things can change rapidly, but only if there's some sort of action to make them change. I put one foot beside the other, and the ledge fell away."

To Paige, that was even worse. Danger here was invisible and ever present. For the first time she questioned the idea that the thermals should remain "wild and free," as Henare Poutapu had demanded. Shouldn't an area with so many risks be constantly monitored? Shouldn't paths be built, the worst dangers cordoned off? As Hamish had said, if Pacific Outreach tamed the thermals, the company might be saving lives.

She tried to calm her growing panic. "At least we're not so high up that you would have died if you had fallen."

Adam's eyes opened, searching her face. She was trying to treat this lightly to quiet her fears, but in her brief seconds on the rocks she hadn't seen what was directly below the waterfall. He dropped his gaze immediately, hoping she would never suspect.

"Adam?" Paige slid her fingers under his chin and lifted it. "You would have been all right, wouldn't you?"

His face hurt too much to smile. He tried to make his voice reassuring. "We didn't have to find out, did we? I grabbed a root and found a toehold until I could swing myself over to the rocks."

"But how did your face get so beaten up?"

"There was a rockslide from above me. When the ledge gave way, it set off vibrations, I suppose."

She imagined the rocks falling toward him as he clung to an exposed root. One root between him and... She clamped her lips shut, afraid she was going to say something she shouldn't.

Adam saw the grim set of her mouth, and suddenly he didn't care about anything except feeling it soften under his. His head was light with more than the aftermath of his accident. He was dizzy with gratitude that he was still alive and that she was here beside him.

Paige was startled when he kissed her; then her arms were around him and she was kissing him, too, with no thoughts of his injuries. "Don't scare me like that again," she pleaded, breaking away to kiss his nose, his uninjured cheek, the lobe of one ear. "Adam, promise me you won't let anything happen to you!"

He laughed, a boyish, uninhibited laugh that echoed against the cliff wall. "How can I make a promise like that?" He kissed her again.

"Promise!"

"I do. And if I break it, I guess I won't be around to listen to your complaints."

She shivered, burying her head against his shoulder. "We need to get you out of here. One of those cuts looks as if it ought to be stitched."

"Granny will treat it."

"How can she? She can't even-see..." Paige thought about her words, then shrugged. "Granny will treat it."

Adam slid up the cliff wall until he was standing. Pleased that he was no longer dizzy, he held out his hand to her. "Let's get out of here."

She couldn't help herself. "Is it safe?"

The same question had crossed his mind. In the seconds when he had hung suspended in the air, rocks jarring his head and shoulders, he had wondered if anything was safe. Until that moment, the ledge that had crumbled under his feet had seemed as secure as any piece of solid ground.

"I'll go first." He took her hand, but Paige didn't allow him to pull her up. She stood without his help, pushing herself against the rock behind her.

"Please be careful," she begged. "I need you."

Somehow everything seemed different. All his feelings seemed to lie along his nerve endings, with nothing to protect them except a thin layer of skin. She needed him, and he was beginning to see just how much he needed her. He needed her as much as he needed air to breathe and food to eat. He needed to be safely on the ground with her in his arms and the sun healing his battered face. "Let's go."

The climb down was uneventful. Once they were safe, Paige clung to Adam, reluctant to let him go. They found a spot in the sunlight, and she sat with her back against a rock and Adam's head in her lap. Since she was too shaken, too vulnerable, to say more about her feelings, she talked about the *mauri*.

"If the *mauri* is there, you'll never find it now, will you?"

"If I organized an expedition and did some fancy rock-climbing, perhaps."

She had been smoothing his hair, but now her hand stilled. "You won't do that, will you? It's too dangerous."

"I would take too much time, and time is something I don't have much more of. There are still other places to look."

She was relieved, but also aware that his time was short because of her own restrictions. It was just one of the things between them. "Will you show me the other possibilities?"

"Are you sure you want to take the chance?"

She was sure, because she knew he would continue exploring whether she was with him or not. Her words were for her own reassurance. "This was just a freak accident. Nothing like this has ever happened to you before." She paused, then spoiled her own display of courage. "Has it?"

"I'll keep you safe, *kaihana*." He turned her palm to his mouth and kissed it.

And she might have believed him if she hadn't asked to see the waterfall and the mouth of the cave from the ground before they went back home. Adam was strangely silent as he guided her along the stream, climbing over rocks and through a small gully that led to the waterfall.

He stood beside her as she gazed at the seething pool at the waterfall's base, its mineral-rich waters muddied with the aftereffects of the avalanche.

Above the pool, the steaming falls poured spurts of boiling water onto the shattered rocks where he had almost fallen.

Chapter 12

During her years at boarding school, Paige had been the house guest of British royalty. Since then her companions had included Wall Street tycoons, Greek shipping magnates and influential politicians. She had learned exactly what speed to travel the fast lane, and when to stand back and view the race from a distance.

But never, in any of her forays into society, had she been this nervous.

Paige smoothed her black skirt with hands that couldn't seem to stop fluttering. A moment before they had been in her hair, a moment before that at the scarf around her neck. Now she forced them to her side, knowing that they would rebel again.

The group of people clustered at the *marae* gate had grown noticeably. When she had arrived, there had only been half a dozen, a nuclear family complete with mama wiping noses, and Papa trying to ignore the squabbling twins who played an aggressive game of tag at his feet. Their games had been interrupted by the arrival of a bus filled to overflowing with people of all ages, shapes and sizes. The bus had disgorged its cargo with the speed of a huge yellow whale ridding itself of not-so-tasty minnows, and three dozen more *hui* invitees had joined Paige and the family at the gate. Five minutes later another bus had arrived.

If protocol had been left up to Paige, she would have strolled leisurely across the vast expanse of flower-bordered lawn to the porch of the meeting house where a row of solemn old people sat. Rather than wait in the deepening shadows of late afternoon, she would have introduced herself, offered her hand, and asked where she could find Mihi and Adam.

Adam had saved her from that disastrous faux pas when he had come to visit her last night. Only an ignorant person, or one of very high standing, entered a *marae* alone during a *hui*. Adam had told her to wait at the gate until she was with a group. They would be welcomed together.

A smile touched her lips as she thought about Adam's visit. Adam had come to explain *hui* protocol, but he had stayed longer than his explanation required. Close to midnight, both he and Paige had found that whatever self-restraint they had been able to impose was fast coming to an end.

Her not-unpleasant thoughts were interrupted by the loud wail of a woman's voice. Paige looked up to see where it was coming from. She knew little about what was supposed to happen except that she was to stay with the group at the gate and do what they did.

No one else seemed surprised. The people she was standing with were paying rapt attention; some nodded in response to the half-song, half-chant of the woman's voice. Paige saw Hira standing on the front porch of the meeting house and realized the song was hers.

As she watched, Hira stopped abruptly. The man who was the leader of the group from the buses stepped forward and approached the gateway. From the side of the meeting house a young man dressed only in shorts and a kilt made of New Zealand flax danced across the *marae* swinging what appeared to be a wooden sword that was almost as large as he was. He executed a complicated drill that left Paige holding her breath until he reached the gateway. Kneeling, the young man took a carved stick from his waistband and placed it crosswise in the gateway at the visitors' feet. A man who had been standing behind Paige walked through the crowd and bent to pick up the stick. Then the young man in the kilt turned, holding his sword high above his head, and started across the *marae*. Paige felt the people around her moving with him, and she followed.

The singsong chant began again, this time from another woman. It was answered by a woman walking beside Paige, and the chants echoed back and forth between visitors and hosts. Paige felt a shiver run the length of her spine. The sound was eerily beautiful, the pageantry impressive. She was surrounded by the tradition of a people she was only coming to know, and she felt the beauty of that tradition flowing inside her.

As she listened and moved slowly across the *marae*, the sound changed to a wail. Surprised, she saw tears streaming down the faces of some of the women on the porch, and she saw that women around her were crying, too. The young woman who walked beside her turned, and seeing Paige's confusion, whispered, "We cry for our dead."

Paige nodded in thanks.

In front of the meeting house, the *hui* hosts were forming ranks, as proud and grave as soldiers. They began to sing songs much like the ones Paige had seen at the *hangi* she had attended with Hamish, but this time the women gracefully waved greenery as they sang. Some of the men stepped forward and shouted challenges, their faces and demeanor fierce and frightening. Paige searched for Adam and saw him near the front. When he participated in one of the shouted chants, she was enthralled. He was an ancient Maori warrior, and she was captivated as surely as if she had faced him in battle.

Finally the singing and chants died away. Paige followed her group to a point halfway across the grounds, stopping when they did to bow her head in silence. Then she sat with the others on a woven reed mat, facing the meeting house. What followed was a fascinating display of Maori oratory, not one word of which she understood. Her new friend explained occasionally in a whisper, and Paige learned enough to know that the speeches made by both hosts and guests were of welcome and acceptance at being welcomed. Each speech began with a warning shout followed by a chanted introduction. The speech itself sought to establish links between the two groups, common ancestors, common interests, and ended with a song-poem.

Just as she was beginning to wonder if this would be the sole activity of the *hui*, everyone stood and moved toward the front of the meeting house, where a reception line of hosts had been formed. Paige passed down the line, shaking hands and pressing noses with people she had never seen. By the time she reached Adam she was dazed. "Almost done," he said, kissing her after their *hongi*. "Are you holding up all right?"

"I'm impressed." She was reluctant to pass on to the next person in line. "What comes next?"

"We'll eat, *kaihana*. You'll sit with Granny and Jeremy and me."

"Adam, will people mind me being here?"

He brushed a strand of hair off her forehead. "A fine time to ask, but no, no one will mind." He couldn't add that there were people here today purely because Paige had come. She had so many people who loved her already, and she didn't even know it.

"Everyone's been lovely so far," she murmured.

He laughed. "Well, we're just a lovely people," he mimicked. "Now go on and finish paying your respects to your hosts. Then come find me."

At the end of the line Paige extracted herself from the arms of an old woman with tears in her eyes. The woman murmured a steady stream of Maori sentences, and Paige nodded uncertainly in response. She felt a hand at the small of her back, and, turning, she saw Mihi. Mihi spoke to the other woman, who smiled, kissed Paige's cheek and wiped her eyes, all at the same time.

"She says she's very happy to see you here," Mihi translated. "This is Materoa Poutapu."

"Henare Poutapu's wife?" Paige asked, wondering how this gushing old woman could be married to the stern Henare.

"Henare's keeper," Mihi joked. "Materoa leads him around by the ear. I should know. Henare is my brother."

Paige tried to imagine anyone telling Henare what to do. "Would you tell her I have great respect for her?"

Mihi laughed, turning back to Materoa, who guffawed in response to Mihi's words. Then Mihi took Paige's hand and led her away. "Come inside. We're just about to serve the feast at the dining hall, and I know Adam wants to show you the inside of the meeting house before we do."

Paige followed Mihi, who unerringly wove her way through the crowd as if her vision were perfect.

"What do you think?" Adam asked, coming up to stand behind Paige when she was gazing with awe at the elaborate room.

In its own way and on a different scale, the lushly ornamented meeting house was as impressive as the architectural jewels of Europe. "It's exquisite," she said, moving up to examine it at closer range.

"We save our best carving for our meeting houses."

"It's all right if I examine it this way? It's not *tapu*?" Paige wandered along one wall, admiring the ornate carvings with paua shell eyes, the intricately woven reed mats that rested between them, the painted spirals of black, red and white that decorated the rafters.

"It depends on what you mean. The whole *marae* is *tapu* in relation to the rest of the world. The meeting house is *tapu* in relation to the dining hall, and within these walls, this side of the meeting house is *tapu*," he pointed to the area behind her, "and the side we're standing on is *noa*. People performing certain tasks here today are either *tapu* or *noa*, depending on who they are and what they're doing. In fact, you are *tapu* because you've never been welcomed here before. The welcoming ceremony modifies that *tapu* so we can be comfortable together."

"So many rules," she said, trailing her fingers along the wall.

"Were you uncomfortable coming here today?" Adam asked, following her as she moved along.

Paige nodded.

"Because you'd be with strangers?"

"Yes."

"And how did you feel after you had been welcomed?"

She hadn't thought about the impact of the ceremony. "Much more certain I should have come," she said at last.

"You see, that's part of the reason for the rules and for the ceremony. As a people, we're very conscious of similarities and differences among us. In the welcoming ceremony we began apart, hosts and guests, then each step of the ceremony linked us together. You'll see the same principle apply over and over today and tomorrow. In order to find common ground, we begin apart, then explore what links us. In the end, we come together."

Paige turned to him and asked the question she had been asking herself for days. "And what if there's not enough to link together, Adam? Is there a ceremony to bind people who have nothing in common?"

Adam knew they were no longer speaking of Maori customs but of the gap that divided them. He told her what he was coming to believe. What he had to believe. "There are always links, *kaihana*. Sometimes it just takes longer to find them."

Paige reached for his hand and realized she was praying that he was right.

"I hear the call to tea," Mihi said from across the room. "Shall we go?"

The dining hall was to the side of the meeting house, a large room filled with tables that sat twenty or more people. Guests walked along the side, while smiling hosts filled their plates with a vast array of foods. Since the kitchen was attached to the hall and only a doorway away, the room was warm from the heat of huge cast-iron stoves and fragrant with the smells of home cooking. Paige watched her own plate being heaped to over-flowing and wondered how she would eat everything.

"Everybody seems to know just what to do," she said, sitting next to Mihi. Jeremy was across the table from her, but he hadn't yet looked her in the eye. Paige was reluctant to make a point of saying hello.

"We do it often enough to know how," Mihi explained. "And everyone contributes, so the burden is shared."

Adam seated himself beside his son. "Everyone contributes what he's able. The mutton on your plate is from Four Hill Farm. The beef we'll cook tomorrow comes from Hira's mother's family, and the eels were brought by truck from the coast, where one of my brothers lives."

Paige swallowed slowly. "You wouldn't mind telling me which of these dishes is eel, would you?"

Adam grinned and pointed his fork at hers, which was halfway to her mouth. "That one."

The room hummed with the cadences of adult voices and children's laughter. There were a few good-natured attempts to quiet a table of chortling adolescents, but no one really seemed to mind the hubbub. Although she couldn't think of a time when she had experienced anything quite like it, the meal, the room, and the warm family feeling seemed familiar to Paige. "Does everyone here get along?" she asked, starting on a bowl of pudding someone had insisted she eat.

"It's too bad you don't understand Maori. You'd only have to listen to our speeches to see how often we disagree," Adam told her. He knew she was examining everything around her as if somehow, by observing his family, she might understand him better. He wanted her to understand, and he wanted more. He wanted her to move past understanding to acceptance, and then to knowledge of who she was. He knew the path to finding common ground was full of twists and turns and seemingly endless. But now, watching the way her hair fell across her cheek as she leaned toward him, watching the way she smiled at the antics of the teenagers at the next table, he wished he knew a shortcut.

After they had finished their meal, Paige stood, admiring the expertly planned hustle and bustle of the cleanup activity. She suspected she wasn't going to feel like she belonged here until she joined it. "I'd like to help."

Mihi nodded, pleased. "Come with me."

"Where will I find you afterward?" Paige asked Adam.

He sensed her insecurity and smiled to reassure her. "I'll find you. I won't leave you alone."

The kitchen was a cheerful madhouse of men and women who seemed to know exactly what they were doing. Mihi guided Paige to a group of women who showed her where tea towels were kept and where to put the dishes she dried. Then, with a squeeze of her hand, Mihi left.

Paige was starting on her second batch of plates when Hira joined her, introducing herself as she reached for a towel to help.

"So you're Uncle Adam's friend," Hira said. She didn't examine Paige overtly, but Paige knew that Hira was taking in every detail of her appearance.

"Your uncle is my friend," Paige agreed. She thought of all the times in the last month when she had stood drying dishes and exchanging confidences. She and Julianna had first gotten to know each other at a kitchen sink in Hawaii as they had waited for Hurricane Eve to make up her mind whether to savage Oahu. And then, more recently, Mihi had shared her thoughts about Adam over wet dishes. Paige was beginning to think a dish towel and a psychiatrist's couch were interchangeable.

"Pat told me about you."

"Is Pat here?"

"Pat doesn't come to *hui* anymore. He doesn't want to be with family."

Paige imagined there was a story there but, not wanting to pry, she changed the subject. "I saw you perform in Rotorua. I was impressed."

Hira looked down at the plate in her hand. "Thank you," she said shyly.

"And Adam said you toured the island recently."

"Just a few places. I'm glad to be home again." Hira reached for another dish. "Do you like Waimauri?"

"I do."

"It must be different from what you're used to."

"Very."

"Did any of it seem famil—" Hira stopped, clamping her lips shut.

"Familiar?" Paige pulled another stack of dishes to the sink's edge. "No, I've never been to New Zealand. Why?" She glanced at Hira and saw the distress in the young woman's eyes. She frowned and wondered if somehow she had said something offensive.

"I . . . I just thought since you travel a lot, maybe you'd seen places like this," Hira stammered.

"Nothing I've ever seen is like this," Paige said, still frowning. "Hira, did I say something wrong? I'm afraid I'm really not sure what to do or say while I'm here."

Hira laughed nervously. "Nothing you could say would be wrong."

"Good," Paige said, still not convinced.

After a few minutes Hira drifted off, to be replaced by another young woman, a school teacher who regaled Paige with stories about her classroom. Someone took her place, and then someone else, until Paige felt as though she had already begun to make friends. By the time Adam sought her out, she was feeling more at home. He dried her hands with the tea towel and left it for someone else to take up, leading her back through the dining hall to the cool evening air. Next to the side of the building, he pulled her to rest against him.

"I wonder how Rambo is," she said, leaning back against his chest and hugging his arms tighter around her waist. Adam had hired a neighbor's teenage daughter to lamb-sit for the weekend, but Paige still wasn't sure that Rambo was going to be all right.

"He's in good hands," Adam assured her. "How are you?"

"Happy, comfortable—" she paused "—proud to have been invited."

He reminded himself again that the path was long and full of twists and turns, but the reminder did nothing to quench the warmth inside him. "Then you like what you see?"

"Why wouldn't I? Did you think I couldn't appreciate it?"

"Have I told you I appreciate *you*?" Adam turned her, wishing for more privacy. "That when I look at you I feel something end and begin at the same moment?" He took her lips with more passion than he had intended. His tongue plunged into her mouth, and his body hardened against her softness.

Paige felt a familiar weakness and something more. She pressed against him, wanting him no matter what the consequences. When he tore his mouth from hers, she clung to him. "Does anything have to matter except what we feel?"

He was aware of the madness of standing in the shadows, Paige in his arms. Any moment they would be discovered, yet he couldn't let her go. Without his permission, his fingers slipped to the soft skin of her back, then between them to her lace-covered breasts. "When we make love, nothing else will matter."

She shuddered against him. This kind of desire was something she had never known. It went far beyond the need for physical release. She needed all of him, and somehow, being here was part of that. "When will we make love? I need to know."

If the shadows had been deeper, the place less sacred... Adam told himself to let her go. No part of him complied. "When it's right," he said through clenched teeth.

"We could hurt each other, and I don't even care anymore." Her head fell back as his hand slid to her buttocks and pressed her against him.

He didn't care, either. He had just enough sense left not to take her here. They would make love; the only choice left was when.

Music floated across the evening air. Guitars and women's voices mixed with the nearby laughter of children. The groan he heard was his. "The rest of the evening and night will be taken up with speechmaking in the meeting house. We'll go find our beds."

The thrill of being part of the *hui* had taken second place. Paige allowed herself a fantasy and a question. "Are you sure we shouldn't just come back in the morning?"

Adam tried not to let temptation overwhelm him. He had experienced second thoughts since inviting Paige to the *hui*. She could be hurt by what she might remember. If he took her home and made love to her, one confrontation would be replaced with another. He imagined the feel of her beneath him, imagined filling her until neither of them could remember when they had been parted.

And if he did, she might never learn who she was.

"We'd miss the best part." He squeezed her wrist, then, lamenting, pushed her away. "You haven't really been to a *hui* until you've spent the night."

"It's that important to you?"

He couldn't look at her. "That important." He took her hand before he could change his mind and pulled her into the light. "Come on."

The meeting house had been arranged for sleeping, with mattresses laid out in rows on the floor at right angles to the side and rear walls. The central aisles had been covered with beautiful flax mats. Each mattress was covered with a snow-white sheet and a pillow with a starched and embroidered pillowcase. Adam led Paige to the host's side and pointed to a mattress beside the one he claimed as his own.

"Beside you?" she asked. For the first time since their mo
ments in the shadows, she met his eyes. "Hinemoa slept besid
Tutanekai and became a married woman."

"Hinemoa and Tutanekai did more than sleep. We all sleep
together here. The speechmaking continues until three or fou
in the morning. The lights stay on all night, and we'll be sur
rounded by the elders. Nothing could happen even if we wanted
it to." Against his better judgment, he touched her cheek and
saw that his hand still shook.

"And, of course, we don't want it to," she said, nodding, "so
that makes it doubly safe." She turned away, pleased at the un
steadiness of his hands. She didn't have to look at him to see his
smile.

The room began to fill with people who settled on their re
spective mattresses to chat, and, later, to listen to the speeches
Jeremy came in and settled on his father's mattress, as if there
was no question in his mind where he should sleep. Mihi joined
them, too, and as the evening progressed, Paige felt sur
rounded by family warmth.

The feeling was a peculiar one, but not completely strange.
There had been little warmth at home, but there had been an
aunt, her father's half-sister, in Mississippi who had tried to
make up for what Paige was missing. And there had been those
rare, wonderful times when her mother had tried to make a fresh
start and give her daughter the semblance of a normal home life.
Still, those times had been very different from this. And yet . .

"You look perplexed." Adam held Jeremy in his lap, rock
ing the little boy back and forth. His eyes hadn't been far from
Paige all evening, assessing her responses. Now there was a
break between speeches, and the huge room was filled with the
low murmur of voices.

"Every once in a while I have this flash of déjà vu," she con
fessed. "I was just trying to figure out why some of this seems
familiar."

Adam stopped rocking. For a moment he wished they were
home, body pressed to body, with no revelations except the
perfection of their lovemaking. "Familiar?"

"You must have had times when you felt you were reliving
something. I've been having that feeling since dinner."

Jeremy threaded his arms around his father's neck and
whimpered sleepily. Adam began to rock again.

Paige watched the man and the little boy. She was always
touched by Adam's devotion to the child in his arms. In no way
did his tenderness diminish his masculinity. One moment he was

the prosperous sheep farmer, the next the Maori warrior, the next the loving father. Not one of the roles was any less a part of him than the others.

"Sometimes we bury memories," Adam said, rocking back and forth. "We can't remember exactly why something seems familiar, but we're actually connecting it to those memories."

"Has that happened to you?"

"Yes." Memories of a dark-haired cousin with dancing eyes merged with the feel, the scent, the sounds of the woman beside him.

Paige shrugged. "Maybe I'll remember what this reminds me of."

"Maybe you will." Adam was glad when a warning shout signaled the next speech. He didn't know how much longer he could continue this charade. In spite of all the reasons not to blurt out the truth to Paige, he was finding it harder and harder to hold his tongue. He had never been certain silence was anything except cruel. Now he wondered if it might be more than cruel. If she discovered what he was keeping from her, would it destroy what they were finding together?

Paige settled in between the sheets to listen to the latest rapid-flow Maori discourse. Adam's words stayed with her, and she thought about his theory. She wondered if it was ancient Maori wisdom or just psychology he had studied when he had attended the university. She had discovered that Adam was not only well-educated in the formal sense, but also well-versed in all the subtle philosophies of his culture. He was both Pakeha and Maori, comfortable with seemingly diverse identities. He embodied the best of New Zealand.

She had changed into a nightgown and new robe, bought just for the occasion, and now she pillowed her head on her hands and listened to the lilting speech of the orator, enjoying it even if she couldn't understand it. She felt at peace, in tune in a way that seemed odd to her, considering that she had never been so completely surrounded by strangers. She let her eyelids drift shut, as others around her were doing, and gradually she fell asleep.

Adam watched peace spread over her features. Jeremy was asleep, too, cuddled tightly against him. He wondered if *he* would ever sleep again.

Paige woke once when the room was silent. She turned and saw Adam gazing at her. Sleepily she reached out and touched his cheek with her fingertips. Then her eyelids drifted shut.

The familiar nightmare began just before dawn. She was in the meeting house, but it wasn't the same. The building was much larger, or perhaps it was just that she was much smaller. Whichever it was, the fierce carvings on the walls seemed to smile at her, their paua shell eyes following each move she made in loving approval. The people surrounding her were much larger than she was, gods and goddesses who smiled and stroked her hair, calling after her in a language she couldn't understand. She felt shy, yet pleased at the attention.

A young boy who looked like an older Jeremy appeared and offered her his hand. She reached for it gratefully, and he pulled her inside, where other children played. She hung back, uncertain. "Come," he insisted. "I'll take care of you." When she still hung back, he gave her a warm hug. "I'll take care of you," he repeated.

She went with him to stand on the sidelines and watched two boys tumble playfully on the grass. When she turned back to her companion, he seemed to have grown. "Are you Jeremy or Adam?" she asked.

"Don't you know?" he answered. "You must know."

"But I don't," she insisted, near tears. "Why am I here?"

"Just watch."

She turned back to the boys, but they had grown into men. Their fight was no longer playful, but vicious, each trying hard to wound the other. As she watched, the man with the lightest skin faced her. It was her father. "Daddy!" she shouted, recoiling at the anger in his eyes. She shrunk back as he came toward her, but a crowd had gathered behind her, and she had nowhere to go.

She began to whimper, and the sound was answered by a woman's cries. Frantically, Paige tried to reach her, because, somehow, she knew without seeing that the woman was her mother. But no matter how hard she tried, she couldn't move. Pleading, she stretched out her hand to her companion. "You said you'd take care of me," she cried. "You promised." But no one was there to take her hand. The man who had been fighting her father began to shrink, slowly, into a boy, and she knew, suddenly, that the boy was Adam and powerless to help her. Someone took her hand, and as she watched in horror the hand began to shrivel, its flesh falling away. She heard screaming....

"It's okay. Wake up."

Paige fought the voice, turning away from it. The voice was a child's and a child couldn't help her. No one could help her.

"Wake up." Tiny fingers gripped her shoulder, shaking her in alarm.

She came awake in an instant, and her eyes focused on rafters painted in ornate spirals. She knew exactly where she was, and she knew something more.

She had been here before.

She sat up, icy cold and numb with shock, to find Jeremy sitting on her mattress, his eyes round and worried. The room was quiet. They were the only ones awake. Adam slept soundly beside her, exhaustion etched across his features.

"Jeremy!" She tried to blink back tears.

Hesitantly he reached up to touch her cheek. When he withdrew his hand, his fingertips were damp. "I have bad dreams, too," he whispered.

She didn't consider the consequences; she just scooped the little boy into her lap and held on to him as if someone was going to take him away. She began to rock. "It was a terrible dream," she whispered, choking on the words. "Thank you for waking me."

Jeremy put his arms around her neck and rested his cheek against her robe. Paige cried silently for all that she had lost and found.

Chapter 13

How could you not have told me?

Adam read the words out loud, then crumpled Paige's note and pitched it across the floor, where it rolled to a stop at the feet of a woman making her bed.

"So now she knows." Mihi stood beside him, straightening her robe. "Just as you wanted her to."

Adam kept his voice low. "We don't know what she knows. A child's memories are hardly fact-filled. But no matter what she remembers, she blames me for not telling her the truth right at the beginning."

"Didn't you know she'd blame you?"

"There was more at stake than my desire for her to know the truth!"

Mihi reached for Adam's hands, aiming through the air for them with uncanny accuracy. She held them firmly. "Don't blame yourself. This was not your decision alone. Now you must tell her why you didn't speak of her past."

"She's gone. And I have responsibilities here."

"Then go to her after the feast tonight."

Jeremy came through the doorway, skipping between rows of mattresses. He wrapped his arms around his father's legs. "Paige went home," he said, squeezing hard.

Adam was silent, wondering what he was supposed to say.

"I watched her go through the gate." Jeremy released his father. "She has bad dreams, too."

Adam squatted in front of his son. "How do you know?"

"I woke her up." He looked down at his feet as if he were embarrassed.

"That was the right thing to do," Adam said, tipping Jeremy's head so they were eye to eye again.

Jeremy still looked embarrassed. "She's soft, and she smells good. I sat on her lap, and she cried in my hair."

Adam wished that he could cry, too.

The oversized phone booth held no charms today as Paige waited for the overseas operator to process her call. As she waited, she tried to calculate what time it would be in New Orleans. Not that she cared if it was blackest night. Her questions couldn't wait.

"I'm sorry, there's no answer at that number."

Paige held the receiver away from her ear and stared at it. She could hear the operator repeating the message, and she slowly put it back to her ear, speaking in a dull voice. "Thank you, I'll try again later."

Only she wouldn't. Because by then the images racing disjointedly through her brain would settle to form a cohesive picture of the past. By then she would already know everything her parents had neglected to tell her.

Neglected? That was a joke. No one had neglected anything. Her heritage, her extended family, both had purposely been kept from her like the most hideous of secrets.

And Adam and Mihi and all the rest had somehow been in on it.

Paige paced the length of the booth until she realized what she was doing and how crazy it looked. She threw open the doors and stalked back to her car, turning the key with an angry twist. She was out on the road and driving before she had even made a decision where to go.

There was one place she certainly wasn't going. She wasn't going back to the *hui*. That was something she couldn't face. How many of the people there were related to her? How many of them knew it? How many of them thought she was a shallow rich girl with values as ephemeral as the smoke that hung like a haze over the Waimauri thermals?

And wasn't she?

The sight of emerald hills blurred in front of her eyes as she blinked back tears. She drove for hours, stopping once for fuel and once to pick up food to eat under the shade of a tree at the edge of someone's pasture. As she drove, images from her dream began to flow together with pictures of a childhood she had forgotten, until she understood only too well why she had forgotten it. When she finally drove up to her house, exhausted and emotionally drained, she was left with only one important question.

How could Adam not have told her?

Stripped down to a wool shearer's singlet and denim jeans, Adam helped four other men tend the *hangi*. The sun just bordered the ridge of trees beyond the green grass of the *marae*, and when it sank a little lower it would be time for the feast that was the culmination of the *hui*. Inside the *hangi* were beef, pork, mutton and chicken, along with *kumara*, a sweet potato brought to New Zealand with the first Maori settlers, potatoes and squash. When the food cooked in the *hangi* was brought inside to be set out with numerous other native and imported foods and a rich display of desserts, Henare Poutapu would call the guests to the dining hall and the hosts would serve them. The hosts themselves would not eat until the last of the guests had finished.

Adam listened to the joking of the other men, but his mind was on Paige. He had thought of nothing else since she had left, and he was no closer to a decision on what to do about her than he had been that morning.

"Adam?"

He turned at the sound of a woman's voice and managed a smile for Hira. "Has it been a good day for you?"

She ignored his question. "Pat's here."

Hira should have been thrilled that Pat had come. The fact that she wasn't was Adam's signal. "Has he been drinking?"

She nodded, and Adam could see that she was struggling to keep her lip from quivering.

"Is he causing trouble?"

She nodded again.

"Why do you put up with him?" Adam asked, more harshly than he had intended. He sighed, running his hand through his hair. "Why do *I* put up with him? Why do any of us? Come on, *e tamahine*, I'll send him home."

"If his father had lived—"

"If his father had lived, *he* would be sending him home."

Hira followed Adam around the side of the dining hall. "He's over near the gate."

Adam saw Pat immediately. He also saw a sight he hadn't expected to see again. Paige was walking through the gateway, her head held high. She wore a printed dress with all the shades of the sea and sky swirled in abstract patterns, and a white jacket that brushed the curve of her hips as she moved. As if she knew he was looking at her, her head turned in his direction. Her eyes looked straight through him.

Adam started toward her, but Pat reached her first.

"So, you've come to see how this half of you lives." Pat began to laugh, as if he had said something uproariously funny. He put his hand on her arm, staggering a little as he did.

Paige realized immediately that Pat was drunk. She tried to free her arm, but his fingers tightened around it hard enough to cut off circulation. "If you want to talk to me, I'll stay here," she said quietly, "but please let go of me. You're hurting my arm."

Pat staggered backward, holding up his hands in mock apology. "My, my. We can't have that, can we? Can't touch the princess. Not the princess."

Adam reached them, clapping his hand on Pat's shoulder. "You're plonked. Let's get you out of here."

Pat shook himself loose. "Just talking to the princess, boss. Aren't we commoners allowed to talk to the princess? The princess and the boss. The princess and the boss," he chanted.

Hira reached them, her face was wet with tears. "I'm so sorry," she apologized to Paige. "He didn't want to come today, and I begged him to. It's my fault."

"It's not," Adam said. "For once, let him take responsibility for what he's doing." His arm shot out, and he grabbed Pat by the shoulder, locking his fingers in place. "Say good-night, Pat," he ordered.

"But I haven't bowed to the princess." He bent his head and almost lost his balance. "A Maori-American princess. First of her kind. Long live Princess Paige, and long live her consort, Prince Adam. As for me, I don't care if I live at all. Not if I have to live here. Hira, come with me. Let's get out of here, Hira." He sniffed as if he were going to cry.

Half-dragging, half-propelling Pat, Adam started toward the gate. "Hira!" Pat called. "Come with me, Hira!"

Paige stood in shock and watched the weeping woman at her side. Finally, with no other remedy in sight, she put her arms around Hira and hugged her as she wept.

"He's not usually this bad," Hira insisted through her tears.

Paige looked up and saw that they were beginning to draw a crowd. "Adam will take care of him," Paige whispered, smoothing Hira's hair. "It's going to be all right."

"He hates Waimauri. He wants to live in the city. He wants to be somebody."

"He just has to grow up," Paige reassured her. "He doesn't know how important his family is. He doesn't see what he has here."

Hira sniffed. "He didn't know what he was saying to you."

"I think he did."

Hira pulled away to stare at Paige, but before she could say anything, a plump woman broke through the cluster of people moving toward them and came to Hira's side. "Did that boy hurt you again?" she demanded.

Hira sniffed, her lower lip trembling with her effort to stop crying. "I'm fine, Mama."

Hira's mother reached out for her, but Hira backed against Paige. "Mama, I'm fine," she repeated. "I really am."

Hira's mother shook her head, as if this was an old scene, re-played too many times. "Thank you for helping her," she told Paige. She extended her hand. "We haven't met yet. I'm Iris Tomoana."

Paige took the woman's hand, admiring the strength of her handshake. "Perhaps we met before," she said carefully. "When I was a child."

Iris held her hand seconds longer than was necessary, then, reluctantly, dropped it. "Perhaps," she murmured, as if she were afraid to say more.

Henare Poutapu stepped forward and said something to Iris in Maori. Iris stepped back as Paige turned to face him. Henare waited, expressionless, for her to speak.

"And perhaps," she said carefully, "I met you as a child, too. Perhaps you are part of my family?"

There was a silence, and Paige knew she would always remember that moment when the New Zealand sun sank over the horizon and the *marae* was bathed in twilight—caught exactly between day and night.

Then the stern patriarch smiled and opened his arms. "I am your family," he said clearly in English. "And you are mine. Welcome. You have come home."

* * *

Through it all, Adam hadn't spoken to Paige, nor she to him. Through the tears, the hugs, the introductions of people who one day before had been strangers and were now family, Adam hadn't once approached her. She, as family and host, had helped serve the *hui* guests, and when they had finished their feast, she had sat at Henare's table, trying hard to follow his explanation of just how she was related to everyone there.

There was so much she still didn't understand. She knew now that her grandmother had been a full-blooded Maori, a Poutapu, Henare Poutapu's first cousin. She had married George Abbott, a well-to-do merchant in Waimauri, and they had lived a long and prosperous life. Paige's mother Ann had been born long after the Abbotts had given up hope of having a child, and although no one was disloyal enough to say so, Paige surmised from veiled comments that Ann had been badly spoiled.

The conversation had centered on Paige's relationship to the Maori families left in the community. Her grandparents and great-grandparents had long since died. Henare and Mihi were her closest kin, third cousins. After that the relationships got even more tenuous. The Tomoanas were related by Mihi's marriage to Adam's great-uncle. When her *whakapapa*, or genealogy, had been proudly recited to her, Paige had understood two important things. One was that, in American terms, she had no close relatives in New Zealand, just as she had been told. The second was that, in Maori terms, that made no difference. She had Maori blood; she was a Poutapu, descended from chiefs and *tohungas*. If she wanted to be Maori, she was. If she wanted to be family, she was.

On her long soul-searching drive, she had discovered that she wanted to be both. Through tear-filled eyes she had driven through the country of her mother's birth and felt a connection flow from the earth itself. Her blood, like Adam's, combined two ancient and honorable cultures. Her bloodlines were no different today than they had been yesterday, but, knowing her heritage, her ties, her roots, *she* was different.

She was different. She was not the person who had come to New Zealand seeking peace of mind. She was not a visitor or a tourist, and New Zealand was no longer a place to escape to. It was part of her.

At last, exhausted, she had driven home to the cottage near the thermals that had once belonged to Jane Abbott. She had climbed the highest hill on the Abbott land and looked out over the countryside. The wind had ruffled her hair, and nearby a bellbird had chimed its sweet welcome. In the distance she had seen the smoke from the thermals and, beyond, the beginning of Adam's pasture land.

Until that moment she hadn't been sure what to do. But as she had walked back to the cottage, she had known. She was not going to run; she was not going to ignore what she had found. She was going to go back to the *hui* and claim what was hers. And in the claiming, perhaps she could discover why her ancestry had been hidden from her.

Now the *hui* was over, and she was alone, although she knew she would never be alone in quite the same way again. The night air was cool and damp; the night smells were heady. Paige sat on her front porch with all the lights off to discourage the large moths that fluttered through the darkness. Cornwall lay at her feet, and Rambo snuggled beside him, disturbing the night symphony of insects with an occasional baa. Wrung out from a day of revelations, she let the dark, cool mists slide over her skin as she tried to solve her one unanswered question.

Why hadn't Adam told her who she was? All his veiled comments made sense now, yet his silence made none. He had known from the beginning, but he hadn't wanted her to know. There had been a conspiracy to keep the truth from her. And although Henare had answered every other question she had asked, when she had confronted him with that one, he had only shrugged. Already she knew that Henare's shrugs were unassailable.

Mihi's answer had been little better. "The time wasn't right for you to know," she had said.

And Adam had never gotten close enough for her to ask.

Even now, confused and aching, she was too proud to go to him. She had been a pawn on a chessboard, caught somewhere between her father and her mother's family, with no one willing to tell her the truth. And Adam, who she had begun to love, hadn't loved her enough to be honest with her.

At her feet, Cornwall sat up, cocking his head to one side. Unhappy at the disturbance, Rambo baaed. Cornwall stretched and trotted to the porch steps, looking out into the darkness.

"What do you hear, boy?"

Cornwall wagged his tail in answer, but otherwise he was still.

Paige listened, but heard nothing. She was deep in thought again when Cornwall barked. She stood and went to his side. There were no cars on the road, and she doubted that Cornwall would do anything so out of character as bark at another animal. She was about to give up and go inside when she heard something, too.

The sound was eerie, a high-pitched sob carried on the night wind. Just as she was sure she wasn't imagining it, it stopped. Just as she was sure she *was* imagining it, it began again.

"Well, you heard it first. What is it?" she asked, scratching Cornwall's ears.

The sound ebbed away, renewing itself on the next gust of wind. This time Paige swayed gently to its rhythm. Somewhere at the edge of her consciousness, the sound was familiar. Once before she had stood just so and swayed to it. Only then the sound had been strong and vibrant.

The pitch changed, climbing higher, dropping to a resonant wail, climbing again in a primitive, modal melody. She tensed and stopped swaying. She knew where she had heard the song before. It was Adam's own composition, and the sound was Adam's flute.

Still tense, she waited. But the sound came no closer.

Cornwall whined and jumped down off the porch. He took a few steps, then turned back to Paige and barked.

"I'm not a sheep, and I won't be led."

Cornwall cocked his head and waited for her.

"And I'm not Hinemoa." Turning, she scooped up Rambo, debating whether to put him in the makeshift pen Adam had built in her front yard or the kitchen. She carried him into the kitchen, reluctant, as always, to leave him outside at night. In her bedroom, Paige began to undress, trying to ignore the music floating in bursts through her open window.

"And Adam isn't Tutanekai," she said, as if her one-sided conversation had never been interrupted.

She paused when her sweater was half over her head and faced the truth. Adam was playing the music for her. She knew, without questioning how, that the music was a gift, a consolation for what she had suffered today. He had been unable to console her with words. He had no way of being sure she would be awake, but even asleep, perhaps he hoped that the music would weave its primal secrets into the fabric of her dreams and comfort her.

Tears filled her eyes as she made herself face the truth. Whatever Adam's reason for not telling her that she was Maori, one thing was certain. It hadn't been to hurt her. The man who had grown from the little boy in her dreams would never willingly hurt her.

Paige pulled the sweater back on and stepped into her boots. She was going to find Adam and ask him to explain. Not only did she want to know why he hadn't told her the truth, she wanted to know what the truth was. She hadn't been able to talk to Henare about her childhood. She remembered enough to know that she had been to New Zealand, and that she had been to the meeting house. She remembered enough to know that she had been dragged away by her father, and that Adam had tried to stop him. But she wanted the whole story, and she knew that Adam could tell it to her.

Outside, Cornwall lay with his paws under his muzzle, waiting for her. At her appearance he stood and trotted across the yard, stopping to wait until she caught up before repeating his performance. The moon was nearly full, washing the ground at Paige's feet with quicksilver rivers of light. After her eyes adjusted, she snapped off her flashlight and tucked it into her pocket.

As she walked, the music grew steadily louder, although it was still far away. Following Cornwall, she crossed the open pasture behind the house and started into the forest. The path was still clear in the moonlight, and the music grew louder. Paige only hesitated once. When the smell of sulphur intermingled with the sweet fragrances of the night, she stopped. They were very near the thermals, and no matter what her incentive, she knew better than to venture into them in the dark.

Cornwall didn't wait with her. He barked once, then plunged on ahead, turning into a thicket of tree ferns, where he was immediately lost from view. "Cornwall," she called softly, not wanting to interrupt Adam's song. "Come back here." But Cornwall was gone.

Now, with nothing but the music to guide her, Paige walked slowly, using her flashlight to scan the ground carefully for hidden traps. Only the smell of sulphur hinted that the earth at her feet would soon change. The thicket hid all but the next tree from view, and she picked her way through it, ready to turn back at the first sign of danger.

The music stopped, then started again, this time louder and more mournful. As it drew her closer, the sound echoed her mood, rising and falling, weaving past and present together in a melody that transcended time. She forgot her questions, her doubts, her despair. She wanted only to see Adam, to sit at his feet and listen to him play. To touch him.

The thicket ended suddenly, the tree ferns replaced by an expanse of sword ferns and slumbering wildflowers. Her eyes adjusted slowly, and she stood under the last tree, gazing across the lush vegetation to the edge of the hot pool where Adam sat on a rock. Cornwall waited just in front of her.

If Adam knew they were there, he gave no sign. He was naked, and, as if he had just come from the water, his body glistened with moisture. As she let her gaze roam over him, he finished one melody and began another, turning so that he was facing her.

His beauty took her breath away. The moonlight touched his body with platinum, and each fluid line of his torso and limbs was a study in symmetry. He moved as he played, bending and swaying with the music, a perfect marble statue come to life.

When the song ended, Paige stepped from the shelter of the tree into the moonlight.

Adam put his flute on the rock beside him and folded his hands around one knee. "You shouldn't have come."

"Then you shouldn't have enticed me."

"You could have been hurt."

"I doubt I would have felt it."

He nodded gravely, but didn't speak. Paige knew he was waiting.

"Why didn't you tell me?" she asked, knowing she didn't need to explain her question.

"Do you really want to hear my answers? Or did you come to tell me you're angry?"

"Both."

He smiled a little, as though he thought her answer was fair. "But you aren't as angry as you want to be, are you?"

Paige had felt her anger fade with each step. Now she couldn't renew it. "You hurt me," she said. "You didn't trust me, and now I don't trust you."

"You trust me." Adam stretched, and he was no longer a statue, but a sleek, dark panther about to begin the hunt. Standing, he held out his hand. "Swim with me."

She shook her head. "I came for answers, not for a swim."

"You can have both." Adam saw the path her gaze took and waited until her eyes were focused on his again. "Swim with me, *kaihana.*"

Paige saw the challenge, just as she'd seen the evidence of his desire. She knew that if she went into the water with him, nothing would ever be the same for her again. "You are not my cousin."

"We are Maori cousins. I figured out our exact relationship the day I led you from the thermals. The common blood we share is a microscopic drop five generations removed. But we have been united from the first time we saw each other."

"I only have my dreams to tell me of that meeting."

"Swim with me and I'll tell you."

Behind her, she heard the crash of bushes as Cornwall disappeared back into the forest. She and Adam were truly alone.

"Swim with me," he ordered.

Paige crossed her arms and, with one graceful motion, pulled her sweater over her head. After, kicking off her boots, she unsnapped her pants with one hand, pushing them down over her hips to tangle at her feet. Then she hesitated.

"Let me see you, as you've seen me," he said in the same commanding tone.

Her gaze locked with his, and slowly she reached behind her back to unhook her bra. She slid it over her arms. In the moonlight her breasts were the pure white of a new snowfall. Before she could change her mind, she undressed completely, until she was naked before him.

Adam's expression was veiled. "You're cold."

She was. Terribly, terribly cold. She forced herself not to wrap her arms around her breasts in protection.

He moved forward, offering her his hand again, but she shook her head. Turning, she made her way to the water's edge and began to ease herself in. She knew Adam had followed by the splashing behind her.

When the steaming water was up to her hips, she sank in, flinching as it covered her all the way to her shoulders. Then, her body concealed from his gaze, she turned to observe him. "You knew I'd come."

Adam stood several feet away and made no move to come any closer. He knew what would happen if he did. "The music was a gift, not a summons. I didn't know you'd be courageous enough to follow it here."

"Was it my lack of courage that kept you from telling me the truth about who I am?"

"How could you not have known?"

Paige had asked herself that all through the long day. The truth had been so obvious, and yet her Maori ancestry had never occurred to her. "There was no reason for my parents to have kept such a thing secret," she said slowly, feeling her way. "It's not as if it's something to be ashamed of. America is a melting pot. People are proud to be part this or part that."

"So you weren't looking for the truth?"

"I thought I knew the truth."

He nodded gravely. "And now, how do you feel?"

"Like an explanation is in order."

"I can only tell you what I know. You'll have to ask your parents for the rest of it."

"You can be sure I will."

Adam lowered himself completely into the water, moving closer to her, but not close enough to touch. "Your mother and father met when she was little more than a child. I've been told Ann Abbott was the most beautiful creature anyone in Waimauri had ever seen, and, knowing her daughter, I have no reason to doubt it."

Paige tried not to be affected by his words. "Go on."

"Your father was in the armed forces."

"Navy," Paige affirmed.

"He came to Rotorua on leave and met your mother, who was working as a reception clerk at his hotel. They were married against the wishes of her parents. Your father never forgave the Abbotts for that. He left Ann here, but when his time in the Navy was over, he came back for her. There was quite a fight, and when your father took Ann and left, he vowed he would never let her come back to New Zealand."

"But she did."

"You were five." Adam moved closer. "The most beautiful little girl I had ever seen. I was nine, and enchanted immediately. You had long black pigtails, and even though you were shy, your eyes danced. You held yourself back from everyone else, but you put your hand in mine and let me take you anywhere I wanted to go."

"I was the cousin you were talking about the last time we were here."

"You were." He stretched out his hand and touched her hair. When she didn't move away, he moved closer. "Your mother was a very unhappy woman, and she came here without your father's consent. She clung to her parents, and they clung to her, frightened she would leave them again. Each time I saw her, she was crying, and I remember how her hands shook."

"And then my father came." Paige wanted Adam's support. When he withdrew his hand from her hair, she reached for it without realizing what she was doing. She held it tight. "Please tell me."

"We were at a *hui*, a *tangihanga* for our great-uncle."

Paige knew a *tangihanga* was a Maori funeral wake. "And I was there, too."

"Yes, and your mother. I took you out on the *marae* to see something, I don't remember what it was. I only remember that a man I didn't know came striding toward us, his eyes flashing angrily. You reached out to him, but when he began to drag you away, you started to scream. I ran after you and tried to stop him." He paused, as if trying to decide what to say next. "But I couldn't," he added finally.

Without even realizing what she was doing, she clasped his hand to her cheek. "He pushed you away," she said, tears welling in her eyes. "Oh God, my father knocked you to the ground. I remember now."

Adam put his arms around her, drawing her close. "You don't remember. You were too young."

"But I do!" she cried. "He pushed you to the ground, and when I screamed, he dragged me faster. My mother came running out of the meeting house, and some men, too. One of them grabbed my father..."

Adam left the words she didn't say hanging in the air. Carter Duvall had experienced Maori justice, but it had firmly cemented his hatred of his wife's people and stolen Paige from all of them.

"In the end, your mother chose to go back to America with your father. I don't know why. Perhaps she was afraid he would take you away forever if she didn't. Perhaps she didn't want to give up the things he could give her. Perhaps she even loved him. Whatever the reason, not one of you ever set foot on New Zealand soil again until now."

"And my father hid my ties here so that I wouldn't come."

"Your father was always ashamed of who your mother was."

"Adam, did he hurt you?" She framed his face in her hands as if she were looking for visible signs of that day.

Adam held her tighter. "No. I don't think he meant to push me so hard. And that was twenty-four years ago, Paige." He forced her chin up. "That was then. And this is now."

"I cried for you," she said, stroking his cheeks. "I cried for you for weeks."

"You can't remember that."

"But I do." She traced the faint scar that was all that was left of the accident on the cliff. "I cried for you and for my grandparents, and finally my father sent me to school in Switzerland to forget. Then I had no one at all."

"And you learned not to need anyone."

"I learned to pretend I didn't," she said softly.

"And are you still pretending, *kaihana*?"

Paige looked into Adam's eyes, eyes that were brooding and darkly adult. There was little left of the boy who had tried so hard to protect her. But the man holding her in his arms was someone she knew even better, and someone she loved with more than a child's innocent affection.

"I need you, Adam. And this time there's no one here to drag me away."

Chapter 14

Adam's hands began a slow glide from Paige's shoulders to her hips while his lips moved over hers. "No one can drag you away," he agreed raggedly, after his mouth had reluctantly left hers. "But memory can't bring us together, either."

"What do you mean?"

"Twenty-four years have passed." As if to deny his words, he pulled her closer until not even the steaming water was between them.

His naked body fully against hers was a homecoming. Instinctively she fitted herself against him. "And you're afraid it's memory that makes me want you?"

"Be very sure it isn't. Because I'm not that boy anymore."

"And I'm not that girl, though I'm not who I always thought I was, either."

Adam's hands stilled as he cradled her hips against his. "Are you happy to be who you are?"

"Right now I wouldn't want to be anyone else in the world." Paige felt Adam shudder, and the sensation sent waves of heat through her. He was holding himself in tight control, but that control was shattering. She moved against him, her body as hot and liquid as the water. "Right now I wouldn't want *you* to be anyone else."

"And later?" His question was muffled against her neck.

Her head fell forward, and the answer came easily. "Later will be just the same."

His hands gripped her buttocks, and he dragged her harder against him. There was nothing gentle about his hands; there was nothing ambiguous about his desire. He wanted her, and the only thing that had kept him from taking her was his integrity.

"And later still?"

"I can't make any promises," she whispered, her lips against his shoulder, "except that I'll never stop wanting you, Adam. Never."

He groaned, his control gone. He lifted her, and his kiss was fiercely possessive. His lips demanded a response as they trailed down her neck, stopping at the hollow of her throat, then tracing the delicate line of each collarbone to her shoulders. She draped her arms around his neck, and her knees rested against his hips as she leaned back to give him access to her breasts. There wasn't time, there wasn't patience, for leisurely exploration. He hungered, and she offered herself to him. When he drew one taut peak into his mouth, she arched against him in satisfaction. When his mouth and tongue made a mockery of control, she melted in his arms.

She had known it would be this way, a circle completed, a wish fulfilled. Adam in her arms. Her hair trailed in the water as she arched spasmodically. Her fingernails dug into his shoulder, and she whimpered, a sound of both pain and pleasure.

Adam clutched her tightly against him, and she slid down his length, her body slick and hot against his. "Not in the water," he ground out. Without waiting for an answer, he scooped her up and carried her to the bank. Her body was cushioned by lush greenery, and she smelled the crushed fragrance of herbs as he set her on the ground.

He knelt beside her, his hands everywhere, as if he couldn't find the patience to stop, to gently explore, to give slow pleasure. His fierce need excited her as gentleness never would have. She could feel her body throb with unfocused yearnings, and then his hands began a rhythm as old as time, and her yearnings were no longer unfocused, but clearly centered, like a white-hot flame feeding on resin-rich tinder.

"No more," she said, trying to turn away from him.

"Always more," he insisted. He stretched out beside her and turned her face to his. His lips were a demand, his hands a demand, too. She felt the first flicker of fear that she might not be able to satisfy him, that she might not be able to give him

everything he was insisting she give. Her hands crept to his
shoulders as she tried to hold him back.

Adam gathered her hands and held them, and the kiss went
on. His tongue demanded that she give up all her secrets; his
body demanded the same. Paige felt him move against her, felt
the heat of his desire, and her fear strengthened.

She had never given all that he was asking for to any man. A
small, untouchable part of herself had been kept sacrosanct.
Like the devil she had once imagined him to be, he wanted her
soul. She cried out in protest, pulling her mouth from his.

One hand stroked her body, but not to soothe her fears. "I
want all of you," he said. "All."

She squeezed her eyelids tightly together, afraid of what she
saw on his face. No one had ever asked for so much. No one had
ever known what she held back. "Adam," she said, and the
word was a plea.

"All," he demanded. He turned her so that her body fit perfectly against his. She could feel the heat of his desire, but she
resisted, stiffening. She was caught between wanting him and
holding back. She knew he would only make love to her if the
terms were his. Total surrender.

"All," he said, his mouth bathing each eyelid with kisses.
"Because that's what I'll give you. I couldn't give you less."

She opened her eyes and felt her spirit melting into his,
bleeding its essence drop by drop into the open wound that was
his need for her. Her fear bled away with it. He released her
hands and they floated over his body, anchoring themselves finally against the velvet smoothness of his skin. She explored
each ridge of muscle, each flexing sinew, until her fingertips had
memorized the man he was.

Adam buried his face at her throat and molded her body with
his hands, creating someone new from the person she had been.
When he finally parted her legs, he lay against her, touching but
not touching, demanding but not taking.

"All," he whispered.

"Adam," she begged, the last remnant of fear in her voice.

"You're mine," he told her. "I'm asking for what's mine."

He wooed her with his strength, with the heat of his body,
with his demands for possession. She felt herself slipping toward him, merging somewhere in a place that she hadn't even
known existed. Then she felt herself giving, giving pleasure,
giving love, giving up control. He made their bodies one at the
moment she gave herself completely to him.

And then, together, they gave each other heaven.

* * *

"There are more stars in New Zealand than anywhere else in the world." Paige lay contentedly in Adam's arms, one leg draped lazily over his.

"You've counted them, then?"

"Every one."

"They'll be gone soon."

"Let's stop them." With a graceful sweep of her arm she dragged out her command. "Stay."

"Do you think they heard you?"

Her hand settled back on his chest. "I'm sure of it."

Adam's laughter rumbled through the steamy glen. "Why aren't you sleeping?"

"I'm afraid to. I might wake up and find out this wasn't real."

"It wasn't real."

"You mean I've stayed awake for nothing?"

"It was better than real."

Paige pushed herself to one elbow so that she could see his face. The hand on his chest moved up to stroke his cheek. "It was everything."

He covered her hand and brought it to his mouth. *"Taku aroha ki a koe."*

"What does that mean?"

"Don't you know?"

She felt a thrill of pleasure as he kissed her palm and wondered how, after a night of exquisite lovemaking, she could still want him. "Understanding the language doesn't come with the genes."

"I taught you those words when you were five. I'd forgotten, but Granny reminded me yesterday. Your grandmother cried when you said them to her."

Paige's eyes softened. "Say it again."

"Taku aroha ki a koe."

She repeated. *"Taku aroha ki a koe."*

"Well done."

"I love you," she translated, knowing she was right. "I do."

Adam framed her face in his hands, then brought it to his for a long, passionate kiss. "Come home with me," he said when her cheek was pillowed on his shoulder. "Sleep with me in my bed."

"There's not much time to sleep."

"Come home with me."

Paige knew what Adam was asking. He wanted her in his life, just as Tutanekai had wanted Hinemoa. "If I come," she said regretfully, "it can only be for the rest of tonight."

His hand left her hair, and she could feel his body tense. "Adam," she started.

He didn't let her explain. "Don't bother." He sat up, bringing her with him until she was sitting alone. Then he stood, moving to the water's edge to search for his clothes.

"I'm going to bother." Paige felt the loss of his warmth and knew without a doubt just how much of herself she had given him. She stood, too. "If I move in with you, how will it look to my father?"

He stopped, his body rigid in the moonlight. "Your father?"

She went to him and circled his waist with her arms. "Yes, my father. No, don't pull away." She tightened her grip and rested her cheek against his back. "He controls this land," she said gently. "And until a decision's been made about it, we can't do anything to put it in jeopardy."

"Jeopardy?"

"How will it look to my father if he finds I'm sleeping with you? Will he believe I've been objective, that I've tried to make a careful decision?"

"And you care what your father thinks?"

She pushed him away, angry. "I care about this place. It's my heritage, too."

"From rich Pakeha to loyal Maori in one day. A small miracle."

She turned so he couldn't see how he had hurt her. "Believe what you want."

She was bending over the damp heap of clothing when she felt him behind her. As she straightened, his arms came around her. "One of the reasons we didn't tell you who you were was because of this land. We didn't want you to think we were asking for favors based on our blood ties."

She knew he was asking for forgiveness, but she wasn't quite ready to give it. "You're very quick with your tongue, aren't you?"

"I felt you slipping away."

"I'm not Sheila."

"But you're not mine, either, are you?"

She sighed, and her anger disappeared. "Give me some time to find out who I am."

With his hands on her shoulders, he turned her to face him. "Your father probably won't sell the land to us anyway, *kaihana*. He hates us. Nothing you can do will change that. We're fighting a battle we can't win, and we know it. But you mustn't let it rule your life."

She shook her head slowly. "I know what you think of my father. What else could you think? But there's good in him, too. And despite everything else, he is my father. In his own way, he loves me. He'll listen when I tell him why the land should belong to the Maori people again."

"But not if you're living with me?"

"Could I ever persuade him that I wasn't swayed by personal feelings if he knew that?"

His fingers caressed her neck. "I want you more than I want this land."

"And what would you tell our grandchildren?"

Adam watched Paige draw a quick breath as her own words caught up with her. "I'd like to tell them that their grandmother was worth all of New Zealand to me." His lips curved into a smile. "Perhaps I'll be able to."

She couldn't bear to see the dreams in his eyes. Turning away, she asked, "Do you still want me to stay the night with you?"

"I'll take what I can get."

They skirted the thermals on the way to Adam's house, choosing a longer path that avoided the greater part of the treacherous ground and brought them to the road that bordered his property.

Once they were undressed and snuggled together under a thick wool blanket, Paige sighed with exhaustion. But she wasn't too exhausted to savor Adam's lovemaking. They moved in counterpoint, one to the other, seeking and finding, giving and taking, until pleasure flowed between them and the only Maori words she knew fell from her lips like a benediction.

She wasn't sure if it was the light or the noise that woke her. A door creaked rhythmically, as if it were being swung slowly back and forth, and even with her eyes still closed, she could tell the room was lighter. Adam was gone. Vaguely she remembered a kiss and a laughing rejection of the sleepy offer of her body. He had said something about humble shepherds who had to tend their sheep and beautiful princesses who needed some rest. She remembered that the bed had felt very empty then.

Now her eyelids came apart slowly. She felt like a woman who hadn't slept enough. As she stretched, the pleasant aches in her body reminded her how little she cared. She was a woman who had been loved thoroughly and well. Her head turned toward the door as she extended her arms.

Jeremy stood in the doorway, watching her. Caught in the middle of a stretch and yawn, her jaw clamped shut, unfulfilled, and her arms jerked to her side, pinning the covers above her breasts. "Jeremy," she said, wondering what she was supposed to say next.

"Do you like eggs?" The little boy cocked his head, and the movement reminded Paige so much of his father that, despite her embarrassment, she couldn't help smiling.

"Yes." She inched the blanket higher.

He appeared to be trying to remember his next question. He worried a curly lock of black hair that had settled over his forehead. "Do you like marm'lade?"

"I do."

"Do you like little boys?"

The question was so off-handed that for a moment she thought he was still reciting the breakfast menu. His stance was nonchalant, but his eyes were grave, and so like Adam's that her heart felt as if it were skipping beats. "I like *you*," she said, patting the bed.

He seemed to consider whether to join her; then he walked slowly across the room and crawled on beside her. He sat just out of hugging distance. "Do you read?"

"Quite well," she assured him.

"Do you sing?"

"Well enough to get along." She hummed a few bars of the overture to *The Mikado* to make her point.

"You're pretty."

She decided that must be a point in her favor, because Jeremy was nodding. "I think I'm being interviewed for a job here," she said, reaching out to smooth the errant lock of hair.

"What's a job?"

"Something you get paid to do."

"If I pay you, will you be my mum?"

She felt a wave of sadness wash over her. The question had been so horrifyingly adult. The only thing that was still four years old about Jeremy was his body. "I would be your mommy for free if I could." Her fingers trembled in his hair, and she wanted to cry. "But right now, darling, I think I can just be your friend."

He seemed to be considering her answer. "Can you still read to me?"

"Anything you want."

Nodding, he climbed down off the bed. "I'll go tell Granny about the eggs."

"And the marmalade," she said, trying to swallow her tears.

He paused at the door. "I have a book about trains."

"I like trains."

He turned and flashed her a big smile before he disappeared down the hall.

Suddenly everything was different. She could no longer pretend that she was just a woman falling in love, a woman with only herself and her lover to consider. She looked up, one rebellious tear trailing down her cheek, to find Adam in the doorway. "He wants a mother," she said, choking on the words.

"He wants you."

She shut her eyes, because Adam's expression reminded her so much of his son's. "Adam, I can't be a mother," she protested. "I don't even think I can be a wife. I've never been anything except a spoiled rich girl, and I don't even think I did that very well."

He took her in his arms and rocked her back and forth, soothing her tears. "I'll bet you've cried more in the last two days than you have in your whole life," he murmured.

"I don't even cry very well," she said, sobbing.

"You're wrong about that." He continued to rock her. "You're tired, *kaihana*. Don't think about anything now. Don't make any decisions. Just be with us today. We'll take Jeremy and look for the *mauri*. We'll bring something for morning tea and eat it beside the cliff."

She jerked away. "Not the cliff. I don't want Jeremy anywhere near the cliff!"

Adam grinned. "Spoken like a mother."

She put her head in her hands and hiccuped softly. "You don't know me at all. I don't have any emotions. I'm not maternal. I'm always in control. This isn't me."

"I like you best when you're not in control," he said, turning her face to his. His lips followed the path of her tears. When she hiccuped again, he laughed, and, reluctantly, she did, too.

"I'm going crazy," she apologized when they both had sobered.

"You're like Kaka geyser in the thermals. It builds up pressure underground, where no one can see it, until it finally blows. No one would ever know there was anything there if it didn't."

All her vulnerabilities were right on the surface. "I've never wanted anyone to know there was anything there, Adam. I never knew why, but now I do. I've been afraid to feel, afraid that if I did, someone might see and drag me away from whatever I loved."

"And banish you to someplace cold and strange, where no one was allowed to love you." His voice was deadly, and Paige knew that if her father were there, Adam would have shown him his own brand of Maori justice.

"I was a child, and I learned what a child learns," she said, wiping her eyes. "But now I'm an adult. I have been for years, but I've still been doing what a child does to survive."

"Because you didn't know."

"And now I do. I can't blame anything on my father now. Only on myself."

"Don't be too busy blaming yourself." Her hair felt like living silk twined around his fingers, and her skin felt like part of his own. He pulled her close and wondered if he would ever find the strength to let her go.

"Everything is changing so fast."

He wasn't sure if the words were a lament or a hosanna. He only hoped they were a prophecy.

"When the shepherd's away, do the lambs play?" Paige swung Adam's hand in rhythm to her words as they walked through the thermals. Her other hand was firmly clasped in Jeremy's. She had insisted he hold on to someone, and he had agreed, with great forbearance, beginning with his father and graduating to her after they had walked awhile.

"This shepherd has enough help not to worry. Four Hill Farm's a family endeavor."

"What do you do besides make sure they have enough grass to eat and shear them?"

He looked down his nose at her. "We tail them, drench them, doctor them, breed them, cull them." He paused, looking to see how she would take the next item. "Neuter them."

She appreciated the delicacy of his language. "Remind me to hide Rambo the next time you come around."

"You've done well with him. Orphaned lambs don't always make it."

She bristled. "He's most certainly not an orphan. He's mine."

"He seems to think so, too."

"Stop smirking. Just because he tried to follow us . . ."

Adam laughed, the picture of Paige pleading with the lamb to behave still fresh in his mind. They hadn't been able to leave the house until Adam had promised to fetch Rambo and let Paige feed him before they began their walk. Now the lamb was asleep in Mihi's immaculate kitchen because Paige had refused to leave him in the barn.

"Rambo won't be tailed, culled, drenched or neutered," she said firmly. "But you can buy him a new red bow."

"I'd be laughed off the Wool Board."

"Your ewes might be impressed." She fluttered her eyelashes. "You might get more lambs."

Adam squeezed her hand. She had been irrepressible after the scene in his bedroom. This was a Paige he hadn't seen before, and one he suspected the rest of the world hadn't seen, either. After breakfast he had actually heard her giggling with Jeremy over a picture in his book. Just yesterday he would have sworn there wasn't a giggle anywhere inside her. Now he knew better. There was a lifetime of giggles stored away.

They picked their way carefully through boulders left from an Ice Age landslide. Fumaroles sent their unholy smoke to perfume the air, and Adam carried Jeremy on his back, instructing Paige on where to step as she followed him through the giant prehistoric maze. Just past the boulders, they scaled a small ridge, lifting Jeremy up beside them. Paige watched the two males disappear through a narrow canyon, then followed behind, gasping as she entered the small valley, which was almost completely surrounded by low cliffs.

"Paradise," she murmured, entranced. The cliff face was striped with colors ranging from a purple as deep as the last moments of twilight to a butterscotch gold. The surface was flecked with tiny crystals that sparkled like the New Zealand stars on a clear spring night. The valley had been landscaped by nature with clusters of ferns and a velvety undergrowth of grass. Tall trees swayed in the morning breeze, and birds, absent in the bleaker parts of the thermals, clustered on branches, exchanging morning gossip.

"I thought you might like it." Adam held her back as she started toward a sky-blue lake fed by a small stream trickling down from a gap in the cliff face. "It's deceptive. Lovely as a jewel and as hot as molten lava."

Paige clapped a hand on Jeremy's shoulder, afraid he might start toward the lake.

Adam covered her hand to pry her fingers loose. "Jeremy's been here before. He knows."

"Then you've come here to look for the *mauri* with him?"

"No. The legend wouldn't refer to this. The valley was a gathering place once, as public as any place in the thermals could be. Women would cook in the lake and use the water to set the mud dyes used in their dancing skirts. There was nothing *tapu* here. Jeremy and I come because it's so beautiful." He rested his hands on her shoulders and turned her around. "And because of the man."

At first Paige couldn't see what Adam was referring to. The cliffs he had turned her toward were just like the ones she had been facing. Then, suddenly, she realized that wasn't quite true.

"It *is* a man," she marveled. "A stone man."

The cliffs parted, an almost imperceptible crack where water had worn away the surface as it seeped down the cliffside into the lake. And there, to one side, leaning down to watch the eternal trickle, was the stone profile of a man, with bulging eyes and a stubborn chin, short thick neck, protruding potbelly and surprisingly dainty feet. "He should have a name."

"No one knows it if he does. My uncle called him the *kai-tiaki*, or guardian. He said that in his youth, when the women came here, they would call on the *kai-tiaki* to keep them safe. He was supposed to come alive if an enemy approached and protect them, although I imagine that was only what they told their children."

"*Kai-tiaki*," she murmured.

"Later we'll go up on top of the ridge and look down. It's beautiful," Adam said, taking her arm to lead her to a flat grassy area near the lake where Jeremy was sunning himself.

"Beautiful and deadly."

"I realize the other day upset you." Adam sat in the grass and pulled her down beside him. "But if we respect the thermals, they'll respect us. I've never had an accident like that in all the years I've been coming here. And no one else has, either."

"No one else?" Her suspicions began to grow. "Adam, I thought you were the only person in Waimauri, in the whole world, who knew enough to explore this whole place."

He smiled seductively. "What made you think that?"

"Everything you ever said about it."

"I was very careful not to lie. I just told you I was your only choice. And I was. Everyone else knew I was to be your guide."

"Everyone else?"

"Everyone else who could have guided you." He reeled off a list of names until she held up her hands to stop him.

"Is there anyone in Waimauri who's *not* on that list?"

He promptly began another list.

She stopped him again. "Why did you mislead me?"

"Because I wanted to be your guide. And I'm the best. I knew you'd be safe with me."

"But if the thermals are so safe anyway..."

"Did you think I'd take even the slightest chance with your life, *kaihana*? Even then, I knew you were mine." He lay down and caught her hands between his, tugging her beside him to rest before they continued their search.

Jeremy joined them, and the three of them lay together, contented, holding hands and staring at the *kai-tiaki*.

Chapter 15

There was a top in the pocket of her jacket, a spinning top carved with spirals and respect for old traditions. Paige fingered it thoughtfully, then lifted it out to caress her cheek with its loveworn surface. Jeremy had shown her how to spin the top on a flat rock near the place where Adam had searched for the *mauri*. Adam hadn't found the *mauri*, but she had learned to spin, watching hypnotically as the spirals intertwined one with the other until there was no beginning and no end, but one eternal circle.

They had gone back to Adam's house long after the sun was high in the sky. She knew Adam hadn't intended to stay so long. Despite his disclaimer, he was an overworked farmer with a successful farm to run. But none of them had wanted to leave the thermals. None of them had wanted to be parted.

At Adam's she hadn't been able to face parting, either. Instead she had lingered, helping Mihi and one of Adam's nieces wash windows when Adam went to oversee the transfer of part of his flock. The women had taught her the beginning of a Maori song and praised her for her singing while they cackled at her pronunciation. Later she had leaned out of a second-story window, wiping and watching Adam and his men working the dogs in a far pasture until the glass sparkled like a diamond and the men were out of sight. Before she could shut it, Jeremy had called to her from the yard where he was practicing granny knots by tying the ropes on his swing together. She had waved, then gone down to help him untangle the mess he had made.

Finally, though, she had gone. Without saying goodbye to Adam, she had shrugged on her jacket, promised Jeremy and Mihi that she would see them soon, and started home.

Home to find Jeremy's farewell gift in her pocket and Adam's name on her lips. Home to wonder just what the meaning of the word was.

From the kitchen, Rambo baaed, demanding his fourth meal of the day. Paige knew she should put him in the pen Adam had built for her, and she had tried. But the house had been so quiet that cleaning up after the lamb seemed a small price to pay for company. Even Cornwall's shiny black body draped across her sofa was a welcome sight.

Most of her life, she hadn't minded being alone. Whenever she *had* minded, there had been cruises and casinos and friends who were one hundred percent loyal to the Duvall name and money. Now she knew that even in the midst of all that merry-making, she had still been alone, and lonely.

For the first time in her life she knew what it was like to have all the empty spots inside her filled. And although only hours had passed, already she missed Adam and his family.

Rambo was halfway through his bottle when Cornwall, who had been whimpering in his sleep, began to bark in earnest. Before Paige could respond, she heard boots stomping on her porch and the slam of the front door. She just had time to stand before Adam strode into the kitchen.

"I didn't expect to see you so—" She stopped at the grim set of his mouth. "What is it?"

"I need you to go to my house and stay with Granny and Jeremy. Can you do that?"

"Of course." She went to him, standing just inches away. "What is it?"

"Pat's been hurt. We don't know how badly yet. I'm on my way to the public hospital in Rotorua now. Granny's very upset."

"Was it an accident?" Paige saw the tension on Adam's face as he nodded, and she knew it was more then just concern for Pat. "Where was he hurt?" she asked quietly.

"In the thermals, apparently."

"Adam, no."

He exhaled, as if trying to rid himself of more than just air. "We think he went there during the *hui*. I took him home after he showed up drunk, but it looks as though he went bushwalking immediately after. His mother wasn't worried when he didn't come home again, because he's always going off."

"Who found him?"

"Your friend, Hamish Armstrong."

"Hamish?" Paige reached up to stroke away the deep worry lines in Adam's forehead. "I don't understand."

"Neither do I, but I will before this is over." He stepped back, away from the soothing touch of her fingertips. "I've got to go."

"Of course." She tried not to be hurt by his withdrawal. "I'll stay with Granny while you're gone. Is there anyone I should call?"

"No, I'll ring you from the hospital." He turned and started across the floor, but at the doorway he did an abrupt about-face. "Why did you leave without saying goodbye?"

She understood his withdrawal a little better. "Because I knew I'd never get the words out."

The lines in his face softened then. "It would have been better that way."

"Perhaps." She tried to smile. "But then you might have been stuck with me forever."

"I *am* stuck with you forever," he said in an amazingly good imitation of her accent. "Wherever you are, wherever you go. Don't you know that was what last night was about?"

And because she was beginning to know just that, she went to him and let a kiss say what she couldn't.

Pat was as drained of color as Hira's tears and the life-giving fluid dripping slowly into his veins. Bandages covered both arms and hid the right side of his head.

Hira turned her face into Adam's side. "He hasn't opened his eyes once. When they put the needle in his arm, he didn't even wince."

Adam stroked Hira's hair. "You need to go home. You need to rest."

"Not you, too! Does everyone think I'm a bloody doob? I'll go home when I know Pat's going to make it and not before."

Adam knew he could argue or cajole, but he also knew how useless it would be. Hira wasn't going to budge unless the hospital forcibly evicted her. "What do the doctors say?" He continued to stroke her hair.

"Both arms are broken. He has a concussion and a gash across his scalp that they had to stitch. He was badly dehydrated, and his body temperature was several degrees below normal. They won't be able to tell anything else until he wakes up." She paused. "If he wakes up," she finished in a monotone.

"No internal injuries?" he asked, ignoring the last. He couldn't reassure her when he wasn't reassured himself. Pat looked like a man walking with death.

"He was badly shaken up when he fell. They're monitoring him carefully."

"They could do a better job of it if you weren't sitting right here watching everything they do."

"Go away."

Left with little choice, Adam did just that. In the hallway he murmured his condolences to Pat's immediate family, then confronted Hira's parents. "She's not going to leave his side until he walks out of there with her."

Adam's brother Samuel muttered his answer in Maori, although his English was good enough to have won him a position at the University of Waikato as a lecturer in Shakespearean literature. Iris Tomoana didn't mutter at all. "That boy is no good. It's no surprise he's almost gotten himself killed."

"Now's not the time to debate his virtues," Adam reminded her gently. "Does anyone know what happened exactly? Hira said Pat took a fall."

"We're just guessing. He was found at the bottom of a cliff," Samuel told him. He ran his hand through his hair. Samuel was a smaller, older version of his brother and a man who was most at home in a library. He had never shared Adam's love for farming or the thermals.

Adam could think of any number of places where Pat would never have been found if he had fallen. "Which cliff? Do you know?"

"We don't. The man who found him dragged him out to the road, so it couldn't have been too far in."

"Did anyone talk to the man?"

"The cops, I think. No one in the family."

Adam nodded. "That's about to change." He kissed Iris on the forehead and patted Samuel's shoulder. "I'll be back later."

Rotorua's rush hour was just ending as Adam pulled his car into the trickling stream of traffic in front of the hospital. He was at Hamish's hotel in only minutes. The lobby was almost empty, but he nodded to the woman straightening magazines in the gift shop as he made his way to the front desk.

He asked the pretty young woman there to summon Hamish, then drummed his fingers on the counter as he waited. At her nod, he made his way to a lobby chair and sprawled in exhaustion.

Twenty minutes ticked by before Hamish made his appearance. Adam sensed that he had delayed his entrance to show that he didn't like being disturbed. Adam couldn't have cared less; he waved Hamish to the seat in front of him without getting up.

"I seem to be spending my day helping the Tomoanas." Hamish sat, crossing his ankles and tucking his hands under his arms.

"It would be interesting to hear how you helped my cousin."

"You people have more cousins..."

"We people acknowledge our own."

"I spent my day taking care of one of your own."

Adam waited silently for an explanation.

"How exactly is that boy related to you, anyway?"

Adam observed the tiny beads of moisture on Hamish's brow and wondered why he was stalling. "He's family."

"Fifth cousin? Sixth?"

The beads of moisture were merging into full-fledged drops, although the room was only pleasantly warm. "It seems to matter to you," Adam said. "Why?"

"An interest in sociology."

"Study this, then. One drop of blood makes him family. Pat has at least two, and he shares my name. We're related in several ways, none of which you would understand."

Hamish looked down the length of his perfectly sculptured nose. "I probably saved his life today."

"For that, we're grateful."

"You probably want to know how it happened."

Adam smiled a little, a smile that was more a challenge than an acknowledgment. "I probably do. Shall we start with why you were there?"

"That should be obvious. I was exploring."

"Exploring land you don't yet own?"

Hamish shrugged away Adam's words. "I will own it, or rather, Pacific Outreach will. Duvall Development has a track record for not letting sentiment get in their way."

"We intend to persuade Carter Duvall with cold, hard cash, not sentiment."

Hamish's smile was thin-lipped. "Carter Duvall will be hard to persuade no matter what you use. He doesn't want to sell to Maoris." He shrugged. "Nasty thing, prejudice. But there it is."

Adam made certain his feelings didn't show in his face. "Just how do you know, Armstrong? Psychics? Fortune-tellers?"

"I just flew back from the States yesterday." His smile broadened. "Duvall and I had several interesting chats. He's coming here sometime this week to make final arrangements."

Adam didn't let any emotion show. "And you celebrated your victory with a walk in the thermals."

"There were places I haven't been yet."

Adam raised a brow. "You went in without a guide? A careful man like yourself, Armstrong?"

"I had work to do." Hamish's smile disappeared.

"It must have been important work. Why was it so important?"

"You think you're the only one who has anything invested in buying this land?" Hamish snapped.

"Not at all." Adam smiled another challenge. "As a matter of fact, I happen to know just how much *you* have invested. We haven't gone to the States to do our research, but we have checked out some things in Oz. You've an interesting reputation there, Armstrong."

Hamish drew his arms tighter across his chest until Adam wondered if he would cut off his circulation. "Oh?"

"Oh. Let me see, how was it put? Something about Hamish Armstrong being Pacific Outreach's boy wonder until a certain deal in Fiji almost fell through because of his mishandling. I believe the resort here in Waimauri is known affectionately as Hamish's Last Chance. Does that cover it?"

"Lies!"

"What important work were you doing, Armstrong? Finding ways to persuade Paige that the land shouldn't become ours again?"

"I don't know what you mean."

"Where was my cousin?"

"Not far off the road. There's a cliff there, just past the geyser."

"How did you know about the geyser. Have you seen it play?"

"No. I . . . I've heard stories. That's why I went there today. I was going to watch and see."

"But you went past the geyser," Adam reminded him.

Hamish hesitated. "I heard a moan," he said finally. "I followed the sound, and I found your cousin lying face-down on the ground. There were rocks all around him, chunks of the cliff,

I think. I carried him out. It wasn't easy," he added defensively.

"Did you think that moving him might not be wise?"

"I was afraid to leave him there alone."

"It's interesting," Adam said thoughtfully. "Paige and my son and I weren't far from Kaka geyser today ourselves. In fact, we passed right past the geyser and didn't hear or see a thing."

"Then he was doubly lucky I found him, wasn't he?"

"Under the circumstances, I'd say he was lucky to be alive." Adam stood, holding out a hand to Hamish. Hamish stood, too, and took it for a perfunctory handshake.

"I've won, you know," Hamish said, crossing his arms again. "I shouldn't take it too badly if I were you. Our resorts will bring jobs for your people. We'll need guides, entertainers, domestic help—"

"I don't see the deed in your hands yet, Armstrong." Adam let his gaze flick to Hamish's crossed arms. "In fact, I don't see your hands at all. When we shook, though, I noticed your palm was bandaged. Bringing Pat out must have been quite an ordeal?"

"Quite."

"You'll want to know when he wakes up and tells us what happened. I'll certainly let you know what he says."

"Right-o."

Adam smiled his third challenge and left.

Paige tucked a blanket around Jeremy, then sat on the edge of his bed. Mihi, exhausted from grief and worry, had fallen asleep an hour before. "I'll be sure to tell your father to come in and kiss you when he gets back."

"He always does."

"That doesn't surprise me." She smiled and brushed his hair off his face with the back of her hand.

"My mum didn't."

Paige's hand stilled against his forehead. "You remember?" She knew that Jeremy had been with Adam for a year and a half. He had been barely three when his mother had abandoned him.

He didn't answer the question directly; instead he covered her hand and brought it to his cheek. Then he shut his eyes.

"Would you like me to lie down with you for a few minutes?" Paige asked, pushing the words past the lump in her throat.

He moved over, his eyelids still squeezed tight.

Paige knew what an invitation looked like. Careful not to disturb their clasped hands, she stretched out beside him and closed her eyes, too.

Adam found them that way, the woman who didn't know what to do with children and the little boy who didn't know what to do with women. Both were asleep; both were smiling as if their dreams were good ones. He bent past Paige and kissed his son's cheek; then he shook her gently. When her eyes opened, he touched her nose with a fingertip. "So, you'll sleep with my son tonight, but not with me."

She slipped her hand from Jeremy's and turned over to rest it on Adam's shoulder. "First part of the night was his," she said sleepily. "The rest belongs to you."

"You don't want to go home?"

"Try and make me."

"What about Rambo? Will he need feeding again?"

"I went back and got him. He's down in the kitchen."

Adam tried not to smile. "Granny's kitchen?"

"I promised her I'd clean it in the morning before she gets up."

"What about his pen?"

"I never leave him in his pen after dark. I'm afraid he'll get scared."

"He's a lamb. Lambs live outdoors."

"He's a house lamb."

"And you're a loony."

"Do you make love to loonies?"

His heart sped up noticeably. "Only if their hair is as black as a raven's wing, and their skin as soft." He drew a line to her mouth. "Only if their mouths curve up at the corners exactly parallel to the tilt of their eyes."

"Only if they want you, too?"

He nodded. "Only then."

"I want you."

"Then you'll do nicely, won't you?"

"Much better than nicely." She sat up, careful not to shake the bed.

"I thought you weren't going to stay, *kaihana*."

She stood, smiling seductively. "Isn't there a Maori proverb to cover this?"

"Me te mea ko Kopu ka rere i te pae."

"Don't look a gift horse in the mouth?" she asked, moving to stand right in front of him.

"She is like Venus rising about the horizon," he translated.

"Taku aroha ki a koe." She rose and brushed her mouth along the shadowed line of his jaw. "Shall I translate that?"

"We'll translate it together in my room."

They were halfway down the hall, arms around each other's waists, before she woke up enough to remember where he had been. "I forgot about Pat," she said, remorseful. "Is he all right?"

"No, but I'm hopeful. The physician in charge said that he's beginning to show signs of coming out of the coma. He's cautiously optimistic."

"How about his family? And Hira?"

"They're holding up, and Hira is being as stubborn as Cornwall."

"Maybe stubbornness will help her get through the next few days without breaking down."

"Has anyone told you that you have a great deal of wisdom in that beautiful head?"

"No," she said, ridiculously pleased, "but you may."

"You have a great deal of wisdom." Adam stopped at his door and pulled her into his arms. "Wisdom, sensitivity, tenderness." He bent his head and swept his mouth across hers once, twice, and then again. "Passion."

Her hands met at the top button of his shirt. "Especially that." She slipped the button through the hole and smoothed one hand over his chest, tackling the rest of the buttons singlehanded.

"Come inside." Adam backed slowly into his room, bringing her with him.

Paige's hands lingered at his belt buckle. She caressed his flat stomach with the backs of her fingers as she leisurely slid the tongue of the buckle from its hole and then back in again. "I've never undressed you before," she murmured against his lips.

"If you don't hurry, you won't have this chance, either."

She tilted her head to avoid his kiss. "Are you in a hurry?" She fluttered her eyelashes innocently. "Such an impatient man."

"I'll find enough patience when I need it," he assured her. His smile was seductive. "But your patience might be tested."

She relished the flutters of excitement building steadily deep inside her. Slipping the belt loose, she fingered the fine leather before she let it hang from his belt loops. Then, slowly, she polished the snap of his pants between her thumb and forefinger. "Have you ever considered how many clothes you wear? So many fastenings: buttons, snaps, zippers, laces."

"Are we doing research?"

"We could compare mine to yours."

"Item for item?"

"That would be one way." She waited.

Adam's fingers brushed her breasts as they made a leisurely sweep to her throat. He counted as he coaxed each pearl button from its hole. "One." His hands lingered at her throat, glorying at the rapid pulse against his fingertips. "Two." Her skin was warm satin, rising and falling, accelerating with each breath. His head dove down to taste the spot where the cleft of her breasts began. "Three," he murmured against the soft mound of flesh spilling over the black lace of her bra. "Four." He felt her sigh, felt the way she leaned into him. He smiled, burying his face so she wouldn't know. "Five."

"Was that a five, Adam?" Paige unsnapped his pants and smoothed her hands under his briefs. "We're even now," she said in an unsteady voice.

His hands covered hers. "Not quite, *kaihana*," he admonished. "There's the small matter of your skirt."

She felt his fingers close around her waist. "It has one button. It's going to fall to the floor if you undo it."

Her prediction was correct. "What a pity," he murmured. "But you're wearing more underneath than I am. That will make up for my zipper."

Her coordination had suffered. His zipper took agonizingly long to unfasten, and, once unzipped, his pants still had to be smoothed over his hips. "Are your hands shaking?" he asked, his smile in his voice.

"Are your knees knocking?" she countered. "You're not holding still."

Adam covered her hands to guide them until his pants were at his feet. "My turn." He left her hands on his hips, gasping as they strayed to more sensitive territory. "Two can play that game," he cautioned. Her laughter was liquid silver, but it quickly changed to a moan as he showed her what he had meant.

"No fair," she said when he began to strip off the remaining barriers between them. "Not the slip and pants at the same time."

"We're counting by twos now."

"I've lost count," she admitted.

"No attention span." He made short work of her blouse and bra, removing them together.

She shuddered as his hands smoothed over her skin, stopping to explore each curve, each hollow. In a second his shirt was on the floor, followed by his briefs. They stood together wearing nothing except their shoes. "Do we take off our shoes together," she whispered, "or one at a time."

"I'm wearing socks."

"Darn your socks."

"Granny does that," he said, nipping the tender skin at the nape of her neck. "We'll kick our shoes off together and call this a tie."

"You're not wearing a shirt, you can't have a tie."

"You're going to be wearing me in a minute," he threatened.

She kicked off her shoes in anticipation.

His bed was soft, his body a fire that ignited her own. He knew what pleasured her now, but the finest nuances still waited to be discovered. Each discovery bound her closer and fueled her desire to know him in the same way. And as they learned, they found the depths of the other's need.

In the brief hours that they had been apart, Paige had wondered if she had imagined the perfection of Adam's lovemaking. Now she knew that nothing she could conjure in her mind equaled his exquisite sensitivity or passion. He was the giver and the gift, the seeker and the sought. He touched her, and she melted. She touched him, and he was molten steel flowing under her hands.

With their first fiery passion a well-remembered blaze to light their way, they strained their patience, reaching for new depth, new control, until there was no control, only fire and impatience and one glorious moment of soul slipping into soul.

And afterward, still clinging together, there was sleep.

Chapter 16

Paige sat at the kitchen table and listened to Jeremy and his father chat over the breakfast she had prepared. As promised, she had risen early and cleaned Rambo's makeshift quarters in the kitchen. Since there had been no sounds of anyone else waking, she had found a cookbook with yellowed pages and read the instructions for omelets. When Adam and Jeremy had come down expecting breakfast, it had been waiting for them.

Mihi had arrived, too, filled with apologies for sleeping so late. She looked older, as if Pat's brush with death had reminded her of her own mortality, and she merely picked at her food, although she insisted Paige was a born cook. For the first time Paige noticed concern in Adam's eyes when he gazed at the old woman. Even his assurances that Pat would get better didn't make her smile.

Mihi needed more rest. She needed fewer responsibilities and more time just to enjoy the simple pleasures that meant so much to her: the sunshine warming the front porch and her favorite rocking chair; the feel of Four Hill Farm wool between her nimble fingers; the sound of Jeremy's laughter without the duties of his full care. Paige knew Mihi would only tolerate so much assistance from her family. She would not give up her place as house manager unless Adam married. Then she would gratefully accept a promotion to consultant.

Adam needed a wife, Jeremy needed a mother, and Mihi needed relief.

Paige was the only one at the table who wasn't sure what *she* needed.

"Do you read tea leaves?"

Paige looked up from her empty cup and realized that Adam was watching her. She wondered how long she had been staring at nothing. "I wish I did."

Adam reached across the table and lifted her cup, swirling the dregs of tea. "I see infinite happiness," he pronounced.

She managed a smile, but when his eyes darkened she knew she hadn't fooled him. He set the cup on the table and shoved it to one side. "I'm going into the thermals. Will you stay with Granny and Jeremy?"

Paige was surprised. "You're going to look for the *mauri* today?"

"Yes."

"With Pat in the hospital?"

"That's right."

Paige knew there had to be something more to Adam's plans, but she waited until Jeremy had been excused to go outside and Mihi had accepted her offer to do the dishes before she questioned him further. Slipping her arms around his waist, she tilted her head to examine his face. "Will you tell me what's going on?"

"First, why don't you tell me?"

She knew she couldn't pretend. Adam was the only person who had ever been able to read her emotions. A lifetime of hiding, a lifetime of smoke screens, was over. "All of you need me," she said finally. "And it scares me."

"It scares you because you don't know if you need us."

"I don't know why I'm scared. Everything is different. The ground under my feet doesn't even feel steady."

"I want to be patient."

"You're not a patient man." She hugged him harder, although she felt his resistance. She wished she could reassure him, but right now there was nothing more she could say about their relationship. "Why are you going into the thermals?"

"I told you. To look for the *mauri*."

"Why today?"

Adam put his hands on her shoulders and pushed her away. "Because time is running out."

"If Hori-i-rangi has been there for centuries, she'll still be—"

He cut her off with the unvarnished truth. "Hamish Armstrong has been to see your father. Your father's going to sell the land to Pacific Outreach. He'll be here sometime this week to close the deal."

Paige just stared at him.

"I saw Armstrong yesterday to ask him about Pat." Adam saw the disappointment and hurt on Paige's face. He decided not to add to her distress by telling him his suspicions. They were only that as yet, and still largely unformed. "Armstrong thinks he's won, but if I can find the *mauri*, maybe that will change your father's mind."

Paige shook her head, upset by the news that she had been totally bypassed on the decision. All her negotiations had been for nothing. "That wouldn't sway him."

"Perhaps not by itself, but if we got the right kind of publicity after the find, he might not have any choice."

Silently, Paige considered Adam's plan. If there was proof of the thermals, significance in Maori history and religion, Carter Duvall would find it difficult to rationalize a sale to Pacific Outreach, especially if the Maoris' offer was just as good. He might be prejudiced, but he was too crafty to be public about it.

She tried to put her own loss behind her for the moment. One fact stood out above all others: Adam was planning to go back into the thermals. Back into the thermals where, in the last week, both he and Pat had almost met their death. She searched for a way to convince him not to go without telling him her fears.

She kept emotion out of her voice. "What makes you think you can find it today when you've been looking most of your life?"

"Because now I'm going to look in the one place I've never bothered with before."

"I don't understand . . ."

"You don't have to." He turned as if to go, but her hand on his arm stopped him.

"Adam, don't go." She went on before he could reassure her. "I'm afraid," she admitted softly. "The thermals are a lot more dangerous then you've led me to believe. You were almost killed, and Pat will be lucky to come out of his accident intact. I'm afraid." Her voice trailed off.

He tensed and pulled his arm away. "What would you have me do, *kaihana*? Turn them over to Armstrong without a fight?" Irrationally angry and growing angrier, he faced her. "But perhaps that *is* what you want. Perhaps you think Pacific

Outreach ought to go in there with bulldozers and cranes and concrete. They could civilize the piece of land God forgot."

Since that thought had occupied her mind more and more lately, Paige couldn't deny it. "The area's not safe," she pleaded. "Look at the things that have been happening. Maybe it does need taming, Adam. Would that be so terrible? Would it be so terrible if no one ever had to die in there? Would it be so terrible if it was a health resort instead of a piece of Hell?"

"What are you saying?"

She was so afraid, she knew she would say anything to stop him. "Maybe Hamish is right," she went on. "Maybe his resort is the best use of the land. Maybe I've been trying to be fair when the fairest thing would be to sell it to him anyway. At this point I don't even know what I'll recommend to my father—if I have the chance."

Adam's eyes were black wells of fury. He grabbed her hand and jerked her toward him. He had shared his dream, his vision, and now she was telling him it was nothing more than a foolish, worthless risk. Her disloyalty was the final straw. He could only read it one way. She had decided not to be part of his life. He shut his eyes, and for a moment he could almost hear Sheila's voice telling him that she was pregnant and leaving him. "Do you know what you're saying?" he asked, yanking her even closer.

She felt a throb of alarm and tried to pull her hand from his. "I'm saying that with money and time the thermals might be made safe!"

"Safe, or profitable? That's what this is about, isn't it? You're afraid to stand up for your own people, afraid we won't have the resources that Pacific Outreach has. Our heritage means nothing to you. I mean nothing to you. You'll take the money and leave!"

"That's not it at all," she protested. "That's not what this is about!"

But Adam was beyond listening. He gripped her hand harder, squeezing her fingers tightly together. "I'll show you what this is about," he said, his voice low and deadly. With one hand he pulled out his pocketknife, flipping one blade. Then with a lightning-swift movement, he nicked her finger.

Paige gasped in outrage and tried to pull her hand from his, but he held it tight, squeezing until a tiny bead of blood appeared. He flipped her hand, and both of them watched as the single ruby drop spilled to the floor. "If you had any Maori blood," he said contemptuously, "you don't now. There's

nothing Maori about you. You are your father's child. You are
nothing to me! Nothing!'' He flung her hand away and turned
on his heel.

"You don't want to understand!'' The door slammed before
she could protest further. Tears blurring her vision, Paige
searched the floor for the place where the drop of blood had
fallen, but already it had been absorbed into the soft, dark
wood.

Adam was almost to his destination before he faced the truth.
He had behaved like a madman.

His finger throbbed. He had cut Paige and watched her bleed,
yet it was his finger that throbbed, as if he had bled, too. She
was part of him; she was inside him.

Adam thrust his hands deep in his pockets. His right hand
touched the cool metal of the knife. Without a thought, he
jerked it from his pocket, turned and flung it high, watching the
sun reflect off its silver surface until it had fallen to the path
behind him. "Fool!'' he shouted, only to have the sound carried back to him, an eerie echo off the cliff walls.

Paige was not Sheila, and he was not the man he had once
been. Nothing was left of the idealistic young man who had
trustingly reached out for love. Instead a bitter tyrant had
emerged, a man who saw disloyalty when it didn't exist.

If he found the *mauri*, would he recognize it? It could be on
the path right in front of him, and he would probably step over
it. It could be at his fingertips, and he would probably bend
down and search the ground at his feet. If Horo-i-rangi were to
be found, it would have to be by someone who could see the
nose in front of his face.

Adam walked faster. It was useless to look for the *mauri* today. But he'd had another reason for coming. It had to do with
the sweat on Hamish Armstrong's forehead and the bandages
on his hand. It had to do with his own middle-of-the-night re-
alization that during their meeting, Armstrong hadn't been
wearing his glasses. Glasses were more apt to be broken and
palms injured during a fight than a rescue. And from what
Adam had learned about him, at any time of any given day,
Armstrong was more apt to be lying than telling the truth.

He would do what he had come to do, and then he would go
home and try to put his world back together. If anything was left
of it.

Adam was close to Kaka geyser. Respectfully he moved closer, listening for sounds and watching for signs that the geyser was about to play. It played rarely. Once he had seen it in its full glory, an enormous, steaming, feathered spout of water, as deadly as it was beautiful. Another time he had caught the very end of the geyser's cycle and watched it slowly return to the crater in the earth where it would grow and expand until someday it exploded again. He had wanted Paige to see the geyser play, but they hadn't yet shared that pleasure. Now he wondered if they ever would.

Today the surface around the crater showed no signs of an eruption. Adam pressed his ear to the ground and listened. Papa, the earth mother, rumbled, her music as mysterious to him as it must have been to his ancestors. When he straightened and stood, he knew little except that crossing the steaming rocks beside the geyser was safe—at least for the next few minutes.

On the other side of the rocks he followed a path that skirted the edge of the cliffs. He walked silently in the shadows without so much as a pebble rolling beneath his feet. As he walked, he listened. Not a falling leaf or the flapping wings of a bird escaped his notice.

There was no difficulty recognizing the place where Pat had been injured. Where once there had been a slick, algae-covered shelf of rock, now there was an uneven pile of jagged boulders blocking the path. The debris reached Adam's waist and extended fifteen yards, partially filling in a spring that spouted angrily from between cracks, struggling to break free.

Pat's survival was miraculous, and, at the moment, Adam was in no mood to believe in miracles. Nor was he in the mood to believe that by coincidence, twice in one week, immense, solid slabs of millennia-old rock had crumbled into pieces.

He picked his way carefully along the edge of the boulders, a feat made even trickier by the spring at the side of the narrow path. Where had Pat fallen? And how had he survived? Unless he had been at the edge of the rockslide, the crushing rocks would have killed him instantly and told no tale.

What tale would Pat tell if he were able to?

Adam examined the boulders closest to the path until he was satisfied there was nothing more to see. Then he scrambled on top of the rubble, his body tensed and alert to the dangers of shifting rocks, and, cautious step after cautious step, made his way toward the cliff. At last, spread-eagled against the smooth surface, he inched along, examining the rock face for faults. But the secrets it hid remained secrets.

He had almost reached the beginning of the pile when one foot slipped, and his boot heel wedged between boulders. He slipped his foot out of the boot, then sat carefully and reached down to work it free. Cursing softly, he threw the boot over the rubble to the ground below. Not bothering to stand, he slid along the final bit of rubble, swinging off to land on both feet. Pain shot through the bootless heel, and, surprised, he lifted his foot to find a spreading spot of blood darkening the sole of his sock. Ignoring the pain, he squatted down to search the ground for the source of the cut.

The answer was only inches from his fingertips. It was lightly tinted glass, a slender shard that was nearly invisible against the rubble-strewn ground. Adam sat and stripped off his sock. The cut was shallow and already beginning to clot. But the glass was more interesting.

With the calculated strategy of an archaeologist looking for artifacts, Adam began to search the ground inch by inch, tossing rocks into a pile beside the path as he worked. He had lifted rocks for almost twenty minutes before he found what he had suspected was there. Under a boulder so large he had been forced to roll it away, were a mangled pair of glasses, the remains of lightly tinted lenses still clinging to gold designer frames.

"And did these just happen to fall under the rock when you rescued my cousin?" he asked the man who had come up behind him so quietly that Adam hadn't heard him until it was too late.

"No." Hamish gave a short, humorless laugh. "They fell off when your cousin attacked me."

"And you lost them in the fight?"

"It seems your cousin was unhappy that I'd taken liberties here and there with sticks of gelignite. He was afraid you'd be hurt looking for your precious statue. I warned him to get away, that the explosives I had just set might bring down the cliff, but he was too drunk to know what he was doing."

Adam turned slowly. Hamish was holding a revolver. "Why didn't you leave him for dead?" he asked, suspecting the answer.

"Because of those." Hamish pointed to his glasses with the gun barrel. "They'd been in my pocket. When I got back to my hotel I realized they were gone. I came back to look for them, but

I wasn't as lucky finding them as you were. Your cousin was still breathing, I heard voices nearby—"

"And you decided you'd be safer bringing Pat to the hospital. That way, if your glasses were found at the scene of the accident, no one would think twice."

Nonchalantly, Hamish lifted his palm in praise. Sunlight glistened off the weapon in his hand. "Excellent deduction."

"Just one thing."

"I'd be pleased to help," Hamish said in a silky voice.

"What if Pat told the story when he regained consciousness?"

"Quite unlikely. You see, Pat was helping me. He kept me informed about your little hunting trips in here, and he kept me informed about your relationship with Miss Duvall. He even acted as my personal guide. Pat wanted a ticket out of Waimauri, and he thought I just might be the ticketmaster. If he told what he knew, his own part in our little drama would have come out."

Pat's betrayal was like ashes in Adam's throat. "And now you're going to get rid of me? A bullet hole might be a bit harder to explain than a rockslide."

"Oh, but there are places to kill you where there won't be enough left of your body to show a bullet hole." Hamish motioned with the revolver. "I've got one all picked out."

"And if I don't go?"

Hamish shrugged. "Then I'll kill you here and drag you there. Most unpleasant, but all in the line of duty." The click of the revolver's hammer underscored his words. "Which shall it be, Tomoana?"

"Adam's never late for the evening meal." Mihi stood at the kitchen door, gazing sightlessly across Four Hill Farm's pastures.

Paige had weighed every answer she had given Mihi during the unending day. This one was no different. "Adam was very serious about finding the *mauri*. I imagine he's lost track of time."

"Adam never loses track of time."

Paige wanted Adam to return, too. Only then could she go home and cry the bitter tears that had slowly strangled her since he had walked out the door. But she couldn't tell Mihi that. Mihi had enough on her mind. Paige walked to the doorway and put her arm around the old woman. "Please don't worry. You should be feeling wonderful. The doctor thinks Pat's going to regain consciousness soon, and the minute Adam comes home, you can tell him the good news."

"Something's wrong."

Paige tried again. "Look, you've had a difficult twenty-four hours worrying about Pat. Now you've got to remember how to quit worrying."

"Something's very wrong."

"Please, Granny," Paige begged.

"You feel it, too, don't you?"

"I'm only worried about you."

"You'd feel it if you weren't so angry at Adam."

"I'm not angry," Paige protested. "He hurt me." She stopped, realizing what she had said.

"I thought so."

"It doesn't matter."

"You didn't want him to go into the thermals. You felt the danger then, just as I feel it now."

"How do you know that?"

Mihi sighed. "Haven't you always understood things that others didn't?"

"No, I'm just like everyone else."

"You've wanted to be like everyone else."

Paige tried to understand the cryptic sentiment. "I'm not psychic, if that's what you mean."

"Psychic?" Mihi gave a harsh laugh. "A Pakeha term."

"What do you mean, then?"

"Guided."

"Guided? Who's guiding me?"

"You'll have to listen to know. But I can tell you this. You are a Poutapu, and your ancestors have been *tohungas*, men of knowledge. You have powers you've always denied, powers even Adam won't always understand."

Paige understood just enough to know that Mihi was talking in riddles. "I'm not like you or Henare," she said sharply. "Adam says I have no Maori blood. He told me I'm my father's child."

Surprisingly, Mihi defended Carter, not Adam. "Your father isn't a bad man. He's ruthless, and he's frightened of something he doesn't understand. But he loves your mother, and he loves you. In his own way he's always tried to do what he thought was best for both of you. If you were just your father's child, that would be no shame. But you are much more. And no matter what my foolish nephew says, you are Maori. You must not ignore that part of yourself."

Mihi was still talking in riddles, but Paige felt her bitterness and pain begin to ebb. "I was afraid when Adam told me he was going into the thermals today," she admitted, gazing across the pastures, too. "We fought. I tried to keep him here by telling him Hamish might be right, that maybe the thermals should be developed."

"That was foolish."

"Yes."

"And Adam saw it as a betrayal," Mihi continued. "Since Sheila, he looks for betrayal everywhere, and he sees it in you when you won't make a commitment to him."

"I love him," Paige said softly. "But I'm afraid. We're so different. We come from two different worlds."

"Which only means that you have much to offer each other."

The slam of the front door resounded through the frame house. "Adam is home," Paige said, relieved and frightened simultaneously.

"No." Mihi clutched Paige's arm with a shaking hand. "Help me to a chair, please."

Paige guided her to the table and helped Mihi sit just as Hira burst into the kitchen. Mihi held out her arms as if she knew what was coming, and Hira, sobbing, flung herself into them.

"Granny," she said brokenly. "Oh, Granny."

The kitchen door swung once more, and Iris and Samuel followed their daughter into the kitchen. The air was charged with tension, but no one said a word.

Finally, Paige couldn't stand the silence. "Pat?" she asked.

"He regained consciousness about an hour and a half ago," Samuel said, looking straight ahead as if avoiding eye contact might make his words easier to say. "He'll be perfectly all right."

"What has he done?" Mihi asked, gently pushing Hira away.

"First, where's Adam?" Samuel asked.

"Looking for the *mauri,*" Mihi answered.

Samuel looked disturbed, but before he could comment, Iris interrupted. "Pat's injuries were no accident," she said, looking at the same point in space as her husband. "Pat has been helping the developer who wants to buy the thermal land."

"Hamish Armstrong?" Paige asked, confused.

Iris grimaced at the name. "Yes. Mr. Armstrong wanted information. Pat sold it to him."

Mihi didn't seem surprised, only distressed. "Tell me all."

"Pat made a deal with Armstrong," Samuel said. "He told him where Adam was searching for the *mauri,* and he kept him informed about Adam's relationship with Miss Duvall.'' He inclined his head toward Paige without meeting her eyes. ''In exchange, Armstrong promised to employ Pat when the resort was built.''

''Pat wanted to be someone,'' Hira tried to explain. ''He didn't want to marry me until he was someone—''

Her father cut her off with a wave of his hand. ''Pat believed his actions were harmless enough,'' he went on. ''Somehow Armstrong convinced him that he just didn't want any unpleasant surprises. Then last week Pat discovered that Adam had almost fallen to his death in the thermals while he was exploring. He was afraid it wasn't a coincidence. So Pat set a trap for Armstrong. He told him Adam had narrowed his search to another part of the area, near Kaka geyser. The night of the *hui* he went into the thermals to see if he'd been right.''

''Right about what?'' Paige snapped in frustration. ''What did he think Hamish was doing?''

''Setting explosives.''

''I don't believe it!''

There was a short silence; then Samuel went on, ignoring Paige's outburst. ''When Pat went back, he found Armstrong in the act. It seems he was an opal miner in Australia, and the use of explosives is one of his accomplishments. Apparently at first he only intended to sabotage the areas where the *mauri* might be found. Then he took a gamble. He got the idea to weaken portions of rock just enough to cause a slide if there was any activity in the area. He hoped to injure or kill Adam and scare off Miss Duvall. His plan worked perfectly the first time, except that my brother has the coordination of a cat and was able to save himself when the cliff crumbled. The second time, Armstrong wasn't as successful. Pat discovered what he was doing and tried to stop him. They fought, and the explosives went off. Armstrong jumped clear, but Pat wasn't quick enough. There was a rockslide, and Pat was caught at the edge of it. That's all he remembers.''

''But that doesn't make any sense,'' Paige said. ''Why would Hamish go to such lengths? He had the advantage anyway, and he knew it. The story is preposterous. I think Pat is lying.''

''Pat's not lying,'' Hira insisted angrily. ''Why would he lie?''

But Paige's mind was whirling. ''Hamish told me his life story. He never said anything about opal mining. I have a friend who's an opal miner in Coober Pedy. I would have remembered.''

''Ring your friend,'' Mihi commanded.

Paige looked up. "Now?"

"You won't listen to your heart. Perhaps you'll listen to your friend. Ring him and ask him about Hamish Armstrong, but do it quickly."

Dillon Ward polished the tip of his pool cue against his white moleskin trousers. The Coober Pedy pub rang with Australia's latest gift to the rock music scene plus the laughter of forty hard-drinking men and six much-ogled women. "Good job it's just me you're playing," he told his partner, Jake Donovan. "Or the Rainbow Fire would belong to a stranger by now."

Jake, a brawny man with a grizzled beard and a perpetual scowl, ran his hand over his chin and glared at the pocket his last ball was supposed to have fallen into. "You haven't won yet, lad."

"Watch me," Dillon said with a grin. He was just bending down, steadying his cue with a pool hustler's finesse, when someone tapped him on the shoulder.

"Telephone. For you."

Dillon didn't question why the call had come to the pub. The operator usually found him there. She usually found everyone in town there at one time or another.

Dillon followed the signals of the bartender and took the call in the quiet room behind the wide wooden counter crowded with opal miners.

"Dillon? Is that you?"

Dillon struggled a moment to place the voice. But only one of the many women he'd known sounded like his fantasies of a New Orleans night. "Paige? Is that you? Where are you?"

"New Zealand." On the other end of the line, Paige felt almost sick with relief to hear the familiar Australian twang. It called up images of curling brown hair and shoulders wide enough to cry on forever. "Dillon, I can't talk long. I've got an emergency, and I need your help."

Dillon wanted to strangle the man who had put the fear in Paige's voice. He had the greatest respect for her strength, and he could tell it was nearing an end. "Anything," he said succinctly. "I'll kill the blooming bastard if you want me to."

Paige didn't question his insight or his loyalty. Together they had survived the crucible of a hurricane named Eve. "Dillon, do you know anything about a man named Hamish Armstrong? He may have been a miner there." She felt rather than heard Samuel come up behind her, but her attention was riveted on Dillon's answer.

"I've heard of him," Dillon said. "Stay away from the bloke, Paige. If he ever showed his face in Coober Pedy, he'd be a dead man."

Paige gripped the receiver tighter. "Why?"

Dillon couldn't think of any way to be tactful. "He killed two men. Blew up the entrance to their mine and sealed them in. They were dead by the time they were found, and Armstrong was in Sydney by then with their opals. No one could find enough evidence to indict him, but everyone knew. It happened years ago, but the old-timers still talk about it. They say Armstrong was the only man in Coober Pedy who could have set the explosives and make it look like an accident." He waited for her response, but when it didn't come, he went on. "Do you need me?"

"No." Paige swallowed the bitter taste of fear. "No. I'll call you back when I can and explain."

"I could be there in a day."

"I have to take care of this myself," she said softly. "But thank you."

"You'll ring me back?" Dillon waited for an answer, but got a dial tone instead. He slammed his fist against the wall and wished he were in New Zealand.

Chapter 17

Y ou're risking your life if you go," Mihi said, looking at Paige as if she were following her movements.

Paige didn't hesitate as she slid fresh batteries into a flashlight. She remembered that Adam had called it a torch, and that silly, endearing detail brought his face vividly into her mind. "I have to go, Granny," she said as she clicked the switch to be sure the light worked. "You understand why."

Mihi was silent. Paige wondered if she were listening to voices only she could hear.

"Does Adam keep a gun?" Paige asked when she was satisfied with the light.

"A shotgun, but it's too heavy for you."

Paige wished she had something more lethal to take into the thermals than the flashlight and a backpack with first-aid supplies, a rope and a flare gun. After what she had learned about Hamish Armstrong, she knew he would be as dangerous an enemy as the thermals.

"Your best weapons will be your ears and eyes."

"I'm going to be careful." Paige checked the contents of her pack once more, then zipped it shut and heaved it to her back. "And Adam's going to be all right. I'll find him before the rescue party does."

"He's still alive."

Since Paige had to believe Mihi was right, she simply leaned down and kissed her cheek. "I checked on Jeremy a minute ago. He's asleep in front of the television. If he wakes up before Adam and I get back, tell him..." She swallowed, forcing down the lump in her throat. "Tell him I love him, would you?"

"You don't have to do this."

"I do." On impulse Paige pressed her nose and forehead to Mihi's. *"Taku aroha ki a koe."*

"Give thought to each step you take. If you find yourself in danger, stop where you are and send up a flare so that the rescue party can find you."

"I'm not going to add to their work."

"Listen with your ears and your heart."

"I'll find him." Paige left the room, taking one last look at the sleeping Jeremy before she closed the door. In front of her stretched acres of moonlit pasture, the somber, shadowed expanse broken only by wooden fences and huddles of sheep. She followed a path over the first hill, walking slowly until her eyes adjusted, then gaining speed until her pace was a safe but steady clip.

She was searching for a needle in a haystack, a changing, mutating haystack that was hazardous in daylight and deadly by moonlight. But somewhere in its depths was the man she loved.

Her phone call to Dillon had confirmed Pat's story. She had repeated Dillon's warning to Samuel, her eyes pleading with Hira in unspoken apology. But apologies and pleas for understanding had been nothing compared to the undeniable truth that Adam had not yet come home, and that Hamish Armstrong was a desperate man capable of desperate acts.

Samuel and his family had listened to Paige and Mihi's concerns about Adam, then left immediately to organize a rescue party. Paige had waited just long enough to hear their car pull away before she had begun to organize supplies for her own rescue mission. She didn't know if she was being guided. But she did know that she was too afraid to wait until a rescue party could form. Adam knew the thermals as well as he knew the blueprint of his own house. But he didn't know that Hamish Armstrong wanted him dead.

She was sure Hamish had counted on Pat's silence. Pat was a confused, unhappy young man, but he had realized something important. Personal disgrace was nothing compared to putting someone in his family in danger. Hira believed that Pat had hung on to his life through the long, cold night in the thermals

because he had wanted to tell the truth about Hamish. By doing
so, he had made up for his transgressions.

Paige reached the thermals sooner than she had expected
Rolling green pastures dissolved into a brief stand of forest. A
she walked between trees, listening to the distinctive cry of
morepork owl, she faltered. Already she could smell the stench
of sulphur and see smoke rising to touch the night sky. Already
the moon, which had been bright enough in the meadows, was
obscured behind clouds.

Nothing looked the same. Paige knew exactly where she was
the Valley of Regrets, the place where she had first encountered
Adam. Each time she and Adam had approached the thermal
from his house or hers, they had come this way. With the onset
of night, however, familiar landmarks were no longer signpost
but shadowed barriers in a maze that led straight to Hell. Like
the stiffened carcasses of dead animals, uprooted trees ex
tended leafless branches to the sky. An innocent rock forma
tion had become a primitive Southern Hemisphere Stonehenge
Thinly slivered shadows were tormented prisoners waiting for
pagan priests to emerge from the forest to begin their sacri
fices.

Paige told herself that she would not be a victim of her own
imagination. There were enough real dangers here; there was no
need to create more. She took one step, then another, letting the
beam of her flashlight guide her way. Once she was out of the
forest, branches of manuka scrub scraped her bare arms as she
twisted carefully to avoid the choking smoke of a fumarole.

"Hell's chimneys." She spoke the nickname, remembering
that it had been Adam's. She wondered what portion of Hell he
had found, and the thought made her push on.

Moving a little faster, she passed the nightmarish Stone
henge and took a sharp detour to avoid a tract of steaming
ground. Where had she and Adam always turned? Was it be
yond the small antimony-orange pond with its rainbow display
of rock? Or was it before it? What had Adam cautioned her
about?

Paige stopped and tried to remember the last time they had
come. She could visualize his face. She recalled the way his eyes
had warmed as he had spoken, the way he had reached up and
touched her hair, then her cheek. His fingertips had been warm
and she had laughed. . . .

"Because he told me I had to decide whether I wanted a warm
shower or a luxurious mud bath," she remembered out loud. I
she turned before the pond and sidled carefully along its edge

he would be safe, but damp from the sprays of a spouting
pring. If she turned past the pond, she would end up in a bub-
ling mud pool.

The powerful beam of the flashlight illuminated her path as
he picked her way between pond and spouting spring. To her
elief, the wind was in her favor, and she wasn't even damp when
he stepped off the narrow path onto a flat shelf of rock that
lowed like platinum in the moonlight.

She knew the path would be easier now—for a while. She re-
nembered no hazards she had to avoid. There were fumaroles
nd a short scramble down a ridge, but compared to what would
e ahead when she neared Kaka geyser, the next part of the
ourney would be easy.

And it was. Until she dropped the flashlight.

She had gained confidence, even experienced the elation of
omeone conquering the elements, when her toe caught on a tree
oot and she sprawled to the ground. Her light had fallen, too,
nd landed in three separate pieces.

Paige lay on the ground and stared, too stunned to believe the
bvious. The beam had been snuffed out as soon as the flash-
ight had fallen. She knew without even trying to reassemble it
hat it was beyond repair.

Three minutes of turning batteries and manipulating the bulb
roved that she was right. Three more minutes of shaky deep
reaths and a pounding heartbeat proved that she was fright-
ned half out of her mind.

She had tried to prepare for emergencies, even bringing more
atteries, although the new ones in the light would have been
ood for hours of constant use. There had only been one flash-
ight in the house, however, and she hadn't wanted to take the
ime to search the outbuildings for others. She hadn't really be-
ieved something like this could happen.

She had been a fool filled with good intentions. Her good in-
entions and the flares in her backpack might get her out of the
hermals in the morning. But nothing she could do now would
elp Adam. He was alone somewhere in the vast acreage, per-
aps injured and dying. And she was trapped on the safest part
f a path with a broken flashlight and shattered hopes.

"Adam!"

As she had gotten deeper into the thermals, she had resisted
alling out to him for fear that the wrong person might answer.
low she was beyond caring. If he were near enough to hear, he
night need the comfort of her voice. Forgotten was the way they
ad parted. Remembered was the feel of his arms around her,

arms that she would never resist again if she were lucky enough to hold him tight once more.

"Adam!"

She hadn't really expected a response, but when nothing re turned to her except the echo of his name, Paige trembled with despair. "Adam," she whispered, tears flooding her cheeks. " need you."

She did need him. Together they were more than a whole Without him, she was incomplete. The truth was so simple, bu the truth had come too late.

More tears cleansed the paths of the first. She had neve known love before, not love like she felt for Adam. She ha married Sim to please her parents; she had tried to fall in lov with Granger to ease their mutual pain. But her love for Adam hadn't been to please anyone, nor to bandage a broken heart Her love for Adam just was. Pure. Fervent. A love out of tim and place. A love that could only come once.

And when it had come, she had questioned it.

She had to find him.

The moon was three-quarters full. It hung in the sky abov her, a shrouded beacon that barely took the edge off the dark ness. What stars there were, were muted by the landscape's gra haze of smoke and mist. Paige stood anyway and took a ste forward. The path was just visible, and she remembered enoug of the terrain to know that it continued for about two hundre yards before it climbed the small ridge. She took another step then another. Her progress was slow, but steady. She was sur that, for a little while anyway, she was safe.

Adam was alive. Mihi had told her so, and now Paige con centrated on that assurance. Adam was alive. She believed it wa true, because if he wasn't, somehow she would know. As chil dren they had been united. Despite everything that had sepa rated them, the bond was still there, tempered steel and pures spirit.

Adam was alive, but he was in gravest danger. Paige walke until she reached the ridge. Beyond it lay uncertainty. With th flashlight she could have chosen the next part of her route; now once she had scrambled up and over the ridge, she would hav to guess where to go, feeling her way. Adam could be any where, and she was reduced to deadly guessing games.

She climbed the ridge anyway, shouting his name when sh reached the top. She tripped on the way down, sliding the res of the distance on her knees. At the bottom she rested, shaken and bruised but not seriously injured. She listened and heard the

ound of running water. There had been a stream beside the path
hat led to the geyser. She remembered it because Jeremy had
plashed pebbles into it as they had walked. Then they had
eached the geyser, and Adam had put his ear to the ground.

Standing, she brushed off her pants, wincing as she did. Us-
ng her ears more than her eyes, she found the stream and
ralked carefully beside it. Clouds drifted across the moon,
appling the ground so that sometimes she could see clearly, and
ometimes she couldn't see at all. When the darkness closed in
round her, she waited impatiently for the moment when she
vould have enough light to continue.

It was one of the rare moments when the moon shone brightly
hat she saw the glint of silver on the path in front of her. Tak-
ng advantage of the light, she walked quickly toward the ob-
ect, reaching down to pick it up just as another cloud obscured
he moon once again.

The object was slender and coldly damp to the touch. She
eld it up to her face and confirmed what she suspected. It was
Adam's pocketknife.

*Her finger had throbbed as he pricked it with the knife. "If
ou had any Maori blood, you don't now," he had told her as
er blood dripped slowly to the floor. "You are your father's
hild. And you are nothing to me."*

She dropped the knife to the ground and hid her face in her
ands. "Adam," she whispered, caught between the pain of
ast and present. "I love you. I was afraid for you. I'm afraid
ow."

The wind began to pick up, and smoke drifted toward her
rom a nearby fumarole. Resolutely she pushed on, stumbling
n her haste to find him. Light drifted back and forth over the
ath, but the sound of the stream guided her footsteps.

She rounded a bend and the stream disappeared. She felt vi-
rations at her feet and knew what she had found.

Kaka geyser.

The kaka, green and brown parrot of the New Zealand for-
st. Adam had told her that when it played in the sunshine, Kaka
eyser was like the iridescent plumage of thousands of parrots.
And, like the kaka, the geyser was elusive, appearing when it
ras least expected.

She walked farther, to the place where Adam had placed his
ar to the ground. He had told her that he was listening to Pa-
a's laments. Papa, the earth mother who cried for her hus-
and Rangi, the sky father.

Paige knelt and laid her cheek against the earth. "Papa," she murmured, "I, too, mourn for my lover. Help me find him."

The earth was silent, its faint rumbles felt but not heard. Surely if the geyser were going to play, the pressure would be building so that it was audible. Paige stood and looked across the steaming rocks that led to the cliff where Pat had been found. Adam hadn't told her his destination, but she knew him, and she knew he would have investigated the site of Pat's accident.

She had found his knife.

The moon escaped its cloud cover, and Paige stepped onto the rocks. She knew she was assured only seconds of light. And if Kaka blew...

Paige picked her way across carefully, but quickly. Her ankles were seared once by a spurt of steam, and once she faltered, almost losing her balance as she teetered at the edge of the steaming crater that was Kaka's home.

In less than a minute, however, she was on the other side.

"Adam!" she shouted. The rising wind took her voice, and she tried once more. "Adam!"

If there was an answer, it was lost to her. She turned to the cliffs, skirting their edge. She was grateful for their guidance. As long as she followed them, she couldn't be lost. She would find the spot where Pat had been injured, and if she was lucky she would find Adam. Alive.

Twenty minutes later she reached the rockslide. She began to shout Adam's name as she searched the rubble. There was no sign that anyone had been there, no sign of anything except one of Papa's mistakes. Only this mistake had been caused by Hamish Armstrong, not a mythical earth mother. Paige felt the malevolence of his presence as surely as if he were still there setting his deadly trap.

The trap had caught Pat. Had another like it caught Adam?

She searched more carefully, looking for a clue that Adam had been here. There was no sign, however, only the feeling, the smell, the taste, of evil. She shut her eyes and swayed, overcome by fear, fear she trusted as surely as she trusted her love for Adam. Something was terribly wrong. Adam had been here and Hamish had been here, too. She could see no signs of fighting, but she felt their confrontation in her very bones.

Hours had passed since Adam had left his house. If he had come here first, confronted Hamish... Paige opened her eyes and tried to piece together the scene that had occurred. Adam had come looking for clues to Pat's accident. Hamish had appeared. The two men had clashed....

In any fight with Hamish, Adam would have won easily. He had the superior strength of a man who worked outdoors and the coordination and reflexes of a warrior. But there were no signs of a fight, and that could only mean one thing. Hamish had been armed.

Paige shuddered. She wanted to believe she was imagining everything. Perhaps even now Adam was back at Four Hill Farm, his search for the *mauri* successful. Perhaps even now he was cursing her foolishness and wondering if she was all right.

Perhaps even now he was lying dead in some smoking ravine, one perfectly aimed bullet lodged in the center of his heart.

"Adam!"

The wind was rising. The sky darkened, and for the first time she feared a storm. She had come this far against great odds, but this had been her final destination. Now she didn't know where to go. She had guessed that Adam would come here, but she had no guesses as to where he had gone—or been taken—after he had left this place. The thermals stretched out before her, a fathomless netherworld. She had no clues to this deadly maze, no knowledge of its dangers or surprises. The day they had passed this way, they had followed the cliff beyond this point, twisting and turning around craters and spouting springs and boiling hot pools to a narrow ravine that had led to Paradise.

"Because now I'm going to look in the one place I never bothered with before."

Adam's words of this morning leapt out of her memory. She had questioned him about his search for the *mauri*, and that had been his answer.

On the day when they had rested in the small valley guarded by the *kai-tiaki*, the stone man, she had asked Adam if he had ever looked for the *mauri* there. And he had told her that he had never bothered because once the valley had been a gathering place. Never a shrine.

He had never bothered.

Is that where he had gone? Was she imagining that Hamish had been here? That he and Adam had fought?

She could find her way back to the farm. She could search indiscriminately, risking her life as she did. Or she could push on to the valley she had named Paradise.

The wind swept across the cliff, keening mournfully. She shouted Adam's name, although she expected no answer. It was a talisman against fear.

The wind moaned again, the sound so human that for a moment it fooled her. She strained her ears, listening for something, anything, to help her make her decision. The wind moaned; the wind cried.

We cry for our dead. The young woman at the *hui* had told Paige the meaning of the mournful lament during their greeting. Now Paige heard the young woman's voice again. Explaining the wind.

Paige put her hands over her ears and squeezed her eyes shut. She was overcome with terror. Her imagination was out of control. She was trapped in Hell, her mind her only weapon against the elements surrounding her, and, slowly, she was losing it.

We cry for our dead. Paradise. Papa, the earth mother cries for Rangi, the sky father. The legend says that Horo-i-rangi resides in the place where night and day meet. It is a place of opposites, earth and sky, fire and water, tapu *and* noa.

She sobbed out loud. She couldn't block the voices, nor could she block the keening of the wind. She opened her eyes and saw one thin moonbeam on the path at her feet. Overhead the moon was covered by clouds. Yet one thin moonbeam was lighting her way.

The wind began to sing. The words were liquid and incomprehensible. She took a tentative step toward the light and it moved ahead of her. Pressing her fingers to her temples, she sobbed convulsively as she stepped toward it once more.

You have powers you've always denied. Powers even Adam won't always understand.

Guided. Guided.

Paige sobbed again and took another step. "Adam."

The wind was a lullaby, its breath caressing her as she moved along the edge of the rockslide, avoiding the angry gurgles of a hot spring. She calmed, swallowing her sobs. Moving with the light, she let the wind soothe her fears. Its liquid song asked her to move to its rhythms, and slowly she began to sway, to move through the deadly maze as if she were performing a graceful Maori poi dance.

Guided. Guided.

Finally she let the dance take her, all fears forgotten.

Adam drifted in and out of consciousness. All day he had struggled to stay awake. Asleep, his head dropped to the ground, closer to the source of the sulphide gas that was slowly poisoning him. Awake, he could lift it enough to find the oxygen to survive. But the effort was impossible to sustain for more than a few minutes at a time. The muscles in his neck were on fire. Soon they wouldn't respond at all.

Then he would die.

He had fought death all day. He still fought it, but he was making his peace with its possibility. His spirit would take the mythical journey of all the Maori departed. He would climb down the roots of the ancient *pohutukawa* tree where the northernmost tip of Aotearoa met the Pacific, and he would disappear into the sea-swirled kelp to find his way to his ancestral home of Hawaiki.

And there he would wait for his beloved.

Paige.

His regrets were legion. He would not see his son grow up, wouldn't see the first time Jeremy rode a bicycle, the first time his dark eyes danced at the sight of a pretty girl. He would never hold his grandchildren, never know the legacy he had left.

And he would never be able to tell Paige how much he loved her. He would never be able to plead for forgiveness, never erase the astonishment and hurt from her eyes. Never tell her that she was his heart, his soul, the breath in his body.

His eyes were wet, either from the fetid sulphide fumes or the emotions tearing at him. It didn't matter which. One was killing him; one was keeping him alive. And he was pulled between them.

Even if he died, he had one satisfaction. His enemy had died, too. Armstrong had left him to rot in this hellhole, but, judging from the screams Adam had heard, Armstrong had met his own death. A death he had deserved.

At the top of the cliff overlooking the stream lake where Maori women had once cooked and gossiped, Armstrong had cocked his revolver, waving it in the air in a parody of a priest's blessing. "Say your prayers," he had murmured as he pulled the trigger.

But he hadn't counted on the swiftness of Adam's movements, nor his finely honed reflexes. Adam had hit the ground and rolled in the split second before the gun had gone off. The shot had missed its target, tearing the flesh of his arm instead, and before Hamish could recover, Adam had rolled over the side of the cliff.

He had expected a clean fall, hoping to land on the narrow strip of ground where bushes grew between the cliff and the lake. He had hoped he would be lucky enough to remain conscious and somehow gather the strength to find a hiding place before Armstrong made his way around the cliff's edge and down the valley below. And if he couldn't have that, he had hoped for a quick death in the lake waters, a death of his own choosing, not his enemy's.

He had gotten neither. Instead he had bounced against the cliffside and landed on a projection of rock that held a deep smoking crater. He hadn't been able to extract himself before he was once more the target of Armstrong's gun.

Except that obviously Armstrong had thought of a better idea by then. If Adam were found beside the crater with a bullet in his heart, his death would be investigated. If Adam were found beside the crater, covered with rock, as if he had been the victim of his own actions...

Adam had blacked out after the first rocks began to fall, and he had regained consciousness to the sounds of Hamish's screams and a burning in his own lungs. He was pinned under rock, his legs free, but his arms and back sandwiched between the side of the cliff, where he had tried to protect himself, and a huge boulder. He had been spared being crushed. Now he would die slowly from the sulphide fumes and exposure.

He knew it was only a matter of seconds before he lost consciousness again. Moments of lucidity were shorter now. He longed to let his head fall back to ease the excruciating pain in his neck. He longed to forget what he had to live for and make his peace with God. And he would have, except that every time his head dropped, every time his eyes closed, he saw Paige's face and the pain he had caused her.

He couldn't die without telling her that he was sorry. He couldn't die without telling her that he loved her.

"Adam!"

He heard Paige calling him and knew it was only in his imagination. "I'm sorry," he whispered, his voice nothing more than a rasp. "I love you."

He was drifting in a void somewhere between time and space. He was comfortable, more comfortable than he had been for hours. He wanted to give in to the comfort, but Paige's voice bedeviled him into opening his eyes again. With an action born of reflex, he lifted his head, crying out against the pain as he did. His brain cleared with the infusion of oxygen, but the pain was so intense he could hardly bear it.

"Adam!"

The voice sounded closer now, coming from the direction of the stone guardian. It was a dream, had to be a dream, yet he seemed to be awake. Had he passed the point of knowing the difference? If so, why hadn't the pain ended, too?

"Adam!"

He groaned, wondering what new torment he was being asked to face. He tried to call out, to silence the voice, but the only sound that came from his throat was a dry rasp. He swallowed, then forced himself to swallow again. "Go away," he croaked. He was talking to a dream, talking in a dream. He tried again, louder. "Go away."

The voice, Paige's voice, was closer. "Adam? Adam!"

His head fell back, no longer held by the neck that had gone into a terrible spasm. "Paige!" He was awake, and the voice was real.

"Where are you?"

Adam moistened his lips. "Ledge under the cliff." His voice broke on the last word, and his head began to swim. Sulphide fumes burned his eyes, and his stomach began to roll.

"I've got a rope. I'm tying it to the tree. If I send it down, can you get yourself up?"

He tried to lift his head, to suck in fresh air, but his neck wouldn't respond. He tried to speak, but the only word he could manage was "sorry."

On the cliff above, Paige was frantically tying a knot in the rope. When it was secure, she grasped it, moving carefully to the cliff's edge. Once there, she lay down and inched out until she could see below. At first she registered nothing except space and smoke. Then she saw a narrow, rock-strewn overhang. It took her seconds longer to identify legs and a body wedged by rocks between a smoking crater and the side of the cliff.

"Adam!"

He moaned in answer.

She knew what she had to do. With trembling fingers she tied the end of the rope around her waist, looping it around her belt several times to secure it. She peered over the side as she did, gauging the sturdiness of the ledge and the possibility that her weight would cause a disaster. The ledge seemed solid, sturdy enough to hold the whole population of Waimauri, but if the last days had taught her anything, it was that looks could be deceiving.

"Adam, I'm sending up flares," she told him, wondering if he could hear her. "We'll be found soon. Just hang on. I'm coming down to help you."

He moaned, as if he were trying to stop her, but she ignored him. The flares went easily; it was a relief to have the old Navy-issue flare gun out of her pack. She settled the pack on her back again; then, giving a final jerk on the rope to be sure it was secure, she turned and, holding tightly to the length of rope above her, began to ease herself down.

The rope burned her hands as it slid through them, and she stifled a cry, using every bit of her energy to hang on tightly. She dangled in the air, bouncing against the cliff until she wondered if she would find the ledge before her hands slipped. Finally her toes touched solid rock, and in a moment she was swinging forward to fully rest her feet.

The rope had enough play left that she didn't have to untie it. She was at Adam's side in a second, trying to roll away the boulder that wedged his body against the cliff. With her hands propped against the cliff wall, she shoved with her feet until she had cleared a space. Then she began to lift the smaller rocks until he was free. "Adam, can you hear me?" she pleaded, wedging herself between him and the cliff. She slid up to his head and, lifting it, pillowed it in her lap.

The foul odor of sulphur wafted toward her from the crater at her side. In the moonlight she could see that Adam's eyelids had opened, but his eyes were glazed. Without moving his head, she wriggled out of the pack, removing the canteen. Slowly she dribbled water across his lips. He swallowed convulsively, and his lips parted.

Encouraged, she dribbled water into his mouth and watched him swallow again. She didn't know how much to give him. If he had suffered internal injuries she might be harming him. "We have to get you away from that sulphur," she told him. "You're not pinned in anymore, but I'm not sure you can move. Can you wriggle down a little? I'll help as much as I can."

"Sorry," he whispered.

"It's all right. I know you're hurt. Don't apologize if you can't move." Her voice broke, and she wiped her cheeks with the back of one hand.

"Sorry I hurt you," he croaked. "Love you."

She washed his face with her tears. "I love you," she said brokenly. "More than anything in the world. Everything's going to be all right, just don't you die on me now."

"Gas," he said. With her help he tried to inch away from the crater, but he could hardly move. "Can't." His head fell back to her lap in exhaustion.

Paige encouraged him to try again, moving with him inch by inch until they were a full foot from the crater. The wind shifted, and even though she wished they could move another foot, the sulphur smell was already weaker. "The smoke's blowing the other way," she told him. "Are you breathing easier?"

She was so soft. Adam turned his cheek against her thigh. The ache in his neck had begun to ease, and, if she sensed the remnants of his pain, Paige began to massage it with her fingers. He swallowed before he spoke, wanting his question to be coherent. "How'd you find me?"

"I'm not sure I understand it myself."

His mind was beginning to function again. With the functioning came the horror of reality. "You're alone?"

"No, *kaihana*," she said cryptically. "Never alone. I'll tell you all about it someday."

"Who?" he insisted.

"Our ancestors." Paige smoothed his hair, then wet her fingers with water from the canteen and smoothed them over his face. "Can you drink some more?"

"Paige."

She recognized the demand in his voice and ignored it. "Did Hamish do this to you?" she asked.

He didn't question how she knew about Hamish. Later there would be time for questions. "Hamish is dead."

Her hand stilled, then resumed its stroking. "Samuel and some of the men from Waimauri should be here soon. They'll need to know how badly injured you are."

He was exhausted, light-headed, and his neck felt as if someone had driven a tractor over it. His arm ached where the bullet had grazed it, and his body felt as if it had spent the day wedged between a rock and a hard place. With a touch of irony, he thought that, of course, it *had* been.

"I'm fine." He turned his mouth against her thigh and kissed it.

"You're not."

"Kiss me."

"You're in no shape to be kissed."

"The breath of life, then."

She was still crying, and she hadn't even known it. With her back curved against the cliff, she bent and brushed her lips across his, then pressed noses in an awkward *hongi*. "You're going to be all right, aren't you?"

"Try and stop me," he said slowly.

A shout from above was a dose of reality. Paige shouted back, giving the men the information they needed to begin the rescue. ''You're going to be safe now,'' she told Adam. ''They'll have you out of here in minutes and into the clinic in town.''

His hand crept up to grip hers. ''You'll stay with me?''

''Will forever do, *kaihana*?''

Chapter 18

 What was this Armstrong chap wearing?"
  The police officer asking the question pointed toward the middle of the lake to a blur ringed by a high-intensity beam from another officer's searchlight. He handed his binoculars to Adam, who took them with hands that still weren't quite steady.
  Adam held the binoculars to his eyes for a moment, then handed them back. "That could be his jacket, I suppose. It's hard to tell."
  Paige rested her head against Adam's shoulder, her arm firmly around his waist, where she had kept it ever since he had insisted on walking down the cliff path under his own power. He seemed to grow stronger with every breath of fresh air that he took, but she still wasn't convinced he was all right, even if the Waimauri doctor who had come with the rescue party and bandaged his arm seemed to think he was.
  "How do you suppose Hamish ended up in the lake?" she asked.
  "It's likely he slipped when he was trying to bury me with rocks. One rolled away from him, and he lost his balance."
  She nodded gravely, trying to summon up a trace of pity for the man who had died such a terrible death. All she could summon was the picture of Adam slowly choking to death on the ledge.

"There's nothing we can do for the poor chap tonight," the officer said. "We'll drag the lake tomorrow and take out what's left of him."

Paige shuddered, and Adam's arm came around her for comfort. "It was over quickly," he assured her.

"I was just thinking it could have been you."

"Or you."

Samuel came up behind them, clapping his hand on Adam's shoulder. "Come on, strong man, let's get you back to the farm before you collapse and disgrace the tribe."

"We're going to need a full statement," the policeman reminded Adam before he and Paige could start out of the valley behind Samuel and two other men who were carrying lights.

Adam barely looked his way. "Let me change my clothes and rest, then I'll be in."

Paige was angry enough for both of them. "Can't that wait until tomorrow? Adam almost died here tonight."

The policeman shrugged. "Someone else did, miss. Adam knows I believe his story. We just want to be certain the Aussies have all their answers when we tell them one of their own isn't coming back alive."

"I'm going to be all right." Adam pulled Paige along beside him. "We'll take the shortest way out, I'll shower and change, then I'll go into the cop shop when I'm feeling rested enough."

"Strong man," she grumbled, making sure he didn't walk too fast.

The shortest way out wasn't short enough, but with some help, Adam walked through the front door of Four Hill Farm on his own two legs. Legs that were almost knocked out from under him by a small boy with a big grin.

Paige blinked back tears as she watched Adam and Jeremy's reunion. Adam sank to the floor and pulled Jeremy onto his lap, and for minutes they just held each other. Then Adam held out an arm to her, and she joined them.

Later, with a sleeping Jeremy on her lap, she told the full story to Mihi while Adam showered.

"Does Adam know how you found him?" Mihi asked when Paige had finished.

"Not really. I'll have to tell him, I suppose, but I don't think he'll understand."

"I understand."

Paige took the old woman's hand and held it to her cheek. "Then you're the only one who does. But I found out something tonight. I don't have to understand everything. I don't

understand what happened to me in the thermals, and I don't
understand how Adam and I were going to make our lives work
together. But I know we will, just as I knew I was being led to
him tonight."

"More has happened than you even suspect."

Paige wasn't sure she wanted any more to have happened.

"Your parents are in Rotorua," Mihi continued. "Your father rang tonight, trying to locate you. They're coming here in
the morning."

"Here?"

Mihi laughed a little. "It wasn't his first choice, I'm afraid.
But I told him he must."

"You told him he must." Paige repeated Mihi's words just to
see if there was some spell connected with them. "And Carter
Duvall agreed?"

"Half past nine."

Adam came in, still rubbing his hair with a towel. Paige
transferred Jeremy to Mihi and stood, circling Adam's waist
with her arms. "You'll get wet," he warned as he pulled her
closer.

"As if I care."

Adam rested his cheek against her hair. "You smell like sulphur."

She decided not to tell him about her parents yet. There would
be time later, when he was more rested. "I want you to drop me
off at my place on your way into town so I can shower and
change. I don't have any clothes here," she said when he started
to protest. "Samuel says he'll drive you in and help you make
your report. Then you can pick me up on your way back."

"Where's Rambo?" Adam didn't want to move. He wanted
to stand holding her this way forever.

"Well, that's the other reason I need to go home," she admitted. "Jeremy and I went over and put him in the pen this
afternoon. I'm sure he's hungry...."

"And he never stays in the pen after dark," Adam finished
for her. "Granny, shall we let her keep that excuse for a lamb in
our kitchen again?"

"I'm of a mind to think she can do anything she wants here,"
Mihi said, nodding. "Anything at all."

Paige slammed Samuel's car door behind her. "Thanks for
the ride," she told him through the open window. "I'm sorry
your stubborn brother wouldn't let you take him into town."

"It's a short drive. Once he's rested a little, he'll be fine driving in by himself. Adam's got the constitution of an ox." Samuel tooted his horn in salute and pulled away.

Paige started up the walk toward the pen, Rambo's bleats a pathetic serenade. "Poor little lamb," she sympathized. "Does Paige's little lamb want to go everywhere that Paige went?" At the pen, she debated whether to take the lamb up to the house with her or wait until she had fixed his bottle. When Rambo was hungry, he sucked or chewed on everything in sight, and she wasn't sure she had the energy to stop him.

She decided to leave him in the pen, although she felt like a traitor. "I'll hurry," she promised as she started toward the house.

She did plan to hurry. Adam was still at home gathering energy for the trip into town, but when he came to get her on his way back, she wanted to be all ready. Not only was she going to shower and change, she was going to pack.

Paige hoped he understood just what that meant. There had been no time to talk, no time for the promises she wanted to make to him, but there would be time tonight. And she wanted to show him that she meant it when she said she was going to live with him. She hoped he would take the next step himself and offer to make it legal. And permanent.

Cornwall was nowhere in sight. "I could have used your company tonight, dog," she muttered as she stepped up on the porch. "For once I would have been glad to see you."

She knew it was just the terrors of the night that were still preying on her, but as soon as she said the words to the absent dog, she knew she meant them. She really wasn't ready to be alone after everything that had happened. With no more adrenaline pumping through her bloodstream, she was tired and shaky and something more. She paused, her hand on the door knob.

She was spooked. She laughed a little, trying to make the feeling disappear. A residue of fear made perfect sense after the night's events, but that didn't mean she had to give in to it. Resolutely she pushed the door open. Adam was safe; she had survived an experience few people would understand, and Hamish Armstrong...

"Get in and shut the door behind you."

Stunned, Paige wasn't able to obey.

A scarecrow of a man stepped out of the kitchen doorway and motioned with the barrel of his revolver. "I said get inside and shut the bloody door."

She forced herself to move. She kicked the door shut behind her. "We thought you were dead." Hysterically she wondered if he was and he just didn't know it yet.

"You'd have liked that, wouldn't you? Is this good enough for you?" Hamish pulled open what was left of his shirt, revealing a scalded chest.

Paige felt nausea creeping from her stomach into every part of her body. His face was burned, too, badly on one side, less badly on the other. One arm hung uselessly at his side. She leaned against the door to keep from fainting.

"Your thermals are a dangerous place, Miss Duvall."

"You fell in the lake." She wondered how he had survived.

"I fell, but I missed the lake. I just didn't miss the geyser on my way out."

After everything he had done, she still couldn't bear to imagine Hamish caught in the midst of Kaka's righteous fury. She remembered her prayer to earth mother. Papa's justice had been brutal. "We've got to get you to the hospital," she said as calmly as anyone could who was looking down the barrel of a revolver.

"I should think you'd like that. The cops could cuff me to the bed while they treated me."

"Hamish, you're in no shape to be worrying about the police at this point. You've got to get to a hospital or you won't be alive to be arrested."

"I'm going home."

At first she didn't understand. "They think you're dead," she tried to explain. "By now the police have probably been to your hotel."

"Home." He swayed. "Sydney."

She edged away from the door, but one wave of his pistol stopped her. "You're going to take me," he said.

"I can't drive you to Australia. There's a small matter of some water between here and there."

"You're going to drive me to Auckland. Then we're going to take a plane to Sydney."

"We?"

"Once we get there, you can do what you want. Sydney's my city. I can disappear. I won't hurt you." As if he saw the doubt in Paige's eyes, Hamish laughed, a horrible, pain-filled laugh. "I wouldn't harm Carter Duvall's daughter, love, unless you forced me to. I'm not a fool, just a murderer."

"Adam didn't die."

"Do you think that matters?" He laughed again.

Paige could hear how close to the edge of insanity he was. His plan was the plan of a man made desperate by agony and fear. It lacked all logic.

"You can't get on a plane, Hamish. You're obviously hurt. Your clothes are in tatters."

"You can buy me clothes in Auckland. I have my wallet, my passport."

"You're too sick. You've got to get medical attention immediately."

"Change your clothes." He swayed, but the gun was steady in his hand. "You have two minutes to get ready."

Adam slowed as he passed Paige's house. There were no lights on in the living room, and he imagined she was in the back taking her shower. His reaction to the thought of her standing naked, water streaming over her breasts and hips, was a good indication of his recovery. He laughed softly at Rambo's pathetic bleating before he accelerated to finish the drive into town.

Paige changed her clothes under Hamish's careful scrutiny. She knew he was too ill for desire, but she still felt sickened by his gaze roving over her body. Her fingers shook as she slipped heels on over bare feet. She wasn't going to put stockings on in front of him.

She was combing her hair with trembling hands when she heard Adam pass. She recognized the chug-snort of his car engine, and her heart lodged in her throat. But the car kept going, and she wasn't sure whether to be relieved or devastated.

Hamish followed her into the living room. "Find me a sweater or something to put on in case anyone sees me."

Nodding, her heart still in her throat, Paige found a loose black cardigan in the hall closet. Hamish slipped it on, gasping in pain as he tried to move the arm that was obviously fractured in several places. Then he motioned toward the door, his lips drawn in a frightening grimace.

Paige's hand was on the knob before she realized what her fear had made her forget.

"Hamish, I don't have my car here." Paige knew she was pleading, but she didn't care. "I can't take you anywhere without a car. I left it at Adam's. His brother dropped me off here, and Adam's going to pick me up on his way back from town."

"You're lying." Hamish took a step toward her. "Don't lie to me."

"I wish it wasn't true, but it is!" Paige backed against the oor. "Look outside yourself. Do you see my car?"

"I couldn't see it from here if you parked it down below."

"But I don't do that. I pull it up the hill."

He seemed to be trying to recall the details of his other visits. His face screwed up in pain. "Open the door and step out on the orch," he ordered. "We'll just see."

She prayed someone would pass by, someone who would uspect something was wrong when he saw her standing on the orch with a man. But the one person who would have known or certain had passed just minutes before.

She stepped away from the door, swinging it toward her.

"Go on, and don't try anything. I'm right behind you."

Paige felt the cold metal of his gun through her cotton blouse. n the background Rambo's hungry baas were like the score of an avant-garde horror movie, and she stepped out on the porch n slow motion, fear walking before her.

The next seconds would remain in her memory forever.

Cornwall materialized out of nowhere, a raging, salivating nonster. Before Hamish could react, Cornwall had attacked, and the revolver was sliding across the porch floor. She watched t slide, too shocked to move. Hamish was screaming, crawling oward the gun with blood streaming from his good arm. His fingers closed on the handle just before they were covered by a nan's shoe.

Adam called Cornwall's name and whistled two blasts that sent the snarling dog to the steps but no farther. Adam shifted his weight forward and listened to Hamish's cries of pain. "Just slip your hand out a little at a time," he ordered. "Without the gun."

"I can't move it."

"I think you can. But if you're not certain, I can get Cornwall to help."

With an effort, Hamish unwrapped his fingers and pulled his hand back. Adam casually kicked the gun to the ground below the porch. Hamish rested his cheek on the floor in defeat and fainted.

Paige moved then, reaching Adam in a split second. "How did you know?" she sobbed. "How did you guess?"

His arms closed around her. "This isn't any way to conduct a romance, *kaihana*."

She buried her head against his chest and wrapped her arms around his waist. "How did you know?"

"I heard Rambo baaing. I was halfway down your road be
fore I realized you wouldn't have left him outside and hungry s
long. Then I knew something was wrong."

"And you brought Cornwall with you?"

He laughed humorlessly. "Cornwall was a bonus, I'm afraid
I always knew he wasn't a sheepdog. He's a guard dog. *You*
guard dog. He surprised me as much as he surprised Arm
strong here."

"I'll buy him from you."

"He's a gift. Just don't give him back." His arms tightened
"Will you stop scaring me this way?"

She knew she was going to have to release him, but she wasn'
ready yet. Time enough when Hamish woke up. "What are you
going to do about Hamish?"

"I was going to the cop shop anyway. I'll just take him along
for the ride."

"In the trunk?"

"Boot," he corrected her, tipping her face to his. "We've go
to work on your vocabulary."

It was with surprising gentleness that Adam loaded Ha
mish's unconscious body into the back seat of his car for th
short trip to town. On the front seat next to Adam, Paige fe
Rambo and continued feeding him at the police station, ignor
ing the amusement of everyone who saw her.

Adam gave his statement; Paige gave hers. Rambo gave his
too, and it was Rambo's that hurried their departure from th
station. Hamish was taken into Rotorua for formal booking and
hospitalization, and although Adam and Paige were told the
might have to clear up the details later, the case against Hamis
was strong enough that justice was going to be swift, if no
merciful.

"I was going to take a long, hot shower and change into
something wonderful," Paige told Adam on the way back
home. She didn't add that she had also planned to pack.

"I know what I'd like to see you wear."

"As little as possible?"

"Nothing."

"I won't need to stop at my house for that."

"Good."

The lights were off at Adam's. They settled Rambo in the
kitchen next to Cornwall, who had arrived before them. "I have

never allowed a dog in my house," Adam said, grimacing as Cornwall and Rambo snuggled together.

"The lion shall lie down with the lamb." Paige stooped to scratch Cornwall's ears.

"I want to lie down with you."

She followed him upstairs. It was a ritual she hoped to observe for the rest of her life. In his room, she held him at a distance. "I never had that shower. I still smell like the thermals."

His eyes glinted in the moonlight-flooded room. "Take off your clothes. I'll run a bath."

Her lips curved into a smile. Adam's water, like the water in her house, was piped in from a hot underground spring. To accommodate that wealth, his tub was huge, a luxury in a house that was otherwise comfortably simple. She stretched lazily like a cat about to get her nightly bowl of cream. "Am I going to have company?"

"I'll be waiting."

"Only as long as it takes to run the water."

When he was gone she undressed, pulling his robe from the closet and wrapping it around her. As she padded down the hall, the robe trailed behind her like the train of the gown she had worn to make her debut. Then she had been told her life was about to begin. Now she knew it truly was.

Adam was in the water when she arrived. The room was fragrant with the good smells of spicy soap and warm, clean man. She unwrapped the robe and let it fall to the floor, stepping into the water and his arms. She sighed as both closed around her.

"Don't ever let go of me again."

Adam said nothing. He just turned her so that her body was sliding wet and warm over his. And then he answered her.

Chapter 19

Paige was wrapped tightly in Adam's arms when she woke up the next morning. Sunlight streamed through the windows, and breakfast perfumed the air. Outside she could hear the baaing of sheep mixed with men's voices.

Still snuggled close to Adam, she fumbled for her watch on the nightstand. "Eight-thirty?"

"Go back to sleep." Before she could sit up, Adam pinned her close with one leg thrown over hers.

"Adam, we can't go back to sleep."

He cut her off. "We can do what we please. I'd say yesterday earned us both a day of rest."

She couldn't agree more, except for one thing. "My parents are going to be here in an hour."

She felt the change in his body as he went from supremely relaxed to ramrod stiff. "How do you know?"

Mentally she berated herself for not telling him the night before. But everything had been so perfect, and they had been too busy to talk. "Granny told me last night." She tried to make a joke of it. "Sometime in between your attempted murder and my kidnapping."

"And you didn't tell me?"

"Well, a few things were going on."

He pushed her away, a gentle push, but a push nonetheless. "I see."

"Apparently you're the only one who does." Paige sat up, brushing her hair off her face. "I'm sorry I didn't mention it, but I don't understand why you're so upset."

Adam swung his feet over the side of the bed and presented her with his back. He felt his world coming apart around him.

"You knew my father was on his way." Paige slid over to his side of the bed and leaned her cheek against his back. "Now we can get this over with and get beyond it."

"Over with?" He couldn't believe she could sound so matter-of-fact about the end of their relationship. On the cliff she had talked about forever.

"Adam, we have to get on with our lives. This decision couldn't be put off." She thought of all the tension there had been between them before he had gone into the thermals yesterday, and suddenly she thought she understood. "My love," she said, holding him when he tried to stand. "The things I said yesterday about the land . . . I was afraid. I sensed something terrible was going to happen, and I would have done anything to keep you here. Even though Hamish is out of the picture, Pacific Outreach will probably still want the land. I want to fight them for it. I want the land to stay with our people." She faltered on the last words, remembering that Adam had told her she had no Maori blood.

She was talking about the land, when the land suddenly seemed unimportant. Adam couldn't prevent his next words. "And what about you?"

She was confused, afraid. During the long night he had made such sweet love to her that she felt forever joined to him. And yet, not once, had he asked her for anything, not to stay with him, not to be his wife, not to share his life forever. He had never asked her for those things in all the times they had been together.

"Adam, what do you want from me?" She straightened, and her arms fell to her sides. It was the one question that had to be answered, but she had barely been able to say the words.

He heard the hesitation in her voice. She had to know what he wanted. She was telling him that he was asking too much. He took an unsteady breath, then another. He set her free. "I want you to be happy, *kaihana*. I want you to think of me sometimes."

She felt his words explode in the place inside her that he had filled. They emptied her until she knew there was nothing left. She gathered together what she could. "I see. Well, you'll get your wish. You can be sure I'll think of you." She swung her legs to the other side of the bed and stood, collecting her clothes from the floor.

"Will you be leaving with your parents?"

"I'm a grown woman, Adam." She lifted her head and realized that pride was all she had left. "I left with them once before. I won't be leaving with them again."

He couldn't keep the hope out of his voice. "Then you'll be staying?"

She blinked to slow the tears she didn't want to fall. "Once you fought to keep me here. Are you in such a hurry to see me go now?"

He felt as if he were swimming upstream, so busy with the battle to reach his destination that he had passed it miles before. "Do you want to stay?"

"I want a shower." She slipped her arms into his robe and belted it around her. "I want some peace." She found her way to the door and closed it behind her.

Adam wondered whether, if he stopped battling and just drifted with the current, he would find enough peace for both of them.

Carter Duvall looked old and haggard. Paige didn't make a mockery of her feelings and go to him for a daughterly hug. She gave him a brief nod, noting the funereal black of his suit, the dull sheen of his silver hair, the ice in his brown eyes.

"I would say it's good to see you," she said coolly, "except that it isn't." She turned to her mother and gave her the hug that Ann Duvall always seemed to need. "You're looking well, Mother."

Ann nodded, as if she were incapable of speech. Paige stepped aside. "I'm sure you remember Mihi Tomoana," she said to both her parents. "She certainly remembers you. And behind her is Adam Tomoana, the man who's offering you the hospitality of his home for this meeting." Paige challenged her father with her eyes. "I believe he's grown since your last encounter."

"That will do, Paige." Adam stepped up beside Mihi, sheltering her beneath his arm. "Please come in," he said, nodding to the Duvalls. "You are both welcome here." He paused, then his lips softened. "After all, we're family."

Ann released a sound like a small sob, and despite not wanting to be, Paige was ashamed. She put her arm around her mother and felt how slender she was. Ann Duvall was too slight to carry any burdens.

"We are not family," Carter said. "We have not come here as family. I've come simply to take care of some business matters. Ann is here—"

"Because Ann wouldn't be left at home," Ann said, seeming to take courage from her daughter's support.

"I'm glad you're here, Mother." Paige gave her a hug. "And I'm glad we can get all this in the open."

"We have come on business," Carter repeated.

"Long overdue business, Father mine." Paige led her parents into the living room and waited until everyone was seated. Before anyone could say anything, there was a knock at the door. Adam came back moments later, leading Henare and Materoa Poutapu. Introductions were made, and they were seated.

Carter levered himself forward, as if he planned to take control. Paige had seen her father in action all her life. She knew what was coming, but she was also her father's daughter. She knew how to take control first. "I've got some things to say," she began before he could. "First of all, I'm resigning my position at Duvall Development." She couldn't look at Adam, because she knew that if she did, she would hesitate, and Carter would take over. "Second, before everyone here, I'm claiming the heritage that's been denied me. I am Maori, my mother is Maori, and I am proud of who I am." She heard her mother's sob, but she went on. "Third, I'm topping Pacific Outreach's offer for the thermals. If you're in the mood for irony, the money will come from the trust fund you started for me, Carter."

She went on over his protests. "Fourth, once the land belongs to me, I'm giving it to the Arawa Tribal Trust Board to be administered as they see best."

Carter would be silenced no longer. "Who do you think you are to speak to me this way?"

Henare broke in, speaking Maori, and although Paige couldn't understand, she suspected that, strangely, he was agreeing with her father. She was breaching all rules of filial respect.

"I am your daughter," she answered calmly, although she felt anything but calm. "I love you."

Carter opened his mouth and let it fall shut again. Paige imagined that in all his years, no one had ever silenced him quite that way. "I love you," she went on, "despite the harm you've done here. I love you because I think you were afraid of something you didn't understand. I love you because I can't believe you ever wanted things to get so terribly out of control. I love you because you've always wanted the best for me and for Mother, even though you've never understood what that was."

"You don't know anything about it."

"I love you even though I know you'll never be able to admit that you've been terribly, terribly wrong."

Carter sat back, paler, sterner. "I'm going to sell to Pacific Outreach. Sentiment has nothing to do with this. I won't let you waste your trust fund this way."

"I'll take this to the board," Paige said reasonably. "Then who will they accuse of sentiment? Me, or the man who's turning down a sizable profit?"

"They will accuse no one, because the land doesn't belong to Duvall Development. The land belongs to me." Ann Duvall sat forward in a graceful imitation of her husband. "Have you both forgotten something? The land is mine."

Out of the corner of one eye, Paige saw Mihi nodding complacently. It was almost her undoing. "Go on, Mother."

Ann ventured one look at her husband, then turned her face away from him. "The land is mine," she repeated. "Not Duvall Development's, not Carter Duvall's. The land came to me in an inheritance. It is mine to dispose of, and I'm giving it to the Arawa Trust Board."

"You don't know what you're doing!" Carter's words were an explosion.

"No," Ann said softly. "I haven't known for years. I'm not sure I will again. But now, I know this is right."

Paige was on her feet in an instant; then she was kneeling beside her mother's chair. She looked up into the face that was so like her own. "Why?" she asked. "Why did you let it go this far? Why all the wasted years?"

Ann reached out and touched her daughter's cheek. "I was young, spoiled. I wanted to be someone different than who I was. All these years, darling." Her hand faltered. "All these years I wanted to come home again and bring you with me. But I didn't have the courage."

"I'm not going to listen to this." Carter Duvall stood and strode toward the front door.

"You've made me ashamed of who I am," Ann said to him, lifting her eyes to stare at his back. He stopped, but didn't turn. "You are the one who should be ashamed, Carter."

He stood, a cast-iron statue; then, without turning, he made his way to the front door. He closed it quietly behind him.

Paige looked around the room. There were many feelings in evidence. Embarrassment, tears, family loyalty. And in Adam's eyes there was unspeakable loneliness. In the silence, she heard the questions he had never been able to ask.

"I'm going to my father," she said, her eyes still locked with Adam's. "Will you take care of my mother for me?"

He nodded, and she rose.

Carter Duvall was on the front porch, gazing out at the meadows of Four Hill Farm. "I hate sheep," he said when he heard Paige behind him.

Tentatively she touched his shoulder. "But you try so hard to make sheep of everyone you love."

Surprisingly he didn't disagree. "I've never been afraid of anything except losing your mother. I came here, and it was a world I didn't understand. She was pulled by it, I could see the hold it had on her." Paige leaned against him, and his arm encircled her waist. "And then I was afraid of losing you."

"You're a real bastard, Carter," she said with a sniff. "But you haven't lost me."

His arm tightened convulsively. "You're staying, aren't you?"

"You've heard of jets. I think you even own one."

"I won't be coming back here." He didn't sound convincing, just older, sadder.

"You're going to be a lonely man if you don't. Mother's going to be spending time here now, I think." Paige paused. "What if I promise you a grandson?"

"You drive a hard bargain, don't you?"

"I've had the best of teachers." She kissed his cheek. "You're going to have to talk to Mother. You know that, don't you?

You've got to talk to her, Carter, and let her tell you how she feels. Don't let her find her answers in a bottle this time.''

He released a long, harsh breath. ''Ann wants to stay in New Zealand for a while, maybe travel around a little. We'll have to talk. What else can we do in this godforsaken place?''

They stood together, surveying emerald-green meadows. Paige hoped a start had been made.

Her parents had gone. After a morning exploring some of Ann's inheritance, they had gone to rest and, Paige hoped, to talk. Ironically they were staying in the same hotel in Rotorua where Hamish had stayed, and Paige had watched them drive away with a mixture of emotions.

Her mother had still looked too fragile, her father too stern. But as they walked toward their car from Paige's house, Carter had reached over and taken Ann's arm, and Ann hadn't pulled away.

Now the house seemed too quiet. Rambo was still at Adam's, and Cornwall was off chasing birds, protecting her, Paige supposed, from magpies and mynahs. She had come to New Zealand for this kind of silence, but now she didn't want to listen to her thoughts.

She wanted to listen to Adam's. But Adam wasn't here. He was home, and if he was thinking anything at all, she didn't know what it was.

They were alike in many ways, too many ways, perhaps. They were both stubborn and proud and easily hurt. They both hid what they felt and denied any feelings that showed. They both had loved and suffered for it before, and both of them were afraid of suffering again.

Did he want her in his life? She wanted to believe he did, but she was too insecure to trust the loneliness and longing she had seen in his eyes. She wanted him to ask her to stay. She wanted a proposal. She didn't want to be told that he hoped she would think of him when she was gone.

''Are you ready?''

Startled, she turned to find Adam behind her. She didn't have to ask where he had come from. The back door was open, and his footsteps were always silent. ''Ready for what?'' She wanted to throw herself in his arms, demand that he tell her what he was thinking, demand that he marry her. But a lifetime of reticence made that impossible. She stood and waited.

"I've got something to show you."

"Will it take long? I'm meeting my parents for dinner."

"We have time."

She walked with him past spreading trees that grew denser as they reached the forest that bordered the thermals. She went that far without a word, but not a step farther. When Adam crossed the boundary she stayed behind.

Adam knew how she felt. He didn't understand how she had found the courage to come after him in the dark. He held out his hand to her. "Come on, *kaihana*."

"No. You're asking too much."

"I don't think so." He stretched his hand a little closer. "I'll keep you safe."

"I'll keep myself safe."

He moved toward her until he was within touching distance. "I need you." His hand rested on her arm. "I need you to come."

He had learned how to manipulate her. She had been that vulnerable. Paige lifted her chin, but the movement brought her face in line with his. What she saw there was the greatest manipulation of all. His eyes were pleading with her. "Please?"

She nodded and allowed him to take her hand.

Sunshine lit their path. Today the smoke obscured nothing. It drifted in dancing, twisting patterns. Steam rose from springs, an invitation to stop and breathe its mineral-rich vapors. The bellbird chimed its crystalline call, and wildflowers bloomed in pastel hues against sulphur-encrusted rock sculptures.

Paige moved without hesitation. It wasn't the thermals she feared. She would never fear them again. It was being here with Adam that frightened her. Somehow, here, neither of them could hide.

At Kaka geyser she watched Adam put his ear to the ground. When he stood, she followed him across the steaming rocks and remembered it was here that Hamish had confronted the true power of the land he had wanted to tame.

They came to the rockslide where Pat had almost been buried. "Pat will be going home from the hospital after the weekend," Adam said, speaking for the first time since he had taken her hand at the forest's edge.

"You've spoken to him?"

"Samuel wants him to give the university a try. He'll be moving to Waikato to work for a while until he can complete his papers to get in."

"Does he know you forgive him?"

He squeezed her hand. "Yes."

They edged along the rockslide and began the twists and turns that would lead them into Paradise. Paige found herself pulling back as they neared the narrow canyon that led to the small lake. "Why would you want to come back here?" she asked at the mouth of the canyon. "After everything that happened."

"If you come, I'll show you."

"You almost died here."

"But I didn't."

She let him pull her through the canyon. They stopped at the entrance to the valley. The cliff where Adam had almost fallen to his death gleamed brilliantly in the sunshine, its rainbow-hued walls denying the evil of the past night. Embedded crystals sparkled like daylight stars, and against the cliff, on the narrow strip beside the lake, trees swayed in the afternoon breeze.

"What am I supposed to see?" Paige pulled her hand from Adam's.

"The place where day and night meet, the place of opposites, earth and sky, fire and water, *tapu* and *noa*."

"So this is where you were going to look for the *mauri* yesterday?"

"You knew?" Adam raised one eyebrow, assessing her. "And that's why you came here last night?"

"I guessed, but that's not what brought me here." She refused to say more.

"I don't know why Armstrong brought me here to kill me," Adam said, sensing her reluctance to share her thoughts. "There were other, better places. I suppose this one was the closest. He took me to the top of the cliff. I think he had intended to push me into the lake, but when we reached the top, he had second thoughts. He must have realized that if we fought up there, he might lose. Then he decided to shoot me. He believed I'd fall into the lake, or, at worst, that he could throw me in and there wouldn't be any evidence to worry about."

Paige shuddered. "Why are you telling me this?"

"Because Armstrong chose the wrong place." He took her hand. "Come with me."

She held back. "You believe Horo-i-rangi is here?"

"I've been so wrong. Where else would she be? A place so emote that her power had no meaning? No, she'd be here, vhere her people came to cook, to make their clothes, to play." He gestured to the lake. "The place where Aotearoa's waters ave their source. The spring that feeds this lake begins at the uardian's feet. There's an underground stream that drains this ake and comes up again in the hot pool where we swam. It's asy to see how our ancestors might have believed all the water ystems were connected."

She let him lead her to the shore of the lake as he continued. 'The cliff is night and day, darkest purple—twilight purple. And golden day."

"Earth and sky?" Paige asked.

"In the sunlight the crystals sparkle like stars. Sky embedded in the earth. At night the moon shines on them, too."

She didn't want to be caught up in the spell of finding the *nauri* again, but she couldn't help herself. And slowly, despite her fears, she was being drawn to Adam, too.

"I understand fire and water." She looked down at the teaming lake where Adam had almost died. "*Tapu* and *noa*?"

"That was the key." Adam drew her along the edge of the ake until they were facing the *kai-tiaki*, the stone man. "I never understood until the first night we made love. I lay there with ou in my arms, and I thought about you having my child." He elt a tremor go through her, but he didn't look at her. "I pictured you pregnant, *kaihana*, large and round with my baby inside you, and then I knew."

"What did you know?" she asked softly.

"That the *kai-tiaki* is not a man at all, but a woman large with child. Our people believed that a woman was *noa*, except at certain times. At childbirth, she was *tapu*."

"The *mauri* is hidden in the guardian, then?" She took a step, as if to begin a search.

Adam held her back. "That's what I thought until last night. Then I lay here dying an inch at a time, and as I looked at the kai-tiaki in the moonlight, I understood. The *mauri* is the kai-iaki. There never was a second statue. The one in the Auckand Museum is the only one. One of our ancestors saw the *kai-iaki*, and understood its significance. She was carved by nature to protect this valley and our people. In every way she was he real Horo-i-rangi, our beloved ancestress who watched over us and guaranteed the safety and fertility of this place."

Paige could see it now. The man's potbelly was a woman's womb, huge with child. There was even the separate outline of pendulous breasts sloping down to rest on her swollen belly. "Horo-i-rangi." She was surprised by tears in her eyes. "She guided me to you last night."

He pulled her closer. "How did you find me?"

"Voices on the wind, moonlight on the path."

"When someone is terrified, their senses are altered."

"Granny said you wouldn't understand."

"I understand more than you think." He turned her slowly until she was facing him. "Last night I understood that I had almost killed our love with my fears. And yet this morning, I was afraid again. I tell you I love you, but at the same time I tell you I don't trust you. I brought you here to tell you I understand that now."

"Here?"

"The place of opposites. Love and fear are opposites. This is where they have to meet." He dropped his arms, but he moved closer until they were almost touching. "I love you. I have since I was nine years old. Will you love me, too? Marry me? Have my children?" He held up his hand before she could answer. "I can wait until you're ready. I can wait until you've found a way to make a life for yourself here."

She started to speak, but he cut her off once more. "I can wait, just not forever."

She felt suddenly light-headed. "May I answer now?"

He nodded gravely, and she saw that he wasn't sure what her answer would be. His fears would die, but not immediately. And she knew the same would be true of hers.

But then, they had a lifetime to learn.

"Yes."

He seemed to consider her answer. "Yes?"

"Easier than you thought, wasn't it?"

His smile started slowly, and his hands rose to grasp her arms. "What about the second part?"

"The waiting part? I think I'll decline to wait. You see, I've been waiting since I was a little girl, and I'm not a patient woman."

"You'll be my wife?"

She could see she was going to have to spell it out. She cupped his face in her hands. "Your wife, Jeremy's mother, the mother of more children, perhaps. And I'll take care of all your ow haned lambs," she added brushing her lips over his. "Cornwall can help."

"You'll make pets of all my livestock and we'll lose the farm."

"But you'll never lose me."

He pulled her close, and in the place of opposites, love and fear merged into forever.

*   *   *   *   *

FOUR UNIQUE SERIES
FOR EVERY WOMAN YOU ARE...

Silhouette Romance

Love, at its most tender, provocative, emotional... in stories that will make you laugh and cry while bringing you the magic of falling in love.

6 titles per month

Silhouette Special Edition

Sophisticated, substantial and packed with emotion, these powerful novels of life and love will capture your imagination and steal your heart.

6 titles per month

Silhouette Desire

Open the door to romance and passion. Humorous, emotional, compelling—yet always a believable and sensuous story—Silhouette Desire never fails to deliver on the promise of love.

6 titles per month

Silhouette Intimate Moments

Enter a world of excitement, of romance heightened by suspense, adventure and the passions every woman dreams of. Let us sweep you away.

4 titles per month

Silhouette Intimate Moments

JOIN BESTSELLING AUTHOR EMILIE RICHARDS AND SET YOUR COURSE FOR NEW ZEALAND

This month Silhouette Intimate Moments brings you what no other romance line has—Book Two of Emilie Richards's exciting mini-series Tales of the Pacific. In SMOKE SCREEN Paige Duvall leaves Hawaii behind and journeys to New Zealand, where she unravels the secret of her past and meets Adam Tomoana, the man who holds the key to her future.

In future months look for the other volumes in this exciting series: RAINBOW FIRE (February 1989) and OUT OF THE ASHES (May 1989). They'll be coming your way only from Silhouette Intimate Moments.
